Forspoken

Ajay Close lives and works in Glasgow.

Ajay Close

Forspoken

Secker & Warburg
London

Published by Secker & Warburg 1998

2 4 6 8 10 9 7 5 3 1

Copyright © 1998 by Ajay Close

Ajay Close has asserted her right under the Copyright, Designs
and Patents Act 1988 to be identified as the author of this work.

First published in Great Britain in 1998 by
Secker & Warburg
Random House, 20 Vauxhall Bridge Road,
London SW1v 2SA

Random House Australia (Pty) Limited
20 Alfred Street, Milsons Point, Sydney,
New South Wales 2061, Australia

Random House New Zealand Limited
18 Poland Road, Glenfield,
Auckland 10, New Zealand

Random House South Africa (Pty) Limited
Endulini, 5A Jubilee Road,
Parktown 2193, South Africa

Random House UK Limited Reg. No. 954009

A CIP catalogue record for this book
is available from the British Library

ISBN 0 436 20492 4

Papers used by Random House UK Limited are natural,
recyclable products made from wood grown in sustainable forests.
The manufacturing processes conform to the environmental
regulations of the country of origin.

Printed and bound in Great Britain by
Mackays of Chatham PLC

For Jim

FORSPEAK, *v.*
Ork. 1774 G. Low *Tour* (1879) 7:
Nobody must praise a child or anything they set a value
on, for if anything evil afterwards befalls it, these poor
ignorant creatures will be sure to attribute to the tongue
that spoke of it, and very probably quarrel on that
account. This they call forspeaking, and pretend to cure
persons so forspoken by washing them with a water
compounded with great ceremony.

Scottish National Dictionary

ONE

I used to think, among my many definitions, the ticks and crosses on the multiple choice which served me for identity, that I was not the type of woman to know my hairdresser. *Too* tacky. All that intimacy over the kidney-bowl sink, strange fingers on your erogenous zones, being ticked off about your split ends like a scabby dug in the poodle parlour. It wasn't snobbery – well, actually maybe it was – but I hated the sugar-and-spice of it, the notion that you weren't a woman, a *real* woman, until they'd rinsed a pina colada through your hair and slapped a couple of quarts of tzatziki on your face. The idea that us girls, we're all the same really, all we want is a Vidal Sassoon conditioning treatment, George Michael turned up high, and a good old gossip . . . it enraged me, made me feel like yelling 'Do you think Homo erectus really cares whether I've waxed my bikini-line?' Although I never actually did, of course. Just went home and said it to Sam instead.

Funny, really, that was more Sam's style. Send in the subtextual police, hunt down the ideological implications: which cheap stereotypes might she be passively reinforcing? But for a while that's the way it was with me too: terrified of contamination, like a beige carpet liable to take on the colour of whatever was on the walls. That's what being on your own does for you. Or at least, did for me. As if I were permanently on trial for my life. Not having secured my matching species, my place in the ark was always open to question. But nowadays I find myself looking forward to these two-monthly appointments at Gil's temple of vanity. It means losing the best part of a day, so I might as well make the most of it: a chance to take stock, a tranche of time out of time, in a setting weighted towards the favourable verdict. I send out for prawn-and-avocado sandwiches and flip through glossy magazines impregnated with sample sniffs of Dior and Chanel, and Gil tells me how when he was over in Santa Monica Rod Stewart walked past in these snakeskin pants that can't have cost less than seven hundred bucks but looked like they came from *Whateveries*. There's usually some canapé gossip about his celebrity clients, that redhead who reads the news or the fashion designer who's sacrificed couture cred for life on the road with a rock and roll band. And to be honest, I'm mildly diverted to learn that Rae Murricane was burgled but they missed the Clarice Cliff tea set, preferring the espresso machine and her collection of porno movies. I like the occasional blast of mindless pop, whisking the blood with a simulacrum of adolescent anticipation, and the artful shopfittings of limed oak and Mediterranean plaster and the flattering attentions of the mirrors, and those halogen spotlights prinking dull eyes and tired skin with the radiance of young love. I even like the shampoo girls, those fresh-from-the-packet beauties with their nose studs and milky complexions, though it's a mystery how he can afford so many, even if he is getting them cheap on work experience. Gil would rather go bust than see them in pink nylon, or any uniform at all, but their street style is oddly homogeneous, those thin floating garments with their drippy sleeves and the bovver boots like gro-bags supporting their sapling ankles. I know they're eyeing my tasselled loafers and my fraying cuticles and my cheeks blotching purple in the miasma of clashing chemicals and thinking *you're so old*, but actually what I feel is affinity, a pure girlishness which in my teens was always compromised by that urgency to become a fully-fashioned woman. Watching them now, white fingers slinking a tendril of hair behind their ears or curling up to the lips to exaggerate a giggle, I have a notion that they're unhappier with the way they look than I am. Always under starter's orders, rerunning the endless beauty contest in their heads, never quite gorgeous enough. As an inch-pinching size eight I felt the same. Now, at thirty-nine and three-quarters, I think: hell, we're not *that* different.

Not that this ease would be possible without my share of sexual recognition, the teasing homage paid by Gil. Flirting's all part of the service, the final touch to send you back out there feeling a little better about yourself. No, he's not gay and I'm not sleeping with him – though Gina claims it was an optional extra in the days when he used to do home visits. He's lean and goodlooking with that lupine colouring found in Glasgow: black hair, blue jaw and the startling pallor that speaks of illness or intensity, a dangerous edge, one way or another. Not a man to trust if he tells you the supermodel crop will flatter your incipient double chin, but there's no one I'd rather spend five and a half hours laughing with through the mirror. I let him know when I've seen something memorable at the pictures, warn him off the gado-gado at the new Indonesian diner; he lent me a book once, I even read it. Luckily I remembered to look out the number of the woman who recovered Drew's chaise-longue.

My name is Tracy, by the way. Don't worry. I'm used to the swallowed sniggers, that avid look that flares and dies, almost in time. I'm aware that you're saving the snorting laughter for later, but your heads are full of white stilettos and strawberry-flavoured cocktails with pink paper parasols. My sister once aired a theory, during that philosophic phase she took up instead of nightclubbing, that I got it both ways. Not conforming to the cliché, I forced their facile assumptions into reverse and was mistaken for a thoroughbred; then, when I fell at the first hurdle, they judged me bogus, guilty of pretension. Like a lot of Sam's theories, it was less than convincing, but there's no denying I've found the name a burden. My friends tell me they don't give it a moment's thought these days, implicitly acknowledging that, once upon a time, they did.

Sam would hate it here: all these women who buy their clothes from dinky little anchor-button boutiques mid-season, not caring that they'll be a couple of hundred pounds cheaper in the sales; those winter tans, the geometrically exact shading of hypothetical cheekbones. They know they look artificial and that's the point, all part of the uniform, a little reminder that the ladies are bought and paid for. But Scottish and bought and paid for, which gives them the edge over me. Like Heidi over there – the Alpine blonde getting her tabby roots tinted, Cox's pippin foundation and a snowdrop-white cashmere, moisturized, manicured, depilated, probably gagging on Gold Spot, too, but none of it counts because she still has that dirty girl's smirk. All the special formula cleansers of Geneva will not sterilize this little slut.

'What are they like?'

The subject of the sentence is not apparent, which means we're talking about Men. She's grinning, raising her eyes to the ceiling spots, sharing a moment of mock exasperation. Staring too hard, I've been taken for an eavesdropper. Still, there's no risk of offence: all girls together, letting our hair down in the community of narcissism, a curiously flirtatious experience, irrespective of Gil. (Even he can't swap meaningful glances with us all.) So I return the smile with a slight shake of the head, the gestural equivalent of the little black dress; whatever the occasion, I find it's just the thing.

I was named after Grace Kelly in *High Society*. Maybe we all were. Being the second child, Sam got Samantha. Thankfully, there was no brother to get lumbered with Lord. Things could be worse. Thirty years down the road they were christening them Kylie: now that will never have any class. Only once has anyone made the connection. We met at an opening. That's the milieu I move in: hip bureaucrats, the mediaocracy, independent filmmakers and warm-up acts, the sort of artist whose muse leaves them considerately alone during the cocktail hour. These people are not my friends, you understand, but my *context*, a distinction allowing me to define myself in contrast to their vainglory while basking in its reflected glow. They get their names in the papers, sometimes their faces too: clustered around an emissary of the colonial power, some Eton-educated bwana taking a trip up country; or showing off the latest souvenir smuggled back from eastern Europe, a stage production in the original Latvian, a string quartet which serenades refugees in bombed-out buildings. I've been in those pictures too, once or twice. Though mostly I attend these events because someone I know has been sent a ticket for two. They all expect to see me; if I don't show they'll let me know my absence has been noted, but it's not quite the same as a personal invitation.

'Everything OK, Tracy?'

Gil heading back from the cash desk. He makes a point of taking the money himself, a bit of chat over the chequecard, the impulsive discount: 'Tell you what, call it seventy.' Bet he says that to all the girls.

Delicately he slips his pinkie under the clingfilm and hooks a curl. Like a party guest raiding the dip. 'That blue rinse is taking a treat.'

Teeth like a pastrycutter, level along the biting edge. The blonde in the next seat sniggers, taking him by surprise. For a second his eye is fishy. The stylist lowers her blow-dryer to give the moment some air. Something tells me this punter will be paying full price.

So anyway, we met at one of those prodigal son shows, the triumphant homecoming of a Springburn boy who'd been feted in Manhattan. Mixed media, full of papier mâché drunks and polystyrene-packed football hooligans. The London critics really rated it, loved the *authenticity*, the echt flavour of the Glasgow streets. To me it looked like money for old acrylic. If he was going to do drunks, and this city already has more than its quota, did they have to be so picturesque? Bored with the installations, I turned my attention to the booze, and then Euan asked if I'd met a name I didn't catch and this big heavy-bellied type in a bottle-green suit tucked his catalogue under one arm and took my right hand in his left: more an invitation to the dance than a handshake.

'Ah,' he said, in a voice so deep as to raise suspicions of satire, 'the fair Miss Frigidaire.'

Euan's puzzlement strung a tenuous thread around us, a ring fence of mutual appreciation. There was an arresting compound of neglect and vanity in his looks. I took in the abundance of flesh, the hair allowed to grow a little too long for its dulling of grey, the shiny seat of those popinjay pants, and thought: here is a man who still reckons he can get away with it. The eyes were shockingly white in their mushroom sockets, the irises the flat blue of faded denim. I guessed he would surround himself with jailbait, despite the candid interest of his gaze. And then something happened, something I knew even then he would see as paranormal, although you can't discount the pivotal role of the Hollywood musical in the middle-class liberal aesthetic, and the fact that we'd both knocked back several glasses of airline-quality free champagne. That said, I find the mutual impulse to sheer blind reckless chance-taking striking enough to rerun the tape from time to time.

Drawing breath, we both sang

'What a swell party this is.'

There's something else too. We sang it in harmony.

After that, the mood could only stiffen. He made some witty remark I didn't get the point of about one of our fellow guests I didn't know. I laughed politely, which is to say insincerely, and asked if he was an artist. He looked offended but I wasn't sure whether this was on account of the assumption (in truth, he seemed a little comfortable to get by on housepainting and Arts Council bursaries) or because I had so clumsily exposed the evanescence of our recent connection. His features were huge: ears, eyes, lips, all to scale with that massive head on its padded pillar of neck and the unashamed bulk of his body, though his nose, I noticed, was unusually narrow, a knife-edge ridge in the rolling contours of his face. Then a crash-dieted blonde in a shantung silk dress too short for her knotty calves swooped in and kissed him theatrically on the mouth.

Back hovering on the margins of an adjacent conversation, I had resorted to eyeing the sculptures until the woman beside me, a Bergman fan by the look of that tortured headscarf, nodded in his direction with the disparaging familiarity we assume in the presence of the famous and remarked

'Looks smaller off-screen, doesn't he?'

So this was him in miniature.

' . . . *I'm warning you, Frazer.'*

The shampoo girls flourish lathery hands; heads lift and turn. Frazer grins fit to muss his goatee. Gil is clowning for the salon, moving menacingly towards the sound system. The song is unfamiliar but we all know the singer, a local boy made good in the mid-Eighties and ever after fondly reviled. That's the deal with Scottish celebrity.

'One song, Gil . . .'

'Is one too many.'

Frazer ejects the compact disc and replaces it with a clash of fiddle and electric bagpipe: thrash ceilidh. Gil squints moodily but lets it pass. The ladies flutter, skin tingling with something better than toner. In case you missed it, we have just had our roots done. A ritual of definition. Glasgow gallus and flash, working-class city with a lust for display, merciless with the unfashionable, tyrant to the naff. Who cares whether it's statistically verifiable, it's what we tell ourselves. Which is the way that myths come true.

Gil's promised I'll be out of here by half three, then it's over to the deli for the Neufchâtel and those Japanese crackers we've a craze for at the moment. The boss-eyed florist will be marking down the lilies and with any luck Xavier won't have sold out of croissants amandes; and maybe a loaf of olive bread to go with tonight's gazpacho. Drew's leaving work early to buy a birthday present for Siobhan so we arranged to meet up in the Quaich at six, which gives me a couple of hours to myself, nursing a glass of Morgon and a fly Gauloise (my sophisticated vices are touchingly jejune, I still get a thrill out of subtitles too). Plenty of time to finish the last forty pages of the new Galloway, providing Murdo isn't propping up the bar, singing along with the jukebox and girning about how he co-wrote that Alex Harvey number and never got a credit. On balance, I believe him, but it's a bloody awful song.

I've been under the lights a good half-hour now and the immobility is starting to get to me; phantom twinges are zipping up my calf muscles, fingering the small of my back. It's not that I mistrust Gil's professional competence, but the tangle of tinfoil threaded around my head brings back the dizzying gamble of adolescent perms, the masochistic submission to sinus-raking chemicals, the tingling scalp under the thermonuclear space helmet, the insane belief that beauty could come out of so much pain. Drew had his misgivings about this appointment. Superstition runs in his blood, he sees omens in torn banknotes and dud light bulbs, portents in racehorses' names. He dislikes small changes, fearing they bring larger ones in their wake. Not that he said anything; just offered me his trilby in case I needed camouflage on the journey home.

'So I can recognize you in the Quaich.'

'No bother: I'll be the one with Murdo's hand up my skirt.'

'Just as long as you keep him away from the jukebox.'

To fall in love at my age: who would have thought it? To rediscover the lost delights of feyness, the card posted to his office Friday night, knowing it won't be read until Monday morning; kisses crossed in the steam of the bathroom mirror; a white rose on my pillow after he's left for work; tears on the station platform . . . It wasn't always like this. I had ideas about love. Not good ideas. Its sterility, the way it would gradually flatten like a glass of water left on the bedside table, always there just in case but over the years rarely touched. Poured out anew each night and in the morning tipped away, unappetizing, brackish with the suspicion of dust. But with Drew it's like pouring the glasses back into the jug, a continual churning that even without fresh source keeps it bubbling with movement and light.

Hard to explain just how different my life is now. Not the body in the bed, although that's always nice, nor even the companionship, someone to sit beside at the Thursday night blues club or walk with along the shore, or misbehave at the superstore when the sociological implications of shopping for two-by-four become too much. I mean the *absolute transformation*. The gauzy palette on a January afternoon by the Clyde, a pinchbeck sun slitting quilted cloud, the water always moving, stealing the ground from under me, but going nowhere; the Georgian merchants' houses, restored with twentieth-century precision, dusted with an antique light. I had seen such beauty before and hated its containment, its refusal to promise passion or change. Yet now I love the cirrus clouds like twisted ribbons, the winter brightness burnishing our pallid faces to chrome, or the softening hour before dusk, a baby blue sky shedding its pastel light on tenement buildings, like opening a calfbound book to find an illustration of familiar streets, a clumsily tinted etching of shadow and sugared stone. With Drew I have acquired the option of tranquillity, and while terrified by the implications of completeness, the philosophical panic of the white endpaper, I know that at thirty-nine and three-quarters I have put away childish things.

And so we wake each morning to the clear air of happiness, a daily miracle like the quartered rectangle of silvered light that travels across the bedroom wall, a domestic slice of cosmic splendour, confirming our place in the planetary routine. I love him, and suddenly everything fits, like the codecracker's grid over the random cipher. Pattern, meaning, initiation into the secrets of the tribe, those rituals I used to observe with a dull, half-hopeful incomprehension: handholding through the park, eyes locked over the candlelit dinner, always wondering *Is this it, are we there yet?* And now the question doesn't even arise, but yes we're here: a place more exotic than the African rainforest or that spice-seekers' fortnight in the South Seas, a life irreconcilable with the priorities and rhythms that went before, no less remarkable for the recognition that this is where I was standing all along.

One or two of my friends were worried at first. To expectations framed by a decade of nursery-rhyming and bottom-wiping and Saturday night TV, such talk smacks of psychotic interludes, a spinster's last throw. But my feeling for Drew is locked into my life, of a piece with its glories and quotidiana, up there with the seagulls like airborne litter in the blue serge sky, or the yearning chords of 'Ae Fond Kiss', or the tweed-swathed braes of highland Perthshire, or the cars clipping their wing mirrors through the corridors of Stromness, or the diagonals of windfurled washing in the back courts of Partick, or the towering container ships in Aberdeen docks. Wherever I came from, this is my home now, this is my country.

About time. Gil seems to have remembered me. Here's his raw silk shirt undulating in the mirror. Oatmeal, a colour so uninspiring only a truly expensive fabric could save it from drabness. He looks concerned, an uncharacteristic uncertainty dulling his black and white sheen. Is it something to do with the drier? But no, there's no urgency in the way he clicks the switch at the socket, wheels away the white-enamelled triffid, removes my clingfilm bubble and starts to loosen the crown of foil. Preoccupied by something, he forgets to meet my eye.

'What is it, Gil?'

His gaze is turned towards the door leading to the wrought-iron staircase which, in its turn, gives onto the street. 'Hmm?'

There are limits to be respected here. However cosy the chat in the mirror, let us not forget that he is selling, and I am buying, his time. But instinct tells me this is not a matter of private grief. I'm feeling my way towards another enquiry when he drops the latest twist of opened tinfoil into the bucket and says

'Did you see that lassie in the brown bootlegs?'

'The one who was sweeping up?'

Hope surges into his features like surgical correction, firming the slight weakness in his chin. Don't say he's developed a crush on one of the shampoo nymphs.

'Aye. Do you know her?'

A slight shake of my head (amused edition). Injured vanity, as like as not.

The jawline sags again.

'I don't know her either. And Frazer says he didnae hire her, but

he just saw her sweep up your hair, put it in an envelope, and walk
out.'

TWO

In the end we bumped into each other on the street. It wasn't as if I hadn't made the effort to catch him on screen, but after a week of combing the listings I decided he wasn't a telly professional after all, just one of nature's blanks, a man so deeply unremarkable that one kiss by the fame-maker, being interviewed about his prize shallots on *Reporting Scotland* perhaps, became ever after his defining characteristic. Drew the Box. Looking back, I admit it doesn't seem likely, nor even compatible with the week's involuntary flashbacks: the way his body redefined its own shortcomings, finding harmony and proportion in its not quite healthy size; the subterranean acoustics of his voice; the come-hither of his aftershave, a high church whiff of Handel and incense, gorgeous rainment and bishop's ring. So maybe I felt the need to belittle him, to even the score for his squatting in my thoughts. That's a Sam theory for you. At least, it would be if she had the facts at her disposal.

He'd had a hell of a morning. Rehearsing his resignation speech every fifteen minutes – and, having heard it many times subsequently, I can confirm that it's a lulu – then biting his tongue. Why make it easy for them? If that devious shite McKinnon wanted him out he'd have to pay. In fact that devious shite McKinnon did not want him out, despite being of the opinion that Andrew Monzie was temperamentally equipped to sing Tosca at the Theatre Royal. Muir McKinnon's revenge fantasies went no further than a bound ledger chronicling all the make-up girls, production assistants, floor managers and research trainees favoured with a private performance over the past eleven years. Or he could have saved on postage and made do with a typed sheet of names: the details were depressingly similar. He could predict the next victim with absolute confidence. There were two blondes left on the third floor, and only one of them had a 38D chest.

I knew this. I knew it from the swing of his navy blue greatcoat, unbuttoned to catch the stiff wind, an ocean of fabric flaring from the shoulder. I knew it from the bruised fruit of his eyesockets and the narrow black hole of his guarded grin (and there I was gumming away, what a gal). I knew it as the heart-case knows from the camber of his fingernails or the pins-and-needles twinge. Choosing not to know.

He spots her crossing the road and registers that she's a looker before she comes into focus. He can tell from the wave of loathing rising to greet her, the preemptive hostility that is always his first reaction to a pretty girl, the assumption that she is judging him too old and staid and sexless. And the other thing. This one isn't so young, perhaps five years left in her, but she walks in that semi-averted way that suggests she still gets her share. She won't look, though she must have seen him. A skittish little trot to cover the final six feet of tarmac. The nearest car is miles away. That tart's skirt they're all wearing now, ankle length, split to the waist, easy access; when she steps up onto the kerb the demure overlap parts for a peep show of inner thigh. Not that he'd give her the satisfaction of gawking. Travelling north, his eyes hit hers. She smiles at him, a not unusual courtesy. And, as usual, he falls in love.

'If it isn't Tracy Samantha.'

He took me to the Highland Hotel, the sort of place I never went, indeed had never noticed, despite its Scots baronial hugeness, its corbie gables and witch's hat turrets looming above the balti houses and sandwich shops and ammonia-scented whisky grottoes in this corner of town. Inside it was august and comfortable with the egregious ugliness of bygone luxury, crammed with objects made to last, to everyone's regret. A sprung carpet with a motif of muddied thistles, tartan curtains, vinyl sofas, freestanding trumpet mute ashtrays, stags on the wall. Through the lounge, past the trio of starched and toilet-watered octogenarians taking tea behind a rampart of Frasers' bags, he led me upstairs to a doomy chamber heavy with the stale stranded air of afternoon drinking. A good twenty feet between the stained ginger upholstery of the uneasy chairs and the nicotine chiaroscuro of the vaulted ceiling; plenty of space for disapproval, or defiance, to hang above the scurfy head of the commercial traveller hunched over the counter, with his one-buttock purchase on the Rexine bar stool. Drawing alongside, Drew ordered a gin and tonic. Now to me, gin is a Home Counties drink with connotations of cardigan gentility, banter on the clay court, friskiness at the amateur dramatic society. The men I'd met in Scotland drank shorts or pints or, occasionally, if they were really making a bid to shake off macho stereotype, glasses of wine. Caught off-balance, I asked for an orange juice and received a couple of mouthfuls of acidic sediment. We took our pick of the empty tables and sat down. When he shed his coat he was wearing a pair of silvery chinos still boasting their storefresh shine and a red sweater which outlined his massif central beautifully. I grieved for the miscalculation in such display. The sweater's round neck showed a peek of tailored denim shirt which didn't quite match his eyes but presumably went down well with the jailbait. Sleeves pushed up, although it wasn't warm. That bloody skirt gaped open again as I sat down. There was an infinitesimal pause, a beat, the sigh of an optic, then the pheromones took over.

There is a theory that all job interviews are decided within the first four seconds. That whatever our post-rationalization, it's all a matter of chemistry. And so it is, the legend goes, with falling in love. Why bother explaining: *you just know.* Which is all fine and dandy, unless it happens all the time. I was born with the knack of intimacy with strangers, no barriers or restrictions, no border controls. People love me. Those textbook signs, the infinitely expanded pupils, the electric whisper of finger on skin, the insistence that they have never voiced such secrets, never felt so intensely, that only I understand . . . all that stuff, I get it every day. So how was I supposed to know when the big one came along?

So much attention had kept me single, and in Scotland single was a state of some concern. They're particular about couples in this country. You can be bored witless, sexually moribund and miserable as sin, and that's OK as long as you supply the sine qua non. And I couldn't. No known associate. I remember the nurse's pen skidding across her clipboard in an almost perfect diagonal. She decided not to start again with a new sheet of paper. 'And have you ever been in a relationship?' she asked neutrally, ballpoint poised. Then she tickled my cervix with a can-opener.

Sure I had past lovers, the way I have past lives: a range of options, severally enhancing without serving to define. If you want to know who I am you come to me. The biographical basics are easy enough. Age you know. Sex and marital status ditto. Height five four. Weight: mind your own business I'm big-boned and anyway beside Drew I'm a waif. Eyes grey. Hair: who knows underneath Gil's handiwork? The roots grow in pesto green if that's any indication. Accent: take your pick, I'll make a fair fist of it after a few weeks. As for the rest, there is an infinite number of variables. I could take you to shebeens down the East End, the punters still passing the hat for the Ra and cursing Celtic's gubbing in the Scottish Cup, where you'd take me for the original dumb blonde. If it weren't for the fact that these days I'm a redhead. Across town at the Loyal, where everyone used to work alongside Billy Connolly in the yards, they know all about my mornings on the picketline: up at four to make it past the roadblocks, putting on a show for the one o'clock news. In the sort of West End apartment where the coffee is Third World direct and the stereo plays vintage Van Morrison, I may recall Godfrey the Rastafarian poet who rolled the tightest joints in Toxteth (among his other less literary talents). I spoke patois in those days; a fluent listener, anyway. And once in a while, just for badness, I'll bring up Duncan the Border raider who made a killing in the City before he blew it all on coke. Or my nights with the dykes in women's hockey. Or that summer on the randan with Class War. I've a story to suit most contexts, and when nothing else will do there's always Darwin. I like to save the best till last.

Drew professes himself awestruck at the multivarious incompatibility of all these pasts; the autobiographical anthology, he calls it. Not that he doubts me: he has far too much to lose. For him, my history is evidence of uncommon worth, like the provenance of an *objet*: proof that he's found something deserving of desire. Though that first afternoon in the Rob Roy Bar of the Highland Hotel I was clean out of anecdote, uncharacteristically tongue-tied, a hoop of anxiety impacting my ribs. That day, the awe was mine.

Drew Monzie was a big man who would have qualified for the term even if he hadn't weighed in at a couple of sacks of potatoes over his starch limit. Looking at him I saw an arrogance which could have been no more than his awareness of my attraction to him, and a vulnerability I needed to believe in to preserve some shreds of pride. But he had one quality beyond mistaking: the charisma of authority which, in the absence of any clue more specific, I put down to birthright. The immigrant is forever seeking out the essence of the transformation she has chosen for herself. Fleeing from a culture where patriotism was the preserve of cheap newspapers and royal souvenirs, how could I not be struck by a country where everyone carried their germ of nationlove, that sprig of heather next to the heart? Envying the fierce pride of their identity, aware that I was resented for the heedlessness of my own, I was always looking for the crossing-point. Knowing nothing of Drew, he took on the colour of his homeland. And I was already more than half in love with that.

'What are you doing over this side of town?'

He interviewed me, that's the only word for it. I know how it's done, being in the information extraction business myself. I also know why: penny-in-the-slot conversation for those wary of making a more substantial investment.

'What sort of information?'

'Guess.'

'You're a journalist.'

'Nuh.'

'Market researcher.'

'Nope.'

'Tax inspector.' (Now he was flirting.) 'Policewoman?'

'Try again.'

' . . .'

So I told him. And he was genuinely touched.

I work in memory. Chipping away at the coalface of identity. Reminiscence work. There was a vogue for it in the Eighties, they started giving grants. It was supposed to delay the onset of senility, restore a sense of participation to outworn lives. It seemed a simple enough way of earning a living, provided I had the patience, and when they heard I was Darwin's daughter they decided I was a natural. As it happened they were right.

I loved it. Or at least loved the niche it gave me, the access to the pulse of a place, its customs and its codes. And then I started to assemble the stories in something more ambitious than the usual Gothic botch-up of photocopier marbling and bleeding print. I've done three books now, desktop published, perfect bound, full-colour cover, and the old ducks tell me no one has ever understood them so well. Inevitably they're chuffed by the sight of their names in print, but there's more to it than a trophy to show the great-grandchildren. Seeing their lives interpreted by subtle but skilful editing, reading the record of penury and injustice, the beatings and miscarriages, the daily grind of whitening the step and blacking the range, can prove a pivotal experience. I take the raw material of their lives and make sense of it, shape the random into meaning, show them the years have not been wasted, that their version counts. I've got a drawerful of testimonials, gushing tributes from grateful relations, approving mentions in the quality press, references to my 'uncanny insight into the poignancy of ordinary lives'. Gratifying, of course, but don't take me for some municipally–funded mystic hunched over the tea leaves. Inevitably there are times when guess-work takes over, when the garbled or piecemeal only makes sense by intuitive leap, but it's all explicable. There's an explanation for everything.

'It must be very rewarding.'

Of course it is, but I still like to take the piss out of their whistling teeth and eye-boggling bifocals.

'Maybe we could get you on the programme some time.'

Oh no. He thought I wanted to be on the telly. So many patronizing assumptions behind that unassuming smile.

'I'd rather just go to bed with you.'

What made me say it? One minute it was in my head, the next minute it was out. But he thought it was funny, and credited me with a sense of humour. The hoop around my chest loosened a ratchet.

Do I really have to go through all this? The Byzantine sophistries read into simple exchange; the tentative alliance implied by circum-spect gossip, bringing ourselves to the boil with the heat of other people's passion; the conjuring of emotion at one remove through books, films and music. That edging towards the personal, all the knowing and not knowing. *Perhaps we're just being friendly, going through the motions, passing the time.* The predictable uncertainty of a very simple drive.

'Do you come here a lot?'

'Often, you mean?'

I didn't mind. It seemed an allusion to the banality of the situation rather than my personal brand, and as such an admission of sorts, a dummy pass.

'*I mean* the barmaid seems to know you.' And, I was not bold enough to add, he had failed to return the courtesy.

'The price of fame.'

It was said ironically, that style of self-deprecation which emphasizes what it purports to undermine.

'Poor you.'

'It's a full-time job opening my knicker mail.'

'They don't *really* . . .?'

'Cupboards full. You'll see for yourself when you come to the studio.'

I laughed, pleased to discover that he could accept my reservations, pleased most of all by the oblique way he chose to withdraw the invitation, relegating it to the netherworld of whimsy. Then he started talking about his plans for a new programme, a twice-weekly show he could sell to the network, sixty minutes of dinner-party-style discussion for people with opinions and wit, and how I could be involved in the pilot. It seemed he wasn't that subtle after all.

He must have seen my expression change, for he said, so low it reached me on a two-second timelag, 'No obligation.'

Aren't we all a little shamed by the formulaic thrills of courtship, the rush when man turns predator? I had given him the cue for this aside, I'd started it, there was even a possibility that he was being no more than polite, keeping the joke in the air. Yet these inconvenient details were banished by the feather twist in my diaphragm, the hiss of blood in my cheeks. Sex kicked in, and subtlety went out the window.

And yet it is never that simple. Drew was a terrible flirt. And I mean terrible. Gauche. Alternately clumsy and diffident. It took all my ingenuity to keep the adrenaline coursing. He came on strong at first meeting, I'll grant you, but it was a case of zero to 60 in 3.5 seconds and thereafter a steady 25. Never do it with a man with a sense of irony. Give me the jut-jawed leer every time, the sit-on-my-face school of badinage, that tang of machismo, unmistakable as Brut, the hormonal code always received and understood. Drew was too proud or fastidious or insecure to hitch his balls. Too civilized. Divining the slow throb of the carotid through that foie gras neck, gauging the too-tight curve of fabric on his inner thigh, I was taking him against his will. His inclination was to perfume sex with romance and make it embarrassing. Too late I realized, he was the type who couldn't manage unless he was in love.

There is a look people get when their minds are elsewhere, a film over the eyes. In my job, you have to be careful. Sometimes I think it's my greatest skill: maintaining focus, no matter how discouraging the raw material. And there is a look men assume when they are talking about one thing and thinking about the other, a furtive glitter. Drew had it, talking about television. In a sense neither of us were listening to what he said. I was nodding and smiling and comma-humming but behind the honeysuckle hedge of all that affirmation not quite believing. Perhaps because his relish seemed less to do with the thing itself than the pleasure of unwrapping it before my eyes. *She's turned on by the glamour, they all are.* Not so. I envied him his world, but not because of television, whose pretensions to universality seem the opposite of life. What I coveted was context, something he would have had in a factory, or an abattoir, or working on the bins.

'Not that I'm in the open-topped convertible league.' He was grumbling, which is the acceptable form of boasting. 'That's strictly for newsreaders whose voices haven't broken—'

I looked suitably sympathetic, though in fact a little bored.

' — still, I wouldn't be rich beyond the dreams of avarice if I'd stuck with the day job.'

'Which was what?'

He stared at me a long moment, then coughed up a sound meant to approximate amusement. I could feel my features taking on the rigor of embarrassment. At last he started to laugh for real, generously including me in the joke even if I didn't understand the punchline. His face bloomed like a peony, turning up the contrast on the grey in his hair. I hoped he didn't have a weak heart under all that blubber.

'I'm sorry – I ought to know.'

He shook his head, riding out the aftershocks of his mirth, and when he spoke it was to enquire

'Another glass of liquefied wood pulp?'

I said no, a thing I used to do sometimes when I wanted the goods on offer very much. This sobered him. Reaching for his coat, shrugging it on, his face showed a flicker of the awkwardness that had marred our first meeting, the pang of mistaken affinity, although you could say we remained united, in disappointment.

'You're probably right. Restraint is not my strong suit: still making up for all those years with the kirk session breathing down my neck—'

I took this as an obscure joke, a metaphor in currency at his workplace.

'—they say you don't miss the collar, but you never adjust to living off the leash.'

He hauled on the door's long brass handle and stepped back to allow me through first. I was getting there, but slowly. The sleeve of his coat had ridden up, his forearm swelling wristless from the pigskin watchstrap, the flesh grey as lard and covered with a fine scrub of colourless hair growing mutinously in every direction. I felt his gaze fishing for mine some moments before I met his eye.

'They're loosening up these days. Even allow you on television on the Sabbath as long as you're spreading the faith. Too late for me, which is probably just as well.'

I slipped through the opening, hair wafting in the draught as the door swung shut behind us. No wonder I hadn't found him in the schedules. It never occurred to me to check the godslots. A spoiled minister. That'd be one in the eye for Darwin. Well, for both of them.

THREE

'And the art nouveau interior streetlamps.'
'In toothpaste green.'
'I think you mean pistachio.'

Drew and I are playing *What is wrong with this place?* A time-passer in those dead minutes when life dares to buck our schedule. Not that I'm particularly vexed. Given our mutual absorption, these reminders of the world outside are really quite a novelty. Almost titillating. Like the chafing of overtight trousers worn for display, the rub between in here and out there . . .

What is wrong with this place is the blonde parquet flooring smack bang next to the dementedly patterned carpet which was chosen not to show the dirt and therefore predicates its presence even if clean. What is wrong with this place is the aubergine bentwood chairs and the tropical rainforest vinyl tablecloths, another misguided hedging between camouflage and taste. Then there's the timeslip between those minimalist Eighties ceiling spots and the Mississippi paddleboat chandeliers; the mindslip between dolphin-friendly tuna and mock-croc flash; the painstaking spontaneity of the chalked crayfish on the blackboard; the Latin American guitar muzak that everyone but the marketing men stopped liking when Nicaragua went sour; the motorway service station clumsiness of the menu, a failure so democratic that anybody could eat here and be equally repelled. In a small town it might be touching, the aspiration to sophistication doomed always to fall short, but this is don't-patronize-me Glasgow and the *savoir-faire* that's lacking, by impli-cation, is our own.

Drew shuts the triptych menu, having reached the conclusion that it offers nothing he would wish to eat, let alone pay these prices for.

'I know you wanted a sugar daddy on PTL-TV but, unfortu-nately, you ended up with me.'

A regular joke: Tracy the Bollinger concubine he can't afford to keep, a rich man's plaything dropped into his lap. Don't worry, I pay my way. It's just sexual game-playing, a form of dressing up, perfectly normal between consenting adults. Even Joan Burnie has started to approve, in the privacy of the bedroom. We're not married, so we can do it anywhere, not just in the twenty-tog sanctity of the double bed. Standing up. Fully clad. In a traffic jam. On the platform at Partick Station waiting for the seven-fifteen. In the Family Changing cubicle at the swimming pool. Not so far in an Esperanto chow house, but who can say what the future holds?

I know what you're thinking: *a minister?* But why the hell should I justify myself to you? I am neither bony nor broad, my hair is not a centre-parted hank of greasy mouse, my eyes are twenty-twenty, my skin is clear, and I do not wear American tan popsocks. Satisfied? Of course I had my misgivings at the start. I'd met the sexy evangelist type before. The boy with the deadly nightshade curls selling Trot propaganda outside Woolworths on Saturday mornings. I agreed to see him for a drink and discovered that he really did want to discuss combined and uneven development. So when the call came after a decent five-day interval and that deep-down voice pushed through the receiver, forcing sweet needles into my spine, I decided to give him forty-five minutes in the Quaich. I wasn't going to get into my gladrags for an evening debating the finer points of transubstantiation. (I needn't have worried: the Free Associateds wouldn't give it the time of day.) Apart from anything else, I'm an unbeliever. But that wasn't what changed my mind about keeping my date with Drew Monzie the television minister; my real misgiving was his reputation as a celebrity fuck.

'What's happened to them?'

Impatient at the best of times; when hungry, Drew is unbearable. The mirage of relaxed chat over a fruity little Chianti is dissolving into the prospect of a wordless refuelling to ward off faintness in the second reel. You know how the conversational impetus flags when you're eating to a deadline. Frankly we're both pissed off, but it's an incriminated ire. If we'd really wanted time to talk, why would we have suggested a film?

We are waiting for Ricky and Yolande, a cosmopolitan couple whose company we sometimes enjoy. The rest of the time we shrug and say: Ach, they mean well. Although in truth that's debatable.

They understand. It's not the first time they've been used to spice up white bread social lives. And it's a two-way street. Allowances are made; you'll see what I mean. In return they lend us their impersonal mystique as emblems of the world outside, which it has to be said comes as something of a novelty to Drew. Lived within twenty minutes of Gibson Street all his life and never tasted curry until he met me. Ricky reckons Drew's guilt over this might be good for an opening into telly, as soon as Drew twigs that there is something to be guilty about.

'Yo fats, what's happenin'?'

Ricky Sidhu. Swinging through the tables with his gum-chewer's smirk and his bedroom eyes. Correction: his Fuck You eyes. Less appealing, I think you'll agree. And here comes Yolande, the little Sherpa, trailing behind with the emotional baggage. A heroine of the revolution, minor division, but major enough to be given a taste of the electrodes from Pinochet's thugs. She has a second-string identity as a séductrice; mother was French, which probably explains it. A crossbreed's knack for languages which manifests itself in an unpredictable demotic Glaswegian. Lips that never quite close, even in reproof; some adenoidal difficulty. An Aztec heft to wrist and ankle which only heightens her allure. According to the minister. On her neck is a small scar, possibly a childhood mishap, but I can never glimpse it without seeing the cement block cell glistening with vomit, the sweating interrogators with their aviator shades. Bad movies. I've never asked, on the basis that I don't really want to know. Anyway, she got out and fetched up with Ricky, who's a bit of an amateur torturer himself.

'How's the lovely Tracy, and that ugly old bigot who's going to hell for you?'

'Hungry. Hi Yolande.'

'Hello.'

Yes, well. She takes a little warming up.

'You should have started without us. The big man needs to keep his strength up.'

Here we have one of those moments that acquaintance with Ricky so frequently provides. Surely you get the picture: me prone below fatso who is chugging away like the Flying Scot; I'm probably thinking of England. Or riding him like a banshee while he clutches his flabby pectoral and tries to stave off the impending coronary. Ricky, incidentally, is built like the models in Austin Reed's window: inverted triangle torso, taut but nicely padded butt. Dresses like them too. Although I've yet to spot an Asian dummy.

He is one of those men who can't resist their own physicality: a pirouetter, a can-kicker, a strutter. Shifting a chair, he boosts it deftly in a needless arc and catches it again in a touchdown quiet as the kiss of an autumn leaf. A talented Sunday footballer, with a coveted blend of unpredictability and control. Yolande is about to take the proffered seat when she reaches over for a pink paper serviette and scoops something slimy off its varnished surface.

Ricky is already scanning the menu. 'I hear Billy Graham has pulled out of his SEC gig – you could step into the breach there, boy.'

Drew has a way of palming the booby-trapped pleasantry, all you know for sure is that it will pop up again when least expected and explode in the sender's face. There's a look, too: his foxhole smile. But this isn't it. Ricky disarms him, not because he's black (although this is certainly the button being pushed with that cotton planter's 'boy'). It's a question of machismo. Don't misunderstand, Drew is not short on testosterone, but something about Ricky's presence unmans him. He becomes overparticular in his speech, a Widow Twanky fussiness settles on his upper lip. I read it as defensive, intimidation bringing out the mammy's boy, a cringe that makes me feel like turning on him too. But that's only my interpretation. Knowing Yolande, she'll hear it as class, the *tottie peelings* superiorism of douce Kelvinside, while Ricky just thinks he's playing the white man. Once or twice I've tried to broach the subject – seriously – with Rakesh Sidhu. He laughs. And maybe he's right, maybe talking it over would merely banish our guilt, not the actual oppression; maybe airing the issues is just another tactic, my way of cheating at Victim Whist. Four suits tonight, though it's too early to tell which is trumps.

'Hey Drew, I was reading in the paper that Christianity's the new rock and roll . . .'

Drew knows he'll have to take the bait sooner or later. 'Not in front of Tracy: she's touchy about the groupies.'

Which is my cue.

'I am, am I?'

'Who gets jealous about the girl in make-up taking the shine off my face?'

'Only when she tries to do it with her breasts.'

I know, it's shameful: this desire to flirt in public, but who's it hurting? And we do so enjoy it. Courtship is a stomach-churning performance, plagued by first-night nerves, all you want is to get through it without slow handclaps or pratfalls, then suddenly the show's over and the lights are off. Intimacy won't play to an audience. There are of course rival pleasures, but occasionally you feel the old-stager's hankering for the smell of the greasepaint, the buzz of the crowd. And besides, it's a marking of territory. In case anyone needs reminding.

'How's the Samba class going?'

Oh yes, she's started giving dance lessons. What *was* Marx's position on the Lambada?

'I had sixteen last week: a couple of Chinese lassies, an Italian, a doctor at the Western from Sierra Leone – he's brilliant, by the way.' It seems this is one of her Parliamo Glasgow nights. 'Too many English, but: nae rhythm at all.'

Drew squints my way.

'Funny you should mention that . . .'

'You drinking red, Tracy?'

Well thankyou Ricky, even if rescue wasn't uppermost in your mind. The blink on hold as he fills my glass: two can play at crossbench alliances. The bottle is almost finished. He signals to an undergrown teenager leaning against the far wall. Babyhair the colour of barleywater, leggings which don't quite meet her socks.

'Sorry Ricky, Lolita isn't our waitress.'

He doesn't pull the bad boy grin, which means it was a genuine error.

'She was looking at us like she was waiting to take our order.'

Drew casts her an uninterested glance; the sort of tiddler even he'd throw back.

'Maybe she's waiting to catch Tracy off-guard so she can whip out her scissors.'

'Pardon?'

Ricky doesn't care for private references in social space, which is fair enough as a general principle, but he makes a fetish of it. His reading is racial, a presumption of exclusion. I don't feel too guilty: he could play secrets with Yolande if he chose. But of course he doesn't choose.

'Has she not told you about the demon hair-snatcher of Renfield Street?'

This is the way we work together: Drew grabs their attention, I tell the tale. Gratifyingly, Ricky yields up a shivering moan in exactly the right place. Then, having created the effect, I undercut it.

'There's got to be a simple explanation. If she was wearing a string of beads that broke . . .'

'You would have heard them hit the floor.'

'OK, a chain then, links. Rather than grub around on the floor it'd be quicker to sweep everything up and sort it out later. That works.'

Yolande pouts. Or is that what passes for breathing? 'That doesnae mean it's what happened.'

'Do you have a likelier explanation?'

'Naw, but there's maybe an unlikelier one.'

Here we go. Sixth sense, the fourth dimension, Yolande's parallel universe. I've only myself to blame. Normally it's Drew who provides the opening. He can't leave it alone, the fascination of the taboo. If I'm honest, it's the reason I wouldn't call Yolande a friend. I can live with her Glaswegian señorita act and her awful, enviable past, and the way she thinks this gives her the right to dismiss me as a floozie, even though I'm not the one whose partner treats me like the invisible woman. But when she gets started on the paranormal . . .

'I had a famous face in the day.'

'Really famous, or a Scottish celebrity?'

Just Drew's little joke.

She took it up in the early Eighties on Enterprise Allowance. They were so eager to get the figures down, they bribed you off the broo. The bank charged eight quid to borrow a grand for the day and suddenly you were a small business. All you needed was a gimmick. Yolande chose the futures market. Tarot, crystal ball, palmistry, a barrel of fortune cookie philosophies Darwin would have loved. From a professional perspective. Ricky swallows the lot with a playground credulity that sadly undermines his cockyboy charm. Drew is so transfixed by terror that even the prospect of holding Yolande's hand won't persuade him to get his lifeline read. I don't believe she has any more faith in it than I do – I mean, she's a dialectical materialist, how many improbable creeds can a person support? But having stumbled on a scam that works with Ricky, she can't afford to admit that it's a trick.

We run through the usual suspects: television presenter, politician, actor, footballer, singer. She's not telling, which rather defeats the object of mentioning it in the first place. Perhaps we're guessing too high and she's staring bathos in the face.

'Devil in the fourth house; ten of swords in the House of Death . . .' Did I mention that her lips look like a haemorrhoid cushion folded in the middle? 'I had to send him home, gie him a refund—'

She's lost us. Being fluent in five languages is no guarantee of effective communication.

'—sometimes it happens because of the way you handle the cards, contamination. But this wasnae physical: it wasnae my reading, and it wasnae his. I knew who it was, but.'

Drew breaks the silence.

'Whose?'

I love him for his moments of inconspicuous grammatical pedantry.

She looks at me. A smile almost closes those inflatable lips.

'It was Tracy's.'

Now I *know* she's a bitch.

Ricky and Drew are staring at me like my nose has just fallen off. Waiting for me to ask. Let them wait.

But the suspense is too much for Drew. 'Are you going to tell us?'

'No' if she doesnae want me to. I'll do you your reading if you want. Save you the bother of picking over Tracy's for the bits about you.'

'It's tempting—' He takes a breath. '—but I'd have to say no. I used to preach against people like you.'

26

Silently I applaud his insouciance. That mischievous pause, the short amused sigh. Only I know the fear that lies behind them.

Ricky shifts his chair backwards, breaking the circle. 'Aye, but you've lost your holy housepoints now, so what does it matter? You're frockless and fancyfree.'

The accompanying grin is only averagely combative, Yolande's glance no more than usually intent. No observable cracks in Drew's equanimity. Am I the only one who treats this as a touchy subject?

'Actually they didn't defrock me, I was never ordained. They just took away my licence to preach—'

But Ricky is not interested in the details. He starts playing with the sugar sachets in the middle of the table, shaking the granules down, folding the loose paper over and over. 'Jeezo' (yes he's a Sikh, but he swears in Glaswegian) 'a guy could starve to death in here.'

Our waitress is threading between the tables. As she approaches he plunges sideways to block her route, thighs still planted on the seat, torso horizontal, a manoeuvre of startling, extravagant, aggressive grace. After her recent flicker of assertion, Yolande's features have reverted to their mask. The waitress giggles, as I would if I did not know him, and promises our order is on its way.

'—though they were talking about a Libel for a while.'

Presumably I'm supposed to ask.

Drew shrugs apologetically. 'Church jargon. Some of them wanted me hauled in front of the Presbytery. Immorality and heresy.'

Ricky is interested again. 'What happened?'

'They couldn't be sure of making it stick. They never supplied me with details of the charges, but "immorality" I could guess.' His head tilts, perhaps unconsciously, in my direction, although the woman in question was a couple of decades before me. 'I'd been discreet: they'd have had problems finding witnesses.'

'And heresy?'

'Ah well, they had me on that one—'

If there's one thing Drew understands it's the impact of timing.

'—Tracy believes. I'm the one who doesn't.'

'Now, whose was the vegetarian tacos?'

Unfortunately, given the flaccid chamois in the waitress's right hand, it was and still is mine.

Drew believes, but it's a bleak faith. After my fleeting encounters with *Songs of Praise* Anglicanism, good-sort vicars who'd marry anyone, a blue-cloaked Virgin Mary in the school nativity play, it came as a shock. I don't mean all that stuff about fornication and tying the swings up on Sundays: we all know how much notice he takes of that. But deep down he's the very model of a modern fundamentalist. Drew believes all right. It's just that he's not sure he's among the saved.

I can see it's still bothering you. Him and me. Calvinism and sex. Of course they *do it* with their tweed-skirted, scone-baking, marcelled wives. They've got the scrubbed, short-sighted, stammering children to prove it. But it's not quite compatible. So let me tell you about standing on the cracked concrete pavement outside the Highland Hotel that long-ago Monday, eking out the smalltalk, the pallid city sunshine strobed by ocean-going gulls. I'm no stranger to men's bodies. I'd gone through a few years of solo flight, but don't imagine I went without. There's an etiquette to adultery. You can hot-breath their balls, tease your tongue into the gathering folds where the red meat gives way to the choicer cuts of white, but you can't spend half an hour on their playground scars or learn their corns by heart. Not unless you intend sucking them. So I'd had the carnal without the intimate, which is better than nothing but after a while seemed worse. And then that day I found myself chatting on the roadside, while the buses chugged past lifting my skirts in their sooty wake, and the pizza parlour pumped out its cheesy heat, and an old boy papped his head out of the bookie's to hawk a greenie onto the concrete, and I realized I knew this stranger's bulky body as well as I knew my own, better than any of my afternoon lovers, though beyond that first hamfisted handshake we had not yet touched flesh.

How many men do you stand next to in a week? Bus queues, supermarkets, waiting to get served at the bar. Nothing more ordinary. Desire, too, can be a workaday thrill. That jumpstart to the digestion. Some days I get hit after hit. A sparking glance on the pavement, the handover of swing doors, a rush of stillness across a room. But not that paradox of excitement and familiarity, positive and negative failing to cancel out. Standing there on the pavement. Knowing each other physically, but not, as they coyly put it, in the

Biblical sense. Knowing I could touch him. And knowing what I'd find.

But time's pressing. We have twenty-five minutes to make the Odeon. The adverts have already started, I know them off by heart so that's not a problem, but I prefer not to miss the trailers. It's part of the complete experience: that eleventh-hour awareness that you'd rather be watching something else. So I change the subject, like the supportive partner that I am, and as ill-luck would have it the conversation swings back to Yolande.

'Nine out of ten, you could tell them their life story just by looking at their shoes. Their clothes. The slap on their coupon. I'm not talking about the truth – they don't want that – I mean the lies they tell themselves. I gie it laldy with the Spanish. It helps. As long as they don't hate the Tims.' She looks to Drew, a lizard lick of those lips, a moment of complicity, or a begging of pardon. 'If you're foreign they think they're one up on you, and then they can take your pity. All these bourgeois women, no ring on their finger, never gonnae see forty again: I tell them' – she slips a Latin thickening into her tongue, pouting more in the delivery – 'there is a sadness in their life. Such a gift of love going to waste, like sweet spring water running into desert sand. I say they feel the lack of a child. I say they have been ill-used by selfish men. I tell them to beware the older ones.' The Glaswegian is sliding back into her accent. 'Once they're past thirty the old ones are the only ones who'll gie them a second look. I tell them I see hurt, deep hurt, at the hands of a married man. One day I'll be wrong, but it hasnae happened yet.'

Yolande does this sometimes, after an evening in purdah. Lets the company talk themselves out and then, whammo, a twenty-minute monologue. This isn't conversation, it's a routine: written, researched, produced, performed. Unable to participate, you see: what we take for modesty turns out to be monstrous egotism, a refusal to share the stage.

'So it's all a scam, is it?'

She drains her glass and empties out the remains of the bottle.

'That's no' what I'm saying. All of us have powers we use all the time, we don't know what they are, we don't even know we're doing it. You go to bed thinking "I've to be up at seven" and you open your eyes just before the alarm goes off. You think "I wonder how so-and-so is?" and the next minute he's on the phone. It's just listening to your instincts. Only I'm maybe more in touch with them than you are.'

Praise be. We got off lightly. I thought she was going to give us the full litany of amazing coincidences, chaos theory, synchronicity, the forkbending works. Notice how, like all the best con artists, she neutralizes scepticism by admitting how much she exploits her clients' need to believe. I particularly enjoyed the claim to instinctual womanhood. (In case you need a translation: she's saying she's better in bed.)

She harpoons a crabstick off her seafood platter, proving yet again that while she may be all sensuous woman in the sack she has one hell of an instinct for the dog dish on the menu. 'We all have our wee superstitions, it's part of being . . .'

'I don't.'

OK, it was a little abrupt.

She squints. 'I bet I could find some.'

'I bet you couldn't.'

'All right: you're on.' She's suggesting some sort of experiment, a tarot-reading for the purposes of comparison with her mystery client last week. ' . . . see if you get the same cards, or cards that pan out the same way.'

That seems to load the dice pretty comprehensively.

'I haven't got time, Yolande. I'm up to my neck at the moment—'

Drew's eyes are luminous with excitement. Ricky seems almost erotically fixed. Across the table she is smirking, knowing I'll say no. '—unless you're free Tuesday night?'

'Thanks for telling Yolande I have no rhythm, by the way.'

Halfway out of his boxer shorts, Drew catches his foot in the elastic in unintended slapstick.

'That's not what I meant.'

'That's the way it came out.'

'Worried that it might put Ricky off?'

Surely it doesn't need subtitles. This isn't a tiff, it's foreplay. Mr X wants to sleep with me. Ms Y wants to sleep with him, there's libido pushing at us from all sides. Drew believes every man in the country would sell his granny to lie between my legs. I counter with the box-watching disciples, the teenage sublimators rolling their eyes to heaven at the thought of five and a half inches of holy fame. And so we have an orgy. For two. You should try it sometime.

'Tracy.'

'That's me.'

'Do you know what you are?'

'Tell me.'

'Whore of Babylon. Subtle as the serpent. Sucking corruption and finding it sweet. Drunk with the wine of her fornication. Sweet bitch of luxury. Jezebel. Slut. Filthy. Perfumed. Delicious. Cunt.'

'And what else?'

'My love.'

Another thing. Drew thinks we are fated. Some women might find it touching, or a laugh, but to me there is nothing in this world, nor out of it, more serious. Such a small superstition, but a jemmy in the crack of metaphysical panic, opening up the eternal questions: predestination, justification, the maker's mark, free will.

Drew believes. I'm the one who doesn't.

FOUR

At thirty-six years old I was still prone to teenage spots. I dragged myself out of bed and grimaced at the mirror and realized there was no getting out of my Wednesday morning session at Magellan Street, and I still hadn't prepared my presentation to the Maryhill pensioners' luncheon club some four hours ahead, which I was planning to recycle at the eventide home in Carnegie Drive next day. And even though my seven o'clock rendezvous with Drew Monzie could make no difference to how I accomplished any of these tasks, it tipped the next twenty-four hours into impossibility. I rang the television studios and the switchboard patched me through to an answering machine. His voice sounded even deeper, as if digitally enhanced. I left my excuses, apologetic but not over-doing it. Our brief conjunction was a mistake, but not a significant one, a spillage from another story, now wiped clean.

I was renting in Never-never land at the time, in a swanky original-fireplaced, crusty-corniced flat the owner couldn't sell because its Victorian glory was being sucked into the labyrinthine mineworkings beneath our elegant street. Taking the long view, this was a tragedy but, like me, most of my neighbours were strictly short-term. Byres Road was full of students, and those who'd spent too long around students, assuming their tapestry fez, ripped jeans and Timberland boots conveyed the authentic carelessness of youth, when what these things actually signalled was the uncared *about*, people stranded on the sandbanks of their own lives. No costume could disguise the walnut complexion and hobbling gait, a handicap often combined, it is true, with a ferocious rapidity of pace, but no bounce. The elasticity had gone: skin, stride, attitude, the ability to face up to the facts . . . All right, the real reason I cancelled: I'd been out to lunch with Euan. Normally he was the one who rang me, but this time I had an agenda, other than the usual of proving to some unspecified witness to my life that, although single, I had no shortage of masculine company. It wasn't necessary to be spotted in the café or the cinema queue or the circle bar, just so long as the image existed, a snapshot of the evening captioned 'I could if I wanted' with the clear implication 'I'm just fussy, that's all'. Wasn't I proving it by positively vetting the latest applicant for the job?

You probably know a Euan: beautifully dressed, even fogeyish, but harbouring wellsprings of anarchic mirth. The point of the wit being its unpredictability. It doesn't always show. On off-days you feel cheated, fobbed off with a pale imitation, one of those men other people's mothers find charming – an attentive escort, good company, what the Americans call a walker. Drew maintains he has the hots for me, and it's one of the rules of the game that I never deny to the point of conviction, Drew needs his illusions like everyone else, but really I don't think so. When I took the call two days after the party and blushed and flustered, and said sure, I'd meet him for lunch, I knew even then it wasn't sexual. For the record, he is even-featured, pleasantly proportioned, regular as a knitting pattern, with a moustache which comes and goes. (It lends him the dashing air of a nineteenth-century cavalry officer, but plays havoc with the libidos of cruising homosexuals.) He works in picture conservation, restoring old masters to their original glory, reaching for the touch of genius through the layers of grime. By the time he's finished the artist himself wouldn't know the difference. Interpreter's vanity is one of the things we have in common.

We agreed to meet in a wholefood café downtown, a long ribbon of glass wall fronting the traffic-blown pavement, where couples gather over candlelight to flaunt their romances and shiver with the frisson of prying eyes. At lunchtime it's mostly menopausal ladies with time on their hands and middle managers hunched over the voodoo of office politics. I found a table and smiled at the waitress and had two glasses of wine poured and waiting when he arrived, all set to tickle up his taste for indiscretion. But first, a little window dressing was required.

So I told him about being taken for Glasgow's only thirty-six-year-old virgin by the family planning commissar. I dished up Rona Black's significant other, who'd developed the habit of fastening his flies in the living room, a process which always took longer to accomplish than it took me to waver from my determination not to look. I gave him the latest on Bridie Condon, one of his favourites, eighty-three last birthday, still teaming her lambswool twinsets with a Tina Turner wig. The home help had found her in the bath singing advertising jingles and feeding Franklin Drambuie chocolates; the dog was paralytic but yapping roughly in tune.

You'll have gathered by now that I'm a talker. Well, not just a talker, a rescuer. Transmuter of base metals, supplier of punchlines, the one who'll take your shopping list monologue and add a flip little wisecrack as if it was meant to be funny all along. Not just a good but a *creative* listener. The perfect punctuator, a flattering tease, a sprinkler of glamour, not panstick and lipgloss, but the real thing, that prickle of static that says we're alive. Drew calls it – since these tributes are more becoming secondhand – my suburban Gothic streak, a knack of seeing the patterns most people take for granted, and drawing out the bizarre. I don't talk all the time, that would make me a bore, I just fill up the spaces. It's a matter of vivacity, of how much life you have to spare. We all know people whose silences hold the clanking echo of eternity, their dead eyes pleading to be reminded that the universe is teeming, that their life, too, can be filled to the brim. I attract people who fear their own emptiness, and sometimes, as I've mentioned, their gratitude is extreme. I've had longing looks and midnight phone calls and poems in the post and one or two other tokens of appreciation we won't bother with right now, but I don't let it go to my head. In America, where they'll describe the loss of their virginity within seconds of shaking hands, I wouldn't expect a second glance. Costive Scotland stands at the opposite pole, but which is healthier? You tell me. Does the skin denied touch become supersensitive or numb? Which is more exciting, the novitiate's ankle or the stripper's crotch? Drew jokes about his repression, putting his faith in an equal and opposite reaction, volcanic passions seething under the crust. But let such feelings out and who knows what shape they will assume: the erotomaniac's obsession or the flat spasm of disgust?

'Oh hi, Carina.'

A tall figure dressed with the thrown-together vanity of girlhood, unbrushed hair gathered into a gypsyish slide leaving plenty of straggle, plenty to push back from the wide open forehead with an automatic flick of finger and thumb. The heedless erogenous zones that women lose through nature's thickening: long, whittled forearms, a blueish knobble of wrist, the washboard ridges of the sternum above those junket breasts, the legginess of geraniums straining for the sun. She was standing over our table leaning on one hip, self-conscious, graceless, charming. Very young.

She sat down at our table. As Euan transferred his smile to me I noticed a slight, forgivable dimming.

'Carina's been temping at Lachlan Lane—'

And reignition.

'—this is my pal Tracy Malleus. Supposed to be attached to the museum though you'll never catch her on the premises—'

A milk-tooth grin. I liked her.

'—so how's it going? Andrew Monzie made a pass at you yet?'

She dimpled, a verb I had encountered in sub-literary fiction but never experienced until that hour.

'I've got two arms and two legs haven't I?'

I didn't like her any more.

I recognized the cringing bravado of adolescence, the precarious tightrope between showing off and shame. She knew she was wobbling, so she made it worse.

'On a quiet news day, you can hear the floorboards creaking. We're sitting underneath an exclusive and nobody'll touch it. I know what the *Record* would do with it: *TV's Drew in Shagging Shocker. Telly Minister Changes Girlfriends Like Socks . . .*'

Something odd within the too-fluent recitation, perhaps the way her phrasing was punctuated with the wrong breaths, suggested that these lines had been spoken before. And not only by her. An office joke, then. This is what it boils down to, our great longing for community: freedom of information on who's screwing who.

Euan was displaying the witless determination of men in early middle age to impress themselves on women young enough to be their daughters.

'You know he had an affair with Avril? Lasted almost four months. She threw a party for her big three-o. Found him in the toilet with the caterer. Spent the rest of the night in the cloakroom. Lesley barged in, miraculous—'

His voice plunged to a conspiratorial register, suddenly aware of the silence around our table, and his own increasingly exuberant delivery.

'—told her he wasn't worth greetin' over: he'd been shagging Clare Pitt for a fortnight and nobody'd had the heart to let her know.'

Carina smiled courteously, but she'd heard the story before and was eager to tell a better one.

'He took up with Mairin when Josie was working for the evil empire. Everyone thought he was after a new job: phone calls every five minutes, afternoon appointments. They were only doing it in the boardroom. Big Malcolm needed to see her one day, they told him she was in conference but he walked straight in. That's when she took that six-week sabbatical. Only she wasn't looking into the future of digital broadcasting, she was in the clinic getting her nose reset – Are you OK?'

Their faces jerked towards me, the peevishness of the interrupted softened by a fractional concern. Euan said I should tell the waitress and make a claim against the restaurant, but I couldn't face the thought of sifting through the bowl and, without evidence, who would have believed me? How often do you hear of anyone cracking a tooth on a spoonful of lentil soup?

After all my worrying the Maryhill presentation went well. I came home, cooked myself a watery scrambled egg served up on the crustless pulp of a morning roll – toast seemed dangerously *al dente* – opened a bottle of Shiraz and wrote to Sam. I always write her proper letters even though she never returns the favour. Instead I get postcards, Mount Rushmore with an obscene speech bubble coming out of Jefferson's mouth, a hillbilly on the toilet from Arizona, '*The Abelard Motel is for Lovers*' from Michigan, a row of topiarian phalluses on a privet hedge from Fire Island, and always on the back a dozen words scribbled across the left-hand side, the two kisses slashed in haste or embarrassment, the echoing margin of unused white space. Birthdays, she sends jokey objects briefly in vogue across the Atlantic, hotdog-flavoured condoms; a rape alarm you wear in your knickers, activated by sudden pressure on the groin; cockroach earrings; a can of Los Angeles Police Department pepper spray; glass cocktail stirrers filled with a clear but viscous fluid through which small plastic effigies of Michael Jackson and someone who looks like Louis Farrakhan make their stately progress.

Doubtless she finds my attempts at humour as wide of the mark. After seventeen years, all I have to go on is the post, so I pick the sort of gifts which would tickle a buyer of cockroach earrings. Maybe she's guessing too, and this dime-store gimmickry pleases neither of us.

Next day I crossed the river to repeat my pitch on the miracle cure of memory in Carnegie Drive. It was Roderick's idea: replenish the customers. Working with the over-sixties, your turnover is high. I didn't have to sign them all up at once, just get enough expressions of interest to produce a waiting list if the council ever threatened to pull the plug. This place wasn't a municipal home, nor a profiteering granny farm: too cosy, with its freshly laundered antimacassars and embroidered firescreens and brass companion sets and the bone china plate on the wall with its hand-painted view of Ailsa Craig. The old girls seemed sharper too; even the noddies looked less like they were wearing each other's clothes. The staff were different from the usual breadline skivvies. Young girls with the willing smiles and on-the-knee skirts and artless hairstyles of Tourist Board fantasy: Highland lassies who would sing you an air or dance you a reel or pot you a herring as soon as look at you. One of them led me to the matron, who shook my hand with an uncomfortably knowing contraction of the pupils. Had I interrupted a mass will-altering? Was I about to undo years of painstaking intimidation into blessed vegetable silence? Then I felt her eyes travel down my legs, toes curling invisibly in my damson suede boots. When the possible is exhausted, we must look to the improbable: it seemed that she objected to my wearing trousers.

The group they had assembled in the day room was older than my usual constituency. All female, though that was nothing new, old age is the territory where we girls finally get our turn. Whiskers glinting like needles from softly folding flesh, scalps showing pinkly through dandelion-clock perms, the draping of liverspotted skin over bones that parodied Carina's oversized joints. Perhaps five of the dozen around me were worth addressing. Why so old? I'd spotted younger residents, knitting needles fencing and parrying, hands of cards played and folded, spectacles raised like quizzing glasses, even a chug of sociable laughter. Evidently Matron had her own ideas about who stood to benefit from reminiscence work.

I was well into my pitch when I realized that even the few with any attention worth holding had started to lose interest. In the absence of an alternative, I persevered. Gazes continued to flutter past me. One old duck was overtaken by a snuggle-down smile. Like the principal boy staring straight ahead, heedless of a hundred screamed *behind yous*, I carried on, bewildered but unbowed, until the punchline finally dawned. Slowly I turned, with as much dignity as I could muster. Drew Monzie was standing in the doorway.

'Do go on, Miss Malleus.'

His voice was as deep as ever, but different, as if he'd put on invisible half-moon spectacles. There was a rigidity in his pose which made me nervous, but I couldn't entirely suppress the teasing lift in my reply.

'I'm not used to an audience under pensionable age.'

'I shouldn't let it worry you: I'm not that far off.'

That strain of hostility that addresses others by turning on itself. Give me a shouter every time. I did that little interrogative pucker about the eyes that sometimes chips through public frost. It got a reaction, but not the one I wanted.

'I'm surprised it should concern you what I do—'

I sensed the rustling of sexual antennae behind me, the dragging out and dusting down of long-defunct equipment. I needed to return my attention to the girls: it was extremely impolite to present my back, and in that generation politeness is taken seriously.

'—it didn't seem to bother you that I sat in a public bar where I'm a stranger for an hour and a half wondering if you were lying on the roadside after a car accident, or left for dead by a rapist.' The perfectly enunciated R gave the word an unintended relish. 'Whereas, I am greatly relieved to see, you were simply too ill-mannered to turn up.'

My cheeks were scorching with the disgrace of the naughty child. Someone was trying to open an umbrella inside my chest, the spokes insistent against my ribcage, pushing hard enough to snap. Such a relief to feel the shame replaced by a small hard lump of opposition.

'I left a message at Lachlan Lane. There was no other way of contacting you. I'm sorry you wasted so much time, but you should have given up on me earlier.'

I seemed to have caught his tone of tweedy reproof, a note not altogether welcome in my ears. 'And now, if you'll excuse me . . .' By the time I'd turned up my last prompt card he was gone.

On the way home I remembered I needed bread. Not to eat – until I made it to the dentist there would be nothing but overboiled pasta – but to hoard in the cupboard. I never had a teddy bear, no ragdoll, no bunny, nothing cuddly or furry, no pet to anthropomorphize. Darwin didn't approve of transitional objects, all that Winnicottian shit, but he fetishized the home-baked, stone-ground organic wholemeal loaf. Sam and I would watch him kneading, beating the clod of dough against the scrubbed tabletop, explaining just whom he was punching out. Sometimes he'd let us have a bash, though he was impatient with the feebleness of my efforts: there was no one I hated that much. It wasn't the bread itself I liked, so much as the solid, salty, cardboardy crust, and, hungry or not, as soon as it was out of the oven, barely cool enough to slice, I'd take the heel and hide it in my bedroom. So you could say that bread was my transitional object. Assuming I ever made it across.

Coming out of the shop I spotted a raven, a rook, a crow: I've never known the difference. Whatever it was, an unusual sight among the *fin de siècle* tenements. It was walking purposefully, jauntily, possibly an infant not yet at ease with flight. Its undercarriage had a fluffiness of feather, subfusc to the gleaming jet of the folded wings, the tarry bristle of the executioner's hood. Its legs were black and skinny, septuagenarian socialite pins, grotesquely neat under the couture-chic body. Making straight for me, it stopped short, deflected by a pile of retailer's rubbish, flattened cardboard cartons bundled together with string, a moulded plastic baker's tray with a cargo of brittle morning rolls. Hopping from pavement to the tray's plastic perch, it leapt the implausible distance between one bright blue latticework edge and the other with sudden weightlessness, as if plucked upwards by invisible string. On a whim it hopped down again and strayed onto the road, pecked at a flattened medallion of chewing gum. It was the car which altered course. Losing interest, it waddled back to the gutter, executed another of its absurd, balletic, gravity-defying elevations to the kerb, and picked up a stale roll, an alarmingly proportioned burden but, through loss of moisture, light as polystyrene. The bird carried it some distance nearer before dropping it and pecking out a few desiccated morsels, lifting its head to swallow so I saw the shivery undulations of its gullet, the efficiency of dispatch. Its black beak was coated with sawdust crumbs, attached by some residue of past scavenging.

I have the citydweller's embarrassment around non-domestic animals. Confronted with the beautifully filmed courtship of the natterjack toad, the pining of the widowed mongoose, my boredom threshold is very very low. Yet I stood and watched. I was I suppose still smarting from the little unpleasantness at the eventide home, but beyond my need for distraction, the black bird with its urban savvy seemed relevant in a way I could not easily fix. By now it had returned to the tray and was addressing the greyish polythene surrounding another batch of yesterday's bread. All that pecking and tugging extorted a lateral peak and finally the plastic yielded an opening. It was not that the bird was repellent, not like pigeons, those flying carcasses with their detachable toes; despite its crusted beak, it had the wholesomeness of the wild. But its fearlessness intimidated me. It knew I was there but it would not look up, caging us both in the charged arena of deception. I was glad to be wearing glasses, eyeballs shielded from that tireless beak. Fleetingly, I harboured the image of a foot, my foot, booting it along the pavement, felt the solid mass amid that bulking of feather, the snapping of those Wallis Simpson gams, the give against my toecap as I propelled it through the air. The bird cocked its head suddenly, abandoning its keyhole surgery to bead me with one brown-tinged eye.

'Tracy!'

Drew Monzie was behind me, both hands clutching at my upper arm. Wheeling round with a twinge of some intercostal nerve, I saw that his head was oddly angled, averted. I almost lost my balance, so abrupt was his grip, so unfeasible the manoeuvre, trying to turn me and pull me backwards at the same time. Manhandling me, though the impulse was too sharp to be sexual.

At moments like this the layers of socialization fall away. Darwin would have been proud of me.

'What the fuck are you playing at?'

His face was grey but with a rosy tint of excitement, a touch of falsity in his panic, self-conscious within the extremity of his alarm.

'Did it cross your path?'

'*What?*'

But he was not accessible to rational scorn.

'Did it?'

Only then, wrenching free, did I make the connection.

'For Christ's sake, it's a *bird*.'

I swivelled with the satiric splayfingered gesture of a conjuror's assistant, to find the trick had disappeared. When I turned back, Drew was restored to an approximation of the man I knew. His hair had lost its parting and his sweater had taken on a corkscrew twist, but he was sufficiently recovered to look embarrassed. Me too. I had sworn at a religious broadcaster. A regrettable moment of exposure from both our points of view. I looked up: it was mizzling, spreading that fine net of atmospheric saturation which is the city's natural state. Behind us was a low wall boobytrapped with the iron nipples of an amputated railing. All that Edwardian craftsmanship melted down for propaganda, a war effort that boosted nothing but morale. Finding a relatively benign patch, I sat down. He looked doubtful, but perched alongside.

Fifty yards down the road a traffic light changed, and the queue of cars in front of us started to move. His eyes travelled with the redhead in the black BMW. Tinted windows, wipers slow-sweeping, but she was wearing Ray-Bans just the same.

'You needn't have bothered,' I said. 'I don't believe in it.'

He smiled thinly, his gaze still following the departing car. 'Then it's just as well you've got me looking out for you.'

Across the road on the junction stood a pub, an all-comers drinking hall with a semicircular threshold of brass and fancy mosaic. I nodded towards it.

'Do you fancy that drink now?'

A wee libation. Maybe we shouldn't need this Pavlovian trigger of altered expectations, this permission to flirt, or philosophize, or feel, denying that life has the freedom to happen anytime. Maybe we shouldn't need it, but we do. We tread such narrow paths of cause and effect. I told myself that in coming to Scotland I had entered a landscape of limitless possibility, but already I felt my choices closing in. Did I want a liaison with a failed Free Associated Church minister? Did he want to fetter his freedom by associating with me? Would the potential pleasures be worth the grief? The honest answer was that I did not know, but I knew it was important to hold on to this uncertainty. One way or another we predetermine most outcomes, forcing a resolution that no one necessarily wants; sometimes we don't even spot the point where we cross the line. I suggested a drink in the Victoria Bar, and from the moment he shrugged his acquiescence it was only a matter of time.

I love the tins in Tullibardines. Enamelled tins that looked the same when Livingstone left North Britain. Embossed tins of Highland toffee. Tartan tins of deadweight Dundee cake. Tins of broth with mock-Landseer labels and 'by royal appointment' next to the seam. Sweet-cured hams in aspic. 'Purveyors of fine foods' it says on the white paper bags, just as it did when rationing was lifted, and the stock has not greatly altered either. Tullibardines is still the place to go for meringue nests, pickled walnuts, ratafia biscuits and other delicacies the genteel housewife of the 1950s held in high esteem. Though I prefer the Continental corner with its eye-watering sauerkraut and pumpernickel densely flexible as cork tile. Once in a while, these were the foods that Darwin would buy, the stuff of our childhood treats, which gives me an odd affinity with the do-gooding golf widows and fur-clad grandes dames buying their candied peel and loose-leaf Orange Pekoe.

I'm bent over the loose-biscuit boxes, wondering if lemon and cinnamon would appeal to Drew, so I don't spot him until the last moment, although I'm not altogether surprised. Such incongruous juxtapositions carry their own inevitability. He is dressed like the men in glossy magazines, in fabrics whose softness begs the exploratory touch. That blue chin is piratically dark this late in the day. A lonely tin of anchovy-stuffed olives rides in his chariot.

'Hello, you.'

It's not that he has forgotten my name. Hereabouts such greeting is a paradoxical token of intimacy. He shunts the trolley to one side and leans in close. Only hairdressers kiss in the confectionery aisle.

His glance combs my damply straggling hair, snagging on a chlorine knot. 'Defected to another salon?'

I laugh it off, though shamed to my exposed roots. 'Sod off, Gil, I'm just out of the pool.'

He grins back and I gather that a hard day at the cutting edge has depleted his stock of smalltalk.

I nod towards those olives. 'That won't keep body and soul together.'

'Aye, well . . .' But what was to follow is lost with the arrival of a mashed potato shampoo-and-set. We separate to let her pass, glancing in expectation of some modest acknowledgement, but receiving only a spinsterly glare. Recently Tullibardines has become fashionable with the Friday night pick-up crowd, its narrow aisles congested with singles getting acquainted over the linguini before moving on to what they might fancy for breakfast.

At least this gives us something to smile over. He looks into my basket, seeking inspiration in a jar of crabapple jelly and a can of cullen skink. What *do* we talk about in those five-hour appointments? The first words that spill from my lips are a slighting reference to a new and much-promoted sitcom, a clumsily acted farce with a mirthless premise, set in our own back yard. Too late I realize that the scriptwriter is a customer of his, maybe even an occasional drinking pal.

He nods, though disagreeing with me. 'I think it's pretty funny.'

There is a slight pause during which I note the old-tech *ching* of the till. A distant voice enquires after haggis. He picks up a packet of Viennese fancies, puts them back again. 'The curse hasnae got you yet, then?'

A while back I went through a phase of dizzy spells. All it took was a cup of espresso on an empty stomach and suddenly I was sweaty, light-headed and spotty before the eyes, seeing an extra insistence in the texture of things, bus stops and buildings swarming towards me, the pulsating sky squeezing my eyeballs. I cut out the morning caffeine and it got better, but sometimes commercial striplights have the same effect.

'Sorry, Gil, what were you saying?'

For a moment he looks lost, despite the poise of those fancy threads. 'The great hair robbery: you've survived it.'

'Oh aye – did you ever find out who she was?'

He shakes his head. 'Never saw her again.'

Further shoppers file between us, and when they have passed, Gil manoeuvres his trolley back into the traffic. I'm relieved, if a little resentful, at his eagerness to go.

'Time we saw you professionally,' he says, with a last-ditch attempt at drollery.

'I'll give you a call.'

I meander along Condiments, swither over the maple syrup, flirt briefly with the focaccia, then race down Morning Goods to catch him at the till.

'Gil.'

He turns, gratified. He likes being the centre of attention, having the checkout lady know his name.

'What was that about a curse?'

Those in the queue who have paid no attention now lift their gaze. He shrugs, rippling the supple leather of his jacket. 'A crap joke.'

'I don't get it.'

'Dennis Wheatley – you know.'

But I don't.

I can tell he is wishing he had never brought it up. 'When they make a wax effigy and get some hair or fingernail so there's a physical connection—' He mugs a sinister grimace for the benefit of the queue. '—I wouldnae lose sleep over it: if there was a curse on you, you'd know about it.'

Drew's biscuits come to two pounds twenty, which is more than I was planning to pay.

FIVE

The artful high shot of the chimneypot lenses, the vast limbo of lino around the snugness of the set: the television studio is one of our stock images of yellowing modernity, like golfing on the moon or Jackie on all fours in the Dallas motorcade, part of the collective unconscious tapped by advertising creatures and headline writers to sell us . . . Sorry, that's heredity talking. Darwin always resented television, a stance of the same order of pointlessness as the Amish resenting the zipper. Now here I am not just parroting the prejudice, but meaning it too. There are times I sympathize with the wackos in Drew's kirk denouncing the devil's instrument for corrupting us with false coin. Not on account of women in trousers or *Masterchef* on the Sabbath. What bothers me is the selling short, downgrading the priceless particularity of the local in favour of the departure lounge anonymity of the impenetrable screen.

Usually I watch *Revelations* at home. It's one of our games. We have nicknames, code words, covert signals: it's the paranoiac's nightmare come true. Should one of his studio guests wax particularly unbearable Drew will scratch his left ear. If their line of argument grows unfeasibly attenuated he may accuse them of 'postmodernism'. Sometimes his lips align with the hint of a smile as he does so, but the pleasure is more complete if they do not. The private semaphore gives me a sense of sharing this part of his life, an illusion shattered whenever any of his public approach him for autographs or launch, unprompted, into fond reminiscence of favourite moments from the show. Then I realize how removed I am from Drew Monzie the flyting minister but – and this is important – no more removed than he. The presenter receives these proprietorial tributes in wonder, knowing that whether they stoop to touch the hem of his garment or circle his shoulder with the commandeering arm, he will never understand quite what it is he means to them.

'How're you doin'?'

A silent mouthing from Cameron the floor manager. I mime

the raised-eyebrow grin of distant cordiality. We're booked for the theatre at seven-thirty so today I'm watching the show from the wings. The studio is a mess of chipboard and blue paint, the splintered edges of his desk unfinished, the snaking cables gaffer-taped to the floor, an underworld populated by the bobbing, creeping, occasionally scuttling figures behind the stockade of cameras. Drew affects to despise the technology, but it's an essential vehicle for his mystic communion with his country. Scratch the urbanity of his telly professionalism, his good microphone voice, and you'll find an acute case of pathetic fallacy, a man who believes the very stones reflect his feelings. Of course he knows better than to admit to the megalomania thus implied. There's a precautionary inversion: he is so susceptible to the spirit of a place that *he* takes on *its* tenor but, funnily enough, its tenor fits his melancholy like a glove. We laugh about this, but he's deadly serious. *L'Ecosse, c'est moi.* Scotland as a state of mind.

He was spotted at Synod as a fresh-faced apprentice, delivered a speech full of soundbites and made the lunchtime news. He'd always been struck on the media: writing letters to the papers; getting the odd topical sermon into print, heavily edited, once they'd run out of secular angles on the latest act of God. And when, on the point of ordination, he had his problems with the Presbytery, it seemed the obvious fall-back: he needed a job, and they were looking for a Sunday broadcaster who'd never heard of double time. At least, that's my understanding, though there may be one or two details I don't know.

Drew has had other lives yet he speaks to me only of childhood. It is as if he has erased the rest, the errors and specifics, the literals of his life. Who was he before we met? I know he existed, he has the videotapes to prove it, five shelves' worth of Sundays minus the annual summer break. But where was he after the credits rolled? Oh I *know* him inside out, in many ways as well as I know myself: his tastes and inclinations, the blackspots in his humour, his kinks and reasonless fears. In love with his country, and imprisoned by what he loves, threatened immeasurably by intimations that another's Scotland might be larger than his own. Sentimental about Gaeldom in the classic Lowland way, and pained that this higher Scotland shuts him out. Champion of his nation, denouncing mush-culture and creeping anglicization and the colonizing cathode ray tube but still chasing the doppelganger, his scaled-down, shiny, perfected self. I can't condemn him. Everyone wants to be changed – all those quick-fix happiness manuals on the bestseller list – we all want to believe it's possible, the only question is how? Drew believes in transformation from the outside in. Mirror magic. Seeing his radiance reflected in the viewer's face and one day, perhaps, believing in it. I take a more prosaic approach. We are what we eat, and breathe, and see: the sum total of our influences. If you don't like the dish, you vary the ingredients. Emigration. It's always worked for me. Although, all things being equal, it's better not to choose a country that holds you personally representative of everything you emigrated to avoid.

Siobhan the PA glides across the floor and points an index finger upwards, inviting me into the gallery. I shake my head, but nicely. She knows I always watch from the floor, where the tension between the man I love and the man I can never know is almost tangible. My other half is a compound fraction. But then, when the red light's glowing we're all on our own.

The first time I went to see Drew at the studio, he had abandoned his blue desk for a round table of politicians: Labour, Tory, Lib-Dem and Nationalist all represented. I was the only one who was fooled. Everyone else knew that the object of this careful balance was to allow Drew to wrongfoot the uncompromising unionist as politely as possible, to needle the devolutionists with slightly less reserve, and to go for the SNP jugular on the grounds that we forgive our own their failings least of all. Under the presenter's prerogative of challenge he posed questions which were actually highly partisan rhetorical denunciations, if nothing compared with the speech that was still to come. *Revelations* is, however unlikely it often seems, a religious programme, and the minister always has the last word, a two-minute sermon of summary which is more reflective of his personal prejudices than of anything his guests might have had to say. The format is a hangover from the Sixties, but seems to strike a chord with its audience, which is, as far as the modish mandarins at Lachlan Lane are concerned, embarrassingly high. Admittedly there's not much competition at five-fifteen on Sunday afternoons, but sometimes the ratings top *Scotland at Six*.

Drew gets the biggest postbag on the station, a source of profound grief among the slimline, suntanned Daves and Marks and Andys in the third-floor canteen.

It was a rainy afternoon, the Sunday streets scoured clean of people and, unsettlingly, of cars. *Revelations* being a mixture of live and prerecorded material, I had been told to arrive early, to catch the taping of the studio discussion, but by the time the commissionaire finally showed me in, finger ostentatiously shushing his lips, the debate was already under way. Drew was sitting in semi-darkness with two politicians at either hand, presenting an almost iconic tableau, a scaled-down last supper. On the vast table in front of them were a carafe of water, a half-drunk glass, and an empty fruitbowl, a pool of reverberant ochre against the midnight of the set.

'You don't really expect us to swallow that?'

The party chairman bared his grey and yellow teeth in a rictus of effortful good humour. Mustn't be rude to the minister, especially on a Sunday. Poor old Farquhar, whose very christening was a joke at his expense. Scraped back in '83 with a majority of thirteen, since when, inevitably, he'd been known as 'Lucky'. Next to him was Tommy Parr, fresh from his Barbara Follett personal grooming session but looking as much as ever like Horace Broon. On the other side sat Jim Lawers in his Aran sweater, pitching for the home handicraft vote (there are an awful lot of wool shops on Royal Deeside) and, at the end, Black Douglas, nursing a paralysing hangover, to judge by the frequency of his recourse to the water carafe. Unless it was a case of rabies.

I won't deny I enjoyed watching Drew rough them up. And continue to enjoy it. Quite sexy in a limited kind of way. Puts him in the mood, too: a bit of antler-locking before bedtime. The experience of broadcasting affects him profoundly, lingering long after the director wraps it up, a possession to be driven out like daemons, his promiscuous reproduction in five hundred thousand homes. But that first visit to the studio I had no inkling of this; I saw only the interviewer's knockabout, that ambiguous mix of aggression and clubbable code.

Despite the safety net of pretransmission editing, the discussion seemed as tense as if the show were going out live. Every so often proceedings would be halted for another prerecorded insert, or to allow Drew to repeat an imperfect link and, while the director fussed over some technical requirement, presenter and guests would exchange that peculiarly impersonal banter that goes with the territory of masculine public life. Then Drew's magic earpiece would buzz him to attention, a rapture at once impressive and absurd, like a mystic entranced, or a German pointer fixing on game. The moment he left their inferior sphere of consciousness, his guests' conversation would lapse, their pretensions to nonchalance cruelly exposed. In the interval between this calling to readiness and the resumption of filming, while Drew communed with his inner ear, they entered a state of suspended animation, expressions self-consciously absent, faculties strainingly alert, trapped in the distress of men of action waiting for a role. Their host, meanwhile, was in his element. As a television presenter, he enjoyed a reverence from the powerful which the status of spiritual leader could never have bestowed. In this immaterial world where political influence hovered, ungraspable as grace, they had no option but to submit dumbly to his will. And when the camera closed in on his face at the end of the programme, banishing them to a hinterland of shadows, they could only acquiesce.

'They tell us that there is no such thing as Scotland. That the gap between Lowlander and Highlander is as wide as that between Englishman and Scot. They say that Inverness would rather be ruled by London than by the tinpot tyrants of the Central Belt. Rebel hearts in Orkney and Shetland have vowed that the day sovereignty returns to the Scottish people is the day they announce their own UDI. Even Glasgow and Edinburgh, the teenage delinquent with his pimples and his blaring rock, and the speccy swot poring over his Latin verbs, cannot agree. They bicker across the lobby, narrow in their prejudices, resenting the parents that feed and clothe them for holding them back. We are as squabbling children, forsaking wisdom and judgement in the pursuit of petty difference, an adolescent nation forever passing the buck. But I ask you, was it not ever the fate of those treated as children to respond in kind? Ach, the cry goes up, to undo three hundred years of history would be a terrible mistake. And this may be so. Is it not the prerogative of other nations to make their own mistakes, and learn from them? No such thing as Scotland: there's a dream. Why not a thousand Scotlands united in diversity? A nation no longer so conveniently introverted, so obsessed with the mistakes of history, that our neighbours can safely ignore us? Why not a country sufficiently civilized to *like* the folk who live down the stair? If we want our nation to grow and flourish, and who looking around them at this desert of inhibition and timorousness would not? If we want our people to reach their potential, secure in identity, embracing the variety and splendour of their race; *if* we want these things, there is one sure way to attain them.

'Goodnight.'

I was astonished. This jettisoned any pretence of balance. He'd given it the works. The sermon might have been a cornerstone of national culture, but even in Scotland you didn't use sepia lyricism and thunderous pulpit oratory in the cause of nationalist propaganda on prime time TV. That was before I realized it happened every other week. The prelude from Bach's cello suite number one in G major played, somewhat tinnily, from a monitor on which the credits were scrolling by. Drew unclipped his microphone and exchanged a few words of bonhomous banter with his guests. They chuckled, moderately, to show that there were no hard feelings. Although of course there were.

I'd only caught a couple of editions of *Revelations* at home, but I'd seen enough to notice that Drew looked different on screen, healthier in complexion, his sluggish pallor invigorated with the glow of studio lighting or the flush of the make-up brush but chiefly, I assumed, changed by the technology. It wasn't inherently implausible: actresses complain the camera adds ten pounds, why should there not be other transformations? But as he strolled across the floor towards me I recognized that this dazzle wasn't dependent on the mediating lens.

'That should get them going in Garelochhead.'

Back on the set, Lucky was looking a little less genial.

'Not to mention closer to home.'

I admit it: I enjoy the pleasures of stagey repartee, the crisp exchange of dialogue banal enough in content but stimulating in form, a rhythm as sexual as any between the sheets.

He extended a formal right hand.

'Delighted you could make it, Tracy Samantha—'

It never seemed worth stopping this Tracy Samantha business. It was a seal of intimacy, a private joke, if I'd nipped it in the bud who knows if we'd have come to fruition; and later, well, later it was just too late. It's not as if I'm keeping anything from him, he knows I have a sister, it's just that he doesn't know her name.

'—I hope you found that of interest.'

They were all in the know, of course. The cameramen, the director, the producer, the PA. Not that there was anything to be known at that stage, but they'd seen the wide-eyed studio tour too many times before. The politicians, on the other hand, weren't privy to his secrets and considering the ride they'd just been given, the formalities made sense. Anyway, he was playing at strangers. Never mind that we *were* strangers more or less, the shared deception created a kind of bond.

'Aren't there supposed to be rules about impartiality?'

'Did I not sound impartial to you?'

'You sounded like you've already picked out the curtains for Holyrood.'

He cast a glance over his shoulder and, in turning back, the porcelain gleam in the whites of his eyes flashed startlingly. 'If Andrea McCracken doesn't get there first.'

This too was destined to become a regular joke: who's in line for the presidency of an independent Scottish republic. Andrea is a paid-up member of the great and good who recycles the arguments for Scottish self-determination with fearsome, numbing persistence. She reviews books, lends her gravitas to radio panels, speaks at school prize-givings, and always, always, says the same thing. In reality neither of them stands a chance: everyone knows Sean Connery has first refusal.

These days, when I drop by Lachlan Lane, the studio looks very different, my perspective sharpened by technical understanding and blurred with the boredom of routine. I see good shows and bad shows, days when working the weekend lends a holiday abandon, days when they're going through the motions zombied with fatigue. I know about Siobhan and her boyfriend trouble, Jacob's flirtation with smack, Gregor's herd of cashmere goats; I'm used to Drew's blatant displays of favour and the rage of his producer after the show; and sometimes I wonder what I ever found so intimidating.

'So what's the plan, Tracy-S?'

Bach has died another death, Drew has shaken hands with the rabbi and granted the British Movement organizer a curt nod, and here he is before me, expanding that mountainous torso with a slow creaking stretch, left arm bent to free the silky hairs plastered by perspiration to the back of his neck. I lean in close on the pretext of blowing across his collar, in reality to inhale a little sabbatarian sweat.

'Well, we could earn our brownie points with Lepage at the Tramway, but I'd rather see that Icelandic comedy they tried to ban at the Citz.'

'Is that the one supposed to make Kelman sound like *Tea at Miss Cranston's*?'

'Treenie Campbell takes her clothes off in the second half.'

'You talked me into it. Let's hope no one shops me to the *Sunday Post*.'

'They'll get you in the end.'

His face is blank, but then indigenous ignorance is permissible; the immigrant can never afford not to know.

'Scotland will never be free . . .' I chant.

He looks at me testily, none the wiser.

'*Until the last minister is strangled with the last copy of the* Sunday Post—'

Muir McKinnon. How did he creep up on us?

'—God knows I'm counting the days. Thought you'd be at home watching the rugby, Tracy: your lot are in with a chance. By the way, Drew, do you think you might inform your producer before pulling a stunt like that again?'

Evidently there were fireworks before I arrived, but McKinnon has decided against a retake, which rather undercuts his footing on the moral high ground.

I'm not fond of Muir McKinnon, and not just because of his thinly concealed loathing for Drew. His sort of normal isn't normal any more. Harris tweed jacket with leatherette elbow patches. Polyester shirt over the trelliswork of a sitcom string vest. Highlander's brogues and Argyll socks. Building society manager's tie with an egg-drip motif randomly repeating on the maroon background. That slightly greasy hair just curling over his collar and the reek of long-forgotten roast beef still lodged between his teeth. That and the pipe. What makes him think these features are socially acceptable? Where has he *been*? Sitting up all night watching Seventies reruns on UK Gold? The most sinister detail is that he may be no older than me. I can't tell any more. Once the old looked old, and the middle-aged middle-aged: that was their most striking characteristic. Now even the Magellan Street crumblies look like people. I register the speculative glint in their eyes, the sensuality or malice in the set of their lips, where once I saw only the dullness of cataracts, the slackening skinbag of an organism in decline. McKinnon looks past it to me, but it's an ageless state, a voluntary relinquishing. He's thrown in the sexual towel, if indeed he ever got wet. This might sound like vulnerability, but actually it's a badge of rank. Freakishness is the prerogative of the powerful, of those whose essential normality is not in doubt. If you're born outwith the Wendy House, it's not an option.

'Come on Muir – it'll bring in the mail, and a few inches in tomorrow's papers. I had Julie send out a press release.'

McKinnon twists his wrist upwards to check the time, a gesture which fails to camouflage what amounts to a strategic withdrawal. 'I haven't got time for this now. We'll have it out on Tuesday.'

Drew is not normally given to *Carry On* double entendre but, as I mentioned, live television affects him in peculiar ways. McKinnon, already walking away, pretends not to notice.

'I've booked us a table at Cressida's for nine-fifteen. The play's ninety minutes straight through, no interval.'

Drew purses his lips as if about to breathe softly into an invisible flute, a mannerism that always stirs my pulse.

'You think of everything.'

The play is disappointing, which is not to say it affords nothing of use. New stock for our repertoire of in-jokes, a pretentious line, Treenie Campbell's defeated attempt at a dominatrix. At home I make a better fist of it; and afterwards Drew brews me a cup of camomile and pours himself a finger of malt and I give him the news.

Preoccupied with a shoelace, he is hardly listening.

'Uh-huh?'

'Must have come surface mail: the postmark's five weeks old—'

He switches his attention to the other foot.

'—she's arriving a week on Saturday.'

Now I've got him.

'What are you talking about?'

'My sister. She's coming to stay.'

'For how long?'

A good question. 'Since she's crossing the Atlantic, we can assume it's not the weekend. I haven't seen her in seventeen years, so it seems only sisterly to have her for as long as she likes.'

'Hold on, I don't even know her name, and now you're telling me she could be with us indefinitely.'

Still seated on the side of the bed, he pulls his socks up and his jumper down, a ritual as familiar as – well, that's the point, there are no comparisons. 'What is her name by the way?'

He had to know some time.

'Samantha. She's called Samantha.'

'Sorry?'

Drew doesn't call me Tracy Samantha all the time. It's a sign of special moments, like singing in the car, or sharing a bath, or licking crème brulée from the same teaspoon; a precious point of focus in the heedless headlong scramble of making love. Now it will never happen again.

He takes his jacket from the chair, spots and carefully removes the curly hair from one cuff. A black questionmark ending in a stricken bulb of white.

'Right.' He looms over the pillow, dignified, daddyish, already bracing himself for the dank outdoors. 'Goodnight, sleep tight, hope the twirlies don't bite.'

Drew is married. Or didn't I mention that?

SIX

The school stands alongside a sparse square of park in what I suppose you'd call the most picturesque part of this least picturesque of neighbourhoods, a wild west frontier settlement with hard rules and rough manners and a certain bleak poetry in its exile from the blandishments of the late twentieth century. The tenements are plain, bereft of the curlicued vines and classical pediments, the joke Jacobean chimneys which embellish even the most basic buildings on our side of the river. The absence of detailing forces the visitor to take the long view and find beauty in the oddly-angled jutting of the shipyard cranes above the red sandstone tenements, the stark refusal of the twenty-foot wall blanking off the blind alleys beside the yard. Drew once bought Cammie an outdated Rangers strip from a house in one of these melodramatically foreshortened streets and told the boy he'd got it in No Future Avenue, a name that could sit comfortably on every street corner, cul-de-sac or thoroughfare. The shops predate the age of cornucopia consumerism, their stock unambitious, almost rationed, in range. Their turquoise tiles and yellow Formica seem to date from an exact moment in the nineteen sixties, a wet November weekend when the forces of international capital decided the place no longer represented a viable investment. Confectioners sell sweets and tobacco, utilitarian jars of cough candy and soor plooms, dusty boxes of chocolates in packaging long since superseded. Fish shops offer a minimalist menu: fish; chips; sausage, battered or smoked. No deep-fried steak pie or grease-sodden pizza. And to drink, just a shelf of sticky-looking Irn Bru with a warning intensity in its synthetic colour, as if some critical chemical change has occurred. You know what it's really like? A fairground. The suggestion of freak shows and urban gypsies; men with oiled hair and exotic tattoos; stookies painted in tender, tawdry pastels; gaudy plastic façades with an edge of panic in their gaiety; and the smell of fried onions heavy in the air. To walk through this quarter is to court a seductive dread. Trying to analyse the drop in my stomach, the sudden hunger that is half appetite, half fear, I come back to that sense of lives spilling onto the pavement, an unboundedness always latent in this city, a spreading lava of vulgar gratification, sex and violence, impulse and phantasy, the swirling soup of id. To share the street with a stranger is to enter their life, to acknowledge their right to address, or accost, you. Which is one of the reasons I came here, or at least, one of the reasons I stay.

There are one hundred and seventeen people in this room, a high-ceilinged, long-windowed chamber of workhouse severity, which the enlightened educationalists of the late twentieth century have painted the gorge-rising colour of strawberry blancmange. I couldn't wait to leave school, yet there is something about the smell of chalk and powder paint and plimsoll sweat that tugs at the entrails, dislodging unsuspected nostalgia. That time the geography textbooks fell on Julie Ancara's head. The bearded, lugubrious art teacher – what *was* his name? – with whom I forged an inexplicable bond; surely not sexual, as a child of barely eleven? But looking back now it feels heavy with the unacknowledged, a dark corner amid the crêpe paper and cowgum and plaster of Paris in the sun-streaked artroom. He used to mention his wife, which struck me as strangely unteacherly, though what he said is beyond recall. To be honest I don't put too much effort into this sort of retrieval.

The meeting is scheduled to start at seven. The clock, brown Bakelite with a vicious unpredictability to its jerking minute hand, shows a quarter to. We'll be lucky to begin by quarter past, but that's OK, in fact it's a bonus, a stolen half-hour with nothing to do but watch and listen, and infiltrate other lives. Another couple of women peer, uncertainly, through the door: one hundred and nineteen. Not a bad turnout. There's Uncle Joe, our local Labour MP, still wearing his rust-speckled 'Ditch the Bitch' badge. He's a bam, everybody says so, which in no way diminishes his status as political saint. And beside him, Stevie Caw, with his consumptive menace, that madman's glitter of compassion and rage, still living off his role in that thirty-year-old play, a boiling broth of social indignation reduced to the slops of annual revival. He's the only one here you'd call famous, but there are several half-familiar faces attracting their share of rubbernecking stares. It suits us to be

57

generous with the gift of parish pump celebrity, for in this way we are all enhanced.

I should have guessed the artistic community would be out in force: the gallery owner with his flapping fringe and polkadot handkerchief; and Manny Rae, a guitar legend who now inspects drains for the Environmental Health. He looks substantially the same, with the accent on substantial, a thickening around the neck and nose: funny where age will get you. That packing crate on legs he's talking to is Pablo, who, about the time Yolande was taking up the crystal ball, got paid off at the yards and conned Enterprise Allowance into paying him forty quid a week to produce the great Glasgow novel. He's still at it, too, penning those unreadable indictments of capitalism that never get past chapter three, wondering why it worked for Zola and not for him. And hello, here's MacCodrum, our foremost exponent of tea cosy surrealism. Acknowledged influences: Beuys, Michelangelo and back numbers of *Woman's Realm*. His current interest is food sculpture, a pageant of Scottish history rendered in confectionery. The raising of the standard at Glenfinnan baked as shortbread (he cheated on the muskets, using Matchmakers made in Slough), the massacre at Glencoe in Tunnocks' snowballs, Bannockburn carved from tablet, the Disruption done in pan drops . . . Once you've grasped the metaphor, there isn't much more to be said, although he's popular with the weans, and the Eastern Europeans. Very big in Czechoslovakia, I understand. He likes me, but it's an affection contaminated with stickiness for my calling: St Tracy of the sweetiewives, patron saint of the undervalued, my own voice subsumed within the babble of their pasts.

'I've phoned you a couple of times but I didnae want to leave a message and upset your man.'

Let's take this as a joke, although of course it isn't. Strange attitudes are abroad. The other day I heard Big Vivien asking the wee man's permission to meet the girls for a lemonade shandy: not a reciprocal courtesy, needless to say. Called in to hospital for one of the *sotto voce* operations, Jeannie MacArthur's overriding anxiety was the rota of neighbours for cooking His tea. Even Euan appends the offer of a spare ticket for *Firebird* with the caveat 'if Drew doesn't mind'. And Drew hates the ballet, so that's not what he means.

'I was thinking you could maybe help me out next week. I'm needing a classical beauty for my Flora Macdonald. We'll be working in Cream-Crowdie.'

He's flirting, silly old sod. Seventy-five if he's a day. He can't expect to get away with a line like that. And yet I let him, tickled by the assumption that I'm eligible to pose as a national heroine, a dimension to the flattery of which he seems unaware.

'Won't it go off before you're finished?'

'That's the idea.'

His good eye has assumed a sly cast; with MacCodrum you can never be sure where the irony ends. Like that peg leg with its barleysugar twist, an ambiguous prosthetic on the margins of bad taste. Hard on the stump, too: he's feeling it now, the seeing eye turns shifty as he scans the crowd for a vacant seat.

'I'm parkin' the bahookie. I'll see you after, hen.'

Abandoned, I'm free to indulge in a spot of cataloguing. First in, and nearest the front, are the Tankies, lean, nervy old men with their oilcloth caps and fishermen's sweaters, the obstinacy of the autodidact in their bird-bright eyes. All that learning, all those quotes from Willie Gallagher and Jack London on the tips of their tongues, though they've still to come to terms with Berlin post eighty-nine. Behind sit the Greens, with their print-outs of urban fauna, their lists of sedge warblers and waxwings and whooper swans; they're even claiming the salmon are back in the river, although from the Brussels sprouts reek in the backwash from the sludgebucket, I have my doubts. At the far side of the room, leaning against the pie charts and spelling rhymes, hogging the meagre heat of the prehistoric radiators, are the inevitable academics. The leather jacket and Trotsky specs will be the sociologist; historians prefer the chainstore trenchcoat and red lambswool scarf. Those Slater suits hovering by the door are harder to read: security consultants keeping an eye on the opposition, or just a couple of store managers worried about trade? Bizarrely, they're trying to blend in with my people, the antediluvian order of Magellan Street bores, nonaligned, nonpolitical, licensed to spill; the citizens who in their first child-hood made these quayside backstreets their playground. Touching that so many have made the effort, braved the rain and their arthritis to assemble here tonight. And with a royal documentary on the telly, too. But then, demolition was always a reliable rallying point. Monarchists or red flag-fliers, we're all conservatives underneath.

Calico Street. Have you *seen* it? Even I have to squint to get misty eyed. Semi-derelict but indisputably their own, a patch of ground no one else could conceivably covet. And now money, foreign money, *English* money, has decided to take a chunk of their precious eyesore, this slum paradise of drifting litter and graffitoed stone, and replace it with a service point for the underclass. We've all seen the plans at the library, the white architect's model with its mysteriously mature trees. A yellow brick precinct with a pile-'em-high-sell-'em cheap supermarket, a burger joint with twenty-five brands of cholesterol for under one pound forty-five, a video rental with a hoochy-coochy rectangle of flashing lights and, the star attraction, a purpose-built bingo palace offering twenty-four-hour play. There's no question it'd be prettier than the current commercial shantytown, a rat run of metal shutters, dropped syringes, and bored, borderline-malevolent gangs of local youth; on paper, Waterside Place is a marked improvement. But that's not really the point.

Here we go: a new batch of arrivals, a dozen or so, and not an accidental bunching, a posse. All men. Younger than the Tankies, if not exactly young, and harder to categorize. Their leader – though I'm not sure how I know this, since he's not actually in the lead – is in his mid-forties and dressed, with a not-quite risible threatricality, all in black. Leather jacket, sweatshirt and jeans. Still fit and lean, but a leanness already showing how the belly will rise into an old man's pot, the shanks shed their muscle. His hair is clipped short in a psychotic crop, the scalping inflicted on American servicemen, now adopted as a badge of youth. He files along the row ahead, making his way to the seat just in front of me, so I can trace the pattern of crowns and whorls, like swarf on a magnetic field. Being cut so short its shade is not immediately apparent, just a watered whisky glitter, but there's no mistaking the redhead's complexion, that pink scaliness of skin. And the freckles: face, neck, the eyelids with their colourless lashes, the translucent crest of the ear. Even the mouth, the lips themselves, caramel pigment spotting the cushioned flesh, a disturbing detail, as if the normal rules, the distinctions between inside and outside, do not apply.

Judging by the stir among the Maggies he's known to them: there's a rustle of realignment. The easy smile with which Cathy Fenessy greets all-comers is unaccountably absent, displaced by a terse nod. Catching Mary Duffin's eye, she makes a face I've never seen before, a furtive twitch like a stifled sneeze.

In front of the blackboard are three men. Only room for one to sit comfortably behind the coveted authority of the teacher's desk, but the other two cuddle up regardless. Piggy in the middle raises his head. Middle-aged, middling height with a bland-featured air of command: a shop steward from the Seventies perhaps.

'Good evening comrades, ladies.'

And if not instantly then surprisingly soon the room is quiet, conversations are finished with an embarrassed smile, the last word mouthed soundlessly, or the sentence left hanging with an apologetic grimace.

'Most of youse know me but if there's anybody who doesnae, my name's Tommy McAfee, I'm an area organizer at Transport House. This meeting's been called to elect a committee to coordinate the Calico Street Defence Campaign. If that's the name we decide to go with. For the purpose of drawing up an agenda I propose to act as temporary chairman. I take it we're all in agreement—?'

This may not be everybody's idea of entertainment but believe me I'm having a ball. Drew wonders that I can stand the greyness of this city after my psychedelic youth. No meditating with men in orange loincloths and trying not to peek; no kaftan-clad bank managers questing for their inner child; no chemical freak-outs to talk down off the roof. I've sat around on beanbags discussing the meaning of life with a Nobel prizewinner and a clutch of paranoid schizophrenics and yes, despite the right-on propaganda, I *could* tell which was which. P.J. Proby once tried to . . . well, perhaps now isn't the time. The point is, being brought up in a state of permanent excitement, I truly appreciate the novelty of the everyday. I like the fact that I know broadly what's going to happen; that I can tell you who'll be voted on to that committee right now. The triumvirate behind the desk, the game old boy in the wide-lapelled jacket and mustard turtleneck, that Unison rep with the Pringle sweater and broken nose, the bearded Tankie in zip cardie and polyester slacks. Stevie Caw for his pull with the press boys. And, of course, the freckled hard man.

'—As you all know, the council is trying to asset-strip our area . . .'

We all know, which is not going to inhibit our temporary chairman from explaining the situation at length. Calico Street is coming down, two rows of derelict tenements and a church no one attends. Honey sandstone darkened to a sooty tortoiseshell, their slateless roofs crowned with an astonishing variety of weeds, shrubs and saplings, a forest of roots anchored fifty feet above ground. And for this we have splutters of outrage in the evening paper, all these quasi-celebrities manning the barricades? Not quite. You see, Calico Street is a political nexus, one of those sore spots of oppression where rival agendas meet.

The major partner in the Waterside development is an Anglo-American conglomerate which runs a chain of food halls across the UK. Most are cathedrals of upper middle-class consumption: in-store bakery, delicatessen, global greengrocery, your first port of call for smoked reindeer sausage, fresh okra or oven-ready salmon en croûte. And then they run what they call their bedrock stores, all three of them, curiously, in Scotland, and all on or adjacent to notorious housing schemes. Once, last summer, finding myself on the less festive side of Edinburgh, I braved the blanked-out windows in search of a banana. Silly me. A distant corner, over which hung the swaying sign *fresh produce*, suspended by unequal lengths of string, housed a rack of spongy carrots, three mouldy cauliflowers, and a suppurating onion. The apples, too, were soft. For the rest, it was a hangar of cardboard cartons and grey striplighting, everything required to maintain our reputation as the coronary heart disease capital of the world. The crisp and confectionery aisle stretched the length of the M74. But more shocking than the stock was the absence of retailing's seductive wiles, of roseate lighting and slick neon signs. Not even the elementary courtesy of pictures on the tins. Why bother with hidden persuaders when the deal was so up-front? Prices were cheap, and the customers had no choice.

Not, if I'm honest, that this is precisely my objection.

At last, the meeting is opened to contributions from the floor. All speakers must stand and introduce themselves, a prospect so intimidating that a couple of opinions sit down again unexpressed. Out on the street they wouldn't think twice, but the air in here is choked with protocol, the suspicion of procedures they don't understand. As ever, the prolix come out best. There is a delayed start to the audience's focus, a hiatus to allow the rapid audit of who, why, and by what right. Those who make their point too quickly simply sabotage their case. Catching my eye, Mary Duffin smiles defeatedly. Unusually for the Maggies, her husband is still alive, a brass finisher to trade, though long retired.

'John Duffin, Tobacco Street. There's always been Duffins around Calico Street. My father worked fifty year at Gordon's, and his father afore him . . .'

His head is huge and box-shaped, the white hair close-barbered, his massy torso wasting into brittle spindled limbs. One of those men whom age has rendered touching; forty years younger he'd have had me on Prozac. Now he's talking about his former neighbour, a game old girl who's had to be moved to sheltered accommodation which is bleeding her daughter's savings dry. A real drag, but hardly to the point. Mary hears him out, eyes trained on a meandering crack on the opposite wall.

' . . . Tuesdays I always take her the *Radio Times* and a wee poke o' butterscotch . . .'

He's starting to falter, losing his thread. Mary's careful expression petrifies. What's the matter with him? We spent half an hour going over this.

Cities can get used to anything. That is part of their vigorous, indomitable charm. A few shops more or less: what difference can it make? But there *is* something to be lost. Whether or not Waterside Place changes the material comfort of their lives, it will certainly change their heads. I know my way round the respectable arguments, I accept the need for development and jobs; but people also need continuity, landmarks, links with the past, atavistic codes of meaning. Take away the pattern and they lose touch with who they are. That's why my biddies are trying to save Calico Street. Even if they don't know it themselves.

'We also need to look at the opportunities in this situation . . .'

The chairman bristles behind his desk. 'Name and interest group, please.'

'Tracy Malleus. If we think about – sorry: Magellan Street community centre.'

Nervousness always sharpens my voice, but I'm a persuasive enough speaker given the cause. I have a plan, a museum, a corner of the past preserved for future generations. A sprinkling of artisan's workshops, a presence to dissipate the dead air, quickening the sterility of heat-soaked glass and floor polish with the zing of cut metal and acetylene sparks. About one in three of the faces within my field of vision have swivelled around to hear me, eyes walling, necks creasing; they seem to think it's worth the discomfort. The hard man presents his profile. MacCodrum bats one eye in a supportive wink. A social history remit, domestic and industrial, the chain of oppression, bosses to workers, workers to wives, the collusion of the churches, of all denominations . . . Not new ideas, but not unsubversive. This is living history: it still works that way. Around those not-quite ginger lashes the skin is translucent, the vulnerable tissue of a child. Community involvement, local exhibitions, the Icarus high of addressing an audience, *I'm flying Daddy.* Then I make my big mistake.

'Even if we don't manage to stop the precinct . . .'

. . . the museum is compatible with a modified version of the developer's plans. The capital costs might be defrayed by conscience money. Being realistic for a second, how likely is it that a hundred and thirty-one people, however passionately committed, will defeat a multinational? Strange that time should prove so elastic. I grow old waiting for the next spasm of the minute hand.

The man in black stands to address the hall. Looking past me to engage with the roomful of protesters, his eyes snag briefly on mine. Gunmetal grey. It's as if we've met before, but he's not a figure I'd forget.

'Bobby Croall. I'm local.'

This seems to satisfy the chairman.

'Let me get this straight here: we're talking about gie'ing them the go-ahead; standing by while they make a killing, advertising half a dozen vacancies for shelf stackers and telling us they're putting something back? Why don't we ask them in to shag the wife while we're at it—?'

His voice has a jagged, rasping quality, an industrial shearing deep in the throat.

'—has anybody here got a memory? Can you think back longer than your last giro? This was a working community. We had the best skilled labour in the industrialized world. But those skills arenae wanted now. We don't need ships, or trains, or cars, or chemicals, or steel plate. Aye, that'll be right. We wanted a fair wage for our labour and the dignity of the right to strike, so they shut us down because they'd rather pay us to sit on our arses on the broo than give us our dues. And now they're even trying to milk our Monday books. Burgers and bingo. Christ. The Romans invented bread and circuses but at least they didnae try and turn a profit out of them. But nae bother: we're gonnae get ourselves a lottery grant. Only, I don't see myself as a museum piece for the English middle classes to come and keek at how the savages used to live. Am I out of line here? The way I see it, we're still a working community even if there's nae work. Aye, we can give in before the fight's even started, go for the consolation prize, see if we cannae get a nice wee museum, but what are we saying? Sorry, our values are obsolete, but we're awfy interesting for a bank holiday outing—'

The full weight of what is happening is slow to dawn. No, that's not true, I know all right, but between knowing and reacting there are layers of deadening. He is attacking me from a distance of three feet. Spittle escapes those freckled lips as his rhetoric gathers force, a wet fleck of indignation landing on my face. He is attacking me, yet with something humiliatingly impersonal in the attack; it's the crowd he's addressing, I might as well not be here. And yet I am here, and my proximity is integral to his fury. I'm catching his adrenaline, the twist in my guts an ancient response that might be murderous, or sexual. Or just simple fear. The faces that were my allies five minutes ago are now in his thrall, mesmerized and perhaps a little relieved that this elemental anger is not directed against them. His neck is stretched, its sinews corded, a rogue pulse fluttering above his cheek. He's angry. And I can't quite understand it, but it feels like something I've lived with all my life.

'—I've watched us kissing the boot. They wanted to shut the

shipyards: we lay down and let them. Macallister's, Gordon's: we took it up the arse. There has to be a line. We're no' weans any more, we're too old to believe in the tooth fairy, or the ballot box. They tell us what counts is the power of the consumer, then they try to gie us a warehouse full of shite . . .'

He's right of course, but still I don't believe him. His words have the canny flow of propaganda, a passionate smokescreen for something else. One look at the bleak light of those metallic eyes and you know that he doesn't share the faith.

I have been told that English voices sound louder and more arrogant, that the stretch and clip of their – *my* – pronunciation strikes the ear with the expansive ease of colonial power, causing a corresponding contraction in those round about. Accordingly my voice has undergone an adjustment, a softening of timbre, a placatory tampering with certain consonants: the Rs rolled gently from the back of the throat, the sharp edges chipped off 'loch' or 'Murdoch', to be replaced with a discreet rattle of phlegm. I have taken trouble to acquire the rhythms of local speech, the sprigs and branches of street camouflage. Above all, I have learned not to push it. No Doric, no Gaelic phrases, no impersonating teuchters to humorous effect. And this is all to the good, as far as it goes. But it will never go far enough. He's angry with me. And now the room breathes easier. He resumes his seat without catching my eye.

It seems we've lost our appetite for further discussion. A list of objectives will be drawn up by the committee and put to the next meeting for proper debate. All that remains is the selection of the team. Nominations are invited from the floor. The man behind the desk is confirmed as chairman. Stevie Caw agrees to do his bit, though we all know he'll have dropped out by Christmas. One by one my predictions are proved accurate, no challenges, no show of hands. A short man in a patchwork leather jacket proposes 'Bobby' – that friendly, doggy diminutive – and the demagogue shrugs his assent. Eight members, one attitude: pure opposition, unleavened by compromise or thoughts of feasible resolution.

'You dinnae speak for me Tommy McAfee.'

A wiry figure in a thin peach anorak, red-rimmed eyes in a face crosshatched with care. There's a creak of resistant shuffling on the moulded plastic seats.

'None of us would dare to, Molly.'

'There should be four women on yon committee.'

'Are you nominating yourself, then?'

Nastily said, through a smile.

Out of the corner of my eye, John Duffin is raising his head.

'I'm proposing Tracy Malleus.'

Fleetingly, but not too fleetingly to be noticed, the chairman's eyes flicker towards Croall.

'Seconded?'

Mary bobs her fingers towards the ceiling.

'Tracy?'

I nod. That's all it takes, a painless goodwill gesture with no fear of becoming fact.

'Right, we have two nominations: Tracy Malleus and Molly Kane. Those in favour of Tracy . . .?'

A coppice of hands, not a humiliating show of support but thankfully modest, until Molly, too, raises her arm. MacCodrum boosts his stick like an orange marcher's mace.

Looks like I'm on the committee.

SEVEN

I forgive myself all manner of transgressions because I catch the bus. Impulse buys of doubtful utility, leftovers slowly furring in the fridge, the sale bargains I will never wear, my £400 subscription to the private pool (you get a better class of verruca there): small deviations from the path of thrift that could easily be misread as seduction by consumerist wiles. We're all post-Thatcherites now, of course, but we rouse at the old war cries still. Which side am I on? I no longer show solidarity with the ranks of sell-by scavengers, the pricetag scrutineers, the ready-reckoners who clog the supermarket aisle comparing thirty per cent free on the premium brand with the jumbo economy of the downmarket range. I don't care what it costs, but I still catch the bus, so I haven't quite lost touch with the people. Look around, we're all at it: a whole generation of consciences seasoned between the Summer of Love and the Winter of Discontent. Doubtless the sociologists have a label for us. Not for Drew though. He is old enough to seek his absolution in other ways; for him public transport is not a question of principle, merely the necessary adjunct of one who doesn't drive.

He's seen me but there's no flicker of recognition. By now the rules are clearly understood: all things being equal I enjoy the perk of the proprietorial hand on the elbow, even leaning-in close for a whispered indiscretion, but should he see anyone he knows we're barely on nodding terms. So he ignores the vacant place beside me and chooses the seat just behind the luggage rail, sitting sidesaddle of necessity, knees looming into the gangway, the hem of his coat brushing the granulated floor. Possessions have never mattered to me yet I fetishize his wardrobe: the heavy white shirt with its horizontal slub and seashell buttons, the charcoal Nehru jacket lined with a flash of delphinium silk, the cashmere mix of that coat. So easy to lean across and lift the natty fabric clear of contaminating silt; once upon a time I would have done it too. Now I'm the type who respects his circumspection. Though not so prissy as to be indifferent to its source. That underfed schoolgirl shrinking against the window to avoid his encroaching rump? The boys with the celebrity striker perms? The overalled drudge with her check-out pallor and poly bag of discount goods? The postman hitching a free ride? My money's on the astrakhan collar and zip-up sheepskin boots: she hasn't missed a trick. Luckily I was already angled in his direction: no craning required to secure a better view. His hair is needing cut, I notice, flipping into the folded wings of masculine midlife crisis. Must get him a date with Gil. And a new electric razor: something to tackle that tricky patch on the underside of his chin. I haven't seen those shoes before.

Don't get the wrong impression. I'm not about to tweak that loose thread from his shoulder, I haven't sewn a button on yet. Domesticity's a handy alibi but really I'm just looking, battening on his flesh as if I'll never get my fill, indulging the gourmande's hunger, desire so compulsive it devours its own comfort, drawing me back again and again to ask *Why him, why this, why never before?* Why that mouth with its slack lip, a split fruit just past the point of ripeness? Why the Buddha's breasts above that low-slung belly? The peaty skin around those dull blue eyes? The sheer heft of that head? Daring myself to satiety, pushing for the point of sickening, needing to know if the spell can wear out, if the bloodrush can pall, if he could ever be just another middle-aged passenger on his way to the terminus.

We have a history of meeting on buses. There was an early encounter, not long after that first visit to Lachlan Lane. Nothing problematic, then, about sitting beside me. We went a couple of stops, flirting in the casual way of travellers unsure just where their companion will get off. Then the bus slowed to take on a lengthy queue. They filed past the driver, dropping their coins into the fare box. First, a squared-off woman in her thirties, younger than me but bowed with the invisible encumbrance of motherhood. Directly behind, her daughter, ginger-haired where the mother was brunette but unmistakably related, the same pinched nostrils, the same distinctive birthmark on her forehead, an inverted triangle, blackish rather than brown. The child took the stairs to the upper deck while her mother chose a seat below. The pubertal war of independence had started already. Or perhaps not: there was a disembodied yelp of 'Mammy' and the child reappeared. Next was a shrivelled man with the oily quiff of a sometime ladykiller, one lank grey lock falling forward from his widow's peak, not quite low enough to obscure an identical birthmark. He sat apart from them, several seats away. And then two old ladies, one tiger-striped with lines and liverspots, the other small and grey and tight; both birthmarked. I watched them, too, sit separately. If they were not all related then it must be illness, some cancerous disfigurement attacking the same spot on every face. Bad enough for the pensioners, but unthinkably cruel to a child. I turned to Drew, who also seemed unsettled.

'Ever seen that before?'

He echoed my ventriloquist's undertone. 'Once or twice.'

'Is it serious?'

Embarrassingly he turned, a pucker of wonder pushing out his lower lip, and, having studied the little girl, he grinned with shocking relish. Then the smile was gone. Grave-faced, he brought his lips to my ear and whispered

'I've never heard of anyone dying of dirt on Ash Wednesday.'

At the stop before St Vincent Street the schoolgirl disembarks. Stepping into the aisle to let her pass he slides in beside me, as if this were simply the most convenient seat.

'Looks like we've seen the last of the good weather.'

I turn my head, surprised, not fully faking. For some reason he's wearing a tie. 'Till next June.'

His new shoe brushes my ankle. The spy in boots has not batted an eyelid.

'Still, a cold snap should put an end to the wasps.'

Inside I feel a bubble of conspiratorial pleasure. 'What's so funny?' Darwin used to say, smiling with the glinting eye of those excluded from the joke. 'What's so funny?' And we'd be off again, sputtering, snorting, knocking elbows, improvising additional punchlines, their humourlessness adding irresistibly to our mirth.

The bus lurches around a delivering lorry and I'm tipped against his shoulder.

'Whooa.' Through overlapping furls of coat his hand makes contact with my inner thigh. 'Going far?'

His fingers push down further, his expression pleasantly neutral. I could almost believe I do not know him.

'All the way.'

I'm bluffing, but is he? I'm not entirely sure. There are bits of Drew so private they can only be exposed in play. Sometimes I wonder if it stops at sex, but this isn't the day to find out. His mood has changed, his hand withdraws. It seems I'm not to be initiated into the corporation bus equivalent of the Mile High Club.

'I've been at Church House all afternoon,' he says in his ordinary voice.

'I thought you were a tad overdressed for Lachlan Lane.'

A perfunctoriness about his smile. Often there's a strangeness after the three-day absence, the dead air of another life. 'How are you?'

'OK. I was at the Calico Street meeting last night.'

'Many there?'

'A few Tankies, Trots, Greens, the local history brigade . . .'

He rolls his eyes. 'A rainbow coalition – Heaven help you.'

'I was hoping He might delegate a little closer to home.'

He gives me a wary look. 'It's a Catholic area.'

I'd never considered it, but technically he's right. 'I'm not asking you to convert them, we just need some media beefcake to sex things up a little.'

He runs a grinning check over his shoulder, but there's no sign of eavesdropping from the seat behind: just two shoppers swapping operation scars. He risks another furtive pressure on my thigh.

'I'll think about it.'

Actually, we both need time to mull it over. Pulling in Drew might look like I'm hijacking the campaign. They could do with the publicity, but I don't need the grief.

He pulls out a white cotton handkerchief and, half turning, discreetly blows his nose. Thankfully the snot-rags don't go in my wash.

'I hope you're not planning to chain yourself to any bulldozers?'

What he means is, free evenings are precious enough without taking on another commitment.

'Mmm. Bit of an accident, really. I'm on the committee.'

'You and who else?'

'A few timeserved trades unionists. Some commando-style nutcase called Croall. Runs a pub in the East End, fancies himself as a bit of a hard man: mine host to the crims.'

'Not Bobby Croall from the Hangman's Bar?'

'Sounds about right. Drawings and quarterings a speciality.'

Drew is quiet, being in that phase of love where he suspects every violent reaction of a sexual payload. And who's to say he is entirely wrong? Bobby Croall makes my skin crawl, a sensation that's a little too close for comfort. The important thing is to deny it as offhandedly as possible. Candour in relationships is an overrated virtue, complete frankness an indulgence not far short of abuse, like unwashed genitalia or the vegetable belch. Disrespect dressed up as intimacy. And besides, the strongest case for secrecy is the fact that I'm dying to tell.

A grey light filters through the urban crust on the outside of the window. At the traffic lights a man waits, restraining a ferret on a lead.

'What were you doing over at Unco-Guid Hall?'

He shrugs. 'We all need a wee reminder that we're worms of the dust from time to time. A scrotum-shrinking stare from the Praying Tomato, twenty-minute wait upstairs, chairs scientifically designed for maximum discomfort. And we wouldn't want to corrupt the flesh by bringing the thermostat up above freezing: couldn't see out of the windows for condensation. My fault for breathing. The lovely Muriel took my coat at the door, in case I was thinking of rigging my chances of survival.'

You may have noticed that he's turned me into an audience, with all the distancing that implies. A shy man despite that streak of greasepaint. Cut him open and you'd find exhibitionism and diffidence layered like angel cake, yellow and pink, a superficial contrast but the same dry texture on the tongue.

'Isn't it a Greek Thomson building . . .?'

'The anthemion frieze is emulsioned babyshit brown, as I recall.' I catch his eye and the performance becomes a little more personal. 'I could always inform the listed building gauleiter, I suppose, but given their general standard of crimes against humanity, it hardly seems appropriate to shop them for plasterboarding.'

His speech, often faintly oldfangled, seems unusually archaic today. Something to do with the church, I presume, although I don't understand the precise mechanism, only that the past has a talismanic purity for him, a virtue he can call on when feeling beleaguered. It was one of the first things I found we had in common, this redemptive impersonal past. He loves Victorian Gothic railway stations and the cloistered buffet with its steam-fogged urn; panelled hotel lobbies fragrant with lump sugar dissolved in tea; the crazed white porcelain of an Edwardian swimming pool early in the morning, a single dead cockroach floating on its flat chill surface; yellow-lit public libraries at four o'clock on December afternoons; provincial theatres where the red plush has the moth and the plaster cherubs are chipped, but they're still staging matinees of *The Admirable Crichton*. These things exist still, though disappearing fast, the municipal ponds modernized with wave machine and flume, the station buffets franchised by burger chains, the libraries echo-proofed with hessian, the varnished panelling ripped out to make way for the flexistrip dado rail and floral border. And this is where we part company, for while he professes outrage at such vandalism he takes a secret satisfaction from it too. Such places touch him all the more because their days are numbered. Drew is a votary of loss, the perfect temperament for an adulterer: he loves me a little better every time we say goodbye.

The bus crosses Argyle Street. To our right is the twilit souk of donut shops and discount clothing under the railway station, a place I avoid religiously. If the cholesterol doesn't get you the carbon monoxide will.

'They could make trouble for me at Lachlan Lane.'

'How?'

We're through the semi-derelict splendour of Jamaica Street and onto Glasgow Bridge and still he hasn't answered. He is staring at the granite piers, all that remain of the old station viaduct; their carved inscriptions in English and Greek, *All Greatness Stands Firm in the Storm*.

'Drew?'

The bus is slowing. He looks past me, out of the window, and rises to his feet. 'This is me. I should have got off at Argyle Street. I'm meeting the children. Don't bother cooking: I said I'd take them out for their tea.'

I could not tell you why Drew threw his chances of becoming a minister. Whether it was bad luck or self-sabotage, whether he lost his head or his vocation. Or his nerve. But then nor do I understand why he harboured the ambition in the first place. Amazing how much there is for us to say without touching on his history. Perhaps twice, maybe three times, has he talked about the past, his personal past, in anything other than parenthesis, and on balance I've regretted it. Too easy to misjudge the mood, treating the offering as conversational small change when it's the most precious denomination in his gift. He finds personal revelation shaming no matter how banal the details to be revealed. I tell everybody everything. Funny that we should be so compatible.

Among the many abominations condemned by the Free Associated Church of Scotland are homosexuality, divorce, Scottish nationalism, in vitro fertilization, pornography (we part company over the designs of Jean-Paul Gaultier), cremation, communism, Catholicism and Easter eggs. Hanging and flogging are heartily approved: a black day for the Church when they did away with the tawse. Women are not permitted to preach, hold Church office or wear trousers, and their heads must be covered in the sight of the Lord. Lest these views strike you as in any way extreme you should know that Drew's Church numbers the liberals of the Conservative Evangelical pack, viewed in some quarters as unscriptural backsliders for their tolerance of such devilish distractions as theatre and cinema, attendance at concerts and, that most fearful of evils, the Christmas tree.

For a long time I had no inkling of any of this. The knowledge took shape gradually, crystallizing out of sardonic references, occasionally bitter asides. Anxious not to seem naive, I received each tidbit with a knowing laugh, but even then I sensed Drew lacked the streak of surrealism necessary to be making it all up. So maybe he really had come close to heresy by neglecting to reset his watch at the end of British Summer Time, an error which put him on the night bus to Yoker in the closing minutes of the Sabbath. What if he wasn't exaggerating about the unholy row over the Women's Guild using Church premises to demonstrate witty ways with filo pastry? Or the time he was censured for taking his niece for a Saturday morning's pitch and putt? (The club permitted access to the full nineteen holes on the Sabbath.) Could it be that there *was* a three-way split at Synod between the antediluvians who favoured the Victorian starched collar and white tie, the back-to-front majority, and Drew, who insisted that since Scripture kept silence on the subject a polo neck should do just fine? And now I know it's all in deadly earnest, what am I to do but laugh? The Free Associateds are one of Scotland's most glittering contributions to the gaiety of nations, a glorious, elaborate joke. Which is pretty much as Drew represents them, if not how he actually feels.

Hard to connect this carnival of eccentrics with the man who shares my life. He carries no trace that I can see, though admittedly I'm no expert. The sum total of my experience is one reluctant evening in the company of a fellow apostate, a Highlander with a muttony look to his receding gums. As soon as I pushed through the saloon doors I knew that Drew was trapped, but I lacked the wit to improvise an excuse and so we had five hours of it before our claims of another engagement became so hysterical that he allowed us to get away. It wasn't the vicarious lechery I minded, not even the way he talked about himself for forty minutes at a stretch and then, having asked me a question, picked up and read the beermat while I delivered my reply. But he had this habit of sourcing every remark, as if no opinion could be ventured without textual authority. He quoted from the Bible, Shakespeare, Nietzsche, Kierkegaard and, excruciatingly, the Rolling Stones. I hated him, but he had that special gift for making me hate myself a little too. Afterwards, in bed, drunk with desperation, too awash to do anything but lie very still, awaiting the morning's hangover, I wondered if Drew had ever been like that. Was there a time when he had annotated every thought with chapter and verse? I meant it as a joke, but to my dim alarm he murmured something about tools of the trade.

'You don't do it with me,' I said in that clogged voice meant to fool the body with an approximation of sleep.

'Mmm.' Eyes shut, he used the same semi-absent monotone. 'But you're a child of wrath. I was a walking Concordance once upon a time.'

'Not like Angus?'

'Nothing like Angus.' He reviewed the sentence. 'Whatsoever. Couldn't fuck without raising a flag to let us all know about it.'

Outwith the act itself Drew rarely used the Anglo-Saxon word. 'Is that why they booted him?'

He gave a shallow pant which I interpreted as laughter. 'They "booted" him because they wanted him out. Same reason they "booted" me. Or would have done if I hadn't made it to the door first. And I did better in Systematic Theology.'

Gently I patted his dormant penis. 'It's their loss.'

'Is it?' he said.

It's not quite true that Drew bears no traces of the religious life. He retains the instincts of a schismatic. He needs his enemies, those of coarser sensibility, or baser morality, those who run the show. And something else: while the heart feeds on its mush-aesthetic and the body gorges on fats, his soul takes iron rations. Drew is a Calvinist, he believes in sin and judgement, and his head is full of both.

EIGHT

Most of us who mainline the big city inhabit about four streets. Discount the cultural hit-and-run, the ten-minute drive to cabaret, play or film, and my life is as geographically circumscribed as any teuchter's out in the sticks. There's the cluster of shops at the top of the hill where we buy our groceries, a mini United Nations of German baker, Italian deli, Punjabi newsagent, and the South African laundress. And Magellan Street, where I ply my trade, and spend those necessarily unproductive half-hours, the restorative blankness between bouts of significant activity. Mostly I windowshop, although there's nothing I'd wish to buy, just mince streaked pale as uncooked chickenbreast, and the tactfully euphemized second day bread. Too unprofitable to attract the attentions of the shopfitters, and strafed by the screaming gulls, these stores present an unselfconscious collage of the past, souvenirs all the more precious for being taken for granted. The butchers' window with its sunburst engravings and cursive neon sign, the unassuming art deco fascia of the dairy, the chemist with her phials of coloured water, and the fishmonger's protuberant golden sardine don't rate a second glance, despite the current vogue for reproduction retro-tat. Which is not to say that they wouldn't be missed. The third street is home to the Quaich and its satellite restaurants. The twenty-four-hour patisserie, Irenka's Irish bar, Jimmy's caff with the chips and beans menu and choice of Darjeeling or Earl Grey. The circle is completed at our flat, *my* flat, but home to Drew four nights out of seven. It might not be classed as cohabitation by the sheet-sniffing functionaries at the Benefits Agency, but it's a shared life to me.

Lured by the bait of 'original features', I went along expecting no more than a nine-inch skirtingboard and a couple of panelled doors. The estate agent, too, was surprised. A double-breasted chancer with a footballer's jiggle, even his breeziness was becalmed. The floors were shellac relieved by frugal strips of tobacco-stain lino, the woodwork a blistered varnish almost aubergine in the murk. The wallpaper, whatever its original shade, had darkened to a greasy gloaming. The light fittings dangled from twin-ply cable sheathed in mulberry silk; brass-nippled switches beside each door. The set-in bed was in the kitchen recess, sheets and blankets still made up. *She died here.* The salesman gathered courage and resumed his jogging on the spot, blustering about white satinwood and German kitchens and how you wouldn't believe how different it would look and I took a deep draught of someone else's death and said I wouldn't change a thing. Not quite true, but the important stuff I kept. The doorbell on its ribbon spiral of pressed tin; the crackling black-out blinds; that box bed behind its moulting chenille curtain; the hell's mouth kitchen range (though I cook on a four-ring Valor in the corner); the splintering surface on the doors and windowframes; even the crazed and yellowed flooring which assiduous scrubbing has revealed as mock-Minton tiles. Made in Kirkcaldy, an apology of a seafront but lino capital to the world.

I have made changes too. The walls glow with colours that shame the mincing vocabulary of the commercial paintchart. Carmine. Viridian. Permanent red. Artist's pigments. The effect is uncluttered by much in the way of furniture or indeed possessions. My most worldly goods – the Georgian decanter, the Susie Cooper vase, the Victorian lacquerwork glove box – all date from after Drew, although he found them in place on his first visit, and regards them with the tender reverence due the defining heirloom. All things, of course, are revealing in their way, all domestica close to home, but in this case he's following a false trail. Unlike Euan, who understands implicitly. I remember the first time he crossed the threshold, a late-September evening when I needed to borrow a three-quarter-inch brush. The sun slanted low through the sitting-room windows, firing the wall with its golden syrup lustre.

'Well,' he exhaled in droll admiration. 'You've really made a statement here.'

So I inhabit four streets. Which explains why I'm unfamiliar with Yolande's part of town. I was looking for something old and atmospheric, an ivy-clad bothy down an unadopted mews. Unbelievers, too, need their illusions. I followed her instructions to the letter, but couldn't see what I was staring at. A flat-roofed breezeblock quadrangle punctuated by a sequence of fireproof doors. An industrial unit. Even the sign is a disappointment. Black lettering on a white board. No sketch of her in gypsy headscarf, crystal ball in one hand, *Kapital* in the other. Just four words and a telephone number. *Yolande. Consultations by appointment.*

By half-past nine the streets are deep in dusk. It's months past the solstice, but these last few days the city has been gripped by a tourniquet heat which would be remarkable in high summer. We're trapped in an unnerving hybrid season: autumn's copper haze sealing in equatorial temperatures, a ballcock sun in a felted sky, now deepened to ultramarine, a set-dresser's colour that craves the swelling yellow moon. There is a scent of foreignness, of hot dust stirred by night-time breezes, a rustle of nature undeterred by dark. A bat circles the street light on its shirring elastic, and I flinch and wonder why she didn't ask me to the flat. Maybe the hokum doesn't work so well at home.

The sheet metal door gives onto an unpainted corridor lit by a single naked bulb. Through my head flashes an image of the torture cell, a secret shrine, some post-traumatic compulsion to repeat. Schlock is part of the culture now, we're all polluted by its atmospheric grime. Television, tabloids, the images in a thousand magazines: a cesspool of cartoon archetypes, one-idea substitutes for life. Pushing through a second door I'm in the consulting room. No sign of her. The walls are lined with dexion shelving supporting hundreds of paperbacks; a Meccano maniac's den of astrology and biorhythms, leylines and druids, auras and numerology, corn circles and pyramid-building spacemen. Yolande is an automatic reader, a pageturner who'll finish up Foucault on the bus, then dip into her bag for the latest Jilly Cooper. I envy her this indiscriminacy, unafraid to be defiled. *Where is she?* The room is large and rectangular but the shelving has been used to create a recess, a shadowy nook just wide enough for the circular table covered with a fringed Indian shawl. Wooden chairs, padded vinyl seat and back. The only light is cast by a ceramic lamp draped with a yellow scarf. You can still make out the paper shade, lovat green with a sprinkling of golden stars, a motif much favoured by the black labrador set. With a foreigner's touching innocence, Yolande has chosen it for its astral associations. On the freestanding shelves are arranged an assortment of knick-knacks. Pharaonic death masks, soapstone incense-burners, brass cobra candlesticks and kitschy china cats, dinky Ali Baba lamps, Chakra stones, a mass-produced crystal ball on its collar of brown plastic, a miniature African carving with three breasts.

'Welcome to my parlour.'

Presumably the allusion is accidental, although in matters of language she rarely gets it wrong.

She emerges out of the shadows. Something unfamiliar. Maybe the clothes: a long blue skirt of clinging cheesecloth and black vest. Her breasts sit wide, making the décolletage respectable enough, but there is an immodest bank of flesh on the outer reaches of each tight black strap. Why that divan the dark side of the dividing shelves? More ambient pornography. That's the problem with women adjusted to the lineaments of male fantasy: they turn the rest of us into honorary men.

This is the first time we've been alone together since that introductory pot of fennel tea in the prosthetic limb quarter and, although the possibility of a second cup has never seriously occurred to either of us, meeting like this conjures a past of missed opportunities and confronts us like a common rebuke.

'Is it always so dark?'

Not inspired, I admit, but better than discussing the weather.

Taking a step forward to indicate where I should sit, she enters the circle of light. Those stocky legs are finished off with battered trainers. A redemptive touch.

'Sometimes it's easier to see in the dark.'

I assume she's joking.

I first saw Yolande standing behind a trestle table selling snow-flake-pattern slipper socks that smelled of long-dead yak. All proceeds went to earthquake victims. I was cluelessly seeking a birthday present for Sam, cursing her chargecard in the land of opportunity, and cherishing a half-baked hope that the knitwear might be Cuban and thus withheld from the jaded tastes of the Yanqui consumer by trade embargo. The woman selling the socks was drinking leek and potato soup steaming with a ferocity that buckled its polystyrene cup. She seemed immune to scalding, swallowing it absently as she turned the greyish pages of an agitprop magazine. Business was slow. Five minutes later she entrusted the stall to the care of her neighbour (pulses and soya products) and led me round the corner to a shop that sold snakeskin gloves. Not politically correct, but perfect. In gratitude I bought her a cup of tea. It was then I gleaned all I know about her political past, a couple of passing allusions which may have been commendable modesty, or a canny sort of boast (it's so much more dramatic when they make you join the dots). A pleasant three-quarters of an hour, but definitely a one-off. The next time I saw her was in a cinema queue, though it was Ricky I noticed first. Drew was mentally revising one of his Sunday calls to freedom, and I found myself studying the swell of deltoid muscle, the way the buttocks shelved from the scoop of lower back. My first thought was that the woman had registered my scrutiny and was about to freeze me with a drop-dead stare. The glossy black of her hair and her escort's race had nudged me into a lazy assumption that she too was Asian, so when she turned I had a double surprise.

We bitched about the inefficiency of the box office, and then, because I couldn't think of anything else to say, I introduced Drew. By the time she'd returned the favour the queue was moving. It was Ricky who said, just as we were peeling off to our respective films, 'We should go for a swally sometime.' Taking a card – *Rakesh Sidhu, quantity surveyor* – out of his wallet he wrote a seven-digit number on the back. What else was I to do? We could hardly give him Drew's home number. I offered the scribbled bus ticket to Yolande but Ricky palmed it deftly, pushing it deep into the front pocket of his jeans where it nestled, I saw before quickly looking away, next to the neatly stashed bulge of groin.

When the call came and we met up at Joe the Toff's – their choice – I realized that we'd booked ourselves in to an open-ended evening with total strangers. I couldn't remember why I'd liked this woman, beyond the suddenly insufficient fact of her being a foreigner with a romantic past. Leftist Latino chic was still collectable, but don't ask me what you were supposed to do with it once you got it home. What little I could recall, I didn't recognize. Struck by the exhibitionism of her sensuality, a knockout touch like bottled musk, I wondered how I'd happened to miss it before. As a couple, their libidos seemed well matched, yet the sexual energy was centrifugal. Impossible to know whether they were nocturnally moribund, or simply juicing themselves up with third-party fuel. And then they became our friends. What the hell: the balanced social diet demands variety and contrast and they were piquant enough as an occasional snack. Only neurotics treat every chance acquaintance as potential incrimination. Neurotics and Sam, I seem to remember. Who must have outgrown it by now.

Looking back, I can spot the defining moment in my relations with Yolande, the point at which Ricky stepped in to claim us and she took one step back. Since then we've been his friends. Even her tête-à-têtes with Drew are tainted with the suspicion of charity, too much fluoride in his smile. Occasionally, in the passing of a wine glass or the handover of a coat, there'll be a click of inadvertent contact; other than this she resolutely avoids my eye. To be frank I find her boring, opaque but not intriguing: the voice which switches hemispheres at the drop of a consonant, that headline past, the consistency of her commitment to the cause. Above all, her hold on Ricky, the ineffable mystery of them being an item, and an item of long standing. She is at least a decade older, approaching the elephant pit of undeniable middle age. That portfolio of tealeaf-reading and cha-cha-chaing and the odd sub-Steadman cartoon on page three of The Daily Prole can barely pay the rent. Ricky, with his mobile phone and his personalized numberplate, has little time for the romance of good causes. Changes his GTI every two years but runs the same old model in the sack. Drew once asked him, apparently without malice, when they were getting married: how many years was it that they'd been together? Ricky laughed and said something about her putting a spell on him. And such is the power of Drew's superstition that the conversation ended right there.

Who can chart the flux of a relationship? Ricky rarely tosses a word her way but the thread between them stretches taut as wire. They have that couple complicity: the united front of undetected lies, a simultaneous instinct for when it's time to leave. Not that you ever notice, but then it's a quality mostly conspicuous by its absence, and we haven't noticed that. She rarely laughs at his horse-play, but neither does she always look away, and sometimes I fancy there's an intimacy in their estrangement, a passion so exclusive no one else is vouchsafed a glimpse. Drew assumes he treats her badly, and he may be right, but these things look different from the inside. There may even be those who feel that an adulterous telly minister has forfeited his place in the feminists' hall of fame.

'Quite a library you've got here.'

She waves a dismissive hand towards the shelves. 'Most of them I got cheap at a bankruptcy sale: a job lot with the crystal ball and the rest of the window dressing.' I remember this voice, the Glaswegian mostly gone: it's the way she spoke the day I first met her. 'People like the full monty. I could read a pack of playing cards on the pavement down Buchanan Street, but they wouldn't want it.' A sudden grin. 'And I couldn't charge them twenty quid a shot.'

Funny that she seems bigger somehow, taking up more space. Maybe it's just the effect of seeing her at work.

'You've not read them all, then?'

'Only just got the last of them out on the shelves. There's one or two real stoaters.'

And another thing: she's not vamping it up today.

She ducks down to the floor and surfaces with a battered volume in shiny banana and lime. *Sexual Fulfilment Through the Stars.* A bargain at ninety-five cents. 'Here: it could change your life.'

So that's it. She's offering me a pact: she makes out she doesn't take it seriously, I pretend that I do.

I take the book. 'Did it work for you?'

'A win for the Rangers usually does me.'

I like women, even, especially, women who are not my type. I enjoy the trappings of elaborate femininity, the rustling, glinting, scented props, the rituals of face pack and massage glove, the fetishized power of handbag and shoe. I love the way we subvert the uniform: the afternoon crease of paint on an artfully shaded eyelid, the lengthening puncture in the load-bearing lobe, the perfect oval of enamelled nail set into a doughy finger, the delicious disgust in a blossoming cloud of perfumed smoke. I like the lanky headgirl types too: brown hair pulled back from a clear brow, the steady gaze free from the peripheral scribble of mascara, the firm stride, each strong white toe with its individual purchase on the ground. Or the punky girls with their raccoon kohl and zigzag-crimped hair, their scent of Old Holborn and Lebanese Red. Even the prim receptionists in this season's shade of viscose. I'm partial to women's

83

company: the rush of laughter when the audience get to put on their own show, the muse's lips misshapen in mimicry, the explosion of raucousness when there's no masculine presence, no soliciting in display. There is a confidence with women, knowing what jokes to crack, how far to tease. I relish the hint of guerrilla consciousness, the secret sorority of the understated, but I'd never grasped the difference between comrades and collaborators until I met Yolande. Her femininity is foreign at every level, a man's woman *par excellence*. And now suddenly she wants to be my friend.

'I saw your car in Kilcreggie the other day—'

Only this isn't particularly friendly.

'—you were turning into MacKendrick Avenue.'

Sexual Fulfilment goes back on the table. 'I don't see any point taking a five-mile detour to avoid the area.'

Yolande raises her hands and pushes damp hair back from her face. I'm wary of unshaven armpits, I tried it once and grew the attenuated straggle of an adolescent boy. Yolande's mat is luxuriant but neat, which may be the result of Nature's favour or some nifty work with the nail scissors.

'As long as you make sure she's out first.'

I inhabit four streets but recently I've added a fifth to the tally. It's not the sort of neighbourhood where you can get away with kerbcrawling so I parked the car and walked. Litter-free pavements, no crisp packets or flattened dowts, no dogturds, no sick; just leaves and twigs. And washed cars in driveways. Stonebuilt terraces and semi-detached villas, frontages painted cream and white and maybe a wee daring hint of minty toothpaste, couthy names across the fanlights in chipped and nibbled gold, burglar alarms and black reflecting windows, front gardens big enough to forgo the deflective net. A sense of lives unfolding generation after generation, secure in the continuity of red pedalcars and hobbyist's glasshouses and kit-assembly creosoted garden sheds. And those gardens. Roses and montbretia and long yellowing lawns. Box privet. Monkey puzzles and raspberry canes, hydrangeas and hanging baskets, trellis-work and cemetery gravel and wrought-iron fence posts finished with a questionmark curl. A little piece of English suburbia squatting on the west side of Glasgow. The streets are even lined with limes, the sticky-leaved canopy of my childhood, pillarbox trunks erupting

84

from the pavement, roots buckling the tarmac, making miniature mountains and volcanic rifts. In summer such suburbs come into their own. But of course this isn't summer. Lammas has come and gone; the Michaelmas daisies are out, brittle-brown leaves on the white-flecked asphalt scuttle like crabs at a sudden breeze, but still the lipstick melts in its tube, the wind blows warm as Hoover exhaust, the days dawn dusty blue and bloated with the past.

Until I saw the house I thought I had no preconceptions. As if that were possible. A semi-detached residence distinguished obstinately from its partner by a different shade of cream, the seam between them like a knickerline in winter dividing pallor and the residue of tan. The deep eaves of the twin front gables were painted grey on that side, green on this. Hers was the left. The one with the lamb's tongue by the front step and the nasturtium border around the precision-trimmed lawn. So that's what he did on Sunday afternoons. You couldn't see much through the downstairs bay window: the padded rejection of a settee back with a pink and white quilt folded on top, perhaps an heirloom, a pioneer blanket, a sign of tenacity in the genes. Two windows upstairs. The one above the door, Donalda's bedroom, with the Batman stickers she'd never bothered to scrape off, and a row of moulded plastic trolls, stumpy naked bodies and lurid nylon hair, marching across the top of the lower sash. Cammie must sleep round the back. The master bedroom was in the eye of the gable, a shallow bay window with a yashmak of buttercream net. A frilly woman, then. They often retreat into haberdashery when their firm-breasted daughters hoist the sexual flag. Donalda, much to Drew's distress, favours midriff-baring teeshirts and cystitic jeans, so it's only logical that the mother would claim the opposite ground. He has a taste for the hasty encounter, the trouser zip lowered, the skirt hitched clear, breasts squeezed up out of the still-fastened bra. Not a fancy indulged by a woman who puts lace at the windows. Lace is for kindly light on puckered thighs, the minister's wife getting the missionary's good works. I don't want to know if he still sleeps with her; he tells me he doesn't, for what it's worth.

After a couple of minutes a silver-pointed tabby rubbed by me on the pavement and passed like a spectre through the bars of the gate. For all I knew the animal might be his, a co-familiar to the contours of his lap. Then I regretted succumbing to temptation. Not because it was tawdry or for fear I might get caught, but because until then I had never quite believed that she existed.

Yolande lights a joss-stick and places it on the shelf behind her. 'Shall we get started?'

She wants to know my date of birth. I give her day and month. No point in adding the year, there's no telling when this temporary truce may end. She returns a diagnostic nod.

'Libra.' She squares up to the table, squeaking the chair legs on the concrete floor, making herself comfortable. 'So. What do you want to know?'

'I get a choice?'

'The questions are part of the answer.'

She catches my eye and we almost snigger.

'Shouldn't we stick with what your mystery client asked?'

For a moment her face empties, then she shrugs.

'It doesn't make that much difference.'

The cards are kept in a balsa-wood cigar box, wrapped in lavender silk, a fancy hankie going threadbare in the middle, all warp, no weft. She unfurls it on the table, invites me to handle the pack. Darwin was a poker fiend, taught me a few shuffles.

'Now cut, three times, using your left hand: it's closer to the heart.'

Her Spanish voice, which means she's playing. She deals erratically, making a cruciform then filling in the spaces to produce a circle, a clock face of twelve cards. Just the colours make me salivate. Indigo and dirty emerald, parchment and old rose: there's no denying their imaginative pull. The Medieval, trimmed to Victorian sensibilities, provided a magical counterweight to the easi-clean surfaces of my repressionless childhood. The thrill of ruby and royal blue in an Anglican transept window; the doll's house of the Christmas crib; Pre-Raphaelite princesses, tiny faces bobbing in an ocean of golden hair, in the cloth-backed fairytales of the India Street library (one colour plate per volume). It was strictly Doctor Seuss at home.

Yolande has finished dealing. Her eyes skim the circle of cards and again she gives that nod, a gesture of confirmation or a gallus act of bluff.

'You see there are seven major cards in the spread.' Her lips pucker and open, an unconscious tic denoting concentration. Or perhaps not so unconscious: you can bet it goes down great with the boys. 'That means it's an important reading.'

I'm really not sure I can go through with this. The air in here is solid, stifling, heat that hits you like an ultimatum, twisting your mood between murder and despair. Yolande's cleavage is glinting with sweat, her upper lip beaded as from the shower. The backs of my knees form an Elastoplast seal with the vinyl seat cushion.

'Is this the spiel you give them normally?'

She looks up. I'll have to watch the scepticism; she has never understood that I have nothing against her personally, just the voodoo that pays the rent.

'This is not a normal reading.'

'No, but I thought we'd agreed . . .'

'I'm talking about the cards.' Her hand makes a circuit of the table, damp palm to the ceiling. 'Seven major Arcana: it's not usual.'

Two rivulets of sweat run down her cheek from temple to jaw, plastering a few stray hairs to her skin. She reaches to the shelf behind her and retrieves a packet of licorice Rizlas and a suede drawstring purse. One deft lick to join the papers, a rip of cardboard rolled into a roach, the match struck one-handed, off her thumbnail, just like Bogart. A different pain threshold. She inhales, sucking the smoke down deep.

'Ricky scored it in Dundee. Not bad for Scotland.' From some-where in this airless room comes a burst of energy. 'OK. What does everybody want to know? Are they going to get a lumber? Are they going to get rich? Are they going to get a lumber *and* get rich, walk down the aisle with a wallet? Who's going to die? Which is maybe another angle on the rich question. Is there anything nasty round the corner? I don't do all that "Watch out for the staircarpet" crap. *Les jeux sont faits.* It's Fate. If you don't believe in Fate don't come to me—'

She hands me the joint, although I think they're back to calling them spliffs these days. If you stand still long enough, fashion always comes around.

'—you want the fuck card now or later?'

'Let's save the best till last.'

87

'That's taking plenty for granted, but OK.'

She's right, by the way: best grass I've had for a long time.

'What do the stars mean?'

'The Seven of Pentacles: that's money coming in by one hand, going out by the other.'

'No surprises there, then.'

She moves across to the other side of the circle, a drip of sweat falling from her eyebrow onto the tablecloth. 'Four of Cups: that's a reunion in the House of Brothers and Sisters.'

'Drew told you about Samantha?'

There's something too neutral in her stare. 'You can start knitting the pink bootees, by the way: it's a girl.'

On second thoughts, I'm not sure it's wise to smoke in this atmosphere, there's little enough oxygen as it is.

'That's a secret she hasn't shared with me.'

'She will.' I recognize the schadenfreude of the childless. 'She won't be able to hide it.'

Something of a hostage to fortune, that little prediction. Still, clairvoyance is a business like any other: you have to speculate to accumulate.

She reaches over and plucks the joint from my lips. 'Around now I usually give the punter some advice.'

'I thought you didn't do staircarpets.'

'I don't, but if the sky's going to fall in on them' her voice squeezes with the effort of holding in the smoke 'I like to give them time to prepare for the inevitable.'

'So I'm to expect the worst?'

She exhales, offering me the final draw, but I get nervous that close to the roach.

'You have real psychic potential Tracy.' She sucks on the stub of cardboard, her eyes slitted against the nearness of the ember. 'But then you know that already.'

'Anything specific or just all-round disaster?'

She smiles, extinguishing the joint in a brass ashtray. 'Keep an eye on your little sister. There's unfinished business there. See the Devil in the fourth house? That's your unhappy childhood.'

As a matter of fact our childhood wasn't unhappy. It may not have been Enid Blyton meets Arthur Ransome, but I'll never go short of dinner-party anecdote. People tend to catch their breath and murmur 'Christ' in an appalled sort of way, but given half a chance every one of them would swap. While they were dressing their Barbies or embroidering cross-stitch panholders I was baking hash brownies and bottlefeeding the B-movie actor who spent two months in our attic in nappies and bib. I read an interview with him in a women's magazine a couple of years later, he'd cobbled together some cover story about a monastery in Tibet.

I point to a card near the top of the spread. Dogs barking, tears falling from a face imprisoned in a luminous orb, a crustacean in water. 'What does this one mean?'

The table lamp flickers rapidly, inconclusively, under its yellow veil, as if the bulb holds an insect batting its wings. Yolande tuts with irritation and fiddles the flex until brightness is restored.

'The Moon: that's me, the sorceress. In the second house it also means false counsel.'

'Sporting of you to let me know.'

There's an iffy smell somewhere behind the joss stick whiff of cloves, a nuance expanding unpleasantly in the heat.

'It doesn't have to be me. Could be anyone you listen to. Could be the leakage from other people's heads.'

If I feign incomprehension, it will only tell her that I didn't know she knew. Better not to react at all. It's not as if it's any big deal. Pay attention to people and you soon work out what makes them tick. Once you've done that, it's not hard to predict what they'll do or think at any given moment. It just so happens that I hear their voices in my head. Not everyone's, of course. Yolande, for example, is just about leak-proof.

The light flutters again. She sighs and reaches backwards for a candle.

'Now the one you've been waiting for: the King of Swords. In the twelfth house, which is the House of the Unexpected.'

'But Drew's the most predictable man I know.'

'Not Drew. This guy is a control freak. Uptight—'

'You should see him the morning before recording.'

'—a bona fide bastard. You've not known him long—'

Sometimes nervousness makes me laugh.

'—but the first time you met him you knew it was going to happen.'

This is how they get you. Pure fishing. Cast the net wide enough and they'll always dredge something up.

The light is worse now, panicky, flickering sepia. Of course: that's the smell. She strikes a match, lights the candle in its Wee Willie Winkie holder, and douses the electric lamp. An aftertang of phosphorus mingled with charred wick briefly overcomes the fishmarket stink of dodgy wiring.

'Watch him, Tracy. He'll hurt you if you let him. You've never met anyone like this bastard before.'

She's good, I have to give her that. For a moment he was here in the room. The shivery current of his presence, those gunmetal eyes.

'So is he going to fuck me or fuck me over?'

She looks at me. 'Do you know the difference?'

The next card in the circle is the same suit, the Queen, the same sword held aloft, a grimly stylized face.

'What about her?'

'That's you.' The candle flame wavers in an undetectable draught. 'How the card-reader sees you.'

Now we're talking.

'And how is that?'

She shrugs. 'Too sharp for her own good, impaling hearts and leaving them bleeding, not caring about the damage that she does. Riding high but heading for a fall. A selfish woman, greedy, blind to her own nature, taking for granted the abundance in her life, thinking the world owes her a living.' She's reciting this like a catechism long since learned, a mantra of invective, though her finger traces the image as if prompted by the card. 'She thinks she can't be touched, but the Wheel turns.' She taps the card sharply, the noise amplified by the acoustics of the table. 'Fate is inexorable. The Tower will fall.' The smell is overpowering, not the wiring after all, a stench that slices under the tongue, contaminates the saliva. 'Your world will collapse. Spell, soul-sickness, loss. The Ten of Swords sits in the House of Death.'

The silence doubts my sanity. Could she really have said that?

'A spell of sickness?'

She drags her attention from the spread, frowning, distracted. 'What?'

The mood is broken. Quickly she moves her fingers round the table, gathering up the cards, speaking in her normal voice again. Whatever that is. 'It's all crap to you, anyway.'

Bitter almonds, that's the smell.

'Hold on. What about our experiment?'

She's still picking up cards. 'What's the point?'

But I've spotted the telephone among the bric-à-brac. He answers at the third ring. TV noise. Some asinine game show playing in the background.

'Ricky: have you got that list of cards Yolande gave you?'

'Yeah.' A rummaging amid paper filtering down the line. He lays the phone down and the noise grows fainter. Yolande puts the tarot deck on the table. Ricky comes back to the mouthpiece, I can hear his breathing.

'Sorry Tracy, I cannae lay my hands on it just now. I know I had it . . .' more fruitless sifting. 'I can remember them if that's any good to you.'

'Sure.'

'There was the Queen of Swords, and the Moon, and the Wheel of Fortune, and the King of Swords – or maybe the Queen . . .'

'You said her already.'

I can feel his frustration. Ricky doesn't often make mistakes.

'Seven of . . . no, five . . . Shite – it was there on the table yesterday.'

'It's OK Ricky, it doesn't matter. I'll see you soon.'

Yolande wraps the cards in their purple silk, replaces them in the cigar box, empties the brass ashtray into her cupped hand, ready to go home. Four, or maybe three, out of twelve. How does that square with statistical probability?

'So tell me about the Ten of Swords again Yolande.' She is crouching at the bookcase, replacing *Sexual Fulfilment Through the Stars*. 'You said something about sickness . . .'

'In the House of Fate.'

I'm not even aware of moving but my foot snags on the tripwire flex and there's a nerve-searing flash as the table lamp explodes. Yolande shrieks something which sounds like *Madre de Dios* though it's hard to tell against the pitch of my own yell. My hands are raised to ward off the shrapnel glass but the paper shade and yellow scarf have already taken the force of the blast. The candle flame gutters but remains alight. My sinuses tingle like a comb played through paper: aftershock, and the noiseless reverberation of the room.

She exhales through clenched teeth.

'I told that bastard to get the wiring checked—'

She has removed the singed yellow scarf from the lampshade and is collecting the vicious fragments in its folds.

'—Jesus.'

She sucks her finger, then brings it to the flame.

I'm aware this isn't the moment to pursue the subject, but there may never be a better: 'You're saying a period of illness . . .?'

'Not a *period* of anything.' She's squeezing the skin on her finger end, forcing a tiny bubble of blood. She grunts, a sound replete with the luxury of justified aggravation. 'A spell. A hex, a . . . fuck's sake: a *curse*.'

There's a long interval which may last no time at all.

'What?'

She looks down at the table, sucking her forefinger.

'Forget it.'

As it happens I did have a question for the tarot. How could I not? I lived through childhood. The usual swill of playground games, skipping rhymes, Hallowe'en mumbo-jumbo, is banked up, imperfectly dissolved, in the U-bends of my brain. I may not believe in it, but it's there.

I had been up north a couple of days and was starting to feel established. Seonaid at the general store knew me by name and the morning we made a foray across to the crofting township, the woman in the post office was already primed to expect me. I was spending the bank holiday weekend with one of my various partners in adulterous passion. It was our first chance to sleep in the same bed, if you didn't count his habit of slumping into a seven-minute coma after climax. Even I can acknowledge that the all-seeing intimacy of Highland life has its drawbacks for the year-round resident, but for the visitor – at least, the visitor with my predilections – it's a thrill. Such instant belonging, a place in the community even if only as the object of censorious scrutiny, a footnote in the timeless saga. Our stay coincided with a summer festival, an ancient pagan ceremony revived by the local authority a few years before in the hope that a papier mâché sheep on wheels, a couple of pipe bands and a municipal bonfire would start the tourist dollars rolling in. Being high season, there were perhaps seventy visitors in the vicinity, most of them a party of retired schoolteachers from Stalybridge who hard-boiled eggs in their guesthouse kettles and partook of a frugal luncheon on the hill.

That morning I foolishly tried to buy underwear. The woman in the ladies' outfitters showed me a capacious garment in a fabric which would have stopped a bullet at close range. I explained my requirements more precisely and she caught her breath. 'Och, you'd have to go to *Inverness* for that.' I love the Highland sense of sin, so ascetic that a pair of Marks and Sparks knickers makes you a whore. I decided to settle for washing my current pair in the handbasin and giving them a blast with a hairdryer cadged from our landlady's teenage daughter. Outside the shop, where Colin was discreetly studying the pavement, the air was just warm enough to feel the lick of breeze along a bare arm: one of those summer days that make the ignorant grue, longing for the enamelled glare of Spanish postcards. A sky with the whiteness of charnel-house bones turned the manse sycamore black, making the low stone terraces lining the main street stand out as if viewed through 3-D spectacles. I've always found this light erotic, the dull glare of studio-shot television serials watched after school, with their half-understood currents of adult sexuality, the promise of a world familiar but transformed. Light that can make a baby's sock on the harbour wall, the tangled mesh of lobster creels on the quayside, a model ship in the chandler's window, seem mysterious, significant, sharp with withheld life.

Turning on to Main Street we came across the parade. The pipers played and children with the painted faces of tigers and monkeys clawed and scratched, and a dozen or so open-backed lorries passed by, painfully slowly, with their thrifty accounts of the lives of Charlie and Flora, William Wallace, Robert the Bruce and, two thirds of the way along, the lifeboatmen, a tin-rattler informed us, dressed to rape and pillage in burlap and hearthrug sheepskin. Most of the dozen or so crew had taken the precaution of wearing vests under their Viking improvisation, although a couple of exhibitionists were bare-chested, one displaying an alabaster slab of gooseflesh, the other insulated in a satyr's thick growth. One man was cased in jogging pants and a sleeveless leather jerkin, its slashed neckline laced with a shoestring thong. A puzzlingly professional garment to find in this ad hoc pageant: obviously not borrowed from his everyday wardrobe, nor yet a fetishistic item of nightclub gear. So taken was I with this costume that I barely noticed the wearer, the fluidity of line from shoulder to bicep, his incipient pattern baldness, the compensating fur of forearm and chest. Then he saw me and the shock seemed to register several thousand volts. At the time I took the look in his eyes for tribute, but it's equally possible that what he found so striking was the tribute in mine. Either way, it's what came next that matters. Like any woman I'm used to the staring, but this was different, a frowning focus, a quizzical knitting of the brows, deliberate communication. I met his look, and as the lorry moved on he swivelled in counterpoint to its crawling progress, keeping that naked, unmistakable, bewildering contact until the corner of Main Street took him out of sight. I didn't know where he lived or worked, I didn't know his name, I was only there on the promise of three nights in bed with a lecturer in hospitality management, I could hardly follow his float around town like a bitch on heat, so for once in my life I waited, knowing that the gift I was waiting for would come.

And I was right. He was at the ceilidh that evening, a noisy smoky drunken hooley in the drill hall. He saw me straightaway and again there was that direct, unfiltered contact, though this time he seemed wary, perhaps misunderstanding about Col. Not that Col understood entirely, himself. The locals were taking it in turns to provide the entertainment. There were airs and reels and Gaelic laments, even a recitation. He sang an old Rod Stewart number, his voice pleasantly unremarkable, beyond the fact that he was holding a tune with a pint of whisky inside of him and holding my gaze through every line. A couple of women looked around pointedly but Col failed to notice. I talked nonsense, vivaciously, gesticulating as if to signal out to sea, laughing too loud, head tipped back, eyes too bright. Across the room, he was playing the same game. Clapping backs with punitive jollity, punctuating conversation with snatches of song, rolling his eyes in drollery I could not make out above the swell of the squeezebox and the heave of the crowd. We left early, the tobacco smoke was aggravating Col's asthma.

Next morning, which was to be our last, our landlady told us we had won the raffle. A bottle of Laphroaig. Ally MacNeill had taken it home with him for safe-keeping and we could pick it up from his house down by the pier. We called in on our way to the postbus. Colin held back at the door, half-in, half-out, within reach of our bags on the roadside. He never felt comfortable with small-town honesty. A pretty woman with a nasty case of young mother fatigue shouted up the stairs and he was down so quickly I had the impression he'd been waiting for her call. But then, they were very small cottages. He wasn't surprised to see me, but he seemed aggrieved to be found there just the same. The baby screamed and the woman absented herself without looking my way, an oversight which felt less like rudeness than sheer exhaustion. He too moved sluggishly with what could have been a hangover but for the suspicion of sullenness, a refusal, at last, to meet my eye. There was too much furniture in this little room, the nearness of the ceiling and the cram of sideboard and dining-table, television and three-piece suite made the armchairs loom hugely. The floor was a battleground of vanquished toys, their once joyous plastic scuffed and grimy. Towelling nappies hung on a wooden clothes horse in front of the ashy fire. And I thought everyone used disposable these days. It couldn't be by choice. Barefoot, hairy-toed, he picked his way through the rubble to the corner behind the settee. I felt myself shadowing his movements with an automaton's glide. This was not will; all bodily power had drained into my eyes, which burned out of my face like acid. As he bent over the settee his teeshirt rode up above his belt, exposing a vivid stripe of whitely muscled flesh. At last he found the elusive bottle. He handed it over, his gaze resting on the plastic clown by the heel of my right shoe. I waited, taking the whisky's weight without quite receiving it until, still not meeting my eye, he opened his hands so that I had to catch it or take a chance on the glass bouncing off the carpet. I cradled the bottle against my summer shirt and only then did he raise his eyes from the floor and, shifting the angle of his head slightly, look at me. A look with something of challenge, even hostility to it, but a look of absolute directness, physical, visceral, so deep I felt the stirring in my guts.

I'm familiar with the process of mutual projection, I knew that what had happened with Ally MacNeill was a doodling of fantasy across coincidence's slate. Each of us had triggered a memory the other had erased: that's how it works. The recognition is real *and* illusory. There's no such thing as love at first sight. And yet I've spent a long time thinking about that stare. Fumbling around with Colin in the weeks that followed, just the flash of it could trip me over the edge.

I know that I love Drew because my body tells me so, because the way I feel about him I have never felt before. Except that day with Ally MacNeill, a meaningless encounter with a man I'll never meet again. But how can it have meant nothing if with Drew it means so much? Unless Drew too is a delusion.

That's the question Yolande might have settled, had I been gullible enough to believe in her powers. But then if I believed in her, Yolande is the last person I would ask.

Drew is in bed when I get back, tucked up under the duvet with last Sunday's papers and a slice of toast. Embarrassed by his own nakedness, he seizes every opportunity for undressing unobserved. Fully clad at the bedside, I lick a couple of crumbs off his chin but he doesn't seem interested in the proffered kiss. I don't know how he can eat after cleaning his teeth.

'So when's the wedding?'

'Sorry?'

'To the tall dark handsome stranger. Or is it to be the long sea journey?'

Strange how loving a superstitious man makes you feel guilty of deception, even when you're open about finding it all a joke. And now, hearing him make light of it, I feel a shiver of presentiment, as if his turning sceptic clears the way for my belief. But of course he hasn't changed. The impulse to levity is not scepticism but fear. He's afraid that she has told me that one day I will leave him; he's just goading me to say it isn't true.

NINE

I started dreaming about Drew Monzie around three months after we first met. Nightmares often, or at least those unsettling narratives that leave you churning with anxiety, going through the motions of interminable drudgery, some marathon packing or tidying session, convinced that only by completing it will you ever achieve peace of mind. Drew would be there, perhaps only peripherally, but sometimes a definite object of desire, so that a straining sexual frustration added its momentum to the treadmill of deferred panic. Occasionally things would go so far that he removed his shirt, but I never had the pleasurable illusion of physical contact, much less a glimpse of hardware. And there was another common thread running through my dreams: I was never at home in them. Fancy hotels, floral-deodorized bed-and-breakfasts, dingy hostels with firedoors every fifteen yards, but no four walls identifiable as mine. Such is the lot of the displaced person. I had been in Glasgow two years then, still excited by its skyline in the early morning, the advent calendar tenements at dusk, yet I found myself drawn to other towns, unable to pass through an unfamiliar landscape without imagining myself transplanted for the rest of my life. The permanence was crucial to the fantasy; promiscuous as my attachments were, I was looking for the real thing. I relished the intensity of the search, the imminence of the climactic detail, any second now . . . Recurrent disappointment simply prolonged the thrill, for much as I craved the idea of belonging, it also seemed a sort of death.

This is the style of abstraction we'd explore in those cosy early evening drinking sessions around Lachlan Lane. Looking back, I find it amazing that I wove this wispy stuff into approximate sense. As amazing as I found it then that he had patience to listen. I winced a little as the words crossed the air between us, but the feyness only made them more dear to him and, mercifully, in the places he selected for our meetings there was no trace of the contemporary to mock. He used a network of bars I was barely aware existed, professional clubs haunted by papery academics or overloudly-laughing lawyers, residents' lounges in the sort of select West End hotel shoehorned into a single house in a Greek Thomson terrace. I could never work out how these establishments made their money, since they were invariably all but deserted during our visits. They possessed a thrilling sadness, an authentic whiff of bachelor life in the 1950s. It was something to do with the scrolling wrought-ironwork against frosted glass doors, the bamboo-strip panelling on the bar, the bathroom-black tiling behind the gantry with its etched motif of clubs, spades, hearts and diamonds, the pewter tankards hung diagonally along the wall. Also the stock, the two sorts of ginger wine (Stones and Crabbie's), that coagulating jar of green glacé cherries, the untouched bottle of angostura bitters, the chrome cocktail shaker slowly tarnishing on its shelf. And of course the customers, skeletal men with brilliantined hair combed back from liverspeckled foreheads, and a faint, perhaps illusory, taint of bay rum. But even this was only part of the picture. The melancholy I so relished, I gradually came to realize, was Drew's own. I too had a craven taste for poignancy, a bitter-sweet rotting tooth, but Drew's cafard troubled me. However delicious as the flavour of a weekly excursion, could he live his whole life in the minor key?

There was another problem with our evenings. I didn't know what they were *for*. I had heard of his reputation, a mild-mannered Lothario who could whirl a conquest from nodding acquaintance to sexual obsession, only to dump her in an embarrassment of slammed phones, smudged mascara and stifled sobbing behind the lavatory door. This had been the basis of my earliest reservations; now I found myself regretting that rumour seemed so wide of the mark. Initial confidence that we were taking the well-trod path to seduction soon drained from me, to be replaced by another suspicion, that he was slowly, deliberately, falling in love. I felt uneasy, disaffected at being so used, an interchangeable object of a passion he was determined to feel. Time passed and a new fear took hold: that Drew Monzie was too much in love with the frisson of romantic anticipation to exchange it for anything else. Once, in an effort to trigger some sort of resolution, I allowed my fingers to brush his wrist. He retracted his hand, casually, without urgency, the sentence he had embarked upon flowing smoothly to its end.

So elegantly accomplished you would almost have thought nothing was happening. Perversely, his failure to manifest desire stirred up powerful hungers. In idle moments I found my thoughts straying to the sleekly padded skin beneath his jawline, the scrub-hairiness of shin when he crossed his legs. We were walking through Kelvingrove Park one day, the late afternoon sky grey as harling, the stripped branches losing definition in the almost-rain, when a sudden slice of wintry light cut across the horizon and caught his head in its corrosive radiance. He halted, eyes shut, bested by the cold brilliance, and I turned my back on the sun and stared, awe-struck, at the hugeness of that head, the unnatural dimensions of the features upon it, the sheer bulk of that coarse-pored neck with its circumferential crease below the shaving line, the undeniable grossness of its fleshly mass. Like a storybook ogre, a fearful thing of delectable threat. And I wanted more urgently than I'd ever felt need to grasp that greying hair turning frizzy in the damp, pulling down the massive head until I could take it between my hands and tear at it with my mouth. The cloud cover shifted, closing off the light, and we walked on.

The sexual subtext was all the more unsettling because on every other level there was nothing that could not be said. We had discovered the trick of conversational texture, the habit of airing those inconsequential details which crowd the mind as you talk of other things. Freed from the fear of uneasy silence, we both started to relax, and then I rediscovered the hilarity of humour which did not have to pass the test of reason, the ricochet so fast it was a second or so later that I understood my own joke. I found a new self: boisterous, wild, of rude animal spirits, a caricature of vitality to counter his gentle despair. An unfamiliar persona, but so flattering I have decided it is real. At first we met once, and then twice, a week, always at six-fifteen, always parting at a quarter to nine, after his three gin and tonics and my three glasses of white wine. He would hail a taxi, while I opted to walk. He never tried to see me home, a courtesy I resent as patronizing in the absence of ulterior motive.

Only once did a rendezvous deviate from the routine. He'd asked that we meet earlier than usual, and fortunately I worked a flexible day. By then I had rehabilitated the Quaich, cancelled its associations with that night I stood him up, but I got there early just in case. Fergie poured me a measure guaranteed to provoke joshing resentment from the extras propping up the bar, quite apart from the havoc it would play with my habitual calculation of when I'd had enough. Still, I'm fond of Fergie, I like the fact that he's a sallow-faced ned with an unblinking prurient stare. He treats me like a girl, any girl, a hole, a splitarse, and where others might be offended, I'm quite pleased. Well, I am thirty-nine and three-quarters. And he *is* safely penned behind the mahogany counter, contractually obliged not to step out of line. So we chatted awhile about the title fight to be held in the city the following night. Fergie has done a bit of boxing himself, although not enough to acquire that flat-faced look or the circumflexes of scar tissue fighters have for eyebrows. He reckoned the darkie would be breathing through a straw by the weekend and I looked embarrassed and puzzled, given that both contestants were black, before it dawned on me that the reigning champ, being British and a regular in the tabloids, had become an honorary white man. I could have challenged him to explore this conundrum but my consciousness-raising days are over. A sudden bunching of punters arrived at the bar, so I retired to a table to wait.

Ever since that night he spent pretending to read the paper from cover to cover she always makes sure she arrives before him, and there she is: in the window seat, self-consciously abstracted that he may take her unawares. He ought to tell her that whatever she's got is not displayed to best advantage in repose. Hers is a nervy beauty, almost too quick to catch, light trapped in eyes and lashes, the glint of saliva on tooth. Without mobility her face is asymmetrical, the jawline more blurred than strictly desirable, gravity taking its toll. But he loves her imperfections, the vulnerabilities she may not even recognize, tiny flaws in a life unrolling like a bolt of cloth, falling into folds and gathers, creasing and doubling back on itself, one continuous colour, seamless and true. There are plenty of younger women already spoiled, marked by other fingers, where she seems virgin. Not intacta – she could probably teach him a thing or two – but intact, unclaimed, no husbands or exes or still-flickering old flames, no kids, no baggage. Her past is just that, all used up in the stories, leaving her fresh and new. He too could be like that, he feels a second self stirring within him. If she could love him. He thinks about her all the time. He can't help it. Their in-jokes are a running commentary in his thoughts, his funniest remarks come back to him in the mirror-panelled lift or the minicab or the editing suite, tripping him into laughter out loud. Her punchlines too, sometimes. He knows her well enough to anticipate what she would say in certain situations, and even alone he'll hear those overcrisp consonants in his head. But best of all is the secret pleasure of comparison, the continual testing of his love, eyeing secretaries and shop assistants half her age, pitting a sexy mouth, a snugly wrapped arse, or a profile of simple loveliness, against the emotional landscape of her face, and taking his share of the glory when she wins.

I stood up to greet him and, leaning forward for a glancing kiss, felt my lips make contact with the street cold on his cheek. As usual, the physical tribute was lost in the flurry of too much to say. We never kissed on parting, when it might have been easier to linger over the gesture. I bought him a drink, standard measures this time, Fergie wouldn't risk it for just anybody, and he told me about his day. He seemed unsettled, distracted, perhaps he hadn't quite overcome the memory of that night of solitary humiliation, still troubled by the afterburn of all those glances towards the door. When he finished his drink he suggested moving on. It was a cold afternoon in May with a threat of premature darkness, a metallic gleam under the lid of cloud at the horizon's edge. Half a mile down the road he suddenly announced 'I'm starving.' Ten to five: not a time that corresponded with my appetite, but maybe when you got to be Drew's size you needed extra fuelling. I shrugged compliance to find him turning up a tenement close. It was a grand stair fallen on modest times, the wall-tiling largely intact, the paint above cobwebbed and peeling, the trapped air pungent with the scent of cats. On the second floor, he tugged the organ-stop bell pull outside a storm door which folded back to reveal the glowing promise of stained glass.

She was well into her eighties, perhaps even her tenth decade.

'Euphemia.'

'Andrew! In the name of the wee man.'

She was the size of a healthily grown seven-year-old but still disconcertingly womanly. Extreme age had brought her back a beauty I guessed she hadn't known since girlhood. He kissed her, bending down with an abruptness that had me cringing in anticipation of collision. She raised a hand to steady his cheek while pursing her lips to make contact with a ringing smack of suction. The flesh covering the hand was transparent, not slack but petrified into folds which revealed each vein and bone and sheath of cartilage as clearly as a medical textbook. Her skin seemed tanned, though it was just the underpinning of blood and muscle showing through. She was wearing a child's printed sweatshirt with a pussycat and butterfly motif and a pair of Lycra leggings which suggested that time did not do significantly more damage beyond the age of thirty-five. Her hair was white and bushy and I remember wondering when was the last time I'd seen an old lady without benefit of shampoo and set? The Magellan Street girls were always out of circulation Thursday mornings: pensioner discount day at Kiss Me Quiff. The hall was dark and smelled of boiled potato but the absence of any complementary flavour told me that dinner was still some way off.

'This is a surprise.'

She was a Highlander, her consonants chewy with Gaelic charm, sibilance whistling through her too-perfect teeth, though it was the candy-pink gums that really gave the game away. I fell in love with her, as I knew I was supposed to, but was it also his intention that she should fall in love with me? She must have known that he was married. Carefully I avoided his eye, not caring to enhance his virile reputation at the price of appearing a whore. At the same time, the likelihood that she had drawn this conclusion lent a pleasurable substance to fantasy's heat.

She sat us on the splay-legged sofa whose nap-flattened velvet creaked with impacted horsehair and straw. There was a rocking chair, and a china cabinet full of greyly translucent teacups I hoped would not be pressed upon us, and a yellow-keyed piano with candle brackets jutting from the walnut case (one of them precariously soldered at the joint), and a mezzotint of Rabbie Burns, and a Reader's Digest condensed set of the Waverley novels, and a multivariously spiky knitting machine with the unfeasible bulk of superseded technology. Between these sociological landmarks were zones of unfamiliarity, the lack of carpet or coconut matting or indeed floorboards in a couple of places, that maypole of electrical flexes stretching from the ceiling rose, twisted together with an ingenuity I hadn't encountered since the reckless days when I would eat a fistful of unidentified mushrooms and pass the night in a bedsit firetrap listening to Lou Reed at sixteen and a half rpm. Dodgy wiring was as close as I ever came to teen rebellion: Darwin didn't object to sex or drugs.

Euphemia's flat had a certain smell, not inherently unpleasant. For me dampness held the evocative mystery of all things old, but it was an unusual outdoor dampness, a whiff of ivy and cold stone. There was no sense of neglect about the place, it felt fully inhabited, every surface stacked with papers, leaflets, envelopes, knitting patterns, newspaper clippings, arranged in evident if arcane order, yet the dust had lain so long it had reached its finite condition, a felted thickness which looked as if it could be rolled like carpet or lifted intact to smother a fire. Don't get me wrong: I myself tend to the sluttish end of the spectrum, but it's not a characteristic much found among women half a century nearer the great housekeeper in the sky. I was surprised to see Drew so much at home there, careless of his well-laundered corduroys against the veiling of grime on the cream-painted door. I had formed an impression of fastidiousness which I now had to amend to a strictly emotional reserve. Either that or, sentimentalist that he was, normal standards were suspended in deference to the spirit of the croft.

'Will you take a cup of tea?' she called over her shoulder, taking the answer for granted. In the hall I saw the looming shadow of an opening door, heard the purposeful rattle of biscuit tins. There followed an almighty thump of airlocked plumbing which forced from my throat an involuntary cry. Drew beamed at me.

'Just filling the kettle,' she sang.

I craned my neck, feeding on detail, the mirror-mounted photographs hanging from the picture rail by rusting chains, the ancient flypaper with its heavily clustered kill, the intricate wooden fireplace with its shelves and nooks and even a tiny mirrored cupboard secured by a dainty brass key. Below it, the cracked iron hob-grate cradled a stash of Vimto cans. The reminiscence business had significantly eroded my capacity for surprise. I'd sat in homes which smelled of shit, and old shit too. I'd met junkies and alkies and

Temazepam amputees. I'd watched toddlers handed a KitKat for lunch, wolfing it down silver paper and all. I'd seen incontinent grannies dumped knickerless on the living-room floor. But I'd never encountered anything quite like Euphemia's habitat before.

'Who is she?'

He twinkled infuriatingly.

'Drew . . .'

He looked warningly in the direction of the kitchen, then said at normal volume 'No point whispering: Phemie could hear a dog-whistle in the middle of Argyle Street.'

The kettle screamed and our hostess returned, bearing a tray. Drew carefully relieved the tea trolley of its cargo of missionary magazines and pulled it in front of the sofa, lifting one end so its wheel jumped the missing floorboard. On the tray were a couple of Melaware picnic cups of the sort I remembered being given away free with pre-biological soap flakes, two china saucers which matched neither the cups nor each other, a handpainted Victorian cream jug filled with thick yellow milk, a jamjar of white sugar contaminated by years of used teaspoons, a hefty handful of home-made shortbread fingers, a slab of cheese, and a plate of Malted Milk cookies spread thick with butter. She made a second trip to fetch the workman's chipped enamel teapot.

Back again, she handed me a plate already loaded with its buttered biscuit, and pressed me to help myself to cheese. I smiled with noncommittal warmth. I have never been able to eat with strangers, the food turns to ashes in my mouth, becomes a quota to be dispatched as speedily as possible, which brings the awkwardness of second helpings.

Luckily her first questions were directed at me, so I had an alibi. And besides, my escort was eating for two. Phemie was a sharp old girl with a courtesy I knew better than to mistake for approval. That would not be granted for a long time, if at all. She addressed me directly, without reference to Drew, as if we had independently made our way to her door. The closest she came to linking us was with the question

'And have you any children yourself, Tracy?'

Hearing the implication of rebuke, I met her gaze. 'Not so far.'

She regarded me with composure, an old-fashioned word to describe an understanding so unexpectedly contemporary.

'No, well, sometimes we don't.' She leaned towards me, causing a moment of apprehension before her fingers swooped on the plate resting on my knees and removed the buttered biscuit, restoring it to its fellows on the tray. Then she smiled at Drew.

'How's the kirk on the hill; have you central heating yet?'

'I'm not there any more, Phemie. You remember: I work with the television now.'

He was picking up her Highland lilt, a contagion it would take all my vigilance to avoid.

'Och yes, the television.' She seemed as unimpressed as I was.

Drew sat up, correcting his comfortable slump. I placed a protective hand over my teacup fearing the seismic ripple of springs, but on such defeated upholstery it was a needless precaution.

'But how are you, Euphemia? Are you keeping yourself busy?'

'I'm keeping myself off other people's consciences, which is what they usually mean when they ask me that.'

She smiled, but not to draw the sting. Euphemia appeared genuinely unconcerned how Drew took her. She had lost the habit of female attentiveness to men's moods. Maybe she'd never had it. It wasn't a feature I'd noticed dwindling with the advancing years: the Magellan Street girls still opened like daisies the moment a bunneted punter hove into view, but then Phemie was a different species. For her, age seemed a privilege. On the streets my girls were acknowledged with the averted glance, bodyswerved like so much litter. My friends felt the same way, and worried about the inexplicable aberration of choosing to work with the elderly. Euan once accused me of being attracted to mother-figures and seemed uneasy when I took the notion seriously, although on reflection I decided he was wrong. I was drawn to the old by affinity, not the desire to have my difference underlined. It was a good five years since I had felt the pavements a river of pushchairs, tears no longer sprang to my eyes at the sight of a crocheted toorie, but of course not having children affected the way I saw my life. A Roman road stretching unbroken until death. Time, which accelerates with the passing years, undergoes a small reversal with the birth of a child, slowing and borrowing the perspective of infinity. The internal hourglass acquires more sand, the ballast of retrieved memory. My own earliest recollection was a dream, and even then what I retained was the memory of remembering, an unreliable carbon of a long-lost original. But Sandra McKeown had told me that, tucking up her first-born child, she remembered being put to bed by her own mother, the careful arrangement of uncoordinated limbs. Such fragments return to the maternal consciousness, so the miracle of new life opens up a second avenue, through an undiscovered country of our own.

Euphemia saw me looking at the knitting machine and spoke as if I'd asked the question.

'I'm not responsible for that repulsive colour, it was a commission. I'm very particular what I make for the orphans. Mrs McGregor now, she'll turn out the most unsuitable clothes. A great big yellow sailor suit in garter stitch and she sends it off with a label, "boy, aged 13". It's a shame.'

Reaching over for another finger of shortbread, Drew was caught in the crossbeam of our glances. I had not seen him around food before, and its proximity seemed an intolerable strain. I had forgotten the psychodrama of confectionery along with the misery of teenage diets, the compulsive allure of forbidden treats. 'She means well,' he commented, trying to move the moment on.

'If she meant so very well she would have taken the trouble to inform herself what the children like to wear these days. At least I knit clothes with plenty of room in them, that's the young style isn't it, Andrew?—'

She dropped a pawky glance to his cords, which were showing slightly more than their customary four inches of empty fabric between crotch-seam and groin. Laughing through a mouthful of shortbread crumbs, he deferred to her superior knowledge. She preened slightly.

'—I like to watch *Top of the Pops*, though it's not so good since they stopped the break-dancing. I always look out for Madonna: a lovely wee girl. I don't believe she's wise having the navel ring, when I was nursing you saw a lot of infection there, but if they'd had the fashion when I was a wee bit younger, I might have had a nipple pierced.'

Just as it was occurring to me that the cabaret might grow tiresome over time, she dropped the roguish manner.

'And tell me, Andrew, are you still hearing the knocking in the middle of the night?'

Both looked over accusingly as I returned the teacup to its saucer. 'Sorry: went down the wrong way.'

Drew held my eye, awaiting some cue which I provided.

'What knocking is this?'

'The three knocks, on the wall, or the window,' Euphemia answered.

Reflexively, I turned to the window to my right. Outside it was snowing, and seemed to have been doing so for some time.

'Bella now, she sleeps right through it.' It was the first time I had heard his wife's name. 'You'll be hearing the water too?'

He raised his head slightly as if to speak. She was watching him in a manner both intent and detached.

'What water?'

If they were going to have this conversation in my presence then I was damn well going to be included.

Again she spoke for him. 'I had a friend in Cruden Bay, the name she had for it was the deid-drap. I've seen people call out the plumber or the joiner or the man who looks for beasties in the roof, they spend a fortune until they find something that will explain it away, but they know what it is, in themselves, all along.'

I turned to Drew, ready to smile, but he was staring at Euphemia like a child. Then he stood up and shuffled precipitately from the room. Down the corridor, through the solid pine of the bathroom door, came the muffled echo of forceful evacuation. The old lady cocked her head in comical acknowledgement. Beyond the window the snow was falling stealthily, grey kapok shedding itself doggedly from a depthless sky, undisturbed by the breath of wind. A layer was building up on the outside sill.

I put my plate back on the trolley. 'Does he bring us all here?'

She looked at me with humorous reproof as Drew reappeared in the doorway, evidently nurturing the hope that his brief emergency had not reached our ears.

'We're going to have to go, Phemie.'

She nodded, rising to see us to the door. This time she moved to anticipate Drew's kiss, placing both hands on his forearm to lever herself up. 'Look after Tracy for me,' she said unexpectedly. 'And be sure you bring her again.' Then she took my fingers in her mothwing hands and puckered up for a kiss. I bent towards her, assuming we would meet cheek to cheek but at the last moment she gave me a darting, disconcerting peck on the lips. We were out on the stairhead and the inner door was in her hand, ready to swing shut, when she offered what I took to be an answer to my question.

'There is nothing I have to tell you that you do not already know.'

And then one day he suggested we visit the island.

I was so shocked by the possible implications, and the impossibility of knowing for sure, that my first impulse was smiling aggression.

'What about your wife?'

His face blanched. He knew I knew, but I wasn't supposed to mention it. Still, I admired his swift recovery.

'She doesn't care for the northern isles. Too wild for her.'

'But her husband going away with another woman: that's tame enough?'

'It would depend on what we did there.' He twitched those outsize lips. 'Since we always behave ourselves, I don't see any reason for her to worry.'

We flew out from Glasgow Airport on a little sky van whose cabin made the runway bus seem luxurious. The seats wore loose covers apparently borrowed from a jumbo, the fabric ridged uncomfortably under my skirt. Drew was too substantial a presence for his allotted place and we swapped seats, me trapped by his spreading thigh and the misted Perspex window, him wedged between the pincergrip armrests with his legs across the aisle. His shoulder and most of his right arm invaded my airspace. My lungs were full of his smell, a smudge of soap and that aftershave with its high vanilla edge. This could have been cosy, had we been on cuddling terms, but the effort not to snuggle was cricking my neck, and I was developing claustrophobia, surrounded by the recycled farts that constitute cabin air. The aisle was so tight the trolley dolly had to use a tray. And walk sideways. And step over Drew's legs. She was a chemical blonde with nicely solid hips and too much brown foundation which blunted her beauty in a fudgelike mask.

'Tea or coffee?' she chanted at each passenger.

'Tea,' I replied automatically, only to see a shadow of concern cross her features.

She leaned closer. 'I should take the coffee, petal. We cannae make a decent cup o' tea: the water won't boil before Inverness.'

I changed my order and made Drew wait until she was fully absorbed two rows behind before giving in to the giggles.

He was making the trip to see a Catholic mystic, an ancient visionary whose continued existence was something of an inconvenience to those who preferred their latterday saints good and dead. When his name was dropped in contemporary contexts people would ask, intrigued and a little disappointed, 'Is he still around?' The promised interview was a scoop, but Drew was nervous about the visit.

'The orthodox brethren will see it as an act of provocation.' He was worrying at the cellophane on his in-flight custard cream. 'Though seemingly he's more interested in spending solstice at the standing stones than celebrating mass these days. Virtually pagan. Not that they'll be thrilled about that either. Still, the old bugger being camera-shy is a bonus. No pictures of me supping with the AntiChrist, and' he smiled with special emphasis 'no camera crew.'

So old and eminent was this visionary that he'd decided the Sunday evening viewer could do without visuals. Tape recorder only. The plan was to match his words to some atmospheric landscape shots and splice in the footage of his younger self available in the library. it seemed a workable solution to me, but mckinnon was not pleased.

Our hotel was a mansard-roofed Edwardian mansion of black and white clapboard. At first sight of it we laughed hysterically, taken silly by such an unlooked-for gift. Inside, as outside, it was a sepia photograph brought to life, the walls covered in tea-stained panelling and watermarked engravings cut from books. The dining room sparkled with white napery and outsize silverware and, above the picture rail, a beaten copper frieze. Longboats featured prominently, as I recall. The hessian-walled public bar with its dartboard and widescreen television suggested an enterprise sustained as much by local thirst as by the tourist trade, yet the village amounted to no more than a couple of farms, half a dozen cottages and a circular walled graveyard. Beyond stretched the impossible blue of the sea, sun catching the kelp on its surface, setting off a black glittering. Rising to the treeless headland was a sloping field marked by parallel lines of mown grass. A haymaking tractor was sucking up the stripes and spewing them into a trailer, leaving the pallid meadow streaked with their ghostly traces. A white line of gulls embroidered its progress. The field, the sea, the cerulean sky. Such good fortune. I felt a surge of gratitude so overpowering it might almost have been love, although strictly, Drew deserved as little thanks as I: the hotel had been booked through Lachlan Lane. Signing in, I experienced a brief, unreasoning flush of expectation before the desk clerk handed us separate keys. I would have been livid at the presumption anyway. We repaired to different corridors to unpack.

Hard to describe quite how glorious I found that island, how unexpectedly its austerity sounded echoes in my heart. A land for the most part without cultivated fields, the drystane seams tracking without distinguishing, a land without trees where a blasted thorn became a tourist attraction, a land of lonely kirks, beleaguered farm steadings and white-harled croft houses squatting into the hillside. Of springy turf and sea lochs and inlets so filigree-fine that the pale horizon seemed a silvered mirror corroding at the edges. The northern light a gauzy wash. It was a place of all-sufficient emptiness, reducing life's questions to the trickling of the curlews, the sweet scent of heathgrass on the breath of the wind, the white-washed wall splashed by sunlight, a low hillcrest blank against the endless sky. One day we stumbled across a ruined village, abandoned yet retaining its red telephone box in working order. A laughing gull rode the thermals above our heads, and we found the leeward corner of a roofless cottage where I peeled and divided an orange, juice running down the inside of my sleeve. Later we set off for a celebrated view high above the perilous rocks but were turned back by the sheep, big and fearless, bodies tight-permed, heads like fisted boxing gloves. Instead, we pushed at the creaking gate into the graveyard, fingering the explosions of lichen on the pitted surface of the stones, finding the same names again and again, tracing the modest inscriptions, the early widowings and infant deaths, the continuity of tragedy and hope.

What were we doing? Sometimes it felt as if we were there, each of us, alone, seeking our own pleasure, and I did not know whether to feel slighted by his self-containment, or grateful for my own. There was an unreality about time passing. Until then the longest Drew and I had spent in each other's company at a stretch was three hours. Now we were together from breakfast till bed. Our separate beds. Previously, we had been playmates and our meetings a match: me on the white squares, him on the black. Now, the island became the focus, and we stood side by side in readiness to be diverted. Until the mood would shift, surprising us both, and we were so absorbed in each other's company that the glories of landscape passed before us unseen.

We hired a car and discovered a new amusement. The first time it happened I was so preoccupied with the road that I hardly realized the sounds were outwith my own head. Then he started singing along, but softly, discreetly, so as not to drown me out. And then it became a habit. Remembering our first meeting in the art gallery it was no surprise that he knew the songs, but I was impressed by his mastery of the words, those meandering introductions before the tune kicks in, full of overelaborate wordplay and outmoded slang. I remember the sense of diminishment when, in the early Eighties, all those wine bars and bistros hit on *Ella Sings Cole Porter* as the perfect foil to yuppie digestion. Suddenly my favourite ballads were the sing-along anthems of the aspirational decade. But not everybody knew every verse of 'How Could You Believe Me When I Said I Loved You When You Know I've Been A Liar All My Life?' I almost choked with laughter. It was clear from the start that we shared a sense of humour, we had spent weeks building up a store of private jokes, but never had we known the helpless, inexplicable hilarity that then convulsed us. Today of course we take it for granted.

On the fourth day he recorded his interview, I took a book of folklore and a bannock-and-corned beef picnic down to the beach. There was an anachronistic flavour to our diet that week: poached eggs and gypsy toast and Branston pickle, over-sweet orange cordial and foam rubber Swiss roll, comestibles I remembered relishing as a child staying to tea in homes which did not subsist on wild rice and mushroom goulash and ginseng root brews. When Drew came back he was brooding, withdrawn.

'So did old Magnus seduce you from the path of righteousness?'

'A little late for that, alas.'

'How was he?'

'Taciturn.'

A trait that seemed to be catching.

My afternoon on the cement-coloured sand amid the scratched runes of birdprints had been restful but markedly short of incident. Certain that his hours had been more exciting, I resented his refusing to share. He must have realized this.

'It's mayhem back in Glasgow: they've sealed off Argyle Street. A couple of flute bands ran into a party of Irish patriots over for the fleadh.' There was a slight pause before he added, 'He had the news on.'

I knew that he had telephoned his wife.

I felt a compound irritation: the surreptitiousness of the contact; the complete lack of need; the knowledge that any show of displeasure would convince him that he'd been right in his instinct to conceal. Above all, the way his slyness showed he'd turned me into a second wife. Unsettled by my silence, he suggested a drive.

The sky was a madness of whirling birds, the wind bent on uprooting anything with the temerity to stand taller than five inches off the ground. Only the lighthouse, clean and unmoved, dared the elements. It was part of my fearless persona when we were together that I should scorn the cacophonous menace of the gulls, but I did not feel contracted to suicidal risk. The ground was dry enough and covered with a pink counterpane of thrift. I approached the precipice on my hands and knees and, having reached a vantage point, lay on my stomach to look over the edge.

'What's the matter?' he yelled. 'Losing your nerve?'

'Come over here and say that.'

'You're joking.'

But reluctantly he crawled serpentlike to the brink.

Out towards the horizon the waves were held in a muted sparkle, but from our perilous bed we could look straight down the cliffs to an inlet where water exploded against rock a hundred feet below. Here the sea was a colour I had always assumed synthetic, a rich bottle green which frothed into white violence and billowing spray. Between us and the water were the birds, puffins, terns, skuas, razorbills, guillemots. Drew reeled off the names confident I could not contradict. Thousands, perhaps millions of them, with a city squalor to their guano-spattered slum. Some sheltered or nested in the tucks and folds of the basalt wall, but most observed a perpetual motion, swinging from cliff face to cliff face as if suspended on pantomime wires, birds in full flight swooping in perfect arcs below us. The world turned upside-down. Then I felt the slow twisting tug of vertigo.

I was a city child, brought up on smog and waxy apples. I knew a nettle from a dock leaf, could identify a robin, although the closest I came to seeing one was on kitschy Christmas cards. I knew that the December starlings bickering in the town hall eaves were migrants, down from Scotland, while the local birds wintered in continental climes. Otherwise the natural world was a closed book. By adolescence ignorance had become aversion. Wide open spaces filled me with a terrible forsakenness, country weekending brought on a desperation to make contact with the works of man, taking any excuse to pass by the petrol station or browse through the tinned goods in the village store. And then I came to Scotland and felt the seduction of landscape. I wasn't a spotter. I still couldn't tell a cormorant from a shag and I really didn't care, but I had felt my body slow to the rhythm of island weather, I had learned to watch the sky, to treasure the endless light of summer and to find some beauty in those grudging days that squeezed out of a marrow-chilling dawn at nine and were dark again by three. Even now, my love of nature isn't the standard strain. I understand the appeal of emptiness, a space unclaimed by others that can be filled to the summit with self, I know that's how it works, but not for me. For me the echoing glen has the teeming life of metaphor, populous with sentiment, a nation's precious sense of who they are.

On the way back to the hotel we stopped at a fishing village, functional, yet with covert flashes of charm. A miniaturized settlement, Nordic in style, matchbox houses on a papier mâché topography, beguiling with the childish fascination of the small. I sensed the life here. Or more accurately, I sensed the men, with their promise of acceptance, however qualified and temporary: the passport of sexual recognition. The wan sunshine had retreated, a high layer of cloud like a dustsheet drawn across the sky above the still-frantic wind. A couple of dinghies jerked between the tines of breakwater and pier. The single-storey harled boxes could have been a couple of centuries old, or merely the worse for five years' weather. Amid the economy of construction each house had its distinguishing feature, its gabled dormer, castellated porch, or trifurcate finial. Some of these embellishments had been painted in gaudy gloss colours, screaming mauve or buttery yellow or Cadillac pink, which lent them an almost Mexican air, a languid touch of dusty heat on this chittery northern landscape. Herrings drying on the lines between them like washday socks. Either side of the neat little harbour was a notoriously dangerous coast, scythed by the Atlantic wind, approached by a treacherous jigsaw of livid grass and algae-slicked rocks on which pottered, surreally, the occasional intrepid sheep. Without needing to agree we took different routes. He was making for yet another of the lighthouses that clustered this side of the island, I was in search of the sea. I kept him in sight for some time, ahead of me, over to my right, now full-length, now bisected by the rocks, now just a bobbing head. As on the clifftop, I had a sense of nature flouting its own rules, changing form to mock expectation. The water seemed so far off, whichever way I turned, those deadpan sheep so unconcerned by the imminence of slippery death. By some geological jape it was possible to be picking a way across the rocks, eyes down, solicitous of your footing, and suddenly, alerted by an unfamiliar acoustic, to look up and find that you were below sea-level, and the crashing surf, as ever at a distance, was hitting the shoreline some way above your head. The path twisted away and the next time I saw the Atlantic it was stretched out at my feet. I found a dry ledge amid the rockpools and settled myself to watch.

The sea was black terror, turbid as flint, yet it broke on the jagged landfall the colour of beach glass. The waves were addictive, calling up that lust for destruction women are told they cannot feel. There was a time with Darwin that Sam smashed everything in sight: cars, crockery, Waterford crystal whisky tumblers, she even snapped the gold nib of his Mont Blanc fountain pen. Just clumsy I suppose. I sat there a long time, watching the breakers, hypnotized by the walls of water advancing on the shore, the rearing up and, once in a while, that eerie moment of hiatus, the scroll of liquid poised so that I looked through its pellucid curl from the underside and saw that, for all the shallowness of that sheet of brine, it too was a glassy turquoise. Then the foam, beaten eggwhite, with here and there a patch of yellow scum. When I checked my watch an hour had passed. He would be worrying. I retraced my steps, lurched onto the same smooth footholds, skipping the same crevices, losing my balance on the same deceiving see-saw stone, and found myself in that same unnerving corridor where the ocean battered above my head, when something made me shift my gaze. Drew was high, high above me, moving over the rocks, unconscious of my presence, his hair tormented by the turbulence, a dot of pink scalp revealed. He was slipping, losing his footing and recovering, yet without mending the carelessness that made him so unsteady. He had unbuttoned his navy blue greatcoat, that great wind-catching sail, and the corkscrew gale was lifting it crazily about him. I felt the exultation of the assault, the noise and push and danger, the wind working him over, searching out every chink in his clothing, every tenderness in his face; his true self, elemental, exposed.

I knew he was determined to fall, felt the focusing of his will and counted, one, two, before I saw him totter, as if trapped in some adrenaline timewarp. Then he vanished from sight. I knew he couldn't swim, not that it mattered, the temperature of the water was enough to kill him. By now I was almost at sea-level, clambering, shinning up the rocks, heedless of the razored surface slicing my knees. At the top I didn't have time to think about launching myself into the sea, it took me, swept me from my precarious foothold and into a coldness I instantly ceased to feel. All I knew was the churning above me, the salt burn in my throat as I struggled for breath, the Atlantic Ocean trying to find its own level, as water will, in me. My saliva came thick as spaghetti, the catfish drool from my lips intact in the saline ocean. Above all I felt the hollowness in my chest, a dent of knowledge: the nameless thing we spend our lives keeping at bay was now happening to me. Of Drew I could see nothing, yet I sensed him flailing in the water, mouth gasping, and I felt a flash of necessary rage. Such stupidity. I wanted to kill him, but to do that I would have to save him first. Limbs thrashing with countervailing strokes, I fought the water, gulping for air past the abrasions in my windpipe, choking, coughing, barking like a seal. And then just for a second, I got my head above the surface and saw him, as he saw me, across the green-furred rocks where he was standing, wind-buffeted but dry, and wearing a look of pure surprise. Then I was dragged down again. I was conscious of the cold and the churning, and the sting of my ribboned flesh, but these were as nothing beside the knowledge. It was a warning come too late. I had heard it and ignored it, and now I saw that it was not within my power to refuse. And even as I succumbed to the inevitability of my death the current caught me and buoyed me and delivered me to land.

I was sick, copiously, the brown and pink chowder of lunch augmented by gallons of swallowed sea. The retreating tide washed it against my face. Perhaps five seconds to make it across the rocks, beyond reach of the next onslaught of water. I had a ghost of a chance and wished that I had none, that I might surrender to my fate. They say drowning is the kindest death, pleasurable, even sexual, to be filled and filled until the body takes no more. But, after all, I didn't have it in me. I lack the temperament for such acceptance; maybe it's a question of trust.

In retrospect, the danger was overstated. A brief dip in the Atlantic, perhaps no more than a minute, and then the undignified scramble for land. Surface lesions only.

'What in the name of God were you doing?'

Getting back to the hotel was almost as dangerous. Drew could barely hold the road, the hired car skidding on the marram grass flanking the asphalt, my right hand changing gear. Only his fourth time behind the wheel: he gave up the lessons thirty years ago. Luckily there was a doctor drinking in the bar, contempt for the idiocy of tourists in his eyes. I didn't care. The anaesthetic of panic was wearing off and I was gradually coming round to a symphony of pain. They gave me whisky, that timeless medicament, and I was sick again, wonderful purging convulsions which gathered my variously defective body into a single clean sensation, one hurt in place of many. My stomach was empty but the retching would not stop, or at least I would not stop it, so they gave me an injection in my left buttock, one of the few bodily parts which had survived the afternoon unscathed. Around seven o'clock exhaustion took over. Which, strictly speaking, was the first time I slept with Drew Monzie. But even as I lost consciousness my mind was teasing out the day. He wanted to bind himself to me, and me to him, held fast by ties of blood. Choice wasn't enough. He chose women all the time, and they chose him, and then he chose again. He needed to change the protocol, to forge a permanent connection that could never be gainsaid, and so he made me save his life, in order that he save mine.

'Delirious,' I heard the doctor say.

'You fell, Drew.'

'I stumbled a couple of times. If that.'

'You dropped like a stone. One minute you were there, the next . . . gone.' I saw that gleam come into his eye and started footnoting. 'Obviously there was some sort of false perspective, but from where I was standing it was the only explanation: you'd gone into the water.'

'And you made straight for the spot you'd seen me fall from . . .'

'You couldn't make straight for anything across those rocks.'

'But I wasn't *anywhere near*.'

'Drew, you don't know where you were. Land, water, land, water: it was a maze—'

I felt anger inflating within me. He wanted to believe in some spookery. He wasn't stupid, indeed there was a censorious streak in his intelligence which wasn't far off intellectual snobbery, yet he was prepared to fly in the face of reason for the sake of a cheap shiver.

'—what are you saying? That what I saw was some eldritch apparition? If you weren't where I saw you, then it's not because of any doppelganger or unquiet spirit or bit of ectoplasm. If you're telling me you weren't there, and you're absolutely certain, then I'm going off my head, and I'm going to see a shrink about it.'

This was the childish stratagem he occasionally employed: stop or I hurt myself. Despicable, but it works.

We were in his room with its outlook over the Atlantic which, thanks to the ox-bow scoop of the natural harbour, appeared as tame as a municipal boating lake. It was one o'clock in the morning and the hospital whiteness of sky was just puckering with the gloaming. Two figures were becalmed in an inflatable dinghy about twenty feet from the pebbled beach. It was one of the delights of staying here that the rooms were furnished as family bedchambers, with mismatched dressing-tables and wardrobes and a general lack of regard for the conventions of hotel anonymity, the drawback being that there was a great deal of clutter and not all that much space. He was sitting on a chair by the window and overflowing into most of the room. I was propped up on the bed, acutely conscious of the darkened but not yet hardened scabs, strips of prosciutto garnishing my shins. No point in dressings, the doctor said: best let the air get to them. No point in bedclothes either, or anything that might stick. Just a big shirt and a pained expression. Not what the vamp-about-town would choose with seduction in mind. That's probably why I said it: I felt absolutely safe.

'I ought to book myself into the nuthouse anyway—'

The hunch of his shoulders relaxed a little, hearing my tone relent.

'—I obviously thought it was worth risking my neck to save yours. If that isn't reason to get my head examined, what is?'

'You don't need a shrink to do that for you.' He got up and seated himself on the edge of the mattress, which pitched alarmingly. 'Here,' he tipped my head forward, working his fingers through the hair to reach the back of my skull, the vulnerable hollow just above the stem, 'you're angry with me because you did something very brave and now you feel it was foolhardy.' Held like this, my field of vision was the stretch of knee to thigh, the diagonal weave of denim holding in his spreading flesh. 'Here,' with the first two fingers of his right hand he applied faint pressure to the crescent behind my left ear, 'you're angry with me because you looked into eternity and understood what it is I believe.' I started to contradict but he drowned me in the slow rhythm of that preacher's voice. 'Here,' he touched the other ear in a symmetrical gesture and lightly cupped my face, lifting it so that our eyes met, 'you're angry with me because I'm looking after you and you can't bear the thought of obligation. And here,' keeping hold of my head, his face bore down on mine; his mouth, a queer not quite live thing like a jellyfish beached by the tide, touched my lips once, 'you're angry with yourself.'

The slow, deliberate reaching for another. The molecules in the air grow sluggish. Light thickens, vision sharpens, the world shifts out of register and realigns. His words glistened like festering ham, self-consciously poetic, as unconvincing as any finely wrought performance, but there remains the moment of reaching. This is true. The nature of the kiss, its sensuality and awkwardness, the something slightly acrid in his saliva, the unnerving, invertebrate softness of his mouth, the reticence of his tongue, all these were secondary to that moment. A point of obsessive interest, the brink of transformation, one pure act of choice. I say choice, but what I mean is being chosen. The slow deliberate reaching in the night.

No matter how well you know each other, how far you've advanced into the monopolistic merger of love, the first time there's always a separating out. The reduction of the transaction to its elemental poles. Man. Woman. Unnerving to act out of the most personal feeling, that heightened uniqueness of another human being, only to find you're going through the motions with someone you don't know.

I was more deeply embarrassed than I could remember being. None of the things that you fear happened: no farts or funny noises at the crucial moment; he brushed my wounds inadvertently, but only once did I cry out. I was worried that my breath wasn't sweet and my toenails needed cut and my labia would taste of garlic from the mussels on Wednesday night, but these thoughts were not as tormenting as the shame that in the midst of an activity so surpassingly intimate, I felt like a cipher in the bed. It wasn't just that this new geography of hair and flesh and sinew, so long desired, should seem a stranger's. I felt like a stranger to myself. What was he thinking? I didn't know. I had his vast stomach beneath me, the slit of navel swimming on its undulant sea of fat; I teased the chevron of chesthair within which his nipples seemed almost androgynous, more succulently erect than others I had kissed; I weighed his balls in the palm of my hand; and all this seemed to give him pleasure, but what was he *thinking*? If it was any relation to my own disorientation, I didn't want to know.

I long since rejected the canon of romantic mythology. No such thing as happy ever after, no such man as Mr Right. But somehow one fairytale slipped through the net. I believe in making love. Here I was looking for transcendence in the arms of someone else's man, awaiting the twinning of souls, the locking of the gaze, that limitless recognition, and I found myself hauling ass in the meat market. What was he feeling? My chaos and panic, in his own hermetically sealed bubble of course? Or an impersonal lust merely requiring that I follow the script? It was essential to give him a good time, otherwise this ordeal would profit no one, but Drew was a gentleman of the new school, and to provide complete satisfaction, it would be necessary to convince him of my own. With so many things to worry about, where was I supposed to find the space to feel aroused? And throughout our coupling, the whole length of this long, long night, one word snagged in my thoughts, gave me something to hang on to, a mantra to keep me whole. *Darwin.* Not the most appropriate lifeline, I admit, but in emergencies you take what you can get.

'So what was it like?' Gina asked me, when we met up the following week. Drunken confessions at a swimming club social: I must have been desperate to tell. 'Oh the usual,' I said. 'You know how it is, the first time.' She was interested in the nitty-gritty: was he tireless, was he skilful, was he big? And frankly I could barely remember. The usual: swarming with anxieties so vivid that they obliterated the actual details. And as the rising sun which had never quite set seeped through the cloud like blood through a bandage, my pelvis went rigid, and in a teeth-gritting dogged sort of fashion, I came. He cried, which he seemed to find satisfactory, or at least, his erection went away. And somewhere in the room a voice stopped repeating my father's name.

TEN

The girl in the fruit shop has a spider tattoo on the mount of her thumb. Swallows on the hand meant a hitter in the days before every kindergarten tough started carrying a blade, but spiders? Sam hasn't noticed, so I say as the girl hands me my change 'Nice tattoo,' because if I nudge Sam in the doorway it will be too late, and the assistant laughs in a way that says I'm old enough to be her mother and thus well beyond the appreciation of tattoos, so what's my game? Sam has seen but takes no pleasure in the embellishment. Another little reminder that we're strangers under the skin. And yet if I take the gulf for granted, as from time to time I do, next thing we'll manifest some freakish symmetry, like those twins separated at birth who meet up to discover both keep prize dachshunds or have the same inexplicable partiality for barbecue-flavour crisps. The last time we met I was trawling through her wardrobe and found a Simpsons of Piccadilly grey and mustard houndstooth jacket, nipped-in waist, patch pockets, single-breasted, circa 1954. I could date it because I had one too, only mine was cocoa and pink. Sam doesn't do Retro any more. She's wearing jeans, pink winklepicker boots, a fitted denim waistcoat with nothing underneath, and looks like she's going sharking at the Grand Ole Opry. We'll put it down to cultural differences.

It must be five minutes now since either of us spoke. I want to show off my town and, silently, subtly, she's thwarting me, just failing to focus as she turns towards the landmarks I point out. We pass a woman on the pavement, her yeasty skin shiny with the threat of pimples in this unexpected heat, breasts straining against a teeshirt which reads 'Which part of "fuck me" don't you understand?' Again I want Sam to have seen, but her attention is caught by that easy grouping of men outside the junk shop, big boots and broad shoulders and the hand-in-pocket slouch. It's the tall one she's watching, the one who flatters his Celtic darkness by dressing all in black, that sooty complexion as if the hair's abundant pigment had leached into his skin. Mid-twenties I thought from that first hurried glance bestowed on men the radar tells me are attractive, only studying those too ugly for it to matter, but I've come across him since and the black hair is touched with a crinkle of contrast like plaster dust, the melanous skin not quite taut across his cheekbones. Not such a hormonal catch, but still plenty to hold Sam's interest. A few weeks ago, browsing through a pile of old sheet music in his shop, I turned for no reason that I can remember, though it might have been the instinct of being watched. Surprised to be caught, he could not recover, standing frozen in that flagrant stare. Not much to justify feeling proprietorial, but I do.

We cut down the cobbled sidestreet to the park. Which is more like an annex to the local psycho-geriatric ward down this end: a refuge for all these jovial men of indeterminate age sunning themselves and wooing the ladies with their sherrydrinkers' gallantry. 'Hello smiler, I've missed you.' Funny that here the trees are mostly green, without that branch-end droop when the chlorophyll gives up. There's less autumn about, as if two days of Indian summer had the power to turn back the clock. In other parts of the city the season is well advanced, orange drifts are banked in the gutter like cornflakes spilled from the pack. On MacKendrick Avenue the limes are almost bare, the pavements too. The good burghers are out sweeping up the leaves as soon as they touch the ground. Those still left on the bough are lollipop yellow, or, caught by the sun, vibrant as those foil-wrapped coins in their little red nets glittering in the shops the weeks before Christmas. Less than a mouthful of chocolate in them, and the taste a saliva-sapping fraction too sweet, but covetable despite the predicted disappointment. Autumn is the nostalgic season for me, holding the past in its pocket, surprisingly complete. When I was nine Darwin hired me out to a patient of his, a parent who sought access to the inner world of his only son, an autistic boy two years my junior. The discrepancy in age and sex was impassable enough, never mind the swirling currents within his head, but I was sent to play with this child, to trail him through the windswept park searching for beech nuts I could pretend were fur-lined pixie hats or, the ultimate prize, a conker still sealed in its contact-mine case. I was supposed to draw him out of himself, put him in touch with the basics of life through our simple, joyous play.

Darwin believed in me. Despising the tyranny of expertise, he subscribed to the democratic nostrum that unites vigorous minds and Dralon philosophers: 'Be yourself'. And who's to say they're wrong? But I was no sort of example, my basic self so far from guaranteed. And so I found myself adapting to this child, trying to make sense of his repetitions and rages and inexhaustible obsessions. But this is old ground. I surprise myself sometimes, the tenacity of these leavings, the way when thoughts are allowed to idle they'll slew into this rut. There is so much more to be said, such pleasurable memories: harvest festivals and classroom handicrafts, the fruits of the earth hoarded amid pocketfluff or collaged with felt and fabric and good sticky glue. Even now I have the urge to collect fir cones and ash keys and the red beads off the rowan trees. It might look like exploitation, with a child so young, but Darwin believed in me. I just didn't merit his faith.

Sam is smiling with a sealed-lipped expression of sunlover's bliss. The sky is hazy gold, the corny light gentle on our faces, without the strength to tan or even tint the skin; the world has turned like a rugby ball, so the rays reach us slantwise. Already, with lunch barely over, I feel the winding down of sunset. It will be dark by six. Here in the middle of the park I can smell frying. It was the same up by the shops: an atmospheric lid sealing in the winter food which ancient instincts prompt us to consume. Beefburger or wildebeest, it's the same primordial stew. People stroll through the park dressed in leather and denim, unwilling to trust the running armpit and blotching cheek. So hot for October. Around us insects are reborn with a grateful teeming. Sam laughs a little with no pretext I can make out. Sometimes I think that all I really want is to regain my childhood playmate. But where would that leave Drew?

You'll be glad to know that the sex got better. Time found a way through the anonymity of flesh, and when it didn't, well, in a sense I enjoyed that too. As the days between our bi-weekly trysts grew longer, my life was ruled by a rhythm not its own. I had often pitied men their unmistakable evidence of amorous pull, the bulging trouser, the stretched cloth, but now I too was prone to erotic trance, on buses, in cafés, even amid the reminiscers' circle at Magellan Street. A stillness so intent my insides seemed turned to rock. I missed him, or more precisely the crease of my pudendum missed him, which displeased me mildly. I had been wont to hold forth about the richness of female sexuality, its infinite variety, its tirelessness and subtlety of response, and here I was fixed by a hunger as reductive as the emery paper's craving for the match. I required his company urgently, aggressively, as the one thing that would make me less distracted. Then it occurred to me that sex might be a displacement activity, a sensual decoy, as smoking or drinking or refrigerator-raiding avoids the issue and helps clog the true. So even as I submitted to this passion I was taking it apart to see how it worked, or to see if there were workings which could not be explained. Anything left over. Anything unaccounted for that might be love.

He offered to go with me to the airport, but I said no.

'I see.'

'Do you, now?'

'You've spent the past hour and a half in front of the mirror. Are we sure it's your sister you're meeting?'

Blind to the irony of his own domestic commitments, Drew dislikes being left behind.

'Don't talk to *me* about marathon grooming – I'm the one who has to go to the petrol station for a pee if you get the bathroom first in the morning. And do you hear me complaining?'

'I rather think that's what you're doing now—'

There *was* a touch of erotic definition about the ritual of face-plucking and leg-shaving, but it was wholly defensible: other people might or might not notice the connecting eyebrows and forested calf, only lovers and siblings have the *right* to look. And Sam was the critical type, or at least she had been last time I'd seen her, deep in the throes of censorious adolescence. The truth was I didn't know the woman I would be meeting off the plane. I wasn't even sure I'd recognize her in the arrivals lounge. I had a date with a stranger who was going to become an intimate, and in these situations first impressions count.

'—anyway she's on the Red Eye: she's going to look like the walking dead.'

That's what I was banking on.

In the event, of course I recognized her, and she didn't look too rough. She was talking to a fellow passenger as she came through customs and took care to finish her sentence before scanning the eager line-up by the barrier. Just a fraction of a second later than she might have looked. But when she saw me her face really did light up. I felt my own eyes kindle and discovered I was laughing.

'Tressy!'

'Sindy!'

There are a lot of things you don't know about me. Some of them I've forgotten myself.

The physical greeting was a problem. An airkiss, a hug? I myself favour a smacker on the cheek, just the one, very different from the finishing school affectation of two/three/four. The intended effect is presexualized warmth, the kiss we were discouraged from as children. Darwin scorned such perfunctory display: it was the bear hug or nothing. In the event I fudged it, grasping her by the shoulders and holding her off in the tension of the let-me-look-at-you embrace.

'How was the flight?'

'The assholes wouldn't let me smoke. Coach was a clean-air zone. You could give yourself cancer to your heart's content if you had the lettuce to fly First. I didn't have a problem with sitting up by the money while I had a cigarette, but no chance: back to the ghetto.'

Reminded, she delved into the raffia handbag on top of her luggage trolley and drew out a softpack of Kool Super Longs. There was something not quite believable about the props. The flash of buckle and talon, that transatlantic sheen, the very colours unfamiliar, a palette worn with a flourish of self-consciousness that reminded me of when we used to impersonate Monroe and Russell in *Gentlemen Prefer Blondes*. The toytown bazaar of Glasgow International Airport pressed uncomfortably on the periphery of my vision; not exactly JFK. She'd put the cigarette in her mouth before starting the search for a light. After ten seconds she looked to me. I shook my head: 'I don't smoke.'

She resumed her rummaging.

'I'm surprised you haven't given up for your voice.'

Why did I say that? She raised her eyebrows with an emphasis that forced her chin downwards: obviously a favourite gesture, but a new one on me.

'No, I'm still squandering the gifts God gave me.' A sideways look. 'Just practising sucking up to your Holy Moly there. Do you think I should kiss his ring?'

I had forgotten I had told her he was married.

'No, but you can bite it if you like.'

'In that case I'm going to need a drink – or don't you do that either? Oh, excuse me sir,' she had spotted a smoker a couple of yards away, 'could I trouble you for a light?'

He started to smile, and I couldn't really blame him. Sam speaks broad Yorkshire. Freddie Trueman was her elocution teacher. The Confederate drawl was just a different sort of joke.

I took possession of the trolley and pushed towards the exit. 'Could you try and hold the vamping until we get out of the airport? I've got the car, so if you want to drink in company we might as well go home.'

She exhaled decisively. 'You're not going to drink at ten-thirty in the morning anyway. Let's go to a bar.'

I didn't buy this bourbon-swigging floozy routine. There was no taint on her breath, and on a seven-hour flight even I'd have had a couple of relaxers. Unless she was easing up on the booze for the sake of a baby.

Sam flew out to New York the week she turned nineteen. Started singing in restaurants. No tips so it paid worse than waitressing but was easier on the feet. Wintered with a friend in Greenwich Village. Slept with a smalltime impresario with rooms off Delancey and got kissed off with a jazz club tour. Atlanta, Birmingham Alabama, New Orleans. Every one a postcard. Lonely at first, always on the move. She married a Haight-Ashbury moustache as a Green Card scam, which ended as a less cynical attachment: she buddied him through Aids seven years ago. ('Taking a week at the game reserve after Joey's funeral': Weightlifters, Muscle Beach.) I don't know if she ever thought she would make it as a singer, but I can't think why else she'd choose the land of the American dream. You know the funny thing: apart from acting the goat around the house – *mi-mi-mi-mi-meeeee* – I've never heard her sing.

After the first shock of meeting she looks remarkably normal, not even that much older, which presumably means my ageing has kept pace. There are small changes. When we were children she was dark and I was fair: one of those handy divisions of the spoils. I got Marilyn, she got Jane. Starsky was hers, Hutch mine. Darwin . . . well, I don't need to go on. Today, her hair is a different colour, but then so is mine – the same different colour. She picked up a strand between thumb and forefinger and fanned it against the light:

'Copper Fire?'

'Auburn Burnish.'

She nodded as if familiar with the product. 'Well, we really look like sisters now.'

That's it: no more thankless sightseeing, normal service is now resumed. I've shown her everything there is to see: the shipyard cranes silhouetted at sunset, the Doge's Palace carpet factory, the crystalline winter gardens across the Green, Charles Rennie Mackintosh's Transylvanian castle. We've had cocktails at Rogano's and cappuccinos in Wiszniewski's rooftop caff, and nothing brought her to life until, slogging up the murderous slope of Montpelier, she lumbered effortfully ahead of me and, turning so she was walking backwards, blew softly into my face. It always worked. Momentum drained from my legs and amid the mutual laughter, that paralysis of mirth, I felt myself sliding down the hill. I grabbed for her but she kept just out of reach, refusing a hand to haul me up the final few yards, and remarking, when I gaspingly made the summit, 'You should take up smoking, Tracy.'

Her voice seems familiar now, which is more than just the exposure of a few days. Most of the American chrome has worn off, and the old Yorkshire bodywork is showing through. That overaspirated delivery Darwin always hated, diagnosing low self-esteem in the need for vocal camouflage, such a desperate longing to speak like the others at school. Overemphasis is a feature of the accent, a century of millgirls miming above the clacking of the looms, so it's a tough one for the impostor. Even the authentic sound like they're putting it on.

We compromised on the drink: I drove her home, got the cases upstairs, then walked her round to the Quaich. By the gantry clock, set seven minutes fast to expedite matters at chucking-out time, it was eleven forty-five. I reckoned I could allow myself a midday swally. After the showstopper debut Sam had gone quiet, jetlag or shyness setting in. I considered introducing her to Fergie, but we didn't need any extra pressure on us to stage the ecstatic family reunion.

'This is where you hang out?'

'More often than not.'

'You got round to balling Pop-eyes yet?'

Fergie was exhibiting his usual close interest.

'He's strictly a look-but-don't-touch man.'

'Want to bet?'

She was feeling for some common ground between us, the old sisterly solidarity, girls against boys, but there was also a trace of sexual one-upmanship, a playful staking of claim to what was mine. Which was fine: I wanted her to feel at home.

This was the first spell of silence. She covered it with stage business, lighting a cigarette, swilling the half-drunk beer around her glass. I noticed her knuckles showed darker than the rest of her hand and there was a biro slash along her index finger. She'd turned into one of those long-boned women who always looked as if they needed a good wash. A sexy type, but she'd have to be careful: gain another ten years, lose another ten pounds and she'd be stringy, a hard-lifer whose lines are a history no one wants to read. Conveniently, I felt the press of my bladder.

Fergie was lighting her cigarette when I got back, so I didn't have to introduce them. I discovered I resented the economy of his relations with fifty per cent of the population. Sam rolled her eyeballs to white as he turned his back. Imbecility or medieval rapture: I couldn't quite tell which.

'So when do I get to meet him, this Drew?'

'He's coming over tonight.' Her eyebrows twitched at that 'coming over'. 'He stays with his family Saturday to Tuesday, spends the rest of the week with me.'

'And his wife . . .'

'Doesn't know.'

'Oh come *on*.'

I was the older sister, the inquisition was my prerogative.

'She knows as much as she wants to know. He works late in the editing suite through the week, she's up with the dawn chorus and knackered by *News at Ten*. They've agreed to limit themselves to quality time.'

'Does he lie to *you*?'

A question I'd asked myself from time to time.

'He's in love.' How insufficient this sounded, considering how all-sufficient it is. 'We're still in the honeymoon period. Ask me again in five years' time.'

Impossible to stop my glance returning to her stomach. Wasn't skin discolouration a side-effect of pregnancy? 'Are you . . .' But the thing about sisters is you can't ask the questions that a stranger could. 'So what's lured you home after all this time?'

She looked offended, as if I were asking how long she was planning to stay. And in truth, the question was somewhere in my mind. But all she said was

'Home: is that where I am?'

She was asleep in the spare room when Drew got in. I was washing the langoustines and brought one wet finger to my lips. He kissed me through the clamminess. For a long time I suspected dental disfigurement was the secret of Drew's close-lipped smile, but his teeth are fine, for a man of his age. The key lies in his eating patterns, the fear that his last snack (never very far behind) may have left its telltale residue. Tonight, however, he was showing a peek of upper set, an unusual honour.

'How's she been?'

He was avid for something I usually provided, but just then I couldn't remember what it was.

'Bit jetlagged. I took her for a lunchtime drink and she conked out on me.'

The teeth disappeared behind their valance of lip and I realized I was shutting him out. That morning I hadn't known her. Now, with an hour and a half's awkward conversation, she had established a parity claim.

We were doing the washing up when she walked in. His body pressed close behind me, four hands in the sink. A certain amount of splashing was going on. She pulled out a chair, knocking it against the table leg to betray her presence, and giving the stiff little smile of the sexual third party. Introductions were effected. She smiled again and said in her best Yorkshire

'And what is it you do, Drew?'

I took her to the Botanic Gardens the next day, hurrying her along residential streets where the yellow streak of sunset was reflected across unlit windows, through the ebb tide of Byres Road students, past the already scintillating lights. The hospitable frenzy was upon me, that compulsion to fill every spare hour. I knew they shut the gates at dusk. As ever the boundary was marked by birdsong. A silver squirrel undulated across a path slimy with decomposing foliage. There was a treacly smell of burning leaves.

'What's with all the walking? You turning into Miss Thwaite: a daily constitutional, with a small sweet sherry before bed?'

' "And two ounces of Stilton and mind they don't crumble it".' You cannot imagine the novelty of a shared history. 'No, I hardly ever get here, for all it's so close. You're a great excuse to do the things I never get time for.'

'You have Saturday to Tuesday.'

The path curved and we came upon a woman sitting on a slatted bench, head averted, a shrinking in her posture beyond ordinary shyness. Sam made a funny face, and I knew she was trying to amuse me, but I felt an overriding sympathy with the stranger on the bench. A woman with nowhere else to cry. Sam quickened her pace, developed a sudden interest in the glasshouses to our right.

The grind of lorries on Great Western Road was louder than in high summer, lacking the muffling of leaves. A bed of roses was just past bud but, this late in the year, would never fully bloom. I huffed hard but couldn't see my breath. Not as cold as it felt, then. We crossed the grass, ignoring the round tin signs, the pair of footprints struck through by a red bar. The earth was mulchy on the surface, iron-hard below. Under the shedding branches of a copper beech Sam stooped to retrieve a couple of pixie hats from the grid of roots and found an acorn snug in its cup, an interloper blown into the arthritic toes of the tree. Such serendipitous finds have the power to compress the years, as if passing time is always retrievable, and nothing irrevocable, nothing quite lost.

'You remember what we used to call him—?'

She was not smiling, but bubbling with some suppression. I didn't know whom she meant.

'—Monziebaby. When he was on telly before. You remember.' But I didn't.

It took a little time to sort this out. Sam maintained that she recognized Drew from some twenty-five years ago, when he was co-presenter of a networked consumer show. Slumped on the settee after getting in from school, waiting for Darwin to finish his group session, we used to watch television. We had a range of abusive nicknames for the faces working the teatime slot. Under her prompting I found I could remember the man with the pelmet-and-curtains haircut, the nervously flamboyant studio cook, the smart-assed Ulsterwoman we both adored (chippy female presenters being thin on the ground). And Drew? The image I retrieved had the cut-and-paste flatness of an old criminal photofit, leading me to suspect my own recall. I certainly didn't remember what we called him.

'Soggy.'

'Are you sure?'

'Abso-fuckin-lutely.'

'*Soggy?*'

'No, not Soggy – Saggy.'

'That's even worse.'

I'm sorry to say we laughed.

ELEVEN

I've always loved the romance of the public library. Autodidacts boning up on Marx and Shakespeare, old ladies getting their Cartland fix, jakeys leafing through the tabloids, all joined in the great community of print. And though the modern librarian boasts of videotapes and talking books and surfing on the net, the Sugar Street branch is sufficiently starved of resources to humour my timewarped fantasies. Here the elitism of literature still holds sway, with not even a rack of scratched long-players to challenge the hegemony of the page. It is of course a shabby kingdom. The stacks are shockingly depleted, jarring the vision with their see-through shelves, an absence mocking the grandeur of that greyly distant ceiling. For Sugar Street was built to proclaim the loftiness of knowledge, an ethos incompatible with the need-to-know horizons of contemporary thought.

I was born on the cusp of the permissive society, into a household shiny with modernist zeal, but the books I read made me a Victorian, and while Darwin preached the good news of emotional liberation, I pored over Charlotte Brontë, thrilling at the febrile tensions within all that delicious restraint. And walking in with Sam today, I suddenly remembered – without ever really having forgotten – that the Mosscliffe library was our secret haven, a warm place to shelter after school, in the rustling silence of turning pages, under the scorchy smell of electric heaters chain-strung from the ceiling. Hours we spent there, clutching our ration of three blue cardboard tickets, skulking around the twinset dictator who ruled the ink pads and date stamps on the semicircular desk. She used to watch us because we boycotted the children's corner, preferring to read off the spines along the dizzying six-foot stacks. She didn't understand that we were visiting the future, a world of adult knowledge safely ordered in its plenitude, alphabetically catalogued by a consensus that Darwin reviled.

'Hello stranger.'

Rose-Marie tends to feel neglected if I don't show up every week, so desperate for the company she's started ordering me books, despite the cutbacks on her budget. I don't feel too guilty: she's building up a nifty little contemporary fiction shelf. Now the students have got wise to it and started crossing the river for a crack at the latest Irvine Welsh.

Sam handled the introductions and the big-eyed questions about the States, then went and spoiled it all by hissing, as soon as we were hidden by the first stack,

'Looks like you've found a fan.'

I moved in close, inhaling a cocktail of smoke and sebacious secretions and pro-vitamin shampoo, to speak directly into her ear.

'She's not a dyke, she just dresses like a PE instructor.'

'Tell that to kd lang.'

I had copies of the Maggies' books at home, but I wanted her to see them in a public setting, with the laminated protection over their paperback covers and the higgledy-piggledy date stamps crowded inside. And I thought that it would pass the time. For time is not yet insignificant, as is only to be expected after seventeen years apart. On the nights Drew spends away from home, away from *my* home, I don't always leave work quite as promptly as I might. Sometimes I stop off for a glass of wine, or a *caffellatte*, or ten minutes' idle gossip in the museum carpark. And once in a while when I get back the flat is empty, so maybe she feels it too.

What does she do all day? I see magazines, the odd plastic carrier from Argyle Street, a couple of new CDs, but nothing that would constitute a life. Sometimes, late at night, I'll delve into the bin to retrieve her evening paper but find no biroed circles on the Situations Vacant page. At first I used to ask her, but she hedged and shrugged and one day she snapped and recently I've left the topic alone. We haven't argued yet but around us are the ghosts of forgotten flashpoints, casual remarks misheard as accusations, tentative suggestions interpreted as spite. Drew has noticed it too, and claims that, along with the surprise, my countenance gains an extra beauty, a harmony of feature, as if one sibling's annoyance was balm to the other sister's soul. Well, he's bound to be jealous.

Disappointingly, all three books were still on the shelf, though they may have been duplicate copies. I laid them out on the readers' table. She picked one up, turned it over, read my carefully chosen backcover blurb, then raised an eyebrow. That killer cocked eyebrow you can see even in her baby pictures, or the only baby pictures we have, a monochrome spread in *Queen* magazine: the young psychiatrist at home in his existential black poloneck. We're both there, striking a piquant contrast to all that book-lined seriousness, Sam fat-limbed in knitted wool and little frilled bonnet, me with walleye and lopsided smile, sweetly precocious in my puffed sleeves and smocking. I can't imagine who would have dressed us so conventionally, unless the photographer brought the clothes along.

It wouldn't have hurt her to skim a sample page.

'They were well reviewed.'

'I'm sure.'

Sam was the one who went all-out for belonging, shoplifting in Woolworths, smoking on the school bus, straight down the front at the Bowie concert, so yes, I was looking for a little acknowledgement.

I seated myself at the table, though I knew she was wanting to leave.

'See this woman, Violet: she had cancer of the colon. When I met her they'd just told her she had four months . . .'

This is my living, listening to stories, giving a voice to the silent and dying. They even say it keeps dementia at bay, which frankly no one believes, though it's easier to swallow than the miracle cure I'm offering. It's a complicated business, the blend of scrupulousness and rapacity one must take towards the past, keeping them talking long past the point where they know what they are saying, coming at them from every angle, asking them questions they've never asked themselves, teasing out memories they barely understand, trusting that when I put them all together, and finally get a fit, I will have a life in miniature. Subjective, objective, psychologically intricate, politically resonant, sociologically precise. A three-dimensional model that can be picked up and turned within your hand. And once I achieve that, all further information is superfluous and I stop asking, like a sculptor who's indifferent to the extraneous chips of stone. After such intimate fascination it can look like coldness. There have been misconstruings, clients who took professional commitment for a lifetime guarantee. There are no known limits to the vanity of old men. But once they read the finished product they understand. I know that text, like truth, is relative, that the vision is always mediated by the lens. Only lunatics or believers would claim a definitive assessment. Let's just say I save things that would otherwise be lost.

Sam was half-smiling, her eyes roaming my face.

'What's funny?'

'I was just wondering if you're saving this country or inventing it.'

'Ask the punters and they'll say just the opposite. They think all I do is transcription. Which tells me I'm generally more right than wrong.'

'Or they're highly suggestible.'

Outside, it was one of those brilliant, blinding days of autumn. Walking westwards, we met a stream of faces pulling the same squint-eyed grimace against the sun. Dazzle caught the graffiti on the Perspex bus shelter, turning it to a platinum blaze of light. We passed the overalled mechanics playing football in their dinnerbreak, the minicab boys drinking coffee outside Downtown Cars. I nodded to Marco who was leaving the post office; a sympathetic pucker for Pat, scraping at the vindaloo crusted to the launderette window; a shared-secret smile for Des. The satisfactions of display are greatly underrated, the certainty of being watched, feeling desire wrap around you like a second skin, the burn of the gaze in your back, the naked admission of the swivelling stare. Harmless pleasures. Some days I feel myself passed like a baton from glance to glance.

'Where are we going?'

'I just thought we'd take a walk.'

'You always did have a taste for the shitholes.'

'Shsh.'

She looked around us, amused. And it was true a recent pedestrian had trailed shoeprints of dogdirt along the centre of the pavement, left foot only. From the street corner you can count eleven solicitors' offices, slotted between the chip shop, the bookmakers, the chemist with its queue of trackmarked punters, the minicab office that launders money for the Revie brothers, and the Drouthy Bar with its three testimonial splatters of sick, one by the wall, one on the kerbside, one bang on target in the gutter. Some local vigilante had sprayed 'McMahon is a grass' in a sloping hand on the five boarded-up storefronts between us and the job centre. I love this neighbourhood.

To broaden her derisive grin I added 'There's a lot of local pride.'

We were passing the off-licence. I waved to Marietta in her cage of hammer-proof glass. In the window of the charity shop next door was a beige nylon underslip conspicuously the worse for wear.

'That's just your colour.'

'But it's *your* size.'

Sam was the one with what we now call, in these enlightened times, poor body image. Never positively anorexic, or as far as I know bulimic, but taking no rice at dinner so she could binge on cardboard crispbread between meals. Our diet, so rich in complex carbohydrates, and her opinion of it as a fatties' charter, was the subject of many a lively dinner-table debate. I dieted too, of course, for five days every summer before giving up and treating myself to a consolatory packet of crisps. But it was easier for me: I was never under any illusion that I was beautiful, but by the age of five I knew how to convince everyone else.

Sidestepping another smeary footprint, she asked 'Fancy a drink?'

The Drouthy is full of men with nicotine-yellow moustaches. They sing a bit, and growl a bit, and sometimes take leave of absence at Her Majesty's Pleasure, and you would never call them unfriendly, but if you fall into their company an aperitif can last three days.

'What's the problem?'

'It's full of cowboys. And round here there aren't any Indians to draw their fire.'

'Don't be so nesh.'

Sometimes she says I'm mardy, or observes that Drew's got the monk on or, nipping out to the newsagents, she'll ask if I want any spice? And I don't think she knows how my heart trips because I hardly understand it myself, the persistent sweetness of words I never used. Sometimes I think her vowels have become even more mushy pea since she left England. Only an accent so artificial could survive seventeen years in America intact.

'It can't be that bad.' She was already pushing at the reinforced door. 'At least they go outside to puke.'

We were lucky, the television bracketed to the ceiling was

showing Italian football. Eyes flickered towards us and back up to the screen. We were the only women in a roomful of rock-faced hardmen, pitted cheeks traced by long purple scars, noses impacted by one blow too many, their profiles a sheer drop. Sam asked for a Budweiser, which they didn't have. Nor did they stock Becks, Schlitz, Michelob or Molson. The barrelchested Irishman behind the bar suggested a half of lager. I intervened:

'Two gin and tonics.'

We took a couple of high stools near the door, an uncoveted corner with a sidelong view of the screen. The Artex walls mimicked the choppy surface of a boating pond, nicotine collecting unevenly on the waves. Sam ran an expert eye over our fellow drinkers.

'If this is the local talent—' I looked at her warningly. It was not the sort of venue where you commented on the clientele. '—Megamonzie makes more sense.'

Formally she hadn't yet passed judgement on Drew, but from the moment they met I knew it was a subject best avoided.

Sliding off the bar stool on to her feet, she asked 'How tall are you?'

'Sorry?'

She flattened her hand, palm down, and administered a couple of feathery karate chops to her upper chest. The third time she did it I realized she was estimating my height against Drew's body.

'A city of midgets, and you go get yourself a giant: funny, that.' She took her seat again. 'What do you see when you go into a clinch?'

'I close my eyes.'

'If you open them.'

Nothing. Everything. Mottled white flesh. The limitless mass of his torso.

'What are you getting at?'

She shrugged. 'Never mind.'

'I didn't expect him to be your type.'

'Nor did I, but I didn't think he'd be—' She splashed a half-inch of tonic into her gin, tasted it, added a half-inch more and raised her glass to me, the ice-cubes clinking. '—still, the girl's got guts.'

Sam reads books, I've seen them splayed on the arm of the settee:

delicately rendered stories by Canadian writers alert to the nuances of domestic angst. Turning the pages, she recognizes details from couples she has watched on trains and buses, in diners and the malls, and yet they're alien to her too, a world away from the session musicians and supperclub managers and commercial travellers who knock gingerly on her dressing-room door to announce that, man, she really has some voice. She calls them groupies but they're not, not really; the appreciative gush is just to secure an introduction, and a way of stoking up their own desire. After that they take the spotlight and her role is as audience, to sit back in the darkness and disappear.

And then every so often she finds a possible partner, or he springs himself upon her, and she's charmed at first, but then she finds something happening to his face, those hopeful features dissolving into the lineaments of another. The old fear, irrational but compelling, that old pain in her lower back, a reaction so violent that the skin tightens under her oxters and her sternum speckles with sweat.

'Oh,' she'll laugh. 'Problems with intimacy – we've all got *those*.'

Or so I imagine. Because she isn't telling.

'So what *is* your type?'

Again she eyed the punters clustered around the television. 'Do I have to choose from present company?'

'We can widen the field to film stars if you like.'

The smile dropped from her lips, the joke suddenly soured.

'What happened in America, Sam?' I saw some muscle tighten in the workings of her jaw. 'There must have been something to make you come home after all this time.'

'*Home?*' Too late, I remembered that this was a red-rag word. 'Do you know that, statistically, "home" is the most dangerous place a child can be?'

Of course I did, it's a commonplace, one of the new pieties of our times. But still I returned the ball.

'It's a real issue in reminiscence work: how you handle people tripping over things that happened fifty, sixty years ago, things they never even had a word for. Getting them to come to terms with the idea that it was what we now call abuse . . .'

She was smirking and shaking her head.

'You're so keen on other people's memories, Tracy. What's wrong with your own?'

'Nothing.'

She finished the drink in a single swallow. 'That's my point.' Her voice picked up a Stateside swing. 'As far as you're concerned there's nothing wrong.'

A menacing note of disappointment rumbled through our fellow drinkers. One of the Italians had missed a penalty. I knew all this was to avoid talking about America, but I also knew that she would never have come here if she hadn't decided to tell.

'Why did you leave . . .'

I was going to say California but she got in before me with

'Home?' Her pronunciation gave the word an advertiser's schmaltz. 'We never had a home. Just a set waiting for the next fly-on-the-wall camera crew. I left *England* because I hated it. OK, because he made me hate it. I bought the propaganda. I couldn't stand the pissy only-one-flavour, don't-be-greedy, costume-drama shabby gentility passing itself off as intellectually superior . . .' She reached for her glass then realized she'd already drained it.

'I know why you left. I'm just not sure why you came back.'

'But I didn't. Come back. This is Scotland, it's a different country, or so you keep telling me.'

A sudden roar went up. The blue shirts had scored. Her tone softened. 'I came back because I'm nearly forty. Not as nearly forty as you, sure, but neither of us can keep on living out of suitcases and pretending the first twenty years didn't happen. We might as well face it: we're Frankenstein's monsters, and it's high time we smashed up the lab.'

While I was touched that she should see us as allies in some common cause, I hadn't the faintest idea what she meant.

TWELVE

'Stop here.'

I'm not a nervous driver but such peremptory command has my foot twitching into an emergency brake, memories of the Highway Code rapped smartly against the dashboard, that driving instructor with his acid-sipper's tidemark of lost tooth enamel. 'Shall I slip it in for you, Miss?' He meant the gearstick, ho ho.

'What for?'

We're heading west along Dumbarton Road.

'Just do it.'

But stopping is not as easy as Sam seems to think. The kerb is crammed with metal and the next turning is, of course, MacKendrick. Here too both sides are lined with cars, the first space fifty yards ahead, almost level with the Monzie residence. Autumn is all but over now and the stripping of the trees, or some heightening of the cloud cover, has altered the street's perspective. A vast water-colourist's sky draws the eye upwards, its high blue crossed by wreaths of vapour too violent for their mass. Battleship grey, a smoking mauve. The last leaves, clenched shells of fossil brown, blow across this wide canvas, right to left. The wind tugs us to take flight with that madly flapping carrion. Sam laughs, a random cackle, and I know that she shares my elation.

'Is this going to take long?'

'Wait and see.'

Actually I've guessed. There's a row of shops around the corner, long-established fruiterers and poulterers and quality pork butchers whose unchanging façades have passed through the shame barrier and acquired the appreciating asset of old-fashioned permanence. Not that this is of interest to Sam, her eye was caught by the off-licence, a flashy double-frontage of mulberry and gold with the inevitable crayoned windows, in this case a caricature of advocate and judge, a would-be comic reference to some port on special offer. She wants me to choose something special, a touching reminder of childhood treats, but a notion next to meaningless for an about to be middle-aged woman whose salary stretches to anything I might fancy. After the jarring double note of the door alarm, the interior of the shop is reverently hushed, as if the shelves were stacked with bottles of silence, not this mysterious hierarchy of liquid and green glass. Sam makes straight for the bubbles, but to me champagne just tastes of weddings, too many summer Saturdays grinning till my face ached and swapping biographical basics with people I hoped never to meet again. Given the choice I'd rather have a Châteauneuf du Pape or, Drew's favourite, Pouilly Fuissé, slips down like water, purifying the heart. Again the door chimes its warning. A new customer has come in, an elegant woman, the adjective owing as much to her carriage as to the cut of her gabardine coat. Head borne like a cork on the fluidity of her movements. Make-up that pretends to its absence, hair a loamy shade of brunette I haven't encountered before. Common sense suggests it must be dyed but something about the complementary colouring, or just the quiet challenge of her bearing, removes the possibility. I never thought she'd be beautiful. A single maladroit touch: her throat, exposed by the open coat, is pallid, and discoloured with faint fingertip bruising. Our eyes meet and she murmurs 'Hello', then slides past me to the New World wines, hovering in the vaguely paralysed way of shoppers confronted with overabundant choice. Her shoes are expensive, two-tone leather, navy and tan, the heels pristine; tights fine enough to reveal a freckling at the ankle. Of course this may not be her everyday wear.

At the back of the shop Sam is still empty-handed. I show her the bottle. She nods, a little disappointed (in truth, she's the one with the fizzy tooth), and we make for the till, all three customers converging at the counter.

'Snap,' the stranger says, and in her hand is a bottle of Pouilly Fuissé.

'Snap,' says Sam, holding up her bottle but angling towards me to disavow the choice.

The woman smiles, her teeth darker than fashion would allow but wholesome-looking, coordinated with her heathery colouring. 'Good to know I've a discriminating palate.'

Sam smiles back. 'Or the same bad taste.'

That slight hiatus while the deferential sex determine who takes precedence. The assistant rolls our wine in ivy-coloured paper. 'Thankyou Fiona,' Sam says and the girl starts violently despite the laminated badge on her right breast. Passing the bottle to me, Sam delves into her handbag. Predictably she's putting it on the plastic. Or not, it seems, for Fiona, eyes fixed on a spot just below Sam's collarbone, refuses the card.

'You're kidding me.'

The discriminating palate is looking the other way, a posture that fools no one, a flutter of impatience stirring in the varicoloured neck.

And for ·a moment I too was staring at an unfocused point, willing myself to absence rather than offer Sam solidarity. A base reflex, I know, but the state of unbelonging skews most responses: without even having to think about it, the outsider's always wrong. For me the accident of birthplace is a deficiency; to those I meet, an oppression. I have to accept the majority view. But Sam, fresh from a whole continent of immigrants, has no sense of being at fault. Against the forces of suspicion, unfriendliness, readiness for affront, her otherness is a feather. And suddenly this mid-Atlantic shopper with the orange hair is the obstinate schoolgirl who spent all one windy lunchbreak standing in the yard outside Mr Osgathorpe's window for swearing at the nit nurse, a nice woman but crawling with manners, forever nagging at you to 'say the magic word'. My sister: such a shock of affinity, like opening a trunk to find forgotten clothes still moulded to the contours of our teenage bodies and flecked with distemper from the patio wall, the smell of summer lingering in the cloth. Our father's daughters after all.

'I'll pay you back at the next cash machine, Trace.'

Tearing the cheque along its perforated join I look up to catch Isobel Monzie reading the printed name beneath the scribbled signature.

I manage the length of MacKendrick without turning around and by the time we reach the car the street behind is empty. Sam swings her plastic carrier into the footwell.

'What's up?'

I've lost my pen.

'Not just any old pen, it's a Waverley. Red and grey marbling.'

Sighing, she shuts the car door.

But the pen isn't in the off-licence. Am I sure I left it behind? Had I even used it? The sales assistant doesn't recall seeing it, and would have to ring the area manager to retrieve the cheque from the countercache and ascertain if it was written in ink. This is happening more and more these days, I seem to be passing through a careless phase, all manner of objects have been disappearing: keys, earrings, phone numbers jotted on scraps of paper, a lipstick still in its box. It's been going on for weeks. I've lost count of the number of stockings I've put my thumb through first time on. Euan gave me six hollow-stem wine glasses last Christmas, I've broken four of them in the past three weeks. I've always had a tendency to rush at life, and for years I've enjoyed a margin of error, more prone to the narrowly averted disaster than to calamity itself. Drew says my luck has changed: just the sort of meaningless remark the superstitious will furnish at times like this. Sam keeps mentioning the early menopause, which is her idea of a joke.

When she invited herself along to Magellan Street I knew it was asking for trouble, but I could find no specific reason to say no. The sessions are open to all comers, though in practice Wednesdays attract the same old faces. Norma Kelly, John and Mary Duffin, Coral Friel, Bridie Condon when she's walking, Sister Cathy of the blessed smiles, the Gogarty twins in their matching outfits, and crackling Rosie, an early convert to the rayon revolution, unaware that the technology continued to evolve. You'll note I haven't described their ailments, the arthritic tuber fingers and cataract-clouded eyes. Everyone has something wrong, some sign of stored-up trouble, but they're far enough past the halfway mark to accept Time's depredations and, after all these years around them, I don't notice any more. The glass is not part-empty but part-full. Hell, at least they're alive.

As we walk in all faces turn Sam's way. They guess immediately, although we're not so alike, and every one of them smiles, delighted by this fresh connection, this new means of binding me in to their world. The presence of an audience brings out the showgirl in her, but behind that megawatt smile she's clocked the crumbling foam rubber exposed by our tattered upholstery, those parched and greying pot plants, the municipal socialist gaiety of the scuff-marked lemon walls. And I know she's turning the same jaundiced eye on the Maggies, seeing only the teeth and hearing aids and jumble-sale nylon knits, those props the Reaper will leave behind.

'OK everyone, last week I asked you to bring something that reminds you of your childhood . . .'

Out comes the swag. Marbles in a paper poke; an ancient-looking blue bag – though I doubt they've changed the packaging since 1917 – an Edward VIII coronation hankie; two Bakelite eggcups (the twins, of course); a licorice bootstrap. Rose has brought a photograph of her sixteen-year-old self in a sailor hat marked HMS Vanguard, her now-vanished lips still cherry ripe, head tilted to one side. I set up the tape recorder and ask them each for three minutes' worth. By now they're pretty well trained, though you have to watch John Duffin, once he hits a roll he'll talk through the whole session. By halfway round the circle it's clear whose memories I want to milk. In a perfect world I'd give Norma her head every time – sharp as a whip, nobody's fool, with a salty line in anecdote – but it doesn't do to have favourites. Lefty Gogarty manages to connect her eggcup with waving off the *Arandora Star*, that doomed tub packed with ice-cream vendors torpedoed by the enemy they were suspected of supporting. Frankly I'm surprised she's not brought this up before. A little caution never goes amiss. I still wince to remember May Bergin's tale of meeting Elvis at Prestwick Airport. One of the printers spotted it at proofs stage.

Sam lights a Kool, which strictly isn't allowed but has the Maggies openly covetous, greedy for a gulp of America. She offers the pack around and they squeak like children at the unfamiliar length trembling between their fingers. With the first drag Rose turns a faint shade of puce, which deepens to a flush in a fit of dry coughing. Her hands don't grip securely so I bring the water to her lips.

'Thanks, hen.'

Sam is watching. I know she disapproves, but don't tell me it's falsification, as if everything else around them is thorny and complex and real. They watch *Take the High Road*, and eat their mince and tatties off tables set with Rabbie Burns place mats, they buy birthday cards of velveteen puppies, they read *People's Friend* and the *Sunday*

Post. So I help them shape their stories: narrative is as basic as the drive to warmth and light. At least by the time I've finished it's good art, multi-layered, thematically ambitious, resisting cheap irony and the Cruel Hand of Fate. I always use their own words, just cut and paste a little. I would never try to claim that what I do is unproblematic, but if they want to take it as gospel, who is she to tell them they're wrong?

Coral is midway through a meticulous account of having her hair washed with blue bag to bring up its blonde shine. Sam fidgets, chipping at a scrap of nail polish overlapping the cuticle, raising a pinkie to scratch at the spot where the lipstick has dried in the corner of her mouth. No one is doing me particularly proud today. Experience teaches that boredom is the reminiscer's friend. The subconscious hands over its golden key at the moment of perfect blankness. Since the present has turned up something so interesting, why bother with the past? Of course, the reminiscence worker bears her share of blame. There are questions to be asked about this interminable bathtime. Why it looms so large. What the hell she finds so fascinating. But frankly I don't care, so I let her persevere with the zinc tub in the room-and-kitchen, the soup pot and the stew pans boiling water on the range, until I can bear it no longer.

'I'm sorry Coral, we're going to have to move on. Cathy: what have you got for us?'

Cathy smiles and offers up a little hand-stitched purse. Coarse pre-synthetic satin with a chocolate-brown warp beneath its thread-bare black sheen. Possibly Edwardian. I assume this is the object and try to pass it around, but no, she wants me to look inside. Gingerly I pull at the press-stud fastening, fearful of tearing the rotting fabric. Normally I have a fairly high disgust threshold, but surprise makes my reaction harder to conceal. Fingernail parings. A small child's by the look of them. Fragile, greyish, three or four millimetres long.

Cathy is still smiling. 'My ma cut them over the Bible on my first birthday. Most folk burned them. There was a woman my Auntie Eileen knew in Paisley threw them out the windae. She woke up next morning, they'd taken the baby, left her with a fairy bairn . . .'

They love this: any excuse for a good old ghoulish blether about

146

cradle freaks and cretins they have known. Mind you, it's good material: a testimony to our ingenuity when it comes to avoiding blame. If the defective child was a fairy substitution it could not be a sign of heavenly disapproval, and so one punishing superstition was deflected by another lie. A healthy response. For the parents anyway. The infant risked a scorching in the belief that if it could be persuaded to flee up the chimney the stolen perfect child might be returned. Regrettably, from the perspective of oral history, by the time of Auntie Eileen's friend in Paisley this practice had died out.

'OK everybody. That's it for today.' The minibus will be arriving any minute: they're due at the pensioners' lunch club by noon.

'Doesn't teacher get a go?'

I know she's joking, but the Maggies are more literal-minded.

'The council pays me to listen.'

Sam's gaze dips to the floor, then back to eye-level. I remember this mannerism, but not what it used to mean.

'We won't tell on you.'

And when was she appointed their spokeswoman?

'They've heard all my stories.'

'You've never told us about when you were wee.'

John Duffin, of course. He salves his masculine dignity with the chuckling uncle act but he's never liked a lassie calling the shots.

'Some other time.'

Sam is semi-supine on one of the foam rubber seats, left ankle across right knee, holding a dowt between thumb and forefinger. When she gets to her feet I assume it's to extinguish the ember in the kitchen sink, but instead she walks over to the potted yucca and plants the inch-long filter in the soil. 'All right then, what about me?'

I really hope she doesn't have mimicry in mind.

'You haven't brought anything that reminds you of your childhood.'

'I've got you.'

She remains on her feet, like the showbiz pro she is, in those evenly faded jeans with the symmetrically ripped knees and the brass-studded cowboy boots and that sleek black leather jacket with

'Harley Davidson' on the back. Trash-glam's so 1980s. Unless it made a comeback when I wasn't looking.

'Once upon a time in the north of England there lived a doctor who claimed to be able to fix people's heads. He was sort-of famous for it. Never had an original thought in his life, but he knew how to dress it up, made a big deal about offering an alternative to Laing and the Philadelphia gang. He had a few gimmicks. And two daughters. And they all lived together in an artisan's cottage with Scandinavian furniture, and too much magnolia emulsion, and a whole bunch of crazy people—'

The Maggies are hanging on her words. They may not be *au fait* with the politics of antipsychiatry, but they know a runaway train when they see one.

'—so these two little girls were supposed to create a normal happy family atmosphere for the crazy people, though nobody thought about what sort of a family atmosphere a house full of crazies made for the kids. Anyway, there was nothing really wrong with crazy people: it was just Society. So sixty-five Wathcote Road opted out of Society, which isn't easy when you go to school and find out the rest of your class don't see their dads walking round butt-naked from morning till night, or you get sent to the headmaster for saying "fuck" ' – out of the corner of my eye I catch Coral tutting in reflex disapproval – 'and you don't know why. So then the Doctor solved that little problem by stopping us going to school, he was going to teach us himself. After a couple of weeks he couldn't be bothered with me, but Tracy here's all set to take her O-levels by post with the local comprehensive half a mile down the road, because Daddy didn't want her contaminated by the pollution of Society. I was bored: nothing to do, nobody to play with, so I went back to school. It was days before he noticed. Then he kept me off again, and the teachers pulled the attendance inspectorate on him, which was just what he wanted: a show trial, Victorian principles of child-rearing versus enlightened family affection. Apparently that's what we got at sixty-five Wathcote Road. Everybody else's families fucked them over.' More lip-tightening from the staider end of the circle, though Bridie Condon shows her three pegs in humorous appreciation. 'We made a few friends when he wasn't looking. Their parents used to drop us home, driving away at fifteen miles an hour, hoping for a sight of him in the rear-view mirror. The "undead" he used to call them. Everything we did with them: games of cricket in the back garden, the odd trip to a stately home, playing Monopoly on wet bank holidays, you know – normal things: he didn't approve. It was up to us what we did with our lives, he would never stop us, we were free to join the undead, if that's what we wanted . . . and we did want to, but he made sure we felt like shit. Do you know what it does to a child's head, when you teach them to look at everybody else on the planet with contempt—?'

We are not the same. I know that. I do not harbour the fantasy that the world outside the skinbag is an extension of the one within. No amount of shared experience changes that. The details sound familiar, but this is not the way it was.

'—one time he took us to California, all expenses paid, to lecture a campus of tripped-out sophomores on the damage patriarchy had done to them. He drags us up on stage, tells them how spontaneous and uninhibited and creative we are, gives us a toke of one of the joints the students have lined up for him on the lectern. And all the spacey chicks in the audience really want to screw the guy who could give them such perfect children, because he had to be really spiritual in the sack—'

Sandi the psychology major walking into the cafeteria stark naked the next morning, her eyes blue discs with pinprick pupils, the carpetburn on her vertebrae, the waitress rushing over with a couple of dishtowels. Red and white gingham.

'—We were his bona fides, you see. So even though we were paralysed with embarrassment, we had to keep smiling, doing our best for Daddy, like good girls. Not too good, in case they suspected traditional child-rearing, all that crap about Ps and Qs and table manners. Childhood was all about freedom. So we worked our little arses off making sure we looked nice and free—'

This is not the way it was, the way it really was. A man with the gift of talk, a man who took tongue and teeth and larynx and produced an event as purely pleasurable as an afternoon at Chatsworth or a picnic on the river or any of our schoolfriends' birthday treats. He was British, but he had the American genius for unselfconscious enjoyment: a sunrise, a home-made sorbet, the lazy heat of the sauna and the pore-closing cold plunge. Some hedonists have the trick of convincing others of their pleasures, making life a sequence of unmissable adventures; and however dull the situation, he had this saving grace. To a child it was like magic, and now, as adults, it's what we call charisma, though really the operative principle was love. Of course all little girls fall in love with Daddy, or so they decide once their earning-power extends to the psychotherapeutic fifty minutes. My classmates — and whatever she says, I did most of my schooling at school — loved their daddies just like they loved their teacher, or their best doll, or the Baby Jesus: with an idealistic passion that, a couple of years closer to the danger zone of puberty, abruptly switched to horses. Meanwhile 'Dad' got lumped in the same musty, irrelevant, vaguely troubling pocket as Cary Grant's jawline and Frank Sinatra's voice. This wasn't my experience. Darwin may have been many things, but he was never a biological archetype. I always knew there was no one like him.

He fed us on miso and wild rice ordered from a Japanese hippy in Fulham Road and put on the night train by a girlfriend in London: last carriage, lefthand luggage rack. The pumpernickel came from the local health shop, run by a trio of balding, bearded men in shorts. This enlightened dietary regime was subject to unpredictable variation: a drive across the moors to Manchester's first supermarket, sweeping the switchback aisles on a white-knuckle ride of gluttony, grabbing whatever took our fancy, cans of pie filling that would never see pastry, great sticky globes of glacé cherry that we would drown in melted chocolate and solidify in the fridge, pink and white marshmallows to be paperclipped to the gasfire, the tongue-searing goo then recovered with a fork. He was a surpriser, less for our benefit I fancy than his own, and *pace* the parenting manual's obsession with routine, I wouldn't have had it any other way. Of course he could be moody, but his absences were almost worth it for the joy of getting the talker back again. Talk was physical with him, sensual, his vocabulary enhanced by that twitch at the end of his nose when he ran with an idea, his delivery accelerating until you were following his meaning three or four words behind. When he was having fun his mouth stretched wider, really grinned from ear to ear, and he had the loudest laugh. He almost stopped the show that night at the Lyceum. We saw *Marat/*

Sade in Paris and *Comedians* at the Royal Exchange, and drove all the way to Oban to catch *The Cheviot, the Stag and the Black, Black Oil.* Even there some old boy recognized him, beckoned us over and passed round the hip flask. It wasn't just the fashionably insane, all manner of people were drawn to him, and Sam and I got our overspill of attention. Which is, if we're honest, all she wants.

'—Tracy got you all to bring along something from your child-hood today. *We* couldn't do that. The Doctor didn't want us hung up on possessions. You know what kids are like: you can't stop them hoarding stuff, so now and again he'd purge our collections, nothing systematic, nothing you could take steps to avoid. Just every so often things would go missing: toys, cracker novelties we'd saved from other people's Christmases, pictures we'd cut out of magazines, even clothes. Some days he'd improvise a game with the Crazies and by the time we got home from school half our stuff was gone. No point arguing, trying to tell him that our friends all had possessions: their parents were the undead, they'd already half-killed their children. And we believed him. The world was full of zombies. And then one day it dawned on me: all the propaganda he fed us, that stuff was killing us too.'

That's enough. Even Bridie's avidity is ceding to a sort of fear. Not so much at what she's saying as at the passion behind it, not reminiscence but a current rage. It doesn't matter what they think of her, but I'm the one who has to stay and work here, I'm the one they'll see in a different light.

'OK folks, time to wrap it up: the minibus will be here any minute.'

She looks aggrieved, as people do when they've just made fools of themselves and someone points it out.

'Let the lassie finish.'

John Duffin again, but Norma and Coral are nodding in support. Even Cathy, our little peacemaker, points out that the minibus driver is often late. I've always subscribed to democracy with the Wednesday crew, secure in the knowledge that they'll do whatever I want. Which leaves me with no option:

'She's had her three minutes. It's my turn now.'

A little too perkily, Sam sits down.

'Artisan's cottages don't have thatched roofs and roses round the door. It was a jerrybuilt Victorian redbrick terrace. Being on the end of the row, we were able to grab a bit of land and build the annex when the Two-Way House got more established. Round the back there was a communal yard and every year we had a litter of feral cats born there. Black and white; tiny even when they were fully grown. They'd come and raid the dustbins and now and then we'd see one with a bird in its mouth. They never let us stroke them but they were nosy enough, and if you made no sudden movements you could get within five feet or so. Mostly you couldn't tell them apart but there was one with three white socks, he was our favourite, we called him Mr P, and when we couldn't get to sleep, our father used to push the beds together and tuck us up tight and sit cross-legged in the middle and tell us a story. The plot was always pretty much the same: about the Persian Blue at number fifty-eight, and how Mr P was always trying to get it to come and live outside, but the lap cat used to say "I drink cream out of a china saucer, and sleep on my own feather bed, I wasn't born to live in the wild." And Mr P would tell her that his mother and father had been house cats, and if he sired a litter of kittens and they were taken away to be reared indoors they'd be domesticated too, even the cats at Buckingham Palace were just one step away from the wild. And we all had to find the wildness within us . . .'

What am I doing telling them this? It isn't even a story: no shape, no punchline, though more than enough to redeem Darwin's reputation with readers of the *Sunday Post*. Sam is rocking almost imperceptibly on the foam rubber cushion, her face strange and strangely familiar, a clean plate of expectation, her eyes locked on mine. I ask her

'Have I left anything out?'

and she looks away, takes out a cigarette, not offering the pack around. I always know they've had enough when Moira Gogarty starts to rub her varicose veins. John Duffin locks fingers and cracks his knuckles. I explain next week's assignment, still wondering where I've seen that expression before.

Then I realize: what she reminds me of is herself.

As predicted, the minibus driver is delayed. To fill in the time I brew tea in the gallon-capacity kettle. Aluminium, but it's too late for the Maggies to worry about Alzheimer's. The kitchen alcove is barely wide enough for one but Norma manages to nudge herself inside.

'Mary was saying Bobby Croall's on yon Calico Street committee.'

She's picking up a teatowel although there's nothing to dry.

'Amongst others.'

'It's no' the others you want to be worrying about.'

She's standing behind me, so close I haven't the space to turn around. By twisting a look over my right shoulder I can just see the distorting plane of one bifocal and the powdered pores of her nose.

'He's a bad man to make an enemy of, Tracy.'

'We've spent an hour and a half in each other's company. He can't be my enemy on the strength of that.'

From the stretch of skin across her nose I can tell she's making her parrot-mouth, sucking in the lower lip. Her clothing smells of naphthalene and lily of the valley. 'Just watch yourself with him, hen.'

I get them safely onto the minibus then return to make sure Sam picks her cigarette ends out of the pot plant. Collecting our coats from the lobby, I conduct a brief search and add a green lambswool scarf to my tally of missing possessions.

We have timed it just right: late enough for the lunchtime stragglers to have drifted back to work, the courts have not yet risen, the journalist's deadline still looms, and the Quaich is all but deserted. Murdo and his pals are drinking a different cellar dry. Fergie's off-shift too, I note with mild relief. Sam casts an eye over our five fellow punters. A couple of shoppers drinking cappuccino, not knowing how Chick hates using the machine. Marcus and Ruaridh have already nodded hello. George is capering about with the barmaid who gives short measure, challenging her to walk the length of the gantry with a breadbasket balanced on her head. Amazingly, this seems to be beyond her.

'I could have said a lot more, you know.'

I'm not sure whether this is some sort of apology, or just a warning that she might go further next time.

'You said enough.'

'I never mentioned the acid, or the love-in, or the night he put magic mushrooms in the star-gazy pie and took us to that coven in Hebden Bridge.'

Did you think we called him Darwin because he was a rationalist? In his way, he was the biggest hippy of the lot. We call him Darwin because he was the origin of the species. I was born in year zero.

Sam sniffs her beer glass suspiciously. The skoosher under the bar doesn't always get them clean.

'I take it that was her this morning—?'

For a second I really don't know what she's talking about. Then I do, but play dumb.

'—in the offie. The Jaeger rail on legs: Madame Monzie I presume?'

Sam could always make me laugh. 'I don't know, I've never met her.'

She misses the ashtray, tapping a tidy grey cylinder onto the marble tabletop.

'Tracy, this is me, remember?'

I take a fortifying swig of Morgon. 'OK: it crossed my mind, I've no way of knowing if I was right.'

The street door swings open and Billy Mac limps in with his fiddle case, which he stows behind the bar. Music night tonight.

'I've worked out what the hook is now—'

Chick comes across to wipe the table, something I've never seen him do before. Sam stares glassily in his direction and he retreats to the gantry.

'—at first I thought: what the hell is she doing with a lard-ass like that? Taking out insurance in case she lets herself go? But it doesn't work that way. Fatboys: they're the biggest body fascists of the lot—'

She reaches for her beer, then changes her mind and pushes the glass away.

'—you think he'd be seen out with a fat squeeze? No chance. Look at the way she was dressed: she was a trophy bride but she got a little tarnished, so now he's found himself a trophy mistress. Big Boy's got something to prove and you, sis, are exhibit A.'

When we first met it seemed to me that he sat amid his fleshliness like a tomcat on velvet cushions. I envied him his insulating layer, not rawly exposed like the rest of us. Now I know there's just more of him to be exposed.

'What if you lost a leg? You think he'd stick around?'

'So it's only monopeds who know true love?'

She raises that eyebrow. 'You could lose a fingerend and he'd be off. Damaged goods.'

'Well, I'd prefer him in perfect working order.'

Her eyes spark with rhetorical triumph. 'Yeah, but you don't want him thin.'

No, I don't. So what?

Her hands flip palm-side-up in her lap, one of those gestures I remember from way back. 'I'm not saying there's anything wrong with fat—'

'Oh no?'

'—but *he* thinks there is. That's why he eats. It's not the problem, it's a symptom, a way of avoiding the issue. Easier to feel like shit because you're the size of a truck than to face up to the real reason.'

Has it occurred to her that she's instructing me in the character of a man I've been sleeping with for years? 'So what are you saying? That I'm with him because he's a shite?'

She pauses and gives this serious consideration. 'No. You might be, but I don't think so. You're with him because he's big, because he makes you feel small.'

'Sam, I'm thirty-nine and three-quarters: I don't play pink.'

'I'm not talking about anything you *do*, it's—' She hesitates, as if she were genuinely trying to enlighten, not just point-scoring because I got the better of her at Magellan Street. The hands do their mini-flip. 'It's big daddy all over again.'

For a minute there I admit she almost had me going. But this is her baggage, not mine. I finish my drink, gather up coat and bag.

She reaches over to place a restraining hand on my arm. 'All right, let's say I'm wrong. You tell me what you're doing with him. I mean, for all I know he may be nuclear in the sack but, Jesus, I've had more fun queuing for food stamps. Maybe I cramp his style, maybe he's a barrel of laughs when I'm not around, but you know what gets me? Every day you stay together you're telling him you haven't a hope of anything better. *He* knows that's not true.

Right now. But give it long enough and he'll start to think he's doing you a favour—'

She doesn't want to leave, but with or without her I'm going. At the bottom of the box remains the elder sister's prerogative, the right to shut her out. I'd forgotten all about it, but after a quarter of a century it still brings her to heel.

'—I know it's none of my business, it's just that I worry about you, Trace. Seeing you so unhappy . . .'

'Unhappy, am I?'

I don't think of myself as a cruel person, but what's the point of having power if you don't use it now and then?

The cigarettes and lighter go back in the raffia handbag. 'You're right, that's not the word. I suppose I mean depressed.'

But I'm the most fulfilled woman I know.

THIRTEEN

The day started badly, but then, how else would a fortieth birthday start? We were in the throes of making love when she tapped on the door. Sam is a late riser with a tendency to grouch before eleven, usually I've left for work before she's stirred, but there it was again: a one-knuckle rap. Drew raised his head, resting his chin on my stomach. He was easily put off.

'*Happy birthday to you.*'

I laughed, but she didn't go away.

Drew lifted his eyes in a silent plea for forbearance and effortfully hauled himself alongside me in the bed. The duvet was arranged modestly, covering our nipples, after the fashion of racy suburbanites in situation comedy.

'Come in.'

She was carrying a tray stacked with toast, cranberry juice, three glasses, a single steaming plate of scrambled eggs, and a foil-necked bottle. She'd bought some bubbly after all.

To be frank, my appetite was not for food just then, but there was no escaping it. The eggs were the deep yellow of children's picture books, as laid by the little red hen. She'd gone all the way to Old Macdonald's to find them: coastal chickens make brighter yolks. On my lips Drew would have found these details charming but, coming from Sam, he could barely force a smile. He disapproves of her dietary idiosyncrasies, the kibbled textures she favours, her habit of reading out lists of ingredients and adding her own jaundiced commentary. Since her arrival he's been on a cholesterol bender, the fridge groans with tiramisu and double-death-by-chocolate and cheeses of maximum matière grasse.

'Just think: you're older than Lulu now.'

I have never been amused by rite-of-passage jokes. The wisecrack overheard in a million conversations before it gets round to you. Cohabiting couples tie the knot and neighbours start winking about honeymoons. New fathers are teased about the milkman. Although not in Scotland. Sean Connery had a milkround once.

Sam looked to Drew, offering him a share of her amusement.

'You know our Tracy's problem? A child prodigy and never lost the taste for it.'

He made the Herculean effort of good humour. 'So what was she good at?'

'Sucking up to male authority figures, mostly.' She turned to me. 'Remember Mister Gunn's special tuition in the books cupboard?'

'How could I forget?' Although I was surprised it had registered with her thirteen-year-old consciousness. Harry Gunn was the modern languages teacher who by an ingenious repertoire of unpleasantnesses steadily whittled the sixth-form Italian group down from seven to, well, one. It wasn't worth putting a classroom out of commission so we used a small storeroom off the upper hall. He never laid a finger on me, though I have to admit that the smell of mildewed textbooks still carries a certain erotic charge. 'They wouldn't allow it nowadays.'

'It's amazing they allowed it then—'

She picked at the gold foil with a fingernail, then opened the bottle with a practised twist. A plastic cork, I was relieved to see: I wouldn't feel so guilty about failing to finish my glass. She poured expertly, the foam forming a chef's hat meniscus without overspilling the rim.

'—this creepy old perv getting his rocks off with a white-sock virgin young enough to be his granddaughter and it's on the timetable. How old are you by the way?'

Drew looked at me, not quite sure she'd said it.

'Fifty?' Receiving no reply, she widened her eyes in stagey astonishment. '*Sixty?*'

'I'm fifty-three.'

Now I never knew that.

Drew left before I was dressed, saying he had to be at Lachlan Lane early, which was a first in my experience. Maybe he was leaving us space for some atavistic family ritual. The birthday breakfast. Only we didn't do birthdays. Us and the Jehovah's Witnesses. Darwin preferred May Day, although even then we were not so naïve as to expect a present. In my last year at college all my friends had twenty-first parties, hire-a-hall affairs necessitating months of excited discussion. Daddy paid for the premises and the flashing lights show and the mobile disco and the special dress that took Saturday after Saturday of hunting down; and as a quid pro quo the aunties got to come, and maybe even Nana for a couple of hours early evening. Only we never had a nana, and if she had existed we'd probably have called her Zoë or Moon or whatever the woman who gave birth to Darwin would have had to be called. But we never met her, never even questioned her absence. We had no relatives. Which, when I think of some of the specimens I've encountered, was probably a blessing. The Malleus birthday ritual, such as it is, consists of those airmailed novelties, approximate observances, sent on their way a hopeful eight days ahead. Duty done, the anniversary dawned forgotten. So it was a surprise to find such festive enthusiasm, the beribboned package placed upon my knee.

'What is it?'

'Take a look.'

She was funny this morning, abnormally normal, unnervingly like anybody else. Dressed in jeans and a checked shirt with pearly press-stud fasteners, but still wearing her towel-turban from the bath.

'Go on.'

And so I snipped the quartering ribbon, slipped the single latch of Sellotape from the glossy paper, took the lid off the box – by now she was smirking with gift-giver's embarrassment – and plunged my fingers into a rustling of professionally crumpled tissue. Violent shades of purple and green. Finally I found it, a jeweller's envelope, out of which slid a chain attached to a small, unevenly faceted lump of glass.

I asked again. 'What is it?'

She nodded towards the envelope and, by tickling the inside with a fingernail I drew out a piece of printed paper about the size of a large stamp.

Rock Crystal. Healing: linked to all the chakras. Promotes positive energy and peaceful thoughts. Encourages serenity and wisdom. Combats negative energy forces. Wards off the evil eye.

I composed my expression to careful neutrality. 'A magic stone?'

'Uh-huh.'

Surely there was a second package behind her back.

'And what do I do with it?'

Obviously I was not as grateful as she had hoped.

'Do you ever wonder what would happen if you loosened-up, Tracy? If you stopped getting through your life by act of will?'

Irritation had untucked her turban and the fabric was starting to slip.

'You want me to put my faith in a glass bead instead?'

'You could do worse.'

I realized then that it was no different from her other jokey presents, but my failure to see the funny side had backed her into a corner. I slipped the chain over my head.

'Thanks Sam.'

She shrugged, and the gesture sent the headdress into its final quarter-turn so that the towel slipped free. She caught it against her lower back. Her hair, which was not quite dry, had the matted, trampled look of stable straw. I must have stared. Self-consciously, she shook it about her shoulders.

'What do you think?'

She'd gone blonde.

I've never understood those women who claim their sister as their best friend. How do they get past the exclusion zone, the fear that, a word out of place and they'll trigger World War Three? All friends have been strangers at some time, not so sisters. The safety catch is off. Other siblings get by on family legend, the easy conjuring of private jokes, memories freighted with love. We try this game but we're fooling no one. Contention lurks around every corner, nothing not open to dispute. Magellan Street was a sharp reminder that her past is a different picture. Psychology was always Sam's religion. I went along with it up to a point: being Darwin's daughter, how could I not? But I've never felt comfortable with the sophistry, the million possible interpretations of the least significant act. No more trusting your instincts. Indifference could be denial, aversion repressed desire, rejection of a theory its conclusive proof. No impulse so simple it cannot be doubted. *How do you know you have an unconscious?* we used to snicker at school. I never did come up with an answer.

Darwin was always suspicious of Sam's obsession with the psyche; he felt, with some justification, that she took it up to rile him, espousing a belief system almost the mirror of his own. But not quite. Don't ask me how much she really understood. Which didn't stop her holding forth at mealtimes. Of course it was sexual, it always is, all that teenage door-slamming and visceral revulsion. I knew it then and resented it as the brow-soothing, apron-wearing hausfrau resents the scene-throwing slattern in the red dress. There never seemed much point in teen rebellion: against what was I meant to rebel? I had everything my schoolfriends were screaming for: sex if I wanted it, drugs lying around the house, the occasional resident pop star who forgot to lock the bathroom door. Darwin relinquished all patriarchal power, handed it back with a shrug so open-ended it didn't even constitute permission. '*It's your life.*' He took Sam's resistance cheerfully, with the odd exception – the compulsive dieting, those Yorkshire vowels, her handholding romance with a local policeman (an inspired stroke, that, I have to admit). Meanwhile I got extra credit, though in a sense it was all my fault. I was such a good girl, what could she be but bad? She flew out to the States the summer I graduated. I was casting about for a career. She told me she couldn't afford to wait for my decision and see her range of options even further reduced. I've no doubt that she meant it. She had to change continents just to find a place where her choices were her own.

So how am I to talk to Sam? There is a no-man's-land between us which neither cares to breach. We've had our moments – that walk in the Botanics, or the morning she helped me clear out the guestroom wardrobe for her clothes – but something in her manner arrests the impulse to move closer. I imagine a lifetime of casual uncommunicativeness, and then the deathbed snapping of delicacy, the blurting of all those words so long withheld. That's one fantasy, but there's also a rival version, where the truth is spoken only to find that there is nothing more to say. Maybe the tongue-tied stand-off is a mercy, a way of keeping alive the empty mystique of kinship. If I'm honest, what draws us closest these days is Drew. Even that hilarious closet-emptying involved the displacement of his spare

shirts. She doesn't care for him and, sometimes, though I know I
shouldn't, I hear myself playing along. It doesn't feel like betrayal.
How often do I get the chance to speak of him, to claim the lover's
privilege of proprietorial analysis? Even when the words are critical,
they're spoken from the heart.

The postman delivered twenty-two cards. Not a bad trawl. There
would be more when I called at the museum. And all of them
carefully, even lovingly, chosen: a hand-tinted photograph, some
luxuriously textured handmade paper, a laminated pop-art strawberry, a couple of speech-bubble PoMo jokes. No flower drawings
or Impressionist masterpieces. Drew's was a pen and ink sketch of
St Andrew's kirk on the palest of grey recycled card. A discreet
remembrance.

We travelled back from the island a couple of days after the accident,
or, as Drew referred to it, my 'baptism'. It seemed the most sensible
option: no point paying for hotel accommodation when I could as
easily sit in bed at home. Throughout the journey he was the soul
of consideration, maintaining a quasi-hysterical vigilance, ensuring
nothing came within twelve inches of my ravaged legs, but it was
a kindness indistinguishable from reserve. Too much fussing to cover
the clamorous silence between us. He tried to see me home but
seemed relieved when I said it would be easier if we took separate
taxis. We said goodbye without arranging another meeting.

A fortnight later he rang me. I had been anticipating his call
every quarter-hour since the afternoon we parted, second-guessing
his routine, inventing lurid emergencies which might keep him
from the phone. After the extravagance of my imaginings, his
quotidian voice on the end of the line was more humiliating than
fifteen days' silence. As soon as I heard that

'Tracy?'

my internal landscape shifted. Hitherto, his absence had stretched
taut, every thwarted second fat with meaning, but no, he didn't
love me, and no, he didn't hate me: he telephoned after a couple
of weeks like any casual friend.

'How're the legs?'

'Itching like crazy – which they tell me is a good sign, but don't
expect to see me in a miniskirt for a while.'

'You won't be feeling much like going out.'

This was not a question.

'Oh I get around. I can even go swimming now without clearing the pool because they're scared they'll get impetigo.'

It seemed he wanted to meet up, but had no idea where or when. He did not suggest falling into our old habit of an early evening drink, and I saw the sense in a new start. Our coupling had cast those encounters as courtship; to repeat the pattern would be futile, and sad.

'Have you. . .' He stopped dead, as if the words had not been spoken. Unnerved, I stepped into the breach.

'Jim Kelman's opening the Sugar Street drop-in centre on Thursday. I've never heard him read.'

And so we started seeing each other again.

He was waiting outside when I arrived, ten minutes early. No kiss of greeting, just an acknowledging heave of the shoulders. All he could manage with both hands jammed in the pockets of his scarlet canvas trousers. I understood then that he had absolutely no interest in literary interpretations of working-class life.

'What do you say we just go for a drink instead?'

'As you like.'

'We'll have to go back into town – you're in breach of the dress code around here.'

He didn't bite, so I spelled it out. 'Red jeans – not a local speciality.'

'Oh them,' he said, looking down.

Do not imagine that I wanted him unequivocally. I might not have cared for the theoretical implications of being alone, but there was much in the day-to-day reality that suited me very well. And there was my pride to consider. I wasn't in the market for a matter-of-fact affair.

'Right,' he said so quietly it was almost to himself. 'Town it is.'

The road into the city centre threads through the empty shells of our industrious past. The odd factory has been converted to a carpet warehouse or showroom for three-piece suites, but most of the doors are rotting within their frames of nails. Their last occupants were manufacturers too prosperous to bother advertising their trade – or too familiar in the neighbourhood to warrant a sign. No guessing now what products were forged in the heat that left its sooty residue on these redbrick walls. We headed for the river, ignoring the bus stops, our silence easier because we were walking than if we'd had to stand and wait. We had reached that point in early summer when dusk is a gradual tuning of the light to a studio flattery, a faint golden note in the atmosphere, but far, far above us, the sky stretched like a held breath. Beside the main road the monumental mason's yard displayed a variety of blank headstones. Draped crosses, fat hearts, teddybears for those snatched in infancy. At length we reached the river and halted on the temporary forsakenness of Albert Bridge, before the Saltmarket lights released their next wave of traffic. The overarching sky was a transparency streaked with violet and green and turquoise and rose, against which the leafy outlines of the trees showed as a mouth-drying smoky blue, a contrast overriding the rules of perspective with a suggestion of magical fit. We counted the gilded clock faces on the towers of Briggait, Tollbooth, St Andrew's. Behind us the mosque dome shone dully.

Drew pointed to the church.

'Built with tobacco money. Half-built, anyway. Then Bonnie Prince Charlie helped himself to the rest of the cash to finance his wee jaunt to Derby. It was another twenty years before they got the wherewithal to finish the job.'

I thought of the king over the water, and old men's half-baked fantasies sending young men to their deaths. And still, in our hearts, we think he should have won.

'Ever been inside?'

I shook my head.

'Lachlan Lane are doing an OB there tomorrow. Early music. They'll be setting up now.'

As he predicted, the grey pantechnicons with their firehose cables were parked outside. The door was ajar. He walked up the crumbling steps and vanished from sight.

Churches are difficult for me. I was not bred to religious superstition, yet few buildings are more evocative custodians of the old and, walking inside, I felt my heart trip with mystery, my breath catch with the sensual apprehension of all that had passed within its sacred hours. As if the new lives christened and the unions blessed and the dead sent on their way had been bottled and unstoppered for a single heady draught. I inhaled the old oak and the Corinthian columns and the parchment light filtering through the vandal-mesh screens over the stained-glass windows. And there were men with beards and duvet anoraks and mobile phones tramping across the dusty parquet exposed by the cleared and upended pews.

I found Drew in the gallery, looking down into the body of the kirk.

'It's over twenty years since I left the Church—'

I was surprised he had detected my presence behind him.

'—I still believed though, for years afterwards. Then one day it was like watching children. A stage they go through. Necessary, but temporary. I could no more wish it back than take up wearing short trousers. Their lives were the richer, but I could not find it in myself to envy them.' He sighed a small juddering breath. 'And then you came along.'

My stomach shrivelled. Yes I was an atheist, but not the proselytizing kind. I wanted no part in confirming the godly in their unbelief.

'I'm no sort of example.'

He turned, his expression full of something I hadn't heard in his voice. Below us, an unknown hand picked out the first few notes of 'Wonderwall' on the organ.

'That's the irony of it.' He swivelled back, looking towards the east window, obliquely angled, as people sometimes are when trying to be direct. 'Have you never known faith?'

'Nope.'

'Not even the impulse to believe?'

Darwin always said you should not dignify the unreasonable with rational debate. I was taught to regard Christians as primitives, emotionally maladjusted and socially undesirable, to be answered as children. Or not answered at all.

When he spoke again I assumed that he had changed the subject.

'I took a cottage up in Sutherland one May. Election time. Eighty-three, it must have been. I'd been working six and a half days a week on a documentary. Then they went and put it out at midnight. The plan was to get plenty of sleep, ease up on the drink, do a bit of walking, maybe lose some weight. The first fine day I set off for a village destroyed in the Clearances. It took me a couple of hours, and when I got there it was as they always are, not much more than a pile of stones, with that . . . sadness, a culture wiped out so efficiently we can't even gauge our loss. I stayed maybe half an hour, then it started raining. The track back to the road went uphill, not steep but a long climb. I took it steadily, reached the road not even out of breath, but I stopped on the verge a moment before getting into my stride again. And then I noticed that everything was moving away from me, I was standing still but the ground was receding, like the tide. I'd watch it move eighteen inches or so and then I'd notice the nearer ground was moving too. At first it didn't trouble me. I thought: that's funny, probably one of those optical illusions that vanish as soon as you really stare at them. But it kept happening. I looked at the horizon, then back at the ground. Everything was shifting, moving away. In time it stopped, but by then I understood. Everything that I took for granted was a lie. There was no God. Or maybe there was, but there was no room for me in His universe—'

He looked away from the window again.

'—Then I found you and it was all here waiting for me: Gershwin and Dvořák and Yeats. Sunsets. Stupid jokes. A clean shave. Linen sheets. All the pleasures of life, the slime of the pit, everything. Even God.'

'And when did He say hello?'

He turned once more to face me.

'When I prayed for you.'

I was crying before I knew why.

FOURTEEN

The restaurant was once a dairy and has kept its checkerboard floor and long marble counter, adding op art pattern black and white walls, ultraviolet lighting, and a ceiling painted pillarbox red. There are a dozen tables of assorted style and date, the requisite number of unmatching chairs, and a life-size fibreglass Friesian cow, but these efforts to capture the bohemian market have not quite banished traces of a recent couthier past. Mockintosh cutlery, twelve-inch teak pepper mills, brandy bowl wine goblets. The menu is a little pricey for the smell of fried breadcrumbs and melted cheese, but the chef has a fancy reputation. The name swinging on the oval sign above the door, a relic of the previous management, is *Ruminants*, a piece of whimsy which has kept me from customer status until tonight.

'And I thought you didn't believe in Hell, Samantha.'

Sam and I are old here but I kid myself that we just about pass, Drew is sufficiently out of place in this crowd of twentysomethings to be attracting furtive double-takes. He is accustomed to recognition on the street, but they don't look the type to watch *Revelations*. Unenthusiastically he studies the blackboard of scribble-chalked specials. Black-eye bean stroganoff, wild mushroom risotto, even a 'non-vegetarian option' (coq au vin). Just in time, I stop myself from pointing this out. *Ruminants* is not Drew's idea of fun, he hates vegetarian restaurants with a passion only partly explained by his lack of appetite for their fare. For him the very concept is self-righteous and socially exclusive. The news that he can, after all, eat flesh will not necessarily ease his sense of grievance; it might even make matters worse, by removing the one acceptable pretext for his ire. He didn't want Sam with us in the first place, let alone dictating our choice of venue with her nutritional fads. And me? I just want it over, this day of macabre celebration for the passing of my youth.

The waiter arrives. Shorn curls, a Roman slave boy crop. The sort of snake-hipped gigolo who pays cheerful tribute to every female who crosses his path. Happy Birthday to me.

I ask for wine and mineral water. Sam says she'll have a beer. He doesn't use a pad, as if our slightest whims were etched upon his heart. He's all set to memorize our choice of food, too, but we're not ready to order.

'—until you introduce a new menu.'

It's just a murmur but the waiter knows something was said, glancing enquiringly at Drew, who lacks the temperament to give offence off-camera and overcompensates with the smile of the professional personality.

'We're waiting for some friends.'

Yolande and Ricky to be precise. I thought the threesome might benefit from a couple of extra angles. We haven't seen them for weeks, not since Yolande started spouting the book of revelations at me. To be honest I can't remember much of what she said, even at the time it seemed unreal, but I'm curious to see whether she's forgotten. And Ricky brings a touch of spontaneity to any evening. In his own predictable way.

Cool fingers over my eyelids, a faint spice on the skin.

'Hello Mr Sidhu.'

He lifts his hands and the first thing I see is Sam's face, wondering.

Yolande comes into focus. Long silver earrings against a short black sweater I haven't seen before. She feels the cold but makes sure her swaddling sticks close to the curves. In her hand is a white envelope and something concealed by orange gift-wrapping. Ricky too has made the effort, the cut of his clothes almost stealing the show from that mannequin's body. He approaches Drew from behind, claps him on both shoulders – 'How's it going, big man?' – and takes the empty chair between us, leaving Yolande to sit on my left. I manage the introductions.

Sam flashes a smile. 'Yo, Yo.'

It must be a line she's sick of, but Yolande merely does her goldfish pout. Ricky sniggers. Across the table, Sam takes off the jacket she is wearing over my chocolate velvet dress, gracing the manoeuvre with the ghost of a stretch, back arching, tits aimed to fire, armpits flooding us with pheromones. These throwbacks to our ape-lives. I believe in the unconscious life in principle, it's just that I have no evidence of my own.

Beside me, Ricky shifts forward in his chair. 'So you're over from California? Needed a holiday from all that sunshine?'

Impossible to check his expression without angling myself too obviously, but I'd guess it's not so different from the look on Sam's face. Lips a camouflaging crinkle beneath the unblinking stare.

'Not really a holiday.' She bats a sidelong look at Drew which, mercifully, he misses. 'I'm not going back.'

This he doesn't miss. His eyes seek mine in urgent question but I can't risk an answering signal. Yolande is watching.

The waiter returns, glancing for longer than strictly necessary at Yolande's double-D torso. Sam and I are champagne cups, a blessing, mammocentric waiters notwithstanding. By Yolande's age gravity is not on your side. Still, she gets to order first.

'I'll have the mushroom pâté and then the millefeuille.'

The pâté was to be my choice too, but in matters of the palate Yolande's judgement is unerring.

Ricky orders lasagne.

Drew's turn. He sighs pointedly. 'Carrot and orange soup, and chicken.'

There's a two-second delay before Sam lifts her head from the menu. 'Same for me.'

Drew doesn't react.

'He's having chicken, Sam.'

'Yeah. I know.'

A bubble of saliva appears briefly between Ricky's lips.

Drew speaks slowly, eyes on the condiments. 'And you're vegetarian. That's why we came here.'

For a nasty moment I'm afraid she's about to laugh. 'I eat organic meat.' She swivels her eyes towards the waiter. 'You use free-range chickens, don't you?'

He smirks at Yolande. 'Sure.' An answer which convinces nobody.

My first boss had the self-righteous gluttony of the warbaby. That greed for steak and cream and butter spread so thick you could take imprints for bridgework in it. No doomladen headlines about coronary heart disease could blunt the craving, no doctor rolling up the bloodpressure cuff with infinite care. At first I thought Drew was another who'd spent his life making up for childhood rationing. But his hunger is different.

Drew eats a lot and drinks a lot, I don't mean the booze, although there's that too. No doubt Sam would say he's filling a psychic hole, treating himself to the most primitive consolation, cramming the gaping emptiness with stodge. And yet, oddly enough, it isn't directed at the stomach. The space he wants to fill is the hollow at the base of the throat, where the collarbones knit and dip, that's where it hurts, that's where he craves to be raked and sluiced so that every fibrillation is overpowered, purged by a tidal wave of irresistible force. Sometimes he walks around distracted, shopping for music, trying on clothes, browsing in the secondhand book-shops; in extremis he even takes up smoking. All doomed to disappoint. So then he eats. His day is marked out by smoked salmon bagels, chocolate-covered Bath Olivers, honey-glazed nuts, wee glasses of Chardonnay. Yet it's not the luxury of indulgence he wants but the bliss of sufficiency after famine, a hardworking morning and a good plain piece, a mug of hot thick tea stripping the topmost layer of tissue on its way down. Although he never allows himself to get hungry enough to face such wholesome fare. The point is, you come between such a man and his meat at your peril. This is not just a question of fuel.

'They tell me you're a singer.' Of course Ricky's a flirt, we all take it for granted. 'Let me guess—'

He tilts his head, the more frankly to examine her.

'—country.'

Sam's lips frame a curve of contempt.

'No, no, I've got it – blues.'

'Jazz.' She picks up the wine bottle and fills his glass without asking. 'Don't worry, I do tunes.'

I sense some realignment under the table. His knee brushes my leg, but he's not deliberately encroaching on my space, merely homing in on the target, fixing her dead centre of the V-shaped trap formed by his thighs. He too removes his jacket, with another cosmetically neutered blast of armpit, revealing a short-sleeved shirt of luxurious linen mix. His bare forearms, out of season, shock with the frisson of nudity.

'Are you gonnae gig here?'

She raises her eyebrows fractionally in mocking acknowledgement of the muso slang. 'It depends, the scene's totally different, I'm not known. Everything I do is based on working with a band. There's no way I'm going to start playing wine bars again, wrecking my nails on a fifty-dollar guitar.'

'But what else can you do?'

I'll admit I could have phrased it more tactfully, but it's a question which had to be asked.

'Who knows? Maybe I'll take up the memory game. You could train me up, big sis.'

I should never have let her wear that dress.

Drew leans across the table and fills Yolande's wineglass, a courtesy Sam seems to have neglected. 'I should stick to what you're good at.' He returns the bottle to the table. 'Assuming you were any good.'

I have not seen him needling her before. Whatever he may say when she's out of the room, in her presence he has always been carefully affable, stilted but polite.

'I'm probably a little freeform for your tastes, but I was never short of work.'

'I wonder that you came back, then.'

With a floor show this entertaining, why is Yolande studying me?

Ricky looks at Sam, then at me, then at Sam again. 'What's the age gap?'

We answer in stereo. 'Four years.'

Absolute seniority in childhood, by your twenties an irrelevance, in your thirties the gulf widens again. The difference between the rhythms of Mother Nature and the interventionist panic of triple tests and amniocentesis, a sudden shortening of disaster's odds. Is she pregnant? She's still drinking and smoking, but then plenty do.

Ricky raises his glass, appraising Sam over the rim. 'I can see the resemblance.'

Now Sam checks my features. 'You think so? Her eyes are grey, mine are green. I tan in the fridgelight, she fries lobster red then peels straight back to white.' Her eyes search my face. 'The mouth, I suppose: Paul always used to say that—'

Did he? Who the hell was Paul?

'—always on about our kissable lips.'

What has happened to Sam? It's not just that she's gone blonde. While I wasn't looking she has become the other sort of woman, a sensuality of fine bones and delicate cartilage, a face that coopts every broken capillary, every pucker and shadow, into a sexual plus. When I talk to her I'm watching two faces, the family genes, the jumbled poohsticks of DNA, and this feminine essence: mystique, we used to call it, though the word has mouldered and the impact stays fresh. It would be fine were she simply more beautiful, bigger-eyed, wider-lipped, fuller-breasted; but *sexier* – that's a different proposition. It's not simple envy that pricks me, the recognition of what I could never possess. This is the fierce pang of possibility, the tormenting thought that, being her sister, it should be within my grasp.

Ricky leers in Drew's direction. 'What's it like having two of them—' do I imagine that fractional pause? '—under one roof?'

Drew pats his trouser pocket, looking for something. Patience, probably. 'It's a daily revelation. Just now, for example, I learned that Sam is not vegetarian after all, and we've been living on chopped grass for the hell of it.'

'Chill out.' She speaks soothingly, that is, in a voice guaranteed to enrage. 'I may have given you an extra fortnight before the massive coronary.'

And now a silence falls and I realize how probable everyone considers this outcome. Yolande takes up the menu as if regretting her order. Ricky stares at my sister's face with naked expectation, but Sam and Drew are locked in low-level social stand-off, neither holding nor quite avoiding each other's gaze.

The waiter is back, not before time, a couple of soup plates in his hands and a portion of mushroom pâté balanced on his left forearm. This is one dish too many, especially with the ramekin of pâté skating about on its rimless china plate. He manages to place one of the soups in front of Sam, but in so doing critically destabil-izes Yolande's starter. As he brings his free hand over to secure the pâté, instinct triggers a complementary movement of his left arm and there is a long second of deferred disaster before the soup spills. Drew sits, paralysed, as the curtain of pale orange liquid descends to his lap and then up again, splattering the creaseless expanse of his buttoned Nehru jacket. Ricky and Yolande watch, astonished. The waiter gapes, appalled. And Sam and I stare, fixedly, eye-bulgingly, at nothing, doggedly avoiding each other's sightlines. I summon truly awful things, moments of horror and scalding embarrassment: failing my driving test by mounting the roundabout, my menstrual blood on the sheets that first morning, Darwin's funeral, but all of it in vain. She catches my eye, and we're weeping with laughter.

The waiter flees for the kitchens, returning with a washing-up bowl and a series of cloths which he moistens and applies gingerly to his victim's clothing. The jacket is spirited away to the kitchen. Our fellow diners are looking over, one or two with wary smiles sanctioned by the brief show of hilarity. The waiter clearly expects us to call a halt to the evening, but this sudden attention, the now-public nature of the occasion, gives Drew a role here, ending his sense of exclusion. He's irritated by the damage to his clothing but, underneath it all, having quite a good time. The other starters are brought to the table. Understandably, Drew decides that he will pass on the soup. Glancing down at the damp patch on his trousers, he offers me a rueful raised eyebrow, my lapse in decorum graciously overlooked.

Sam, too, acts as if the moment were forgotten but I can't let it go. Judging by the responses of the rest of the company it wasn't that funny. Why, then, did we find it so? Rationally I question the pieties of kinship. On any objective basis, be it loyalty, love, or just shared good times, Sam has less claim on my affections than just about anyone in my circle. With the possible exception of Yolande. But such laughter suggests an affinity beyond reason. Humour is the stuff of life, taking nourishment from poisons, subverting what threatens into a sort of joy. Or maybe it's just that we share a common taste for slapstick, a coincidence no more uncanny than a thirst for sweet liqueurs.

'So what was wrong with California?'

The boy's got persistence, you have to admit.

'Too many blondes.' She glances coolly in my direction. 'I don't know, it's like anywhere: you find the people you get on with, the rest are wallpaper. I had an apartment in Venice, ended up with the beat revival crowd: coffee bars and black turtlenecks and too many guys who thought they were Lenny Bruce.' She never talks about this life with me. 'It had its charms. I used to wake up around eleven, swimsuit under the jeans, blueberry smoothie to go: ten minutes later I was on the boardwalk. Wave at the dog walkers, watch the ocean . . . The Heaven's Angels used to hang out by the drugstore. They'd keep hold of your purse if you wanted a swim.'

For a few moments all five of us breathe a different air, then Sam switches off the magic lantern, leaving us newly trammelled by the smallness of our world. Ricky especially:

'There's something real about living in the heat. They don't understand it here, frying themselves on a Spanish beach two weeks a year. You forget there's anything else. And then you go back and it's like—'

'A world without neurosis.'

Yolande doesn't usually finish his sentences. A risky business, I would have thought, although in this case it seems he agrees with her.

I top up my glass, since no one else is going to. 'Maybe in the Punjab, I'm not so sure about a state full of Stepford Wives starved to anorexia and pumped up with silicone.'

Sam puts down her spoon and reaches for her handbag. She smokes between courses, another habit that incenses Drew. 'California's OK, great if you have boundary problems – such a freak culture you're never going to blend in with the crowd – but it's not a place I could ever feel grounded.'

I get nervous around psychobabble. Has she not noticed that Glasgow is a different West Coast? Ricky probably thinks that if all the bored housewives got themselves a good seeing-to the psychotherapy industry would go bust overnight. Not that Sam necessarily cares what Ricky thinks. She seems a little bored by his monopolizing. Realizing this, Yolande joins the party.

'Is this your first time in Scotland?'

Sam lights her cigarette, answering through the first breath of smoke. 'More or less. When we were kids our dad took us on a seven-hundred-mile round trip one weekend so he could nail some actress—'

That wasn't the reason.

'—but all we saw of Scotland was this freezing cold cabin halfway up a mountain. We sat in this bedroom seven hours, too dumb to open the door and find out what had happened to him. Thought he'd got lost in a snowstorm. Turned out he was across the hallway humping this guy's wife.'

'You don't know that.'

She chucks me under the chin with her index finger, a touch which triggers every nerve end into revolt. 'Come off it. When he got back: how cold was he? Were his shoes wet? He wasn't even wearing a sweater, so whatever he was doing it had to be pretty fucking strenuous.'

There is something about waiting for an imminent return that sabotages all other activity. The ear is always cocked, the mind distracted, the eye straying to the window. He told us he wouldn't be long. I remember a man wearing two sweaters; the look he gave us when we were ushered into the croft, though we were used to being looked at. I remember Darwin driving us back down the glen singing excerpts from *The Sound of Music* with scurrilously amended lyrics. But how much more do I not recall?

'Anyway, we stopped off at Loch Lomond on the way home.'

'Loch Lomond: how could I forget?'

'And you did the Edinburgh Festival in the sixth form.'

I know that this sort of ventriloquism doesn't work, but in times of stress I tend to fall back on the habit. It used to drive Carl crazy. I should have kept my mouth shut and let him bore the company catatonic.

Turning to Yolande, Sam repeats 'And I did the Edinburgh Festival.'

But for this routine to work she needs a comic stooge, and guess what? I'm not playing. Smoothly she changes gear. 'Thousands of adolescents away from home for the first time, two weeks to lose their cherry, walking round with chins red raw with stubble trouble, acting like they'd written the *Karma Sutra*. No one else thought it was sordid, not against that classy backdrop, all that antiquity pimping for them.' She rolls her eyes in my direction. 'You would have loved it. That's when I decided to get out, go someplace without history, find out who I was. After twenty years you realize your history *is* who you are.' She looks to me again. 'Do you fancy making a trip home?'

Only I detect the sarcastic aspiration in the word.

'I am home.'

Her eyes close briefly.

'This is my home, Sam. This is where I'm "who I am".'

'Scotland the land that changes strangers?'

Yolande emits a grunt of amusement, which is rich, coming from a Chilean.

The cultural studies brigade have a pet theory: Scotland, country of mists and mountains, cradle of the Romantic movement, inspiration to Mendelssohn and Bruch, the Victorians' playground wilderness, is in effect a colonized imagination, seeing itself through other's eyes, trapped in its own souvenir paperweight. A fairy kingdom, not a living, breathing land. Brigadoon, the village that changed strangers, came to life for a day once every hundred years. Sam is not supposed to know this.

Attack being the best form of defence, I say 'It seems to have had a pretty dramatic effect on *you.*'

She fingers a strand of hair, grinning. 'We couldn't have both of us gingered up: Chummy here already thinks we look like twins.'

She won't have forgotten his name, which makes this a calculated slight. Ricky's face betrays nothing although he seems to be sitting further back in his chair, and now turns his attention to me.

'Hey birthday girl, you've spilled avocado on your birthday suit.'

So I have. I'm reaching down to retrieve my napkin from the carpet when a figure from the kitchens approaches the table. Jeans and workboots, not the blonde suede of current street-style but dun-brown ankle-chafing foot armour. He enquires how we like the food, repeats already-tendered apologies to Drew, adds assurances about cleaning bills and an offer to underwrite the meal. A Highland voice. Presumably the proprietor, despite counter-indications below the knee. Drew insists he is drying off satisfactorily, declining the offer of a hairdryer aimed at the groin. I snicker discreetly under the table, you'd never notice except that Drew knows I'm laughing and breaks into a snicker of his own. I come up for air, brandishing my napkin, pink with bloodrush to the head, smiling into the face of Ally MacNeill.

He handles it, I'll give him that; his expression hardly changes. My own performance is less accomplished. I don't know what to say, which instinct is true: that I have no right to claim acquaintance, or that we share a guilty secret which must be kept from Drew.

He resolves the dilemma.

'Tracy, isn't it?'

Other than 'hello' and 'goodbye', the first words we've ever spoken. Now my turn.

'I wasn't sure it was you for a moment: I didn't expect to see you in Glasgow.'

But why should I hold any expectations at all? What little I know of him is circumstantial: a lorry full of lifeboatmen, popularity at a ceilidh, that pierhead cottage with its nappies and scuffed toys. These days he could be anyone.

'I left eighteen months back. They stopped the ferry and that was me out of a job.' His monogrammed teeshirt, some brewery giveaway, sits lightly on his musculature as if he has only just pulled it on. His torso shames Ricky's designer pecs with the compacted gristle of hard physical toil. A confident body, though his hand betrays some fracturing of ease, loosely clenched as if circling an invisible baton. 'Mhari and the wee one are still at home: she didn't want him growing up here, learning the evil ways of you city folk—'

Despite this teasing he doesn't quite meet my eye. I find myself watching his hands, that springy hair on his fingers, the faint line of grime under his nails. He tucks them into the back pockets of his jeans.

'—she's looking out for anything at home, but I'm not holding my breath.'

Now he has to return to the kitchens and, a couple of hours' hence, we will pay the bill and walk out without seeing him again. There remains the possibility of driving over here on my own, any time, but I'm not looking to replace Drew, not even in the market for a little extracurricular activity. So why not let him go?

'You've been here all this time?'

His eyes flicker around the restaurant, uncertain of the parameters of 'here'. 'In Glasgow, uh-huh. A friend of mine has just taken over this place so I stand in Tuesdays, Wednesdays, give him a couple of nights off. The rest of the week I'm working over in the West End. Luxury conversions, if anybody's got the dosh to pay for them.'

I would have sworn that he was dark-haired but in the refrigerated light of the restaurant he seems closer to a dingy blond. Not that this discrepancy bothers me. Already I've reinvented him, reading off his character from these quickfire first impressions: a vaguely laddish haircut and the burn of his green eyes.

Sam is staring with an intensity that unsettles me.

I smile breathily and already he's moving off, anticipating the dismissal before I've mustered the words. 'Good to see you again.'

He stops too abruptly, turning with unexpected suppleness. Gristle and grace. Now, finally, he looks at me. The look I remember from that morning by the pier, part homage, part hostility.

Then he walks away.

Tacitly we all agree it's a good time to open the presents. Yolande hands over the orange package which turns out to contain *Sexual Fulfilment Through the Stars*. If this is an apology it is cryptic in the extreme. Ricky grins delightedly, not having been party to the choice, though he claims his share of the credit, cupping a hand round my neck to steer me sideways for a kiss. After this, I have no option but to lean the other way and pay Yolande the same thanks. Our cheeks bump perfunctorily.

Now Drew pulls out the reason he brought his briefcase to the restaurant. I had a hunch it might be a painting. Our first Christmas he gave me a woman wearing a cloche hat done in oils. This time it's a watercolour seascape with the boiling waves of that all-changing-day on the island. The frame in itself is a work of art. This is no junkshop find.

'It must have cost a fortune.'

He does not deny it. 'The man in the shop thought it might be a Gillies. Judging by what I paid he wasn't that convinced, but you might get Euan to look it over just in case.'

The spectators create a certain awkwardness; an opacity in his eyes as we close in for the kiss.

Sam excuses herself and heads for the Ladies, Ricky brings out a couple of cigars. Drew takes one, although I know he doesn't care for them. Yolande snares my elbow between fingers and thumb.

'How've you been?'

The intimacy of the gesture demands more than a reflex 'Fine'.

'My tower hasn't tumbled, if that's what you mean.'

The ultraviolet lights lend her eyes a purplish depth.

'Give it time.'

Across the table Drew's features are transfigured by a smile. Turning, I find the waiter bearing a cake, candles blazing. Even the suspicion that there are forty of them can't dissolve the lump in my throat. Sam clears a space on the table, claiming ownership of the gesture, and then, her new blonde hair back-combed by candle haze, sings 'Happy Birthday', taking the childish melody and brushing it with pain and night and the stratagems that get us by. Ricky was right: she was born to sing the blues. The other diners are clapping before I've blown out the candles. The waiter steps forward to serve what, under the phalanx of wax, seems to be a chocolate roulade. Sam draws me out of his way.

'What's it like, coming of age?'

'Don't push it, junior.'

Now we're relatively private I might as well ask.

'That stuff about our mouths – were you making it up?'

She laughs extravagantly. She's always been a performer, lit up by an audience, even a dining room of twenty-five.

'Don't *you* think our lips are kissable? Holy Joe does. And I'm sure your friend with the muscles would give you a second opinion.' She passes me a plateful of cake. 'If he hasn't already.'

FIFTEEN

Since childhood I've been a bathroom singer. Not at Darwin's, where the Crazies might have heard me and started joining in, but in the home of whatever best friend I was inseparable from at the time, amid the candlewick pedestal mats and crinolined-lady lavatory roll covers. And, on schooldays, in the catacombs, a stone-built block in the middle of the girls' playground housing a dozen shortarse toilet bowls with screwed-down wooden seats. Even now, working at Magellan Street, I'll pay the odd unnecessary visit for the professional ring of the white china acoustics and forty-five seconds of reliable joy. Once in a while, as I gaze down the precipitous slope of Montpelier before starting the accelerating trot of descent, the wind will catch a shred of paper and whirl it above the chimneyline and it's almost as if, with a little leap of faith, I too might hitch on to an aircurrent and launch myself into flight. Which is just how it feels when I sing. Not a virtuoso performance, no coloratura or crystal top C, just a sense of my own lungpower, a little letting go.

'Enough. I'll confess.'

Sam was outside the door in her towelling robe. I must have woken her, though it was early afternoon. I followed her into the kitchen. Her movements were still sluggish but she sounded sharp enough.

'You'd better call the animal welfare and let them know it's a false alarm.'

'I thought you were out.'

She picked up the note of apology in my voice. 'It's your apartment: you want to simulate the clubbing of a colony of baby seals, you go right ahead. You sing them blues, girl: I would in your shoes.'

She smelled of sleep and the depths of the laundry basket, a sheet-crease like a chibmark across her cheek. No knowing how bad she was feeling. In the years that I smoked, I awoke to a headache every morning and downed two aspirin along with my vitamin E.

'I've no call to sing the blues.'

'From the way Fatboy was looking at the Señora last night, I wouldn't be too sure of that.'

I hadn't noticed.

She sidled around me to put the kettle on. That snow-white dressing-gown was turning slushy at the edges, cigarettes and lighter in the lefthand pocket, a brown burn mark on one of the sleeves. 'Of course you had something else on your plate. Mu-u-uch tastier.'

'What? A guy I collected a raffle prize from four years ago?'

I don't know how it sounded in her ears. Personally, I wouldn't have been convinced, yet it was only the truth. If I'd failed to register Drew flirting with Yolande then that was because I was preoccupied with Sam, not with Ally MacNeill. He was a face in the crowd, a walk-on part; the sum of our acquaintance an evening in the company of a hundred and fifty people and last night in the restaurant when we'd spoken twenty-five words. How many men did I know as intimately? Hundreds, thousands. Bus drivers, petrol pump attendants, news vendors, old boys at bus stops. Though Drew was funny when we got home. Went straight to bed, bypassing the bathroom, and was snoring when I climbed in beside him.

She pulled up the window sash to create a half-inch draught, a smoker's sarcastic courtesy. 'Save the alibi for big D.'

'You think I should have paid him more attention?'

She lit the cigarette, holding the match burning in her fingers until she was ready to exhale. 'Get a life, Tracy.'

The robe's crossover neckline gaped as she leaned forward to drop the match in the grimy saucer we keep on the table these days. I had a twinge of anxiety about that open window. She feels the cold, coming back to draughts and bloodless radiators after the hothouse interiors of America.

She rubbed at the sleep in the corner of one eye. 'If you're worried about driving him into the arms of another woman you could always give up singing.'

I put it down to the hangover and poured the kettle for her tea.

'I know you don't like him, Sam, but it's hard for him too when you won't give him his place.'

'Hold on a minute: his place is thirty-one MacKendrick Avenue. It suits you right now to pretend he's Mr Best-You're-Going-To-Get, but let's not kid ourselves: when it's all over he's going straight back to the fireside and slippers. And amen to that. Maybe the next one you pick won't be such a—'

Suddenly she was playful. '—what you need is a questionnaire. To be filled in by all applicants: do you weigh over three hundred pounds? Is there a wife and kiddies back at the homestead? Does your nose whistle when you walk upstairs? Do you believe God has personally selected you for lifelong torment?'

I picked up her spent teabag from the draining board and dropped it into the bin. If she noticed she didn't show it. 'Or we could always make you sit the Sam Malleus infallible love test.'

'Which is?'

She walked to the fridge, took out the milk, poured a splash into her tea.

'Sing "Tupelo Honey" for him.' I smiled but she remained straight-faced. 'Go on.'

'Don't be ridiculous.'

'You can't, can you?'

'According to you I can't sing anyway.'

'We're not talking about technique here, just feeling. Although you may find that harder than hitting the notes.'

What does she think I do all day? Feelings are my business. Yes, I work with the bric-à-brac of pokey hat and chanty, but that's where you find the true stuff, not in the drowsy abstractions of the couch. People are like apples: the goodness is just under the skin.

'Tell you what: I promise to work on my feelings for Drew, if you promise to try to suppress yours.'

She took a last drag of the cigarette, made a move towards the saucer, changed her mind and dropped the butt in her half-drunk mug of tea. Then, surprisingly, she enquired

'Fancy a walk?'

No, was the honest answer. I had made other plans. Knowing the morning after my fortieth birthday would be a bummer, I'd booked the time off work and promised myself a day of doing nothing, or at least nothing most people would recognize as something: roaming the city streets, a habit since schooldays, tracing the pattern of privet and railing, renewing my acquaintance with every cracked paving stone and double-stepped kerb. Dullness was always a novelty. By learning the urban landscape, conning the street furniture off by heart, I made a place for myself in the world Darwin taught us to distrust; from the constancy of telegraph pole and hydrant plate and the tail-twitching familiarity of the neighbourhood dogs I took a sense of belonging, even a sort of love. These days I talk to the people too. I am known here now, my culinary habits a running joke in the fish shop, the cheesemonger granting me tick, the pâtissier popping an extra croissant in the bag: everyday blessings which still open the gates of wonder and gratitude. This is my city.

But now I have to share.

Outside the bookshop we bumped into Craig and I asked after his movie. Tempting as it was to broach some other topic, to have done so might have suggested that I knew it would never be made, so we trod the same flattened grass and parted. In the cheese shop we met Annemarie, who mustered a skilful simulation of delight and murmured something unspecific about how we must come round to dinner. Then, waiting outside the newsagents while Sam stocked up on tobacco, I heard a theatrical wolf-whistle and looked up to find Euan crossing the road. He squinted doubtfully when I told him about the watercolour, but promised he'd drop round.

We had left the shops and were heading towards Excelsior Drive when Sam noticed the stairway. The land there, rising sharply from the river, is tiered with elegant terraces underpinned by high, soot-blackened walls. A rare treat to find an expanse of dressed sandstone still uncleaned in this city, like a lumpen brunette in a dancehall of peroxide blondes. We had reached the point where one of these brindled cliffs met the blanched severity of a tenement end. In the cleft between the two rose a flight of steps, a smuggler's passage far from the sea.

'What's up there?'

I hesitated. But as I really don't know why I dislike Ancona Street there was no good reason not to show her. I even came close to living there once. The estate agents had me pegged as an Ancona sort of girl and fixed me up with a relentless schedule of appointments to view, but I always pressed the intercom buzzer with heart-thumping reluctance, made my way exhaustedly up the extra-wide stair, and fled thankfully at the first hint of Himalayan Artex or avocado bathroom suite. In the end I stopped wasting everybody's time and limited my search to those areas of the city which did not fill me with inexplicable dread.

The neighbourhood is in the final throes of gentrification, the sitting tenants gradually dying off behind windows screened by mildewing net; the students' Indian bedspreads ripped down; the yellow skips steadily filling with rotted linoleum and polystyrene ceiling tiles and the hedge-clippings of the respectable bourgeois who bought in to the area before prices rose. Once the builders have departed it will be a highly desirable street. The tenements are top of the range, with a massy, sober opulence. Bay windows stacked five storeys high. Glimpses of cod-classical detail in the etched glass of the inner doors. Already there are gleaming brass letterboxes and covetable cars and even the odd geranium windowbox, but the feel of the place is dour, looming, oppressive.

'It must seriously cut down on your repertoire—'

We'd started with a desultory post-mortem of the previous evening but now she was talking about Drew again. Or, more accurately, about his weight, a constant theme of hers. Those years in America have left their mark. She is obsessed with deviations from the mean, disgusted to the core.

'—the missionary position must be a total no-no for a start. Not that I'm a big fan.'

I said nothing. Ancona Street was getting to me.

'Must be pretty boring.'

I know him inside out, I can predict his every mood. And yet. However familiar I may be with his voice and gestures, the stretch of skin across the knife-edge ridge of nose, his sulks and piques and lusts and waves of philanthropic tenderness, however well I know all these, there remains a Drew I do not know. Only, sometimes, in bed I brush against him. So no, not boring.

'Of course I'm forgetting the Daddy factor.'

I sighed. 'Darwin wasn't fat.'

'He looked fucking big when you were four years old.'

We were back to formative experiences, a whole wardrobe's worth of hang-ups acquired in the first five years of life.

'Let me tell you a story, Sam . . .'

'No.' I was surprised by the urgent way she said it. 'No stories. No funny little anecdotes. No punchlines. I don't want life processed into bite-size pieces.'

'Isn't that what songs do?'

She smiled unpleasantly, matching my tone. 'Not the way I sing them.'

As a rule I am not greatly exercised by what Sam thinks of me. I can tolerate the knowledge that another Tracy Malleus exists inside her head, I can even allow this rival some validity; after all, she has been around for thirty-six years. But once in a while Sam parades my puppet-self in such an ugly light that I'm reminded of the baby in Punch and Judy: only created to be beaten with a stick.

Second siblings arrive to find the flag already planted on the icecap. The cut tooth, the scribbletalk, the stiff-kneed totter: each breakthrough a little less marvellous the second time around. They get by, develop the aptitudes not yet mapped, the skills still on the shelf, but the firstborn is always the privileged one. Sam thinks life's golden apples just tumble into my lap. An enticing notion. Why on earth would I want to convince her that she's wrong?

At thirteen I went to the big school down the road, two years later than my contemporaries on account of Darwin's first experiment in home tuition. Which hadn't been a total failure, I knew things beyond the imaginings of most third years but, overall, I had some catching up to do. Darwin's curriculum had few points of contact with that of the Joint Matriculation Board. Those were the days when geography dealt with sheep-farming in Australia and rubber-tapping in Malaysia, priorities Darwin would have derided as the scum of post-imperialist stagnancy. I went to elaborate lengths to make sure that he didn't find my textbooks, dreading anything that might lead him to the school, the ritual denunciation in the headmaster's office, or worse, the article in the *New Statesman* (he scorned the reading-room obscurity of the *British Journal of Psychiatry*). Next thing he'd be on *Any Questions*, using me as an example, enlivening my tepid experience with his own rhetorical fire. It had its flattering side of course, being mentioned on the radio, but such brushes with fame left me strangely diminished, staring at the tranny while my life was looted by passers-by.

History was equally problematic, mathematics not too bad. One of the Crazies was a delusionary genius in the field of nuclear physics who explained quadratic equations lucidly enough. The biggest lesson I had to learn was social. At my last school I had played hide-and-seek with prepubertal classmates, savoured the oddly pleasurable enmity of the boys, exploited the ambiguities of tig and pillow fight. I had looked for faces in the glass at Hallowe'en, conducted numerological divination on my true love's date of birth, engaged in prophecy by skipping rhyme. But at Bessemer Comprehensive childhood was left behind. No more games. My first day at the big school was the first day I ever saw anyone beaten up, the first day I heard the word 'virgin' outwith a Christmas carol, the first day I met a girl universally acknowledged not to be one. She too was thirteen, although she had 'become a woman' at the age of eight. As I say, I had some catching up to do. Darwin had ensured I was familiar with the mechanics, not just the reproductive nitty-gritty but techniques of clitoral stimulation and a stage-by-stage guide to physiological changes during orgasm, but all this had little to do with the arcane rituals practised by my new schoolfriends, their fervent lusts and elaborate catechisms. Whom did I fancy? Did he have a nice bum? Had we played chicken? Had he touched my bra? Slipped his hand down my tights? Inside or outside my pants? I understood these questions sufficiently to be wary of answering them in the negative, taking them home to study as runes that might yet yield some meaning, but they were fragments of a belief system entirely outwith my ken.

As with Commonwealth geography, the important thing was to pass. So I took a crash-course in desire, developing a fetishistic appreciation of hard-eyed sixth-formers, hirsute chemistry teachers, sullen librarians, leather-faced gardeners with their milk-white biceps and forearm tans. It seemed to me I had no natural bent, no instinct for lust, and because I would not take lessons from the teenage magazines I had to create a personal aesthetic, tastes acquired – as Sam would say – by act of will. And sooner or later this effortful self-seduction would reach critical mass and I would taste the hyperventilating proof of passion. As I got older the game grew easier, I became quite adept at spontaneous desire, and more often than not I got what I wanted. But in due course the spell would be broken and I would feel a seeping of disillusion, acknowledging the inevitable: it had always been an iffy trick. And then one day I really fell in love.

'Is he seeing to his wife as well?'

She was rubbing her shoe against the kerb to dislodge a pellet of chewing gum.

'It's really none of my business.'

In other words, it was also none of hers.

'You must be able to tell—'

I wondered how, but suppressed the urge to ask.

'—still, I suppose our friend last night is sauce for the gander.'

'Look, Sam . . .'

She widened her eyes. 'I'm all for it.'

Drew brought me gifts I had not known before. The shivery intimation of his presence, the racing heart stirred by the wind-whipped trees, his voice resonating in my sternum long after we'd said goodbye. Follow this thread and it leads to the beguiling mumbo-jumbo of the meant-to-be. We are in the suspect territory of meaning, pattern, even Fate, those pretty tales we tell the children, all that stuff I can't abide. And yet the body eroticizes what the mind fears most. Behind the sceptic's wall of qualifying clauses, what I really crave is romance, a love beyond the limits of reasonable doubt.

By my age you get to know the body's quirks and foibles, you have catalogued most variants of sexual response. I know the leaden warmth of morning lovemaking as the senses are dragged out of sleep. I know the compression in the lungs at a stranger's double-take. I know that in the first moment of mutual desire I may feel a sudden access of gravity behind the pubic bone, a vortex like the sucking of a drain. But when I saw Ally MacNeill on the night of my fortieth birthday I experienced something new, a tugging in the breast, flaccid cells filling, fatty tissue tightening like a drawstring bag. An unmistakeable reminder of the biological miracle. So tell me, what am I to make of that?

'I hate this place.'

She looked at me oddly: I suppose it was an odd thing for me to say.

Her shoulders hunched inside her borrowed cardigan. 'The weather's pretty creepy.'

The day had dawned misty but shirtsleeve mild. There was a seasonless feel to the clammy air, overintimate against the skin, subtly fogging the vision, objects appearing as if through a faint layer of rosin. Look up and there was brightness behind the cloud, a hint of the bigger beyond. I had a sense of spatial laws subverted, the world shrunk to a commodious room, the smell of the shore in my nostrils, a stink of weed rotting on shingle.

Across the road my eye was caught by movement at a top-floor window, a sash swinging inwards on the ingenious hinges that allowed it to open like a door. A figure appeared, muted to monochrome by the filtering mist, a man in jeans and grimy sweater who heaved himself up and out on to the sill. Sam looked alarmed.

'Don't worry: he's not going to jump.'

But she stood rooted to the spot.

'What's he called?'

'Who?'

'Your friend from the restaurant.'

'Ally. Ally MacNeill.'

Only when I saw her throat thicken with the shout did I recognize him.

'Don't, Sam, you'll make him lose his footing.'

She closed her mouth again, but showed no sign of moving. The humid air held on to every sound and scent. I could hear the scraping of some tool, a faint taste of linseed oil on my tongue, along with a ghostly cigarette. He was sealing the window frames, working with a palette knife in his right hand, the tub of mastic in his left. Nothing to secure him to the supporting sill. I wanted to walk away, as if we had the power to unbalance him, as if the presence of witnesses and their lurid imaginings significantly increased the chance that he would fall. Mad thoughts.

'Fuck.'

The swearword swelled and blossomed in the strange acoustics of the mist. Guiltily he looked down, into our faces.

'Hello again there.' He seemed as little surprised as we were. 'Come up. The door's open.'

The whole building was under renovation, lengths of timber in the closemouth, sacks of plaster on the stairhead, floorboards thick with floury dust. Somewhere a radio was playing. I tried the wrong flat, then, revising the topography in my head, pushed at the opposite door. The walls of the hall were stripped of paper and gouged with channels for rewiring, the light bulbs were bare, the lavatory seatless. There were turquoise curtains hanging at the kitchen window, a profusion of palmette and lotus flower at cornice and ceiling rose and, stronger here, the smell of linseed oil. When I walked into the living room he was still out on the window ledge, looking at us through the upper pane of glass. Then came a heartstopping moment of confusion as he ducked his head and jumped lightly from the sill.

There was a smudge across one cheekbone and his skin was grained with a layer of stour most obvious when I looked into his eyes, the lashes clogged around the red scored rims, the contrasting whites, each green iris lighter towards the pupil.

Now we were there, I wasn't sure what was supposed to happen next.

He hesitated a beat too long before striding over to the wall behind us and crouching on his hunkers beside an electric kettle, a period piece with a wedge of mock-teak handle and a bell of scuff-finish steel. From above, his bald patches were clearly visible, the surrounding hair grew vertically, not curly but wirily kinked. A stub of pencil was tucked behind one ear. He lifted the kettle and swilled it from side to side causing water to slop out of the spout and fall as a darkened tear-shape on the dusty floor. Satisfied, he depressed the red plastic button.

'Is tea OK?'

Drew peels his jumpers off from the hem, arms crossed, a feminine tic. Ally MacNeill pulled from the neck to reveal a pale blue teeshirt in need of a wash. His jeans were long past the point where laundering could help, an anatomical frankness in their accumulated grime, darker at the seat and in the long ovals of the thigh muscles, a contour map more telling than naked flesh.

'Black, no sugar for me.'

We both turned, only fractionally, but enough to show that until that point she had been excluded.

'I'm Sam by the way. The little sister.'

I wasn't sure I'd seen him smile before.

'How do you take it, Tracy?'

I decided to tease his shyness with deliberate misunderstanding.

'After thirty-odd years you get used to anything.'

Sam stared back unsmiling. '*Thirty*-odd?'

Ally MacNeill was watching too shrewdly.

'Milk, no sugar,' I replied.

He turned to the door and I saw how the teeshirt clung to his trapezius muscles but creased loosely over his lower spine.

'I'll need to wash some cups.'

In the kitchen there was a Formica-topped table with a plateful of dowts, four coffee-streaked and black-fingerprinted mugs, a tabloid turned to the sports pages, and a half-eaten bacon roll.

He grimaced, but whether at the ashtray or the tabloid I could not tell. 'Twice in twenty-four hours.'

Which was when I realized he thought I had tracked him down.

'The odds against must be phenomenal,' I agreed drily, 'given the chances of us remembering each other at all . . .'

I had the impression that he was smiling, though he was facing the other way. Still he was shy of me, still not sure if we were anything more than strangers. Not a question in my mind. I knew him well enough: my gala day Viking turned born-again Glaswegian, a pint-sinking, chip-eating aficionado of the beautiful game. I knew that Iggy Pop and Portishead would feature in his record collection, and that when he read, his tastes would run to Martin Amis and Iain Banks, and he could still pick out Pink Floyd's 'Money' on an unplugged electric guitar, even if these days he listened to trip-hop and dropped a Saturday tab of E. And if I was wrong on one or two details, still I knew him just the same: he was all the boys I was wary of at school, the ones I didn't bother to fancy, not the heart-throbs or the playing-field studs but the regular Joes, the ones who were normal. The type I knew without question would never be interested in me.

'I've seen you around Byres Road.' He spoke to the window without bothering to turn. There was the rush of the tap and the chink of crockery as he did the washing-up. 'With the big guy.'

Over his shoulder stretched the West End of the city. From so high the view should have been panoramic but each row of tenement roofs was fainter than the one before until, beyond a point I could not determine exactly, the world ended, whited out. The unspoken put a vague pornography into the dust-thickened air between us. There was a provocative intimacy in the domesticity of that filthy kitchen, a tease of insolence in his turned back, but also an invitation, the limitless possibility of the blank screen.

'Kettle's boiled.'

Sam's call sounded jarringly close. We carried the cups through to the living room.

On balance it was a successful tea party. Given that we had never spoken at length, we did well to fill twenty minutes. He told us about the building, the architect's plans passed by the council although patently unfeasible. He suspected a slap-up lunch and a slim brown envelope tucked into someone's pocket at the end of the meal. I returned the ball with a reference to Calico Street. And so we swapped the lingua franca of desire for the leaden exchange of smalltalk, our streamlined understanding for the rubble of social unease. I tried to look on it pragmatically, as a laying of foundations, but it felt like wilful despoiling of the sublime.

Yet when the tea was drunk and he showed us round the tenement, a current still stretched between us. Half-appalled, I caught myself taking a frank inventory of bodily parts, standing too close, inspecting the merchandise. I heard in my voice a rough familiarity bluffing its way to old acquaintance, pushing for the point where it was allowable to touch.

'I remember my granny opening the windows to let my grandpa's soul out—'

We were talking about a recent anthology of Highland customs. The reviews judged it more scholarly than the usual tourist-twee, more accessible than those insulting transcriptions of every grunting elision and discharge of phlegm, an approach regarded as highly principled by my more patronizing colleagues in the oral history game. We all receive, and extend, the courtesy of editing. It's what makes life possible.

'—I was going to do social anthropology before I chucked the uni.'

It was said casually enough, but the message could not have been clearer if he'd told us his IQ.

'That's what you ought to have done, Trace—' I should have seen it coming. '—aboriginal studies.'

Ally MacNeill smiled quizzically, thinking she was joking, so then I had to explain.

' . . . just local reminiscence, nothing academic, not in the twenty-four ninety-nine hardback class.'

'Twenty-five quid?' He was interested in the Highland book, thinking he might even buy it.

'Well it could be twenty.' I gave a credible impression of forgetfulness. 'I've got the details at home. If you give me your—'

I hesitated. He had seen me on the street and never said hello. Admittedly Drew was an inhibiting factor, but I could not be certain that he desired further contact.

'—I'll give you my number.'

I tore a sheet out of my diary and, before I had time for second thoughts, reached over and slipped the pencil from behind his ear. His skin felt hot, the wiry hair harsh with dirt. Again he gave me that look, which was what I had been waiting for all along. When I gave him the square of paper he folded it over and over, as if we were playing Consequences and cheating to get to the end.

A door banged below, followed by the sound of workboots on bare floorboards, indistinct talk, a snatch of laughter. He nodded in the direction of the stair.

'That's the boys back from the lumberyard.'

They looked surprised to meet us in the closemouth. As surprised as I was to realize that Ally MacNeill was one of them, the same dirty jeans, those gunslingers' toolbelts aslant on their hips.

Outside, the promise of brightness had gone from the sky. The gloomy street held a wintry expectation of curtains to be drawn and lamps to be lit. Sam grinned.

'Now that's what I call a body. Or is it a little scrawny for your tastes?'

'No. It seems pretty adequate to me.'

She was looking healthier now, rosy with the vitality of those whose hangover has passed. 'I didn't know you went for construction workers.'

'He's not, really.'

I realize this was an admission of sorts.

Furtively she glanced to either side then brought her face close to mine. 'Minor royalty travelling incognito?'

Before she arrived, my life with Drew was hallmarked by our common humour. Now more and more it's Sam who makes me laugh.

'He's from the Highlands. People can have two or three jobs. It doesn't define them in the urban way. The postman does weddings, the taxi's driven by a crofter, the special constable runs a B and B: it's a different mindset. What you do is not who you are.'

She shook her head in vaudeville pity. 'You've got it bad, girl. Still, if it means you dump Daddy . . .'

'Can we just drop the incest gags?'

'What?'

I thought maybe she hadn't quite heard.

'His name is Drew.'

She looked at me for a second, then echoed

'Yeah, Drew.'

There was something I had been wondering.

'Why four years old?' Again I saw I'd lost her, though her expression was less stricken this time. 'You said Darwin looked fucking big when I was four?'

'Don't know.' She chewed her lip, intrigued. In Sam's universe nothing is said by accident. 'What happened to me when I was four . . .?'

'You got pneumonia.'

'Yeah?'

She seemed pleased, so I dredged up further details. 'And the woman from next door knitted you a nurse's doll with a red cross on the apron. She gave it to me in the back yard.'

'And you thought about keeping it—'

Even at this distance I was mildly stung.

Sam gave a short laugh. '—but not seriously. You were too much of a good girl for that. Darwin took it off me, you know—'

Yes I knew. I told him about it, with the intention that he should.

'—and wasn't I four when I cut my foot open on that broken glass the Crazies laid across the kitchen floor? And I was definitely four when—'

This was turning into a game.

'—George Harrison came to tea.'

'I don't remember that.'

'He had a yellow jacket on. You weren't there—'

When I was four I used to dream that I was an empty milkbottle and if I didn't walk very carefully with all the other milkbottles then I would smash. Just that. No narrative progression I'm afraid, but very frightening for a four-year-old.

'—and I used to go to bed every night and wish that I could be five, because that was when he'd told me I could go to school with you—'

The pavement in this dream was of cracked stone flags gleaming blackly silver in the wet night. No gardens or verges, just a ribbon of paving between the road and the shadowy wall of terraced houses. I once visited Belfast to join the chorus proclaiming its essential otherness to the British mainland, and was shocked to find those same two-storey redbrick rows, doors onto the street, grey slate roofs with postage stamp skylights, each chimney with its two short pots.

'—and I must have been about four that time I climbed out on the flat roof and a policeman came in to warn Darwin and was told to fuck off for his trouble.'

I followed her gaze up to the roofline and laughed in long-deferred recognition. So that was it.

'What does this street remind you of, Sam?' She shook her head. 'Look at the colour of the stone: it could almost be brick. The way it cuts out the light. These must be about twice the height of a terrace, we were half as tall—'

She screwed up her eyes and looked around. Evidently it rang no bells with her.

'—it's Ollerenshaw Road!'

But already my flash of revelation was fading. She wrinkled her nose sceptically, though when she spoke her voice was gentle.

'Come back with me Tracy, just for a few days.'

'A quest for our roots?'

'Why not?'

Whoever it was, it was not George Harrison.

'Because there's nothing to find.'

Euan was sitting, uncharacteristically, on the floor. Not even on the Afghan rug. I felt guilty about this, but also a little offended: clearly he preferred the perils of splinter and furball to the prospect of sharing the three-seater with me. I should have changed places with Sam and given us all a shot at the soft furnishings, but it was not a move to be effected discreetly. She was sprawled extravagantly on the deck lounger, a relic of some ocean-going liner jettisoned in an alleyway and spotted by Drew from the top of a bus one Saturday morning. I remember his laugh, a single shocked bark, when I suggested returning to retrieve it. We carried it along Dumbarton Road, an exertion which induced visible signs of distress in him; not, as I feared, the imminent heart attack, but sheer terror of being caught. Once we had manoeuvred it up the stair he was profoundly grateful and, ever since, it has been his proudest possession, though installed among my furniture, Bella Monzie not being the midden-raking type.

Within seconds of answering the door I could see that Euan and Sam had taken to each other. Nothing panting, at least on her side, but an instantaneous ease. He was carrying two bottles of Montepulciano, and opened both, although I already had a couple of Chiantis breathing by the fire, and a bottle of Chardonnay in the fridge. I decided not to interrupt our drinking with the complicated business of preparing supper, and laid out a ballast of olives and exotic crisps.

'So where's Drew?'

Sam rolled her eyes and mouthed the word 'tantrum' in Euan's direction.

I denied it, though I wasn't entirely sure. We had returned to an answerphone message that he would not be home that night. No explanation. It was a gesture calculated to trigger hours of frantic solitary speculation but, fortunately, I had company to distract me. The evening was taking a raucous turn, with a touch of theatre in our exchanges, a staginess I hoped Sam was not mistaking for the other sort of camp. She had found the boxes of seven-inch singles I was keeping for Marco until his da took him back, Marco's Mobile Disco being temporarily off the road, and every so often she switched from compact disc to vinyl and demanded that we identify some anthem from the Seventies. We laughed a lot, though they laughed longer, and I was pleased about that, thinking that by playing the gracious gooseberry I might make amends for eclipsing her with Ally MacNeill.

'The set's looking good.'

Sam raised that eyebrow, but he was right: I have created a backdrop. Sometimes in fancy I leave the building and stand, nose pressed to my own window, watching the play of light against the jewelled walls, hearing the click of wineglass on table, spellbound by the dusty refractions of the Venetian mantel mirror and the luxury of those aubergine damask drapes. You assemble the props and from time to time the drama slots into place. Just then a witty Scottish conservator, a Californian jazz singer and Mnemosyne's handmaid seemed the perfect cast.

'What are you staring at?'

Euan never seems quite casual in casual clothes. Even his jeans have that just-pressed look. I once asked him if he possessed such a thing as a cravat and he was mightily offended, but if you met him you'd know just what I meant. That night he was wearing a Breton sweater, long-line, which gave him the air of an off-duty chorus boy. But that wasn't what was nagging at me. I squinted at him.

'Gonnae not do that?'

Euan was a Kelvinsider but sometimes spoke Glesca for humorous emphasis.

'What have you done to yourself, Euan?'

He appealed to Sam, his brown eyes wide under those perfect arcs of eyebrow (tweezer-tidied I suspect). His face was still warm from his annual fortnight in Tobago, dingy beige with a pink stripe along his upper lip.

He had shaved off his moustache since the afternoon.

He laughed, delighted that I had noticed, fingering the tender-looking strip of skin. 'Got to move with the times. It's a changing world out there. As you'd discover if you ever made it into the building.'

'Clarky the Parkie's started sacking people with face furniture?'

'You never know. Someone's got to go.'

This was news to me.

All at once he seemed embarrassed. 'You read the papers: they're all screaming about the incredible shrinking grant.'

'But they promised no more cuts—'

He made a humming noise I took for dissent.

'—they didn't even sack Ron when they found out Langhill Road was on the mailing list of every porn shop from here to Bangkok.'

But shop talk was best avoided. Sam was hunched over the records, not even pretending to listen. Euan noticed too.

'Hey Sam. Be a babe and give us a break from the garage band, will you?'

She lowered the volume. 'Just reminding Tracy what it's like to be young.'

'We were out last night,' I replied too quickly. Maybe I should be giving her a better time.

'So we were.' She turned to Euan. 'Shame you weren't around: I could have done with an escort.' She mimed a yawn. 'Still, it livened up towards the end. That's why Drew's sulking: sits there all night playing footsie with Yoyo, then takes the huff when Tracy's kissogram turns up—'

Seeing Euan's eyes widen, I murmured 'She's talking mince.'

Sam spoke over me: '—fair put the big eater off his food, it did.'

She selected a record from one of the boxes. 'Hey, Trace, here's one to play him when you kiss and make-up.'

She guided the stylus across the turntable and out of the speakers came 'Hey Fattie Bum Bum'.

They seemed to find this hilarious.

I decided to cook us supper after all.

We were picking over the cheese when the conversation returned to my birthday meal. Euan had not been invited, although if he believed Sam's version of events, this had to be a matter of some relief.

'—I knew a guy just like him in Santa Monica: dressed Wasp, screwed the Spics, didn't know what he was—'

I looked anxiously towards Euan, but it seemed that racially abusive language was just another glamorous example of demotic American.

'—couldn't pick up a soup spoon without clocking his reflection.'

Euan glanced slyly in my direction. 'Sounds familiar.'

'I think you'll find Sam at least as interested in her appearance: she wasn't always blonde, you know.'

He dropped his voice to a shocked whisper. 'Never.'

'Lay off, Tracy.'

'What?'

'You know. Yeah, I'm blonde. Just stop going on about it.'

'Like when?'

'Only every quarter-hour. I think the last time was when you told me I looked like a dollar prostitute in a Moscow hotel lobby—'

I didn't remember saying it but found it witty enough to hope I had. Euan smirked too, which I knew she wouldn't like.

'—you don't have the world patent on hair tint, Tracy. You're not even blonde any more yourself. And since you're so sensitive about people treading on your toes, why don't we talk about the trailertrash look you're into all of a sudden? Where did that come from I wonder?'

She was right. Not just the clothes either. Mannerisms too. Seeing them again jogged my memory, details so familiar as to seem long-buried parts of myself. I am even standing differently these days, weight on one hip, pelvis out, as if leaning backwards into a stiff wind. (It makes the legs look longer.) And why not? We were children together, we played dressing-up for days on end, trying out other people's trademarks; when did it become a crime?

The music was turned down low, so low I had not really been aware of it, but now in the silence the volume seemed to rise. Sam began to croon along, then, as I looked at her, picked up the lyrics.

It was a traditional Scottish folk song which had been covered by a couple of famous names and become a favourite on the football terraces. Apart from that drawling 'Happy Birthday' the previous night, it was the first time I had heard her sing. Euan listened in fascination, with an infant's shining gaze, and it wasn't that I was jealous, I can hold a tune, I'm as familiar with the song as any Celt of my generation, but she was using familiarity as a departure point, teasing us now and then with a fragment that came close, and with her next breath veering away, every note an arpeggio, cramming whole new phrases into the line, speeding up and slowing down but still marrying her interpretation with the melody playing beneath her, the clarity of her voice making every hiss, every growl, inevitable the second it was uttered. The music seemed to effect a physical transformation, not from within, but as if she were swimming in it and the notes coursing over her, turning her face to liquid, smoothing her features, dissolving the bone. And me too: my element was changing, the way the world met my skin, the shrill of the air in my sinuses, a taste unignorable as metal in the mouth. Her voice was like a dank-walled garden heavy with rotting blooms, or the sound of the surf behind a white haar, or a starling swarm above the rush-hour traffic, things random revealed as the fabric of life, all the promises I can't believe.

It wasn't that I was jealous, but I could not comprehend how I was not the one singing. As in dreams impossible skills are a matter of instinct, so I could not accept that this trick was beyond me. So inevitable were the notes, I *knew* that if I opened my mouth the right sounds would surely come. So inevitable, and so unpredictable. My lips parted, but I was not so reckless as to sing.

Strange how close distance can make people. I really loved my sister all those years I did not see her. I recognized her essential qualities with a pure regard inconceivable now she's living in my house. My love made her a part of me. Her humour, her looks, her living as a professional singer, were facets of my life too, a sliver of my identity, like a recessive gene. And now I see how impossible that is.

I discovered a couple of things that night. The first was Euan's dislike of Drew. Not that he said it in so many words, but he had understood Sam's contempt so readily that there could be no other conclusion. The second revelation came later, after he had decided he really had to go.

'Not without authenticating the masterpiece.'

He blew out his lips in a flubbery sigh. 'C'mon: lead me to the Crying Boy.'

'It's in the bedroom.'

He twitched his eyebrows in homage to Groucho Marx and followed me to the picture.

'What can I tell you? It's shite.' He was drunk, but not drunk enough for this. 'No. It's very pretty. More Kate's sort of thing, really. I could take it in for her to give it the once-over if you like. But I don't think we need worry about insurance in transit.'

This came as no real surprise. Though perhaps it was as well Drew was not around to hear.

'Now this—' His attention had switched to the woman in the hat. I braced myself for some wisecrack '—is much more my cup of tea.'

He had moved in close and was standing straighter, as if the picture had restored his coordination after that bottle-and-a-half of wine. Abruptly he said 'Can we have some light on this?'

I fetched the Anglepoise.

'May I—' He had unhooked the frame from the wall and was nodding, possibly for effect, albeit fruitlessly. Sam was studying my BSE print, *The Slaughter of the Innocents*, a graduation show purchase in the style of Ken Currie.

'—happy birthday Tracy.'

I looked at him, bemused.

'Bring it in tomorrow and I'll get you a second opinion from Dugald. Or you could take it straight to Charlie Forbes in Edinburgh and put it into his next sale.'

I tried to read mischief in his face but all I found was excitement. Still showing off for Sam, no doubt. Belatedly he added the crucial detail.

'It's a Fergusson.'

Perhaps it was the amount I had drunk, but I took this information in my stride.

'Thanks Euan. You've finally given me a reason to worry about burglars.'

'He's hot right now. You could be talking seven or eight.'

'*Million?*' He eyed me in a way that induced brief compunction. I wasn't being very gracious, but now that the news was sinking in, I was conscious of a curdling disappointment. This thing, so precious to me, was valued by others too. 'I wonder if I should tell Drew?'

Sam looked up from the cattle print. 'Worried he might ask for it back?'

It was time to call the minicab.

Goodbyes took longer than expected. We walked him down to

the closemouth where he offered extravagant tribute to Sam's charms and expressed the fervent hope that they might meet again very soon.

She smiled, disengaging her hand. 'Glad to know you too. I was beginning to think Tracy's many friends were a figment of her imagination.'

He laughed uncomprehendingly. Then, turning to me, he urged 'Think about Charlie. It might fetch ten grand.'

'The last time I heard it was seven.'

He puckered and made a feint at my cheeks, then pointed himself in the direction of the taxi. 'Bottom-line figure. Could be a lot more.' Clownishly, he rubbed one buttock. 'Enough to get the living room carpeted, anyway.'

Once the cab had turned the corner, Sam removed her smile.

'Thanks, sis, but I'm a little old for your cast-offs.'

Drew came home at half-past three. I heard his keys in the lock, the clatter as they dropped on the concrete stairhead, his muttered curse as he headed for the kitchen. Then a long wait. I assumed that he was swallowing gallons of water as a precaution against hangover, yet when he finally slipped between the covers I smelled no spirits on his breath. I stretched out an arm to switch on the bedside light but he wrapped his hand around my fingers and brought them to his mouth. His nose was so icy I thought it might be wet. He suffered from poor circulation which, with the chilly properties of subcutaneous fat, made him a cold bedmate.

'Where have you been?'

Since Sam's arrival, all nocturnal conversations are conducted in whispers.

'I went for a meal with the team, some place near the Necropolis.'

The team. In other words, Siobhan. Which was fine. I couldn't see them getting any further than a long moment of eye-contact over the third glass of wine: enough to make him feel he'd evened the score and send him home contrite.

'It stays open until three?'

'Then I went for a walk.'

Drew in the graveyard at midnight: he would as soon say the

Lord's prayer backwards. I propped myself on one elbow so that, had we not been in darkness, I could have looked into his eyes.

'Making a deal with the Devil?'

As soon as I said it I knew that I should not have done. Drew did not joke about such matters. He made a breathy bitter sound:

'Renegotiating terms.'

I smirked uneasily and burrowed back into my warm patch under the duvet, where he joined me: the two of us enclosed in our soft cave.

'Sing to me, Tracy.'

I struggled back up the bed and surfaced into the cool air of the bedroom. His head followed.

'Tracy?'

He forgot to whisper. I put my finger to his lips.

'Not now, it's late, we need to sleep.'

But I knew that I would never sing to him again.

SIXTEEN

The alarm goes off at 6.30, as it always does. And, as always, I snap down the button and treat myself to another forty-five minutes' sleep, the most pleasurable of the night, skimming along just under the lid of consciousness. At 7.15 Drew heaves himself out of bed and I steel my nerves for the grind of the juicer. Sam's capacity to sleep through it is a daily marvel. He leaves the glass at my bedside and at 7.40 I'm in the bath. By 8.05 I'm washed and dressed, leaving ten minutes quality time for Drew and/or yesterday's paper. I'm always a day behind the news, by which point it's too late to care. When the kitchen clock is moving towards 8.20 we exchange the lingering kisses of the recently reconciled and, rashly, I promise something special for tea. He leaves for Lachlan Lane on foot, having read in last Sunday's lifestyle pages that a gentle stroll five days a week is worth half an hour's competitive sweating when the heart-attack fairy tots up your score. By next Friday I'll be back to dropping him at the door. At 8.25 I'm in the newsagents, buying a can of grapefruit seltzer and the paper I won't read until next morning.

At 8.29 I discover I have lost my credit card.

Thankfully I'm a regular at the petrol station so they're willing to let me pay next time. I check the car, look through my handbag again just to make sure, drive home, search the kitchen, upend my handbag, ransack the cupboards I have already investigated, and stand, immobilized, in the middle of the hall. Sam is still asleep.

At 9.25 I phone Magellan Street to say I'll be late.

I have an ordered mind. I know how these things work. You retrace your steps, piece together the hours since last you saw the missing object. I do this, feeling frantic, but only distantly. I know it will be all right. It is always all right. I have survived four decades of mislaid possessions. Things always turn up. Earrings between the cushions of the settee, knickers down the back of the chest of drawers, the driving licence marking the lemon pudding page in

Mrs Beeton. Catastrophe is always averted. So I look hard, but in the same places, turning out that handbag again and again, patting the pockets of my raincoat, fingertip-searching the kitchen floor. I have narrowed the list to a limited number of locations. The kitchen, the car, the ten-metre walk from closemouth to kerb, my handbag, my coat pockets. The card is waiting in one of these places. My confidence of this makes its continued absence bearable.

At 10.25 I come to terms with the fact that the situation is not so contained. It's not that I have done so very much since paying for my three bottles in the wine merchants the previous afternoon. We're talking about two hours in the outside world. But this world is not a safely sterile space. There are a million variables: scaffies, pickpockets, schoolchildren, well-meaning old ladies. A million disaster movies flit through my head, each aborted before its climax because *it will be all right*. It always is. But still the scenarios swarm around me, breeding with infestational increase. Did I put the card back in my bag? Or merely slip it in my pocket? And if so, which pocket – raincoat or jeans? Could it have fallen as I bent to retrieve something from the pavement? Maybe I made some later purchase, now forgotten, something left behind in the shop, along with the missing card. My life is fragmenting, atomizing, with awareness of its infinite permutations. And of all the options, strangely, theft seems the most preferable: the certainty of another's agency, the reassurance of knowing the worst. I might have lost a hundred, two hundred, three hundred pounds, but a line could safely be drawn under the episode. No need to worry any longer. No point pursuing the phantom of absentmindedness, the actions of a body I don't quite own.

And still I do not telephone the bank.

Drew is in the studio recording an interview but they promise he will phone as soon as he is free. I wake Sam. It takes a while and even when she opens her eyes I can't be sure she is fully conscious, but it seems clear enough that she has not touched the card. Face squeezing with the effort of wakefulness, a bas-relief of muscle erupting from that flat belly as she sits upright in the bed. You're not telling me there's a baby in there. Conscious of my gaze, she pulls down the sleep-twisted teeshirt.

'OK, let's think about this.' She reaches for a cigarette from the pack on the bedside table, opens the matchbox to reveal a couple of stale-scented dowts. 'You know you had it when you left the cheese shop . . .'

Do I? The worst of it is that I do not know anything. I remember taking out the bank's complimentary plastic wallet, all but split in two. I remember thinking that I must be careful, that it could easily sever completely. I remember removing the card and replacing the wallet in my handbag while I queued to pay for the cheese. I foresaw the likelihood of loss and took steps to avoid it; as far I *know* it could not have happened. And yet it has.

My one hope is Drew. He could have found the card last night, pocketed it for safe-keeping and forgotten to hand it back. Already I can hear the laughter, his gentle admonition. It will be all right.

'I haven't seen it.' His voice is preoccupied with work, his concern purely notional. 'Have you rung the emergency line?'

'No.'

'Well I suggest you do so.'

Drew does not often play daddy, whatever Sam might think.

'Right.'

'Is there a spending limit?'

'No.' And just now I don't wish to think about it.

'In that case we'll have to hope whoever it is hasn't bought themselves a Porsche.'

And suddenly it occurs to me why I failed to find it in the car. I was on foot yesterday. It was the day that Sam and I took tea with Ally MacNeill.

It is one of those seasonless days that can happen in October, the high white sky brittle as seashells. A mild wind is blowing from nowhere, tussling hair and clothing without touching the trees. Ancona Street is deserted, no cats, no kids, no young mothers pushing buggies, not even the customary kerbjam of cars. A black sheen to the endless windows. The skip has gone. I'm fairly confident this is the house. Number ninety-eight. I press the bell but the wiring is disconnected, push at the door but find it locked, wade through the woody thistles in the hillocky scrap of garden to peer through the ground-floor window. No sign of life. Strange. It is twenty past eleven on a Thursday morning, even the tardiest of builders should be at work. From across the street you get a better view of the upper windows. No lights. Gone to Rio on my credit card. At the end of the block there's a dustmen's access, an unadopted lane that runs behind the houses, its puddles black with mulch.

Ninety-eight, the number written on the bins, the back door locked, the kitchen bare but finished, walls pinkly skim-plastered, new skirtingboards dulled by a grey skin of primer. I listen for the buzz of a drill, the pop of a transistor radio. Nothing. So I continue along the rest of the street, thinking maybe I've got the wrong house. Then I inspect the tenements on the other side. Ten minutes to confirm what I know already: the conversion work is finished and there's nobody home.

Walking back to the car, I train my eyes along the pavement until my neck and shoulders rebel, stretching skywards, straining for air and light. Now. My neck snaps in shock. Something flickers at the edge of sight, and is gone. No image to wrestle with. No sound to make sense of. Just the feeling that it has happened before.

The first leaves of autumn appeared almost three months ago, in the last days of July. Not one or two but enough to line the cobbled gutter the length of the street, a tidemark of yellow strips detached from the unadulterated green of the trees, a touch of smokiness in the air alongside the pungent breath of flowering privet. That's how it is with the Scottish summer: one minute not quite here; the next, almost away. Towels and teeshirts flapped horizontally on the line in a kind of desperation. The roses needed deadheading in the Botanic Gardens, which was full of summer people wrong-footed by the weather, cotton prints and beach-bright colours absurdly out of place amid the suddenly muted foliage. Tendrils of sky brushed the skin, teasing between chill and rain. However lingering the finish might prove, no matter how many molten skies ahead, the season was qualified by the inevitability of its passing, and spoiled. I have no special affinity for summer; as Sam so unflatteringly pointed out, while others baste to a golden brown I am one of nature's broilers. But June, July and August we'd enjoy a short lease on normality, languid aimless days spent on other people's lawns with the spread tartan blanket and jugs of lukewarm orange squash. We'd go paddling in the park, water sharp as the stones under our feet, crumbled earth between our toes as we trod the parched grass. And sometimes there was a Mr Whippy from the red and blue ice-cream van with that tinkling tune I never named, nor ever knew I was supposed to.

I was killing time in the Botanics, waiting for Drew to finish at Lachlan Lane, and decided to step into the Victorian glasshouse to warm up. I had a yen for the smell of moist earth and bark and the stealthy pallor of the koi carp in the ornamental fishpond, the cicada ticking of the rotating sprinkler, air that wrapped around the throat like a mohair blanket, and the cool of the alabaster statuary amid darkly germinating life. For once there were no children tormenting the fish, no old men easing their arthritis on the benches, it seemed I was alone under the high dome of pearly glass. This hothouse is one of the city's proudest landmarks, large enough to get lost within and cunningly laid out, the rainforest surprisingly convincing, so densely planted with palms and creepers as to seem infinite in extent. The brick pathway follows a circle, returning the stroller to the point of entry just when you least expect it. The trick has caught me so often that I have all but lost the wonder. And so it happened that I made a complete circuit and came upon the man in the brown car-coat. His back was turned so I did not see his face at first, only the furtively anxious motion of his head with its salt-and-pepper razor-cut hair. Noticing the concentric path in the thick of the jungle, quickly he scissored over the barrier and took a few steps into the undergrowth. Then he was back and, briefly lost, swept a look from side to side. I was quite close behind him when he saw me, and I felt his shock like a thump in the solar plexus. The colour left his face. He seemed stricken, even paralysed for a moment, then, rapidly, he walked away.

I thought perhaps he was some pervert who had been exposing himself in the bushes. Not being in the habit of monitoring male groins, it was even possible that he had displayed himself to me. Though, strangely, the connection had felt more personal, more like recognition. I was sure I did not know him. He was short and broad with a waxy strata of acne-scarring over his cheeks. And he was wearing gloves.

It was six o'clock: Drew would be finished at the studios. I had the car outside, all packed for a night away in Perthshire. A Victorian hotel with the tiered cake stands and sailcloth bedlinen and deep overhanging eaves of a Mittel-European spa. He was set for two days' filming, I was equipped with a good book and an insufficient quota of patience. By eleven o'clock I was slamming my overnight bag back in the car and wrenching the key in the ignition while Drew leaned in at the side window, flustered with midges and furious embarrassment. I got home in ninety minutes and took a leisurely bath to review the ruined evening, gingerly probing what damage might have been done. It was hours later that I awoke to the cabbagy water and the thought of how chilling the most ordinary detail can prove out of context: a car's headlights full beam on a sunny suburban street, a newspaper picture of your lover wearing a wedding ring, the elaborate clicking of the answering machine without warning from the telephone bell. I erupted out of the bath in a single heart-pounding movement, and stood dripping on the bedroom carpet, the receiver to my ear.

'Drew?'

Nothing at the other end of the line.

He was remorseful, or in trouble, or maybe drunk. I waited, but he did not speak. The bedside clock said three a.m.

'Drew?'

The connection was broken, the other party hanging up.

I dialled one-four-seven-one, as is advised on these occasions, and a 1950s debutante informed me that the caller had withheld their number. Furious, I rang the hotel and, wielding the unquestionable authority of his employers, demanded to be put through to his room. The phone rang for perhaps fifty seconds before he lifted the receiver. No doubt about it, he was fast asleep.

'Did you just call me?'

He was groggily perplexed, which rendered apologies easier. But he hadn't made that call.

Back at the flat, Sam is out. A buttery plate and the saucer-ashtray still on the table, a muddy inch of cold coffee in the cafetière. So I face ordeal by administration on my own. The voice on the bank's emergency line is reassuring as a milky drink, his questioning streamlined, fingers moving soundlessly over the computer keyboard, the warmth in his voice just another page of the manual. He doesn't mention liability.

The Maggies are still at Magellan Street, gossiping over tea and biscuits, so appalled by the enormity of my misfortune that an idiot repetition of its key features is needed to reintroduce me, decontaminated, to their world. Their shock helps consolidate my acceptance, leaves me marvelling at their horror, the blinding unthinkability of financial loss. I am one of the credit generation, for me money is a column of figures on a pink statement, not a finite number of notes and coins in a weekly envelope. I have friends who have walked away from the cash machine leaving five brown tenners fluttering in the slot, and laughed about it next day. Mary Duffin would never recover, but then she would never allow herself to make such a mistake.

I'm collecting the cups for return to the kitchen when Norma approaches, stealthy in her cushioned vinyl lace-ups, a sleekit glance over the shoulder. There is a sheeplike quality to the Wednesday group: if one moves towards you the others are never far behind.

'Gonnae be careful the night?'

I return a look of perfect blankness.

'Calico Street,' she prompts. 'John was saying you've a meeting.'

There goes Drew's special supper.

'He's a bad man, Tracy.'

Most of the Maggies are thinning on top, but Norma has a good head of white hair threaded, if you look closely, with fine black filaments. As always, my gaze is drawn to that deep crease below her septum which, in certain light, suggests a drop of clear snot. She would be mortified if she knew.

'I take it you're referring to my pal Bobby?'

For weeks now she has had something to tell me, something so unwelcome that it requires my permission.

'I hope you're never so short of pals you look to him.' Her glasses magnify the lines around her eyes into crevices. 'His wife was feart to see her own family in case he found out where she was staying.'

So he's a batterer. I can't say I'm wholly surprised. 'Don't worry, Norma, I'll keep him at arm's length.'

Behind the bifocals her diluted gaze darkens with some sort of decision.

'See Kevin, Janice's man? He was drinking in the Hangman's and a crowd of them were shouting the odds about yon supermarket they want to build. Seemingly two or three of them were all for it. Then Kevin said about me coming here, and knowing you, and Bobby Croall just lost the place—'

The flesh-stripping horror of being talked about: a doppelganger roaming the streets, ugly, contemptible, morally condemned. I have been stalked by this terror since childhood, the shadow side of the Tracy Malleus passed from mouth to mouth in glowing report.

'—Nobody was interested, but they couldnae shut him up. Kevin says he was obsessed. He just kept going on about how you shouldnae even be . . .'

'I'm sorry, Norma.'

Over the other side of the room the twins are about to leave, I dump the cups and hurry across to catch them before they go.

Funny how much we forget. The cloakrooms with their back-breaking sinks and munchkin coathooks, the chromium drinking fountain with its four-inch liquid plume, the clotted cream light from those beehive shades. The first time I spotted the yellow-varnished plywood cupboard I was surprised into laughter out loud.

Schools were never meant to be occupied at night. A blood sausage sky presses on the curtainless windows. The painted walls of the corridor collect a sickly hospital shine. Tonight we're in one of the tiered classrooms, the desks fixed to a hollow wooden slope with iron stanchions, a roller blackboard that wobbles when you chalk. I'm careful closing the door behind me, remembering the way they slammed in the wind, the playground lore of missing finger ends. Inside, I head for the heavy-duty radiators just as I used to before the first bell, bare thighs burning through my gabardine skirt. Some things don't change. The smell of hot pipes running along the skirtingboard, thickly painted and insulated with fluff. The far side of the classroom never felt the benefit, though some-times, called to the teacher's desk, I would walk into it, a wall of warmth against my knees.

Props get results: first rule of the reminiscence business. So it's difficult to know just who attends our fortnightly meetings in St Joseph's High: these paunchy men with their threadbare scalps and calloused sensibilities, or their tender schoolboy selves. They're dotted around the classroom, chatting, idling, smoking a fly fag, deciphering the graffiti scratched into the desk tops, examining the wall charts and the card-mounted poems, but under this listless behaviour I scent the vestigial excitement of an obsolete taboo. School plays, open evenings, concerts in the hall. For me they had the deliciousness of double transgression: first the fact of institutional life, a forbidden culture of regulation, and only then the thrill of breaking with routine. That was the Sixties: everyone mouthing off about overthrowing the system while I had only just discovered it existed, and no one was less sorry that it was there.

'Hi there, Tracy.'

Gerry is writing up pledges of financial support on the blackboard. A gas fitter to trade, at the second meeting he reminded me that he'd once visited my flat to clean the boiler and informed me that I was 'under-radiatored'. He wanted to know whether I'd converted to double panels, at which I made a thoughtless joke about extra jumpers and had to spend an hour in the bar at the end of the meeting, coaxing him round.

There are nine of us on the committee: Gerry, Kenny, Tommy, Harry, Jimmy, Davey, Bobby and the so-far absent Stevie Caw. At first I thought of them as a type, the men of my childhood, glimpsed hauling the bisected carcass in to the rear of the butcher's shop, or wiping their hands with an oily rag in the backstreet garage that did dodgy MOTs, men who had fought in the war and stood in line at the Labour Exchange during the Depression. They have the same faces, the same industrial-coloured hair combed back from the forehead, the same meaty hands and bulging cuticles and a tendency to the unlucky blackened nail, but Davey is a RunRig fan and Gerry never misses a Van Morrison gig and Jimmy has his footnote in the history of Postcard Records. Despite the years between us, culturally we are contemporaries, fellow travellers on the long road of middle age. By now I know them well enough to have developed subtly differing relationships with each. I know that Davey and Gerry are Irish and Kenny a Highlander, though all three are natives of Glasgow town; I can tell you who cheers for Rangers and who for Celtic; I know their trades and their fathers' trades, albeit nothing of their mothers; I remember that Tommy smells of ancient sweat and Jimmy has a jigging leg and Harry's teeth are acquiring the porous look of the extra-strong mints he sucks so compulsively, and Kenny half-smokes his cigarettes, pinching the ember between finger and thumb before dropping the stub in his pocket. Above all, I have acknowledged that my co-campaigners are men. Nothing so crude as flirting, merely a moment of biological recognition, a teasing out of the sexual from their battered and sunken faces – an overprominent stare, a black hedge of eyebrow, a larcenous mouth – before storing the knowledge unused. It doesn't alter the rules of survival as a token woman. Don't run yourself down, even in jest. Join them at the bar and stand your round early. And always, always use their first names.

'You missed yourself last week, Tracy. We ended up in the Bounty with they boys from Keoghs. They were having a right get-together.'

In other words, drinking themselves under the table, with maybe a moving platter of sandwiches and a handful of softening crisps. Still, I'm sorry I wasn't there. I passed it over in favour of dinner at Finlay Burns's and feel mildly apprehensive about what happened in my absence. Not that anything will have been decided, we're far too early along the road for that, but I'll have to play things by ear, attentive to every pointless digression, just in case. And then of course there's Bobby Croall.

He was absent from the second meeting but any edge I might have gained was frittered by missing the following week. Which leaves him with the advantage. We've had no contact since that first night. Or none of which he's aware. Four or five days ago, taking the bus along Argyle Street, I saw Sam up a side road, a carrier bag in her hand. She was talking to a man in black jeans and a leather jacket, his shorn head covered by a knitted blagger's cap. At home that night she denied it, had no idea what I was talking about, then finally tipped her head back in recollection.

'Oh him. Yeah. He asked me the way to Sauchiehall Street.'

'*Sauchiehall Street*? He's lived here all his life.'

She was unsurprised. 'I thought he was probably on the pick-up.'

'And that was it?'

'More or less. I said I didn't know. He asked me where I was from, did a bit of welcome-to-my-fair-city schtick.'

It didn't sound like Croall.

'Did he not try to repatriate you at gunpoint?'

She shook her head. 'Nice as pie.'

Kenny breaks off his contemplation of the periodic table and shuffles across the room.

'How're you doin', Miss?'

However it sounds to the ears of a middle-class feminist, this is a term of endearment, so it's a smile and a wink in return. On Tobacco Street a girl picks her battles.

'No' bad, Kenny. How's yourself?'

'I think gentlemen—' Tommy McAfee has stationed himself alongside the teacher's desk. Noticing me, he breaks into a smile. '—hi Tracy – we'll come to order.'

Kenny taps me gently on the upper arm, deferring his reply, and we sidle round into a ragged parody of a class, spaced at regular intervals, facing the front. By now we've played out the best joke, the Cinderella's slipper trick of pushing down the hinged plank and sitting at one of these midget-sized desks. Expectations of cramped knees confounded, Davey, Gerry and I still fit neatly into the slot; though for the purposes of the meeting we take more dignified positions, perched on the writing surface, feet resting on the seat in front.

'Item one: apologies. Stevie Caw cannae make it the night.'

I'm waiting for the second name, but already he's moving on. My eyes circuit the room, just to make sure: no Bobby Croall.

'Item two: pledges of support.' He turns, gesturing towards Gerry's blackboard. 'Folk have been very generous. The defence fund stands at . . .'

Again he defers to Gerry, who announces 'A hundred and sixty-three pound.'

'Rose-Marie Costello at the library says we can use the photocopier for correspondence, and what the council don't know won't hurt them . . .'

The classroom door swings open with the dazzle of an event, its reinforced glass panel catching a reflection of the beehive shades. Bobby Croall steps in from the corridor wearing the same hood's outfit as on the other occasions I have seen him, doing that redhead's trick of colourlessness struck by light. Real redheads, I mean: it doesn't work with the bottled kind. He scans the room, nodding to Tommy and a couple of the boys, Jimmy and Harry, his special pals, then walks up the wooden gangway to my right. I feel his heat through the stiff leather, catch a seam of his jeans in the corner of my eye, amber tracking on the black cloth. The desk behind me creaks as it takes his weight and I experience a slight shortness of breath, studying the landscape of the desk in front, the concentric ovals of its grain, the metallic sheen on that purple stain of ballpoint ink. The wood beneath me gives a little as he plants his feet on the sloping lid of my desk, a matter of inches from my rear. I see his boot lifting, the rutted sole almost vertical before the measured kick. And it's not that he might do this, since clearly he will not: what worries me is that I possess the paranoia to imagine it. A volley of coughing issues from the back of the room. I'd recognize Jimmy's phlegm anywhere but it's an excuse to swivel around, taking my eyes that extra quarter-turn. He stares back with dramatic absence of expression, a challenge that from another I might even receive as sexual.

'Item three: it's time we sorted out our tactics . . '

An area of some disagreement. Gerry has implicit faith in the powers of petition, Kenny thinks we should use the press, Harry wants a fly-posting campaign comparing the exploitative wages paid by the supermarket chain with their half-yearly profits. (I detect the hand of Bobby Croall.) Tommy is pushing for a vanity publication edited by Stevie Caw, mixing community contributions and rent-a-celeb good will. As long as tub-thumping agitprop can be kept to a minimum, the idea has potential. I might sneak in some reminiscence. A few high-profile names never do any harm, even those invariably attached to the week's good cause. However, it would have to be supplementary to my own favoured strategy: a velvet revolution down at the City Chambers. Let's try bending the ear with blandishments before we denounce them in the streets. They won't give us everything we want but, squeezed between the jaws of glory and guilt, they might be persuaded to offer us something. One side of Calico Street saved with housing association cash, the church converted into a museum, the past clipping the heels of the soulless present. Assuming we're not going to achieve the downfall of international capitalism and the reopening of the yards, it seems a respectable outcome. But before the enemy can buy this solution I have to sell it to my friends:

'Right now they're taking decisions behind closed doors. By the time we find out, it's too late. We need to get inside, split the opposition, convince the councillors there's good publicity to be had from consultation with the local people, a bit of community architecture—'

A breath of bitter mirth behind me indicates that Croall has made the Prince Charles connection.

Kenny leans forward, showing a top set of cinammon-coloured teeth. 'That's what I've been saying. We want to use the papers, get ourselves some headlines . . .'

Kenny's a sweet guy but he misses the point sometimes. It's best that I take it slowly. 'We've already had our headline. We don't get another one until something changes.'

'That totie wee piece in the *Herald* and a few letters in the *Evening Times*? We want to be in the *Record*.'

'And why would the *Record* want to put us there?'

Again I sense a bristling of resistance, but this time it's harder to pinpoint the source.

'It's important.'

Hard to tell if they're being deliberately obtuse.

'*I* know it's important, but that doesn't mean the editor of the *Record* thinks the same way. I can't see it shoving Father O'Feely and his bastard offspring off the front page.'

A bad idea, bringing religion into this.

'They'll print shite if it's the developer's shite.'

Now I have reason to turn around. Strange how fear can heighten perception. I swirl in the sculpted hollows of his ear canal, cushioned by the firm pads of his freckled lips, pulled with the membranous seal as they part in speech. I'm not sure I've noticed his hands before: long, capable, unexpectedly white, a surgeon's hands, or some other trade that plies the knife.

'The developers are talking about doing something, that's why the papers print what they say—'

His upper lip tightens derisively but I can't stop now.

'—OK, let's say they print it because they're part of the capitalist conspiracy, the point is we've got to work with them as they are.'

'Maybe we should ask Samantha Fox to get her tits out on the chapel steps: put us on page three of the *Sun*.'

Only Croall could take the high ground on tabloid sexism and throw in a subliminal slight on my breasts. You think I'm oversensitive? Believe me, this is war. He doesn't care about the media, and nor do I, but both of us are ready to fight to the death for the underlying issue, whatever that might be.

'Hold on, I cannae hear you down here.' Tommy has a problem with impacted earwax. It must be bad tonight, if he's giving up the dignity of the only adult-sized chair in the room. Unless I underestimate him, and what we are witnessing is a diplomatic interruption. He lumbers up the wooden hill. I take the chance to move to a desk two rows away, sitting sidesaddle on the sloping lid, savouring its hardness, a comforting discomfort, wood to bone.

Jimmy's leg-jigging takes on a seismic quality. 'Just because they're more interested in which royal's shagging the corgi doesnae mean we have to play their game.'

'Aye it does.' In case you're wondering, I'm aware how unpopular I am making myself, and not sure why I can't stop. 'That's exactly what it means, if we want media exposure. They don't need us. They want news, what *they* call news: a concrete idea of how things might change. If we provide a blueprint for the way Calico Street could work, old and new side by side, that's something the councillors will want to be in on—'

I have the impression that he is attached to me by invisible wires. If I hunch my shoulders, he will shrug; if I scratch my ear, his will itch. But this is not the mirror of sexual attraction, more like the exclusive communion between predator and prey.

He shunts off the desk, on to his feet, taking the floor. 'Aye: heard it. Are you blind or just stupid? They've taken our jobs from us, there's whole streets living on the social, men pushing buggies round the park because they've fuck-all else to do, and what are they offering? A bingo hall so the women can blow their giros and put more business the moneylenders' way. We need jobs, jobs that make things, not profits for pinstriped bandits down in London. These guys are scum, we all know it, but now we're gonnae cooperate with them?' He never acknowledges me, I have noticed, neither addressing me directly nor referring to me by name. 'They've got us up against the wall but maybe we'll get to tie our own blindfolds? Is that what we're holding these meetings for? Because if it is, I've better ways of wasting my time. We let them build the bingo and if we're good boys and girls they'll help us out with a wee museum. That's a good one: two parasites on the community for the price of one.'

'Museums in this city get three million visitors a year: working-class, middle-class, right across the board . . .'

For perhaps five seconds we have been speaking simultaneously, in similarly aggravated tones, and at similar volume. I can't keep it up. His rage is awesome, mesmerizing, his skin barely able to contain it, his outline shimmering with psychotic energy, his body perfectly still.

'A museum doesnae preserve a community, it's got fuck-all to do with continuity, it's about taking working-class lives and gie'ing them us back, with labels, so we can go and visit ourselves on Saturday afternoons. Then the middle classes won't have a problem with us, there'll be nothing to remind them that they're the living dead, because we'll be just the same. We've still got blood in our veins, the last thing we need is a professional vampire telling us how many pints we're allowed to keep—'

I can't say he's not acknowledging me now.

My fellow committee members appear strangely out of focus, but the blur that is Tommy is emanating concern. Not on account of anything Croall might do. Nothing he says will ever be challenged in this circle. It's my face: this madman has got to me, my sinuses are humming with the imminence of tears.

'—you think the savages need educating?' His habitual rasp changes timbre to some sort of mimicry. ' "They're pissed all the time, God knows if they can read and write, they barely know what day of the week it is." ' To my relief he drops the funny voice. 'Did I miss something? Were you born here? Did you grow up here? No? So what the fuck gies you the right to tell us how to run our lives? Christ, the way you speak, you cannae even understand the half of what we say. You want to pickle a community in formaldehyde: go home, do it there.'

There is no answer to this, nothing that I can say. I accept the logic of his argument: a place for everyone, and everyone in their place. But I have no place, no home but here. Which is not my home. I belong nowhere. So where am I supposed to go?

There were no kids who hated me at school. Strange but true. As a white blackbird it was plain I was due a severe pecking, so for a year or two after being plunged into the state of emergency that was Bessemer Comprehensive I kept my head down, perfecting the bored expression which was as much part of the uniform as the brown blazer and curry-coloured tie. But blending in to the background is not the only form of camouflage, and later, older, longer-established, I switched to dazzle paint. Amazing what they let me away with under the token conformism of school colours. Sam chose the leaves and twigs of full assimilation, with some success as far as I could tell, passing her in the corridor on the way to double maths. Neither of us had much sympathy for the cringing four-eyed victims the bullies unerringly picked out. They should have played it differently, worked out which cover it was safe to wear. That's what adolescence is all about.

So in this throwback to high school dynamics, I don't know what to do. I've made my adjustments to this peer group. Too late now to bring up my Scargill stories. As soon as I opened my mouth I was lost. My voice said it all: English and middle-class. A cold, arrogant, genetically selfish race. This is not merely the opinion of the blood-and-soil brigade. After not so many years of living here, I think of them that way too. They trample over us, impose their alien ways upon us and, in the last resort, they appropriate us. Only here of course we're talking about me.

'Somebody got out of his bed the wrong side the day.'

This is Gerry's attempt at consolation.

We're in the Bounty, in the public bar, on our feet despite being spoiled for choice of bar stools and vinyl banquettes, cultivating varicose veins while consuming alcohol being an authentic Glaswegian tradition (white, male, working-class). And they say I have no cultural insight. Naturally I was tempted to go straight home, but they'd only talk about me in my absence. The emotional mauling is nothing, the bruises will heal, but I must emerge from the post-mortem with honour. As yet the event has no fixed meaning, by the time we leave the pub it will have assumed the calcified form of ancient myth. But the discussion cannot begin with both of us present. Gerry only risked this timid allusion because my opponent is visiting the Gents. So I'll be sitting it out to the bitter end.

Kenny replaces his pint on the bar. 'I'm tellin' you: it's sexual.'

'Move out of the cave, Kenny; do you really think if I was after a bit of rough that I couldn't do better than . . .'

'Hold your horses, Tracy: I reckon *he* fancies *you*.'

The barman smirks, perhaps thinking of something else.

'Oh sure. It'll be the dozen red roses next week.'

That was embarrassing, but a Freudian slip? I don't think so. I'm aware of the bull market in brutal lovers; I've seen those pastel-coloured paperbacks pushing aggression as the currency of desire; I know plenty of women who'd fall all-aquiver at a single harsh word from a leanly muscled sociopath; but over the years, I've found, the archetype loses its charge. Men seem more fallible, more human, less thrillingly in control, and what's the point of being dominated by someone as powerless as yourself? Not that I see much vulnerability in Bobby Croall.

He's back. I can tell by the way my companions have drifted away from me. He takes up his former station and drains his glass, running a swift check on the progress of adjacent drinkers, considering whether to order a round. But I'm already buying.

I nod towards his empty glass. 'What are you having?'

For a second he stares. 'No thanks.'

In the mirror behind the gantry I see him glance at the woman washing glasses; hear the click of two pound coins upon the bar.

The barman hands me my change. 'See what you think of that one then.'

Having decided that the white wine has a bouquet like neds' aftershave on a Saturday night, I'm taking a chance with the red. One sip and I realize it's no better. I sniff the glass like a connoisseur. 'Ribena with a Benylin nose.'

Over to my right Croall takes possession of his lone pint. 'It's a shame they don't sell Pimms on the Soo'side.'

His voice is so low I'm not sure I was meant to hear, but Harry titters, which puts it in the public domain. The shock of what happened in the schoolroom is still reverberating in my blood and now, belatedly, I feel a surge of injustice. The crudeness of the fox-hunting, City broker, public school caricature: fifty million people reduced to a playground insult.

'What the hell do you know about me?'

Even I didn't know I was going to say it. Gerry looks profoundly embarrassed. Tommy, Harry and Jimmy are suddenly even further away. There are five clear feet of floor space between myself and Bobby Croall, easily enough for a bar-room brawl.

He takes another drink of beer, as if he had not heard the question.

'More than I want to know—'

His voice is very quiet.

'I know they pay you to convince working-class women that the men they buried after forty, fifty years were bastards to them. I know you poke around in their memories until they gie you something you can twist into propaganda to keep your social worker pals in jobs. Then you're back to the West End and a cheeky little wine in the Ubiquitous Chip where you talk about these terrible people who eat fried food and watch satellite television, and don't look at the Zero Tolerance posters because they're printed in black and white. I know that you're conning them, telling them what's wrong with their lives, coming out with all this bullshit about personal politics. But you're not interested in the fact that the Social doesnae gie them enough to live on, and the local Co sells a quarter of what you can buy on the Byres Road, at twice the price, and they cannae afford the bus into town, and the council operates an unofficial no-repairs policy because they're waiting for the walls to dissolve in the damp so they can sell the land to a private developer—'

He must have rehearsed this, it is too fluent, its rhythm straight out of the rhetorical textbook. And he doesn't fluff a line.

'—what I don't know, but I don't gie a fuck about, is whether you're sucking our blood because you want to wipe us out, or just so you don't feel so lonely on that fucked-up planet where you stay.'

I know I planned to stick it out to the end, but sometimes you have to cut your losses.

I finish my drink, release my jacket from the brass hook under the bar, and nod in a shaky impression of unconcern.

'Like I thought: you don't know anything about me.'

SEVENTEEN

I still remember the shock of discovering that I was too old for old clothes. One day I was an urchin whose coltish limbs and snowfall pallor were charmingly offset by a baggy-breasted crêpe de Chine in a fevered floral print; the next I was a madwoman whose frock didn't fit. That is, of course, an exaggeration. The truth was more intimately insulting: I looked like a fey hangover from the salvage society, a whale-saving, carrot-cake-nibbling, paper-bag-recycling hippy who imagined those sixty-year-old armpit stains signified a poetic soul. A drippy woman who thought she was still a girl. I was well past the watershed when I actually noticed. The revelation came courtesy of a pair of Women's Land Army britches, modelled by a perky brunette with an unselfconsciously spreading bum, though what really struck me was the anaconda-grip on the calf muscles. I had fully digested the pitying thought before I realized that she was a good five years my junior. That was when I packed in the jumble sales and started browsing in Princes Square.

Although I have stopped buying, I still visit the rag shops, those poky hideaways down in the whitewashed basement or up a cork-screw flight of uncarpeted stairs, warm with the insulating layers of tweed and alpaca and flattened musquash. It's the smells I love most: moth balls and Yardley's Lavender and the atmosphere peculiar to pincer-clasp handbags of the nineteen fifties: a compound of lipstick and powder and brass thru'penny bits. I used to watch for those handbags opening as avidly as any child scoured the heavens for Santa's sleigh, waiting for the embroidered hankie to receive its pink-tainted bubble of spit, and then the vigorous rubbing of the chocolate moustache. I longed to be so womanhandled, to feel my shoes yanked off the pavement as I was frogmarched across the junction, to wince at the tug of a sharp-bristled brush, to be smacked by a loving hand for smearing my face with a clown's mouth of Estée Lauder. Darwin never laid a finger on us. I was the envy of the class.

So of course I understand what draws me to these places. In so far as I have ever felt at home, I have felt so here, in an abstract of the past on which no one has prior claim, an archive dependent on the reader for its meaning: junk or riches – for me part treasure chest, part intravenous hit. Morning coats, evening scarves, pork-pies, homburgs, taffeta, grosgrain, art silk, fabrics weighted with humanity, not just the surplus dandruff and shed skin, or that bus ticket in the pocket, or the safety-pin glinting in the hand-sewn lining, but whole histories rendered in the intricately coded data of the cloth. Every meal cooked, every dance partner favoured, every walk in the rain, every kiss squirmed out of or lingered over. It's all there, if you can retrieve it. Like many extroverts I'm tempera-mentally shy. I find it hard to entrust more than a casual word without making the recipient a lifelong friend. But in a secondhand clothes shop, burrowing into the yielding density beneath the chro-mium rail, I can press against the surface of indifferent strangers, taste the promiscuous pleasure of other people's secrets, feel the thrilling touch of normal lives.

And yes, the clothes that so excite me are women's clothes. The smells I sniff for are women's scents. Femininity turns me on. I never had access to this stuff, never clutched at the reassurance of a micromesh leg or ransacked the jewellery box on the skirted dressing-table, never paraded in clacking stilettos and the creaking wedding gown from whose stiffened petticoats a horseshoe of con-fetti might yet fall. She could have stuck around and made us hate her, or fought a messy court battle to kick him out, or picked a favourite and divided us forever. But she didn't. She left us nothing of her but the names that she had given us, and we enjoyed an anti-Freudian, non-sexist, socially progressive upbringing courtesy of one of Britain's hundred most eligible men (the *Sunday Times Magazine*, 1971). Not a bad bargain by anyone's reckoning. And as a byproduct, I'm fascinated by secondhand clothes.

I've called in to Vi's a handful of times on the slimmest of pretexts: elbow-length evening gloves, unturned linen sheets, a wine-red Tootal dressing-gown (size extra large). I wasn't sure Drew would have worn it anyway. He is phobic about living in anyone's shadow, already troubled by the possibility that he is understudying his own life. To date I've never bought anything, but Vi, a spry seventy-two-year-old in an acrylic cardi and Crimplene slacks, seems to appreciate the company, given the invariable absence of customers and the unsociable personality of her grossly overweight cat. But today it isn't Vi. The figure in the Lloyd Loom chair is smaller and less charged with ambient static, a little old lady in traditional old lady clothes: shoehorn shins in sheer nylons and a schoolmarmish suit of brown houndstooth check, with a string of milktooth mother-of-pearl to deflect the eye from where the neatly buttoned blouse meets the crosshatched folds of neck. Head bowed. Hair so white you just know it was jet-black. She's talking to the cat which, unprecedentedly, seems to be mewing back.

I bestow a reflex smile, although she's not looking, then start to flick through the rails. Behind my back the cat continues its petition, encouraged by the woman's rhythmic, sibilant speech. A Highland voice speaking the textbook English of the Gael, words skimmed off the top of a language that lies deep in the throat.

'Talk to me then, yes, talk to me, come on, you can tell me, yes, you tell me, how is your sister?'

Some seconds pass before I turn around. She is looking up at me and smiling with a set of perfect dentures. For a moment I have no idea who she is.

'Phemie! Sorry. I wasn't expecting. I was miles away.'

'I know.'

I had forgotten about her Delphic streak.

'Are you a friend of Vi's?'

She looks at me vaguely, so I prompt

'I haven't seen you in here before.'

'No,' she agrees. 'You won't have.'

The cat mews at her feet and rises on its back legs, pawing the air in soft, slow-motion entreaty. Many would consider this gesture appealing, even sweet, but I am not one of them. It is an animal for buyers of telephone deodorant and quilted toilet tissue, an overstuffed toy, its coat a patchwork of lavender and peach. Euphemia lifts her foot in its tiny leather lace-up, teasing the cat, perhaps mimicking its gestures, then with a slow, measured movement she brings her shoe down hard just short of the piebald tail. The cat, traumatized into silence, shoots up the stairs. The old lady looks up calmly.

'He'll come back when you're leaving.'

Seeing that I too am a little shocked, she continues 'And how is Andrew?'

'Fine.' We've met once, so I'm surprised to hear myself confiding 'Finding it hard adjusting to my sister being around.'

She nods. 'That must be gratifying—'

I can feel my face falling into the open-mouthed grin I do when I'm uncertain whether to laugh.

She smiles back at me. '—as long as he doesn't withdraw from the contest.'

Which, if Sam were a man, is exactly what he would do.

Carefully I ask 'Has he said anything?'

'I haven't seen him since the day you both came to tea.'

'But you know about Sam?'

She angles her head more precisely in my direction. 'I'm not sure that I do.'

'My sister: you asked after her.'

'Did I?' She furrows her vanished eyebrows, and when they uncrease again the topic is gone. 'Well, what can I interest you in today?'

I glance round the shop. 'Nothing special. I just . . .'

She nods, curtailing the explanation. 'You have a look around and tell me when you know what you're here for.'

So I look around. I have no idea of the dimensions of Vi's shop, I could not even swear to the presence of solid walls behind the close-packed shopfitter's rails. The most prized garments – beaded cardigans, an ostrich shoulder cape, lace-trimmed camiknickers – are strung across the ceiling to form a gorgeous ragged canopy. Three or four layers of carpet yield fibrously underfoot. The window is screened by another rail of evening dresses, above which drifts a little dusty daylight; further down the shop illumination is provided by three transparent forty-watt bulbs, their scribbles of filament searing the eyeball. The back wall is indented by a changing cubicle screened by a mustard chenille curtain, the shelving beside it swathed in a length of purple satin held down by a standard selection of bric-à-brac: Woolworths deco sundae dishes, a plaster Alsatian, a honeypot crawling with glazed bees . . . But to list the contents is to alter the experience. Seen in isolation these are only things, chipped, cracked, faded, sad. Together they form a backdrop, a stage set for the suspension of disbelief, not the glossy fictions of the professionals but the clumsy subversion of amateur dramatics, a game somewhere between acting and pretending and the self you never knew.

The miniature cowbells tinkle on their red dressing-gown cord and a young woman enters the shop, pushing at the frosted-glass door with her rump, then turning to reveal a baby in a harness on her chest. She has an eyebrow ring and split ends and a dulling henna rinse and, I see where the sling is pulled awry, a dark circle of leaking breast milk soaking her shirt. From these details, and her extreme youth, I judge her an incompetent mother, as the childless are wont to do.

Phemie rises from her chair and extends her arms to take the baby. For an instant its knobbly luminous head and the beanbag body in its brushed cotton sleepsuit hang suspended in the air. Phemie takes the weight without sign of strain, though against her tiny frame the infant seems gigantic.

'What's your name?' she croons to the baby.

'Lauren,' the mother replies.

'Oh, you're an ugly one, Lauren—'

The mother flinches. The baby is watching Phemie with absolute intentness, its wide eyes all pupil.

'—yes, you're an ill-favoured child.'

The woman is staring, as mesmerized as her offspring, and Phemie winks, but so naturally that it might just be a tic. Then she angles in my direction and gratefully I step forward, for I too want to fuss the baby.

'I think she's lovely,' I say.

'All the more reason that she should not be forspoken.'

Clearly unnerved by Phemie, the mother looks to me.

'Forspoken?'

'Overpraise a child and you may cause her to decline—'

Funny how close our folklore comes to the dour precepts of Calvinism.

'—or so they say,' she adds demurely.

I think of Cathy's changelings, the wicked fairies waiting their chance to steal each perfect child. I have a reminiscence project in mind, one that might tickle the tourist trade, which never goes amiss when grants are handed out. 'Do *you* believe it?'

Phemie looks at me shrewdly. 'I would not lightly praise a child.'

'But if you meant no harm . . .?'

'If I meant no harm I should not do something so harmful.'

The baby, clutching my index finger, breaks into a sudden toothless smile. Taking advantage of the infant's distraction, the mother hoists her out of Phemie's arms and back into the harness.

'I'm looking for a snowsuit. . .'

Leaving them to their transaction, I return to the tightly compacted rails.

'So what have you found for me?'

Phemie is at my side. The customers have gone. Feeling the need not to disappoint, I reach for a russet cotton duster coat which briefly caught my eye. She takes it from me. With the hanger in her hand the flared hem sweeps the floor.

'Let's look at the label.'

I steel myself for the loss of a tenner. Not the end of the world. I could always give the coat to Sam. Not that it's her style either. But Phemie ignores the price tag, fingers working over the fabric, seeking out the oyster satin ribbon stitched to the lining, its brown signature-style trademark. *Bella.*

I laugh, because it is a good joke. 'I'm not so sure I want it now.'

Phemie stares back unsmiling.

I still recall her tenderness the first time we met, the loss of this favour is surprisingly painful. 'You think I'm wasting my time with him.'

'I'm not aware of having said that.' Her eyes glint like glass buttons in the artificial light.

'It was a question.'

Her face softens a little.

I shrug. 'It's not as if he denies me anything, but then I never ask.'

'Perhaps you should start asking.'

She takes the duster coat off its hanger and holds it out for me, an impractical courtesy in one so small.

'Well?'

We inspect my reflection in the cheval mirror.

I shake my head.

Evidently this is the right answer. 'The colour makes you look three days dead.' She hands me the coathanger. 'Is there anything else?'

'I could do with a scarf and a pair of gloves. Things have been disappearing recently.'

'And you think someone else is responsible?'

An odd question, to which I answer

'No.'

'In that case it can only be yourself.'

I see what she's driving at. Clumsiness, carelessness, being accident-prone: such failures of attention can be read as refusals. 'You mean like an unconscious cry for help?'

The cat pads back down the stairs and makes for the evening dresses, disappearing between the skirts of a grey crêpe.

'If that's what you want to call it.' She seems disappointed in me. Outside there is a rumbling sound which might be thunder.

She has escorted me to the door before I realize I'm about to leave.

'Come and see me again one day,' she says, pulling the handle, jangling the little rope of bells. Looking down at her, she barely reaches my chest. Strange to be the lofty one, surprised by the minutiae of the world below. Poor Drew, exiled in the stratosphere.

'Take care, Tracy.' Fleetingly I wonder if she's going to kiss me, but she takes a step backwards, putting herself out of reach. 'And remember: not everyone can be your friend.'

EIGHTEEN

When we first started sleeping together I'd lie awake all night. Electrically aware of him, of the definition of his body, the duvet mountainous over his shoulders, the pillow shrunken beneath his head. The world had become a Caulfield canvas, each contiguous object bounded by its thick black line. My own body, too, refused the blurring of drowsiness, that molecular merging with flannelette and down. He slept solidly, huddled in to the wall like an anchorite, his snoring a rich and complex sound like a radio roaming the dial. It broke my heart but I could not claim him, drag him from the cold plaster to the press of flesh and blood. He had his reasons. And so I lay there reading secret scruples off the bulwark of his back. Those nights were the loneliest I have ever spent. In the daylight he was all devotion, captivated by my sneezes, hanging on my words, but in the dark we lay like cellmates, shoring up proprieties against the intimacy forced upon us, limbs not touching, careful not to pollute each other's airspace with our breath. Once, when I thought he was asleep, I kissed the nape of his neck and he shuddered with a sound of patience pushed beyond endurance, turning to excavate a crater in the mattress and impact himself, face down. Through four long weeks of adulterous assignations this went on. The ingenuity of his excuses hung over every meeting, another thing we could not share: those murmuring late-night phone calls behind the stealthily closed door. I was nodding off at work, walking the streets through my lunch hour in an effort to rouse myself, feeling my feet strike the pavement as if through cotton wool. Until one day, in jest, he referred to our night-time exclusion zone and I realized he did not always sleep so soundly in my bed. He had his reasons, but it seemed that they had changed. That night, for the first time, we did our nocturnal dance, a strange slow tango ever on the brink of wakefulness, winding between the bedclothes with blind grace, twisting in each other's arms, legs entwining and slipping free, our bodies turning like compass needles in a foreign magnetic field.

And now we dream each other's dreams. There's a rational explanation, but it's unnerving all the same. Not that we match each other frame for frame: that would be merely banal, like watching the midnight movie on separate portable screens. And it doesn't happen every night. But sometimes, drifting in the shallows of the morning, still breathing out our exotic nocturnal fug, we'll exchange details. 'I dreamed I was a footballer,' I mouthed into his ear one thin blue dawn, only to hear him murmur 'So did I.' A couple of weeks later it was ballroom dancing, the next occasion we each cooked Chinese food. Another night we dreamed of peacocks. For Drew, this is proof of our status as twin souls, at which point I remind him that the most significant aspect of coincidence is all the times it doesn't work. Most mornings I awake to find he has spent the night in the studio or the edit suite or some ecclesiastical court, while I have been padding the corridors of yet another labyrinthine family hotel.

Today is Saturday, most precious wakening of the week. We exchange dreams in the dark, tumble back into unconsciousness, and start the day afresh with a seal-coloured sky pressing between the curtains. This is what passes for daylight in late October. It is our habit to spend an hour or so in talk, sifting through our recent pasts, sharing the news too slight to be worth reporting during the week.

'I saw Euphemia in an old clothes shop the other day—'

He rolls over on to his side and exhales luxuriously, his warm breath sticky against my neck.

'—she said she hadn't seen you since that day I met her.'

I nudge his chin with my shoulder and, reluctantly, he speaks.

'That's how she is: no sight of her for years, then suddenly you can't move without bumping into her.'

'She looked different from how I remembered.'

'Mmm.' He's coming round, his voice settling to its habitual baritone. 'I've known her thirty years and she's never looked the same twice—'

His skin smells savoury between the sheets, something topped with melted cheese.

'—I sat at the same table at a ceilidh once, even passed her the tea and biscuits; still didn't recognize her until she asked me up to dance.'

'I hope she survived with all toes intact?'

Despite what they say about fat men, Drew is a terrible dancer.

'All eleven of them.'

'You're joking?'

I am oddly gratified by freaks of nature.

'Six on her left foot. Very common, I understand. With hospital births they tie a piece of string around the offending digit and it drops off—'

And there it is. Just when you least expect it. In childhood I could alter the perspectives in my bed, draw out the long tunnel under the covers, smell the dizzying blackness of cavernous space, feel myself tiny as a speck in the vast vaulted chamber. And though these fancies pass, there are allied transmutations in my morning life with Drew. Sometimes within the bedclothes seems a firmament, a weightless atmosphere in which we float like space debris. Then I feel us closest, and yet distinct, sensual but disembodied, released from the heaviness of his flesh, and the burden of my desire for it. In these moments we find a brief and precious balance, to be tipped a moment later by the inevitable sexual stirring, the mercenary's pulse that puts all comfort to use. I, too, turn on to my side, aligning our bodies, allowing that half-inch airlock of charged space between our skins before slithering close, belly to belly, thigh to thigh, breast to . . . He rolls away from me and delves under the pillow for the handkerchief he always has ready, this one pristine, its four sharp creases still intact. Bella irons them. He blows his nose, although I didn't know he had a cold, and replaces the hankie, settling on his back.

'—she'll be out on her broomstick later.' The calloused pad of his heel accidentally brushes my instep, followed by the whistling of the sheets as he swiftly withdraws his foot.

'Who will?'

'Phemie.' He is staring at the ceiling as if he sees her there. 'Hallowe'en tonight. Soon be Christmas.'

The first cotton-wool snowman appeared in the chemist's three weeks ago. The post office is already nagging about parcels for

Australia. Have you any idea how depressing it is to look out on a hundred tenement windows, every one of them framing a tree?

He yawns. 'Will Sam be with us?'

Us? I don't recall last Christmas in the first person plural. I spent the day with Euan and his mother, shelling half a hundredweight of hot roast chestnuts to make a tablespoonful of greyish stuffing for the greasy festive goose. On my way there I happened to drive by MacKendrick Avenue. The Monzies had two Christmas trees, one in the bay window and one, decked with red and blue Chinese lanterns, beside the front door. As if they were advertising the joys of the season to the heathen passing by.

'I haven't asked her.'

'She's been here seven weeks now.'

There are a number of reasons why I might feel justifiable irritation. At being wrenched out of a lover's lassitude. At being asked the one question I have deliberately deferred. At the fear that Sam might leave us, or the fear that she might not. At Drew trying to arrange my life for his convenience. At the inconvenience of which I can never complain.

When I first knew him I thought that he was single. No ring, you see. Not that this excuses a naïveté I can barely credit now. How could he not have been married? Think of the advantages: the flattery of definition against the contemptible other, the drabness of domestic life to throw every solitary pleasure into sharp relief. Every escape an adventure, a release from guilty obligation, from the concern and revulsion and occasional shaming safety he feels around his wife. For this marriage is not a contract to be terminated as both parties see fit, it is destiny, signed by God, and sealed by Fate. Under such circumstances it is pointless to imagine ever taking her place. And who would wish to?

He's unnerved by my silence. 'You have to admit she's changed things.'

Of course. But to hear him say so makes it far worse.

'I've tried not to criticize her in front of you—'

So that daily litany of complaints represents the edited version.

'—but I don't believe for a moment that she shows the same restraint. Sometimes when I see you together I don't know you, Tracy. Sometimes I get the feeling you don't know yourself.'

I might lose him. A fact so obvious I wonder it has not occurred to me before.

'Drew . . .'

A faint nausea scoops out the base of my throat. I abandon the sentence, having nothing to say, and too much that must not be said. On no account should I point out that having to share me redresses the balance, that my sister is merely a counterweight to the unmentionable Bella M. Drew is not interested in the level playing field. He could never compete on an equal footing with anybody, the very thought is annihilating. Which means, when you come to think about it, that he can never really win.

'I heard the postman,' he says, pulling on his trousers.

I must have opened the letters but fallen back to sleep again before I could read them, for now I find one on my pillow, three fragments of type visible through the torn envelope.

regret
appreciate
unable to renew

The other half of the bed is empty. There is a crick in my shoulder and the arm outwith the covers is cold. I snake it back into bed, shrinking when the bloodless fingers inadvertently touch my thigh. Using my warm hand I extricate the single sheet of paper, scanning it quickly, then reading it again because I recognize such perfunctoriness as a loophole, a way of keeping alive the possibility that I might have misunderstood.

I live well, forgoing nothing, drinking the wine I like, eating the food I fancy, forever swinging carrier bags back from the midnight delicatessen. I am under the impression that, should it become necessary, I could live on buttons, but not since my student days have I had to try. On Sugar Street you can purchase a gauzy slice of reconstituted turkey (min 62% meat) on a white roll for thirty-seven pence. I ate one once, and vowed never to repeat the experience. How do people stick to a budget? I have a vague recollection of mornings when I never left home with more than fifty pence in my purse, let's say a pound to allow for inflation. That's a lunchtime sandwich and a little something left over for emergencies. Could I really go back to those days of bulking-out on coleslaw, half a red cabbage dressed in a five-ounce carton of natural yoghurt, having raided the cupboard floor for sultanas and nuts? Evenings in the public library because it's cheaper than putting the heating on at home? These questions, however uncomfortable, remain evasions, ways of ignoring the new fact of my life.

I am a reminiscence worker.

I have lost my job.

My job is what I am.

I am nothing.

NINETEEN

There are always things you can do. An appeal to submit, councillors to lobby, anything to foster the illusion of taking control.
It's the helplessness that destroys you. Now's the time for silver
linings, the counting of blessings, those platitudes we sneer at until
they're all we have left. The Maggies have been wonderful, and
Sam's a tower of strength. Most non-Drew days I come home to
find a casserole in the oven, a salad in the fridge, and no hint that
her savings are running out. Jazz clubs stateside must pay better
than I thought.

Of course I haven't told her. She'd only say I should start billing
Drew, and I really don't want *him* to know. He reacted badly enough
to the other drama, a couple of days later. The morning had dawned
dramatic, an orange skyline crossed by vertical columns of indigo
vapour. I'd opened the curtains and was dressing at the window.
(My exhibitionist streak I get from Darwin.) I watched Paula and
Lorna playing peever, wee David Swaine copying their movements
on the safety side of the yellow chalk line. Plumbing problems at
the local school had given them a couple of days' unscheduled
holiday. If it warmed up Linda and Stephanie would be setting up
shop on the pavement across the road, selling off their brother's
toys. The near side of the street was strangely empty of cars, even
for a weekday: just the Renault there on the corner where I'd
parked it, minus one wheeltrim, needing a wash, with that dent in
the passenger door where Drew nudged it shut with his bum (and
Drew's gluteus is more maximus than most). And then I noticed.

Roy's friend with the recovery truck wanted to know if he
should take it straight round to the scrap. If it had been drivable,
there was a guy he knew would have eased it into the river, no
questions asked, but he couldn't risk anyone seeing the truck. What
was my policy? Honesty, I said. 'Third party, fire and theft.'

He made a noise like Donald Duck and shook his head. 'Sorry
darling.'

Drew insisted on coming round to the flat. I was glad to see him, although his lipsmacking sense of crisis left me feeling somewhat wan. Lovingly he inspected the damage, the impacted bonnet and half-sheared wing.

'Did you not hear it in the house?'

No, I had not heard.

He ran his fingers over the buckled metal, pursing his lips into a wincing O: 'Someone really made a job of it.'

After another ten minutes of this he decided to cheer me up.

'Well,' he said brightly, 'you get a nice new car.'

So then I had to explain about the insurance. Which was when he started to explore his talent for despair. How could I tell him I had lost my job? He might have thought I was making a claim on him, looking to upgrade my status from cohabitee to kept woman. It might have occurred to him that he owed me a little more than a weekly bottle of Burgundy and the odd Marks and Spencer sweetmeat, most of which he consumed himself. Anyway, secrecy was becoming a habit. He never did ask what happened about my missing credit cards, so I never got round to telling him that someone had spent four thousand eight hundred pounds of my money – that is, money I never had in the first place – before I telephoned the credit card hotline. After that they stopped shopping. It wasn't that they were nabbed by a sharp-eyed sales assistant, or that the bank failed to notify me of further transactions, being bound to cover all subsequent debts. I checked: whoever it was stopped, voluntarily, the moment I reported the theft.

I had an appointment with the union at two-thirty, and as I didn't feel like catching a bus over to Magellan Street for a couple of hours' work, I walked to the museum, along Montego Road, past the drive-thru' burger joints and glass-walled car showrooms, and that eerie barrier of wind-buffed polythene lining the chain-link wire fence of the secondhand lot.

I was upset about the car, but not in Drew's way. Not as an object of value suddenly made worthless, or a memento mori of mechanical things, or a shaming implication of carelessness, or a stigma of failed luck. For me, the car was part of our story, prosody in motion, a witness to our shared life.

It took us singing through the zigzag bends of Loch Lomondside, and over the sea to Skye, the single-track road unrolling like a ribbon over the blind summits and plunging slides. And on those summer runs across to Gullane, with a lukewarm bottle of Cava and a Thermos full of crushed ice. We'd make love on the tartan rug, wary of joggers and excitable retrievers and the jag of the marram grass screening the dunes. We're both suckers for the Hollywood cliché of passion beside the crashing waves. Once, the week before his birthday, we drove all the way to Morar for a four-hour honeymoon amid the Caribbean colours, the sparkling sand so white and fine that the wind blew it into smoke. The beach's soft ridges a Sahara in miniature, but scribbled with desiccated seaweed, broad ribbons shrivelled to curlicue and thorn. Bladderwrack capsules dark as olives. The shells bleached to coconut meat and the sea so clear that it revealed its shelving contours and sudden depths in stripes of indigo and turquoise right across to where the bumpy mauve of Rum marked the horizon. I lay spreadeagled, sockless, sinking fingers and toes into the warm sand, while he sat hunched forward over his knees beside me. Drew has difficulties with unsexual abandon, quite apart from the unwieldiness of his two hundred and fifty pound frame, but some inner loosening made him say 'Let's stay here forever.'

And even though we were on the road by six, in a way we had stayed there forever. Folded up the memory and stored it in a drawer of possibilities. Until the loss of the car. No jaunts to the sea. No impulse trips to the hills. No picking him up from the studio. Maybe he'll get a lift home with some comely young trainee. Either that or more waiting at bus stops, more scanning the rain-driven streets for the taxi's orange bar, more opportunities to ponder the metaphor, going nowhere. More time in the flat, wondering if these four walls are different enough from the other four walls to make it worth the lies.

And then I saw the hatchback. It was the colour I noticed first. Bronze. The livery of soft-top Mercedes and the yuppie's shelf-backed Porsche. After that I saw the price. Interest-free credit over three years. Offer closing today. The salesman was there before I knew it, a boy with a pigeon-plump neck constricted by his merciless collar and tie. It was the flesh that snared me, the itch to unfasten his top button. New to the job but not so green that he failed to spot the fractional ebbing of resistance. I wouldn't enter the showroom so he did his schtick there on the street. Amazingly popular promotion, never to be repeated, the manufacturers had shot themselves in the foot, they were actually losing money on the deal, but by the time they had worked it out they were all tied up by the Supply of Goods and Services Act. Come midnight they'd be breathing a sigh of relief.

I was running so late I had to take a taxi to the museum. Even then, he only let me go because I said it was an appointment with my bank manager. As I walked away he was propping the 'sold' card under the windscreen wiper. He'd keep it there until four o'clock, just in case.

The union was a washout. Full of sympathy, but little practical help. Jack and Gordon received me in the office with its unmistakable pollution of cannabis smoke. They made me an apple and cinnamon tea but didn't offer me a toke. I was one of a few dozen staff on short-term contracts. For the past five Novembers I had received the standard renewal letter. It had seemed like a formality. If it was any consolation Gordon reckoned others would follow, in ones and twos, nothing too provocative. Someone had to be the first to go. If they'd booted a batch of us there might have been a chance of goading the rank and file into action, but he couldn't see them manning the barricades for a reminiscence worker. Most of them were sitting on permanent jobs, glad that if folk were getting their jotters, the contracts were in the front line. Which was exactly what management was banking on. Typical of the sleekit bastards, he said, clearing away my half-drunk mug of tea. Jack had already put in for the appeal, but I wasn't to raise my hopes.

On my way out I stopped to check the doocotes for internal mail. The usual Tradecraft pricelist. A photocopied flyer with a number to call about a litter of kittens. The latest union news-sheet. And another letter, dated twenty-three days previously, giving me notice of the lapsing of my contract.

'Do you want the good news or the intriguing spin on the bad news?'

Euan in shirtsleeves and silk waistcoat. I wondered who the lucky lady might be.

'Tell me the worst.'

'Well,' he adjusted his expression to something more appropriate to the recently bereaved. 'It's no worse than what's happened already, just funny really. The word is that your—' I could see him struggling for the tactful phrase '—departure is political.'

'Baillie Billy, you mean? He never got the point of reminiscence.'

He shook his head. 'No one listens to him. I mean *political* political.'

'Dunnet?'

He was no longer trying to conceal his excitement. I couldn't blame him, museums are dull places in November. 'Or McLauchlin, or Greer. Someone on P and R.'

Mentally I ran my eye down the list of Policy and Resources Committee members. No. I didn't believe it. I once caught Greer keeking up my skirt when I dropped some papers outside the members' lounge: that was about the extent of my contact with our political masters. I couldn't be sure McLauchlin even knew who I was.

Euan leaned in closer. 'The good news is *very* good.' He paused, milking the moment. 'I showed your Fergusson to Charlie Forbes.'

I looked at him, not quite believing. 'He's sure?'

He rolled his eyes in imitation pique. 'Oh ye of little faith.'

'You were stotious, Euan, but yes—' I kissed him on the cheek '—you were right.'

Though nothing moved, I had a fleeting impression of panic.

'You'd better take it with you now. It's not covered by our insurance and it'd be a shame to say goodbye to fifteen thousand pounds. Guaranteed minimum.'

'You said ten.'

'I was being conservative.'

I looked at my watch. Twenty to four. I started to run, calling over my shoulder

'You take it home. I'll pick it up around nine. In my new car.'

The important thing is to take control. Turn things around. Even if Charlie Forbes was gilding the lily he wouldn't do so by more than a couple of grand. I could pay off the bank and still have eight thousand to play with. The car was a bargain. And finding a new job was going to be tough enough, without relying on public transport. Besides, I loved the colour.

Back home I felt cheerful enough to sing. But Sam was there, so I contented myself with tidying the sitting room, returning the books to the shelves, retrieving the oven gloves from the mantelpiece, removing the pile of old newspapers beside the settee, restoring the order that had started to slip.

'Sam, have you seen that book I left by the lounger?' Most of her appeared in the doorway, one arm trailing back into the hall. Strictly speaking she was only supposed to smoke in the kitchen. 'The big library book.'

'The one you were talking to Ally about?'

There was something about that 'Ally' I didn't like.

She slewed slightly to prop herself against the door jamb. 'He took it.'

'I'm sorry?'

'He called round to pick it up.'

'When was this?'

She shrugged. 'Day before yesterday.'

'But he doesn't know where I live.'

She scrunched her face as if I were being deliberately annoying. 'He phoned first.'

'Sam, it's a library book. If it goes awol *I'll* be the one forking-out twenty-five quid. But you just hand it over on the doorstep . . .'

'I didn't hand it over on the doorstep.' She met my eye and I read sullenness there. 'He came in, had a cup of tea. He's working on a house just round the corner from Ancona. Architect's conversion.'

'So did you take him into the front room?'

She produced a less disfiguring edition of that scrunch-faced look.

'His jeans were a bit mucky for the furniture so I kept him in the kitchen. He used the blue mug with the stars on it and sat on that chair there.' She pointed with sarcastic precision. 'And he used the bathroom before he left. Is that OK?'

Every home has its trademark smell, its distinctive cocktail of cooking odours and cosmetics and carpet-must and farts, which may be as close as we ever come to the essence of a life. You can never really experience your own, but to a stranger it is an intensely vivid evocation. I saw him in the hall, on his way to the kitchen, looking at the pictures, struck by the portrait of Darwin taken for *Nova* magazine, and later, maybe popping his head round my bedroom door on the pretext of looking for the loo. From his chair he would have had a clear view into the front room, providing both doors were open. He'd have seen one of the aubergine curtains, tied back by its gold-tasselled rope, the Moroccan marquetry cabinet and an arm of the mazarine chair. But what would he have made of them? Perhaps he had taken me for a North British Sloane, a suburban deb in her own cut-price stately home. But this was pure paranoia, I knew then that my savaging in the Bounty Bar had left its mark. Why shouldn't he have seen my setting in its true colours, as pleasure rendered in fabric and paint?

'How long did he stay?'

She shrugged. 'Fifteen, twenty minutes. I said you were out at Magellan Street and we talked a bit about that. I got the impression he was checking you out with a view to nominating you for the Nobel Prize.' Cue the raised eyebrow. 'Unless it was a more personal curiosity. He seemed very interested in Drew's dry-cleaning.'

Two jackets and a pair of trousers I collected as a favour, hanging from the kitchen door so he wouldn't forget them. Which of course he had.

'He said he'd bring the book round next week. I told him to make it Monday—'

When I had a funny feeling I would be in all day.

She looked at me slyly. '—since it's not one of your Monziedays.'

'Makes no difference to me.'

She brought the cigarette out of exile, to find it burned down to the filter, supporting an inch and a half of precarious ash. 'Well, we wouldn't want to frighten him away.'

Naturally she'd have flirted with him. Tapping her cigarette against the rim on the saucer, fiddling the ash into a cone, easing behind his chair to get to the teabags. But there were worse women to have as sexual brokers. Not that I was about to do anything that might threaten my life with Drew, but faced with flattering affirmation from a perfect physical specimen, what woman just turned forty would refuse?

Drew loved the car, the nostril-buzzing newness of its moulded plastic interior, the aviator's panel of dashboard lights, the self-conscious glamour of that colour. As a rule he hated the brashness of high-priced consumer durables, felt excluded by them, as by so much contemporary paraphernalia, but this was a toy he had a stake in, something he almost owned. His mouth hung slack with excitement at the sight of me behind the wheel, his eyes sliding down my forearm as I wrestled the unfamiliar gearstick. At times like this I'll bump against his idea of me and feel almost embarrassed, as if I've caught him alone in a darkened room. Once, in that early stage of drowsy, slurring nonsense-talk between epic bouts of sex, I asked him if he loved me and, on receiving the expected reply, wondered what exactly he loved? His index finger aborted its journey along my spine, and in his serious voice he said

'You're the world.'

Back then I had no idea what he meant, nor why I felt so stirred, but now I understand. Drew's universe has two compartments. The narrow corridor leading to salvation, and everything that lies outwith it. Delicious to be so voluminously swathed, and still to feel the selvedge of definition. The World. Its beauty and corruption. All that. And something more. Surely you didn't think that he'd see me in hell? However titillating it is to lie down with a scarlet woman, he believes that ultimately I will be saved. And it may not be consistent, but I hold this faith most dear of all his love tokens, a detail strangely redeeming, in this life if not the next.

'See if it'll do a hundred.'

'What, at eight o'clock in the evening with speed cameras every quarter mile?'

We drove out to Balloch, just for the pleasure of turning around and driving back again. I was surprised when he asked how I had managed to afford it. Normally he shunned the contaminating considerations of hire purchase agreements and interest rates.

He was silent for too long.

'Drew . . .'

He returned my left hand to the steering wheel. 'I think it's best you keep your eyes on the road.'

I flicked on the indicator and pulled in to the side. We were at the point where Great Western Road is at its greatest, the dispiriting scale of the arterial highways of North London, those towering prewar mansion blocks set well back from the road.

'And when did you take this decision to swap a work of art by a minor Scottish master for a piece of aerodynamically streamlined tin?'

Now I saw his hurt I wondered only at my failure to anticipate it, a slip as unaccountable as so much else of late.

'I know it was given in love, Drew: nothing can ever change that. But I've got to be practical, I don't even know whether I can afford to insure it, and there's talk at work . . .' Not yet. Not until I had another job, and there could be no suspicion of my trying to trap him, asking him to choose. 'I know you're upset . . .'

'Not upset, just surprised that I've known you all this time and never knew you at all.'

He will never forgive me. Only the desperate fear of losing him if I did nothing could have blinded me to the risk of making things worse.

'Still, I suppose it's handy for Sam to have something to chauffeur her around.'

'I bought it to chauffeur *you* around for Christ's sake.'

He didn't like me blaspheming, and I hardly ever did. One of the odd points of congruence between the atheist and the believer.

He shifted in his seat and I noticed the flaccid belly-fold over his waistband. He must have skipped lunch, a rare occurrence. Either that or he was losing weight.

He laughed down his nose, a brief but painful sound. 'Funny: I always thought you understood.'

And of course I did. He is a romantic. No explanation, no matter how detailed, would do. So many words in our hours together, so much discussion of books and plays and politics, but no navel-gazing, no tedious chewing over The Relationship. Neither of us much fancy working it out, talking things through, all that effortful negotiation, the compromises they recommend in women's magazines. He can get all that at home.

He bought me the painting two weeks after we first slept together, but handed it over six months later, the day before Christmas Eve. I was all for opening it on the spot but Drew is a stickler in such matters and insisted I save it for the twenty-fifth. It was a way of being with me on the day, he said, eyes softening at the imagined scene, a Victorian mezzotint: *Alone At Christmas*. And so it was that I removed the scarlet paper with its quartering of gold ribbon on Christmas morning, a day like any other for me, save that the supermarket was shut. Euan and I had ripped open our mutual offerings a couple of days previously, and Sam and I have never bothered, so it was my only present. Refusing any hint of ritual, I was tugging at the paper with one hand while eating a slice of cheese on toast with the other. I already knew it was a picture, and frankly I feared the worst. A jar of wildflowers, or a harbour scene, something pretty and banal. There are pockets of the suburban in his taste. Then I saw her, and put down my snack.

Her clothes, a grey, crossover coat and black cloche hat, suggested the nineteen-twenties or thirties. The background, too, was sombre, a paler curtain echoing the draping of the charcoal-coloured coat. Her gloved hands rested lightly in her lap, finger-ends merging in the dark paint. The canvas went no lower. At a guess I'd say it was unfinished, perhaps a trial run for a later work, but still arresting, almost narrative in its hold. An art critic would have dwelt on the vivid way the flesh was rendered, the blood warm beneath those full cheeks, the animal health of that sturdy pink neck against the oppressive monochrome of the surroundings; but for Drew, I knew, the picture's power lay elsewhere. There was no literal correspondence; she was brown-haired under the hat and, on another day, in a costume less prim, her looks might have been described as coarsely sensual, but I caught the resemblance immediately.

She looked like me.

It seemed a face the artist had painted dozens of times before, the features stylized, almost mask-like, and yet that day something in the sitter's character had reasserted itself. In tension with the blowsy fullness of the lips, the composure of those shadowless cheeks, was a vestigial sadness. Nothing so crass as melancholy, she was not self-pitying, merely caught off-guard. Her downcast eyes

seemed to be turning inwards, contemplating something regrettable
but unalterable, that she had finally learned to accept.

TWENTY

We live in a city of rival populations, each one curfewed to meet only its own kind. At eight in the morning Glasgow is a city of office workers, tailored professionals with their click-open attaché cases and beeping car keys. At nine-thirty the buses are taken over by the pensioner pass-holders: spun-sugar hair under plastic rainmates, ruminative old men with their nippy little dogs. By midday the pavements swarm with buggy-pushers; five-thirty and the supermarket aisles are clogged with singles bumping baskets full of Jaffacakes and beer. I have always known this, as a peripatetic worker I crossed most social timezones, but with all the people I noticed, somehow I missed the poor. That youth with no teeth, the woman whose ankles swell like proving dough, a hard-faced toddler sifting through the gutter, all the unscheduled and the unloved. And now the world is full of them.

So you see I would never underestimate the comforts of routine. In precisely five days my life as a reminiscence worker will come to an end, along with the standing orders that guarantee my contact lenses, telephone calls, refuse removal, building insurance and so-cially selected daily swim. Yet for the time being I still wake at six-thirty, doze, shower, wince at the tartness of Drew's machine-extracted juice. I still pop into Gino's after work on Mondays, fighting through the fug of underage smokers to order a sarsaparilla float. Tuesdays and Thursdays I take my usual sauna, Wednesday is my Spanish class, Friday I visit the gym. And on Saturday, as ever, you'll find me in the secondhand bookshop, hoping to happen across Darwin's *Not Normal,* which was pulped by the publishers for legal reasons, though reviewers' copies were never recalled.

I tried to return the car this morning. The voice on the line was so cold I hardly recognized the chubby boy who schmoozed me out on the pavement. Of course he's a salesman, synthetic warmth is his stock-in-trade, but still I was pained. He referred me to the many magazines listing secondhand prices. I replaced the receiver and totted up my debts: thirteen thousand pounds. Maybe seven if I manage to offload the car, a sum that can only increase. Sam's savings won't last forever and I've had no sniff of a job.

There is nothing else for it: I will have to sell the painting. I could I suppose come clean about my motives, confess my dilemma to Drew. Sometimes when I picture the scene he gives the sale his blessing. That's just before I'm reinstated by the council, win five million in the lottery, and find that his wife has put in for a quickie divorce. Meanwhile, back on Planet Earth there's no knowing what he'd do. Bolt straight back home to Bella? Drop down on one knee? He's quite capable of harbouring a rescuer's fantasies and hating me for trapping him. So when I declined his chivalrous offer he'd carry a double resentment. On the other hand, I could hardly be blamed if the news of my straitened circumstances were to spill from a third party. Indeed, my suffering in silence would put *him* in the wrong . . .

Charlie Forbes' telephone manner was everything I expected: upper-class English strangulation and a strong Scottish rrrr. My guess was Edinburgh Academy compounded by several years in that pink-tinged, gilt-edged pocket of the 1950s behind Piccadilly. He's a fixture on the social circuit – gala performances and anything in a marquee – so I know him by sight: a big-limbed aesthete with a pass-the-port flush and dense white hair that, newly shorn, resembles some rockery plant, hardy and inimical to the touch. Left untended, it grows vertical as a shaving brush.

'Oh yes, *Tracy*.' The distaste was almost undetectable. At least I wouldn't have to explain why I was selling. In Charlie's world women called Tracy aren't meant to own works of art.

'I'm terribly excited about your treasure. I've a sale next week but I'd rather save it for my mega at the end of the month. What do you think? As it happens I shall be over your side of town on Monday. Why don't you wrap it up safe and pop along to the salerooms on Gruny Street so I can take possession? You know where I mean? Behind that rather good wine chappie who sells the very reasonable 'poo.' He giggled and I gathered that I was being treated to a spot of self-parody. 'It's mostly furniture, which means a heavy presence of the great unwashed, but the week I don't go they'll knock down an Eardley for fifty quid. And you might find it fun . . .'

As a rule Drew and I maintain telephone silence during his domestic three-day week, but this was not a matter that could wait.

'Monday's impossible: I've got sessions end to end. I checked out my insurance policy last night and there's no way I'm risking leaving it in the car . . .'

He couldn't quite believe that I was recruiting him as courier, but a refusal might have compromised his role as injured party, so curtly he agreed.

'I told Forbes I'd meet him there at three.'

'Three o'clock then.'

It would be our first appearance in public since my birthday.

Gruny Street sits in one of the city's flux-fields, once prosperous, then an immigrant staging-post, now rising again, colonized by teachers and social workers and other underpaid but epicurean sources of disposable income. Hardware stores and denture repairers and sellers of formidably reinforced foundation garments nestle cheek-by-jowl with continental bakers and scented candle-makers and the odd vendor of speciality teas. There's even a mock-Barcelonan bar. My watch says two-thirty, but the light offers the same promise of imminent gloaming it has held all day. I drive past a couple of spaces and park a hundred yards from the door: dulled reactions, an inertia I find myself feeling more and more.

A blackboard chalked with a pointing finger indicates a small brick-built warehouse tucked between tenements, piquantly out of place. The doorway gives onto a narrow stair of brown-painted brick, fragrant with old machine oil, stirring the blood with romantic obsolescence. An ancient fire hose is coiled untidily in an open-fronted box up on the wall. A series of nameplates, mostly laminated plastic but one of engraved steel, announce car spares in the basement, kick boxing on the ground floor, office stationery above that, a charity I've never heard of above *that*. The concrete steps are cut so steep that my knees ache by the second storey, and there are many more flights, many more perished-rubber hoses, before I reach the stairhead smokers, a couple of baldies companionable in the accumulated tar of twenty years, who nod minimally as I pass into the saleroom.

There is a primitive pleasure about issuing from darkness into the light. It's how I imagine heaven must seem to a believer: an airy room at the top of a dingy stair. Second impressions adjust to something less poetic: a huge studio lit by sloping windows set into a mansard roof. A touch of Paris in that greyly peeling distemper. The door bangs shut too loudly behind me, causing a half-dozen faces to turn round, and I catch the sexual hit of surplus adrenaline, a throat-catching pungency in the air. I've been here before: the absorption of the boxing gym, or the advocates' robing room, or anywhere men go about their business and women feel that ambivalent pang of exclusion, the thrill of the voyeur.

The room is thick with hubbub, and it takes me a moment to single out the auctioneer's goading. There she is: raised above the plateau of heads, a country beauty run to ruin, blue eyes bloodbathed, rosy cheeks crazed with broken capillaries, yet her blonde hair has the unassuming silkiness of the ponyclub sweetheart. She possesses the impersonal charisma of those who speak in public, interpreting the nods and finger-twitches and meaningful stares in a sarcastic monotone, weighing the pause after a flurry of bids, closing the sale with a finality that needs no rap of the gavel. It seems she knows most of the bidders by name.

A swift glance over the heads of the crowd confirms that Drew is not yet among them, although he could be somewhere within the city of furniture crammed into the other half of the room. Huge wardrobes with their secret scent of cedar and mothball. Chests of drawers lined with waxed paper and the odd flattened lavender sack. Tables balanced on tables. Chairs straddling sideboards and bookcases, teetering halfway to the ceiling. Bedside cabinets and cracked marble washstands missing a couple of splashback tiles. Pine kists ready for the stripping tank. Tallboys and enfilades, items we could never have named as modernist children in our Swedish birch beds. Even now I have a hankering for superseded home comforts: embroidered table linen and those puffed-up satin eiderdowns, so plumply insubstantial, like candyfloss to the touch. I once asked Darwin why we didn't have furniture like other people, why I couldn't have a bed like Susan Moody, with a headboard and a footboard and a lumpy mattress that turned trampoline in an ecstasy of jangling springs. It was one of the few occasions I ever challenged him, uttering words that could be parsed as a complaint. He told me that people died in old furniture, as someone would most certainly have died in Susan's bed, and although until that time she had been my best friend, I never slept over at her house again. Looking back, it seems a strangely superstitious observation, but undeniably effective, which is maybe all that counts. And now here I am, all that bad ju-ju in delicious proximity, a whole room full of other people's furniture bound for the bedsit, pieces so scratched and chipped and cigarette-scarred that no tenant would bother supplementing the giro by trying to sell them off.

Filing through the labyrinth, between high walls of walnut and oak and the flimsy constructions of plywood and melamine that came after, threading the narrow passages, exploring depths that seemed impossible from the outside, I feel the old deliquescence, his static crackling on my skin. Hard to explain, but I know he is behind me, catch the asthmatic breath of imminent laughter, whirling around to find

Nothing. My mistake.

In the early days, the body is always primed to meet your lover. On the subway, in the check-out queue, you're waiting for the arms to encircle you from behind, back flexing in anticipation of that nudging pressure between the buttocks, neck stretching, lips softening to match his in a kiss. When was it that we stopped all that?

Back at the business end of the hall the auctioneer has moved from crockery to the pictures stacked unceremoniously against the far wall. Fishing boats in harbour, storm clouds at sea, village streets and orchards and lonely ladies gazing wistfully out of the canvas, a range of artistic visions chiefly notable for their frames. I push myself into the crowd of dirtied sheepskin and scuffed leather. You know the type: street-traders, secondhand car dealers, semi-legitimate operators, the men-who-know-a-man; grizzle-haired, dull-eyed, but with something indefinable that earns even the most nondescript a second glance. The edginess of the unregulated. The women are a different breed, of varying ages but every one of them blonde and intensively accessorized, nails polished, lashes thickened, ears ringed, each carrying her own microclimate, a chill of unblinking purpose.

And now I recognize Charlie Forbes, ostentatiously apart from the other dealers, surveying the lots with the stagily jaundiced expression of one who trusts he is being observed. Amid the guddle of outdoor clothes, he is dapper in blue flannel blazer, canary yellow weskit and paisley bow tie. Though I'm careful not to meet his eye I sense interest, an angling in my direction. He's coming over.

'You must be Tracy.' His difficulty with the name doesn't seem to improve with practice. 'Let me get you a coffee.'

A couple of women are installed behind a table equipped with electric kettle, leaning tower of polystyrene cups, three plastic spoons and a box of Tunnocks Caramel wafers. Charlie Forbes presents himself at the table and, after protracted negotiation, deposits twenty pence in a saucer, handing me a cup of greyish liquid on whose surface swirls a powdery comma of brown. He does not take a cup himself.

'Thanks.' There is no chance of drinking this foul brew. 'Sorry I'm late. I hope you haven't been approaching every woman who walked through the door.'

His mouth parts in a smile that is mostly beetroot-coloured gums. 'Fortunately, I had a description.'

'Red hair has its uses.'

'Yes, he really should have mentioned that.'

I'm curious, so I ask 'What *did* he mention?'

Forbes smiles blandly. 'He said you were English.'

He registers the silence with no idea why it has fallen. 'Is this your first time?'

'At an auction, no.'

'Selling, I meant. Heartbreaking, I know, but we've all done it. *Reculer pour mieux sauter.* Who knows what you might pick up next time? I started collecting architectural drawings at school. Sold them last year and bought myself a Bellany. Much cheaper than it should have been. That's why I still drag myself along here.'

His vowels are barely believable, cruder than playground mimicry. His proximity brings out the Croall in me. This is cultural imperialism made flesh, a music hall toff with a tartan pocket-lining, oblivious to the possibility of giving offence.

He leans in confidentially but does not adjust the megaphone voice. 'This lot wouldn't know a Bellany if it bit them on the cock.'

Up close he has a paradoxical butchness, a layer of muscle beneath the slangy affectations of camp. He could knock you flat with a little finger while pulling out a silk hankie to mop his brow. Once upon a time I would have had his measure, certain of whether he was flagging his gayness or making a move, but just lately I seem to have lost the antenna that tuned me into other people's heads. Take that top-heavy type with the narrow margin of forehead between hairline and eyebrow. He seems fascinated by us but I could not tell you why.

Forbes follows my sightline and smirks. 'I see we've captured the attention of the Missing Link. That's Shuggie.' I recognize this tone from the way he pronounces Tracy. 'Born in the Gorbals, though these days he's living in Bearsden and eating with a knife and fork. Charming company we're keeping today. That's Joey Gryzies over there: he's a "property developer" I believe. Let's just say I wouldn't buy a secondhand Fergusson from him.' He pauses for another beetroot smile. 'I don't know his chum in the brown sweater . . .'

But I do. Even from behind, his pattern baldness cosied by a boatman's cap, his movements have a trademark ease, not self-consciously sinuous like Ricky, but functional, frictionless, their unobtrusive power exerting a strong magnetic pull. On me. Ally MacNeill a gangster's in-house muscle? I admit the idea has its titillating side. Gryzies certainly looks the part: that square-shouldered camelhair coat, the coconut mat of hair, the bulging forehead I associate with used metal recovery agents and minicab bosses. And, of course, a certain sort of property developer.

But something is troubling Charlie Forbes. 'You have brought the picture, haven't you?'

'I've asked a friend to bring it along. He was the one who gave it to me, in fact: he saw a likeness.'

'Really?'

He's bored. And not bothering to disguise it. Not so long ago this would have been impossible. I would have won him over; nothing so crass as conscious manipulation, merely a creeping awareness of him falling under my spell.

'In fact that's something I wanted to talk to you about. I'm afraid he's a wee bit offended that I've decided to sell, but I really haven't any choice. I suppose Euan told you that I'd lost my job . . .?'

'No, he didn't.'

The ambient temperature has just dropped twenty degrees. In Charlie Forbes' world it's not polite to mention money, disturbing the civilized consensus that everyone has enough.

'Actually my friend doesn't know yet either, and I was thinking that if you happened to mention it – how important it is in my predicament that you get me a good price – he might think more kindly of me.'

'I get all my sellers the optimum price.'

'Yes I know, but it would really help me out. Just a cryptic reference to my very difficult situation . . .'

His eyes hood briefly. 'I'll see what I can do. Excuse me a minute . . .'

Gone. The humiliation of being abandoned at social gatherings. Always make your getaway first. But then you have the alternate embarrassment of stalking the room, waiting for the extended eye-contact, the permission to approach. Where is he? I only saw him a moment ago. Outside for a smoke maybe. I check the stairhead. Even the baldies have ground their last dowt under heel. I shout

'Ally'

but there's no reply, not even the accelerating echo of footsteps. So it's back into the hall.

'I've got your library book at home.'

That's what he says, though the words come to me collaged, cut up by our proximity and the fractured rush of my experience of him, all that panicky vivacity. I see him in snapshots, a glint of eye, a sweep of lash, one corner of his parted mouth showing two creamy teeth, the Adam's apple pricked with stubble, that tidbit lobe of ear. We are laughing, which means I must have contributed something that passed for wit, but my overriding sensation is gidd-iness, the two of us whirling in our own private vortex.

'All this weird shit out of the Dark Ages and then something that could have been written about my granny—'

The book. There are issues we might discuss. The light it casts on our pagan Calvinist country. The adaptability of faith, with its suggestion of eternal needs. The blurring between magic and religion, the Bible and the biscuit under the pillow. And Knox really believed it could all be swept away. I have no shortage of things to say, and if he were Drew I might well have said them. Though Drew and I have silences of our own.

We are standing too close but I don't know which one of us took the decisive step.

'—we peasants must seem totally off the wall to you.'

Will I ever get over the shock of it, the gulf I never see until it's too late? Two choices now: the high road leads to cultural resentment, the low road to sexual games. I never much fancied the role of Lady Chatterley, but it's preferable to Lady Muck.

'Don't knock the peasants. Gaels are hip. Like Liverpudlians in the Sixties – everyone's aspirational fantasy.'

'Not mine.' The air sharpens with something other than flirtation. 'I like hypermarkets and all-night cafés and buses that run more than twice a week, and knowing I can get a lumber without hearing about it in every shop on Main Street next morning.'

For all the coded glances this is our first explicitly sexual exchange, and something of a disappointment. However we dress them up, they're the same old urges.

'Is there nothing you miss?'

'Saturday nights. Getting blootered at the pier with a carry-out, or stuck in front of the telly watching a movie people like you saw in Glasgow three years ago.' His lips compress derisively. 'It's a tough choice.'

This isn't what I want to hear. Whatever happened to shearing the sheep and the peatsmoke of the blackhouse and the tragedy of the clever child sent to the big city, there to be taught to despise his own tongue? And if I can't have that, at least let me feel a flutter of reciprocal desire.

And right on cue he obliges, angling towards me, his arm reaching round me, so that instinctively I'm pushing him off, my fingers on his chest, the yield and the firmness of it. His hand reappears, holding a small china shepherdess.

'You nearly had it on the floor.'

'Good job you're so quick off the mark then.' The feel of him still there in my fingertips, the imprint of the transgressive touch. 'Sam said you're working round the corner from Ancona Street.'

He gives me a knowing look, if only I knew why.

'I've a job for as long as I want one, seemingly. As fast as we can finish the conversions they're buying them. I gather you're to thank for one of the sales.'

'I am?'

He thinks I'm being playful. 'Tell the big guy he'd better watch his head in the bathroom. That cupboard over the sink is lethal.'

I suppose I could seek further detail, but only at immensely humiliating cost.

'Lot two one eight, a gouache composition signed David Thomson.'

Over by the auctioneer's lectern the camelcoated gangster looks our way and I feel my companion's attention pulled across the room.

'Thirty pounds.' The auctioneer's tone is one of statement rather than question. 'Thirty. Twenty. Ten.'

The pause between each number is fractional, she is a realist going through the motions of a ritual everyone understands.

A raised eyebrow from Joey Gryzies.

'Ten bid. Fifteen?'

A sallow-faced man in a raincoat flaps his hand.

'Twenty.

Twenty-five.

Thirty.

Any advance on thirty?'

A barely perceptible nod from one of the women. Three in the bidding now.

'Forty.

Do I hear fifty?'

Gryzies again.

'Fifty.

Sixty.

Seventy.

Any at eighty?

Ninety with the lady.

One hundred.'

The bidders seem strangely detached from the contest, the ratcheting tension disclaimed by poker faces, indifferent stares, yet we all feel their animosity.

'One-ten.

One-twenty.

One-thirty.

One-forty.'

The woman drops out, the other two hesitate.

'One-forty. Any advance on one hundred and forty for the gouache?'

Grimly, Gryzies raises that eyebrow.

'One hundred and fifty. One-fifty with Mr G. Any advance on one-fifty . . .?'

Her tone is querulous, nagging, hinting at a future of incalculable regret, and suddenly it's over.

'One hundred and fifty pounds. Sold to Mr G.'

Ally MacNeill replaces the china figure on the table. 'Back to work.'

'What about my library book?'

He shrugs. 'I'll give it to Sam next time.'

Behind him, the door opens. Drew is not a graceful mover. Too heavy and too old, though probably never supple. He has stature, and presence, but no fluid charm. The picture is clutched against his belly. His face is livid with a terrible excitement, skin blanched, eyes scored. Those stairs. Maybe a heart attack. They say the fingernails go black. I'm moving towards him, churning through treacle, reaching for his hands. *What's wrong? Just tell me.* Time folds into itself and out again, like origami. He's an old man now. He looks at me and I read pity in his face.

'What is it Drew?'

He's framing his lips into speech, but I haven't the patience to wait.

'Are you all right?'

Slowly he shakes his head. A muscular man in a brown sweater is staring at us. A ridiculous old fop with a yellow stomach prises the painting from Drew's grip. Comically, his expression changes to a gaping disbelief. Drew closes his huge arms around me but I push him away. Charlie Forbes studies the canvas. His face too is ashen. Slowly he angles the frame towards me. The subfusc backdrop, the gloved hands resting in the folds of charcoal coat, the pink-flushed throat, the black cloche, the chipped crater where the paint has been scraped down to nothingness.

She has no face.

Sam is in the kitchen painting her toenails, yellowing heels up on the table, a red line running over the rim of the bottle. *Brazen Hussy* on the cap.

I slide the butter dish away from her left foot. Such a hunger suddenly scouring my guts.

'Sam, have you seen the bread knife?'

'Nah.' She's intent on the tricky little toe, which curls under, almost out of sight; even when straightened, its sliver of nail is overshadowed by the calloused tuber of flesh. My feet are the same, a genetic legacy, though not from Darwin. The bagel is stiff as cardboard, the newly sharpened knife unwieldy in my hands.

'Oh.'

It's one of those cuts where for two or three seconds after the incision there's no blood, and you think you've got away with it. But now it comes, an inexorable welling over the palm, crossing the lifeline, running down the wrist, a vivid red from deep in the muscle. And I know that whatever it is that is happening to me, it's something very bad.

TWENTY-ONE

For days now beyond administrative necessity we had hardly spoken, filling the vacuum with the television's babble, eating convenience meals of individual size, shared living room, separate lives. Isn't that how most families get by? It didn't seem strange until she tried to break the pattern, suggesting we step out for an early evening drink. As it had been her idea, I let her make the conversational running.

'I met Euan in the deli.'

'Uh-huh?'

'He was just off to the Tramway to see that Dutch dance company. He said we could probably blag free tickets, they're desperate to paper the house.'

She paused in case I was going to respond.

'I told him he should let us know if it was worth seeing. He didn't sound that optimistic. The reviews were pretty bad.'

She picked up her glass and took a swallow, then, before replacing it on the table, took another. I suppose I'm tough going these days.

'He's been meaning to drop round.' Another fractional pause. 'He said to tell you, if there's any way the insurance people would . . .'

'There isn't.'

I knew she'd get round to the subject sooner or later, I was only surprised it had taken her so long. Surprised and grateful. In a weird way her silence had almost persuaded me that it had never happened.

'He said he was sorry, you know.'

'Yeah, I know.'

She reached for the cigarette packet, then had second thoughts. Her stash of Kools ran out weeks ago and she has yet to find a satisfactory substitute. Recently she's been cutting down. Maybe Ally doesn't like it.

'Why didn't you tell me you were selling it?'

I looked her in the eye. 'Don't we have secrets, then?'

She looked away. I quite enjoyed the boot being on the other foot, her acting so shamefaced. In so far as I was in the mood to enjoy anything.

'How much were you expecting to make?'

'I don't want to discuss it, Sam.'

I turned my head and examined the place she had chosen, a basement café I had not visited before. She haunts corners of the city I never knew existed. To my right was a bar counter fitted together from polished driftwood, one of those fanciful pieces of furniture which aspire to the condition of art. The chair was another: undulant wrought-iron, like a Cocteau illustration brought to oddly substantial life. Molten plastic lampshades diffusing their misshapen gloom, Ricard ashtrays on the tables, an unframed canvas by a would-be Peter Howson on the bare plaster wall: once upon a time I might have deconstructed the décor, picked out the post-modern allusions, explained the tensions of playfulness and style. Now I'm sickened by my literacy in this bastard language. Our days are spent in witless self-consciousness, seeing ourselves in ever more ironical perspective, a dot in an infinity of contexts. Godless, soul-less, withered at the root, owning nothing outwith our skin, not knowing what we mean, assuming of course that we mean anything, and finally deprived even of the tragedy of our uncertainty, reduced to a nexus of spending power and tastes. Did I ever wonder what would happen if I stopped living by act of will? Not really. The next time I looked, my dot would have disappeared.

She sounded nervous, aware that she was pushing her luck. 'Euan asked me if you were getting the police involved.'

'To find out who did it, you mean?'

Oddly enough it never occurred to me. Though now she mentioned it I could see why it seemed the logical thing to do. Invite some plain-clothes constable in to check my faulty window locks and interrogate my friends, investigate their movements, draw up a list of suspects.

'Maybe it was your friend Ally.'

She returned my look expressionlessly.

'You know: your friend Ally that used to be my friend Ally. I suppose you had him round.' Her features did not flicker. She was waiting. I waited a while too, but eventually I grew bored and asked quietly 'Is it worth it?'

She shrugged, but affirmatively.

'Serious?'

'As serious as it gets with a wife and kiddie a couple of hundred miles away.' She decided she needed that cigarette after all. 'You're the expert.'

As it happened I couldn't be bothered taking offence, but she regretted it anyway. 'I did my share in the States. Enough to swear I'd never do it again.'

'If you thought they were all going to be young free and single in Scotland you were making a *big* mistake.'

She finds it harder to read me these days, I've noticed. I'm not trying to be opaque, though not displeased about it either.

'Yeah well, this is probably another one.'

'Why?' My pulse quickened. Was there less to that covetable body than met the eye?

She stubbed out her cigarette, although it was barely smoked, and fished into her glass for the half-slice of lemon. 'I wouldn't bet my shirt on him sticking around. Coming from a place that small, there's a lot of pressure on him. It's not just Mhari. He's obsessed with making money, showing the folks back home. I still can't believe he was dumb enough to try pyramid selling.'

I never knew this about him. Just as well, starry-eyed capitalists not being big on my wish-list. I made an exception with Duncan the border raider, but that was back in the Eighties, it was part of the zeitgeist, and besides, he was good at it.

'Anyway,' she said, which was how she cut short any topic that made her uncomfortable. 'Knowing exactly how it's going to end when you've hardly started takes some of the excitement out of it.'

I smiled as convincingly as I could, which these days is not very. 'No false hopes: no getting hurt. Sounds good to me.'

She eyed me warily. 'You reckon?'

I bunched my pout into an approximation of lust. 'Yeah.'

Still she was watchful, and it came to me that she might have misinterpreted my current mood, might even be on the point of sealing my humiliation by asking if I minded, so I added

'You've had a lean time of it recently, you're due some fun. Enjoy.'

It wasn't convincing, not my idiolect at all, but it seemed she needed absolution as much as I needed to give it.

Her teeth teased the lemon from its crescent of pith. 'Mmm,' she said, sucking.

I thought then she might be rubbing it in.

As she waited at the bar while they opened another bottle of headachy yellow Chardonnay (twenty thousand pounds' worth of décor but they still couldn't serve a decent glass of wine), I wondered who was manipulating whom. She was keen all right, maybe even something deeper, but underplaying it for the additional frisson of hearing me egging her on. Meanwhile I had my own agenda. Injured pride, of course, but also the need to injure myself, to feel something that would amount to inclusion in the experience. Though their coupling seemed to count me out, I knew better. I was the pivot, my role as displaced bystander central to her illicit thrill and, who knows, maybe also a component of his pleasure.

She returned with the drinks, cheekbones flushed from some exchange with the barman. That's how sexual homage works: a little confidence-building and suddenly everyone pays court. Her skin has lost that dingy look of late, and she's dressing differently, the Rodeo Drive garishness has been toned down, leaving her less eye-catching but more sexually approachable.

'Any word from Drew?' she asked, sitting down.

For the first week of absence I thought he would come back, if only to collect his scattered wardrobe. In the second week I decided to gather together his things so I could thrust them at him, ready-packaged, the minute I opened the door. I rounded up a couple of rumpled shirts, a change of underpants and socks, his second toothbrush, a shaving adapter point. His navy check suit was gone, and the sand-coloured chinos, the five days' worth of shirts and underwear he liked to keep freshly laundered, the couple of books he always had lying around. He must have been sneaking stuff away for weeks.

Sam did not know this, though it was possible she had guessed. She pushed my wine towards me, spilling a little of the buttery liquid; her admirer had filled both glasses to the brim. Not wanting to risk a second spillage, she stooped and supped from her own glass where it stood on the table.

'Nothing, eh?' she said, licking her lips.

'It's funny,' the wine was opening me up, in spite of myself, 'I've never known a man who told me so often that he loved me. Adored me, he said.'

'If he'd adored you a little less he might have treated you a little better.'

'What's that supposed to mean?' I was aware of some slippage back to the status quo, my brief edge over her was lost.

'Put himself in your shoes, thought about how you were feeling, you know the way lovers look out for each other.' Being with Ally was making her smug. 'You were an exotic for him. And he for you, for that matter. Understanding each other wasn't part of the deal.'

Who can resist the fascination of hearing their life dissected by another?

'I know him backwards.'

'Sure you do, you love him: you learned him off by heart. Understanding him is something else.'

She used to talk like this as a teenager, having sorted the world out in her head. I felt a twinge of nostalgia, while putting a sarcastic spin on the question

'So what don't I understand?'

She shrugged. 'Why he's still with his wife, still obsessed with the Church. Correct me if I'm wrong, here. Why he screwed all those bimbos—'

Why he loved me and none of the others?

She took a breath and added quietly '—why he hates himself.'

'He doesn't.' But as I said it, I knew it wasn't true. 'All right: why?'

'Other than the obvious, you mean?' Her lips twitched but I didn't see the joke. 'It's nothing very original. He's a type. They're ten a penny in television. My line of work too. Show People. Hoping if they're flash enough on the outside that means the inside's OK too. Hanging out with the blondes, the big tits, the personality-girls that everybody loves.' From the way her eyes widened I took it that she meant me. 'Shopping around for the diamond with the right combination of sparkle and flaw . . .'

'And that's why he hates himself?'

This time she lifted her glass off the table to drink. 'I'm getting there. It all comes back to guilt. Born in sin, isn't that what they say? Even as a kid he's bad. Every moment a moral choice, the world a delicate balance he could damage with one evil thought. And if he does something right it's vanity: trying to pass himself off as a good boy, hoping somebody's watching – besides God, who knows he's rotten to the core. To live is to do wrong. Every impulse, every breath is taken at somebody's expense. So he's good most of the time, because he's so cowed, but sometimes he hates himself so much he thinks, fuck it, if I'm going to hell I'm going to take a few with me. What does it matter? The game's rigged before I start. And then after he's done it—' She snapped her fingers, a sound so sharp that the barman looked over '—more guilt.'

She meant it. Without question. But I wasn't sure it was Drew she was describing.

'When did you gain insight into the religious mind?'

She glanced at me, maybe hearing the words I hadn't spoken. 'It's basic psychology, Tracy. What do you think is happening in these godforsaken places where they pray five times a day? It's fucked-up families writ large. Never being good enough. Never being accepted for what they are. God the parent fucks them over. But the propaganda is He loves them, and them being so sinful, they're really grateful. And anyway, they've no option: if they don't toe the line they're definitely going to hell. So they feel angry and guilty but the only thing they can afford to hate is themselves. Then they grow up and pass it on.'

How I envy the comforts of the all-sufficient creed. Marxists explain the world away with money, Freudians blame the home, environmentalists put it down to pesticides, with Calvinists it all comes back to sin. And me: what do I believe in?

She saw that she was losing me, and brought the subject round. 'You know I used to think that he adored you too. At first. You've always been a show-off and I thought: great, she's finally found someone who can love her for it. Better than being shacked up with a punisher. But then I started to notice. You were doing it to please him. This routine about how much he worshipped you, how clever you were, how much you made him laugh, the sex, the all-singing all-dancing Tracy Malleus act: it was a bloody good impersonation, but it wasn't you.'

'Like the picture—' I smiled, although it was a grim joke.

She gaped at me a moment, I suppose not understanding. Funny how confusion can almost look like fear.

'—the thing is, I can't get past feeling I deserved it. A touch of the Dorian Grays.'

Somehow the advantage had returned to me. She scratched at the webbed skin between thumb and forefinger, a nervous tic left over from childhood eczema, though Darwin permitted no psychosomatic complaints.

'Still . . .' I said, having nothing to add.

She reached towards her glass then, seeing that it was empty, opened her handbag. A black leather tote, the dayglo raffia bit the dust long ago.

'My turn,' I said, forestalling her.

'No.' From the depths of the bag she drew out a wad of traveller's cheques and placed them before me on the table. 'I don't want another drink.'

'What's that for?' Fifty-dollar denominations, at least on top of the pile.

She zipped up the bag. 'Let's call it rent.'

So Euan had told her.

I sat there, not looking at the money, weary with the knowledge that I had to turn it down.

'I'm just having a few temporary problems, Sam . . .'

'Yeah.' She retrieved the wad of cheques and, folding it in half, stuffed it into my shirt pocket. 'Just let us know when you expect the plague of locusts.'

The phone rang so I picked it up.

'Is that Sam?'

'Uh-huh,' I said. There doesn't have to be a reason.

'It's Bobby.'

'Oh hi.'

It seemed this hit the required note of enthusiasm.

'How you doin'?'

'Not bad. Yourself?'

'Oh I'm crackin'. Listen, I'm ringing about that swally. What're you doing tomorrow?'

'Nothing much.'

'D'you fancy meeting at the Salutation? You know it?'

Yes I knew it.

'Eight o'clock?'

'See you there.'

We don't sound that alike; he just didn't know her very well.

First I dialled one-four-seven-one, to get the last caller's number, then I rang Tommy, to check the date of the next meeting of the committee. They hadn't seen me for a couple of weeks, but he hid his surprise. Thursday, at the high school.

'Oh yeah, and you can do me a favour, Tommy.'

'Nae bother.'

'Bobby Croall asked me to give him a call about something but I think I've lost—'

Obligingly he recited the number I had just scribbled down.

I retrieved my short black skirt from the guddle on the floor of the spare bedroom and, while I was in there, tried on a skinny-rib button-through top. It fitted. Sam was over at Ally's, as she so often is these days.

TWENTY-TWO

I awoke at half-past eight this morning to the slurring grinding sickening sound of cars failing to start. The sky had lightened to a flat sheet whose whiteness was disgraced against the startling roofs, their nylon brilliance painful on the eye. The shipyard cranes, faint through the atmospheric blurring, pointed their accusing fingers at the sky. The view had that bogus air of the past always lent by snow, a Christmas card promise of fur muffs and sleigh rides and firelight's flickering glow, the flavour of other people's childhoods.

We live in an unknown landscape, revealed by its fresh cover: iron railings individually picked out, the bumpy profile of the bowling club wall exposed, along with that never-noticed outhouse. So much street furniture, freestanding cabinets of switchgear, telephone cables strung across the street like musical staves, traffic lights winking in futility. In the back court the washing posts balance precarious mob caps, each crosspeg coarsened by its blob of white; between them, a criss-crossed craziness of wire and washing line. When I left the house at lunchtime the streetlights still leached their orange stain onto the daylight, our urban world in crisis at Nature's sudden coup. Sparrows flustered to find purchase on the hedge, displacing minor avalanches. The black and white cats, our local vermin, gingerly padded the uneven ground. In the park a flock of pigeons settled, then rose in a swirling arc, disconcerted by their sinking purchase on the ground, their cold and inadvertent roosting. Even I could see the scene was beautiful. The spiky branches under their toothpaste layer, and children playing, with that clinging of white powder around the hem of knee-length coats, packing the snowballs tight with sodden wool. I used to love the safety of new-fallen snow, that shrinking of horizons.

Locking the door now, the stairhead has the comforting gloom of the airing cupboard or the tented sheet. The slab of snow on the skylight creaks. *Coronation Street*'s dirgelike theme leaks through each door as I descend the stair, louder from Mrs Devaney's than the rest. Outside, the sky is midnight blue and storybook-starred, a three-quarters moon with an encircling mist as if it had just exhaled a little patch of breath.

The Salutation Bar is a city institution, a pawky little pub with brandysnap panelling and a ship's cabin snugness that, together with the listing floors and stooping ceilings and the constant population of benignly swaying drunks, creates an unshakeable impression of life below deck. The landlady, Evelyn, saw the commercial possibilities twenty years ago and while her rivals were busy chasing out the old-timers she was spreading the fame of a hostelry where they could sit undisturbed over a wee hauf and hauf. With them came the folkies and the autodidacts and the odd famous name and suddenly the 'working men's bar' was booming. But Glasgow's a sceptical city and most claims to authenticity end up tainted with suspicion. The Sally has a reputation as a bit of a posers' palace, which means that Croall has shown a weakness, if only the instinct of gallantry in selecting a rendezvous where Sam would not feel too exposed.

The interior is as smoky as ever, but warm and bright with a wartime cheeriness that derives, at least in part, from Evelyn's cunning in lighting the place with shadeless sixty-watt bulbs (the smokers' nimbus cutting down on glare). The usual echt faces around me: old men grey-skinned from years of working with asbestos; shaggy-haired folkies spared the same fate by the closure of the yards; and a scattering of women, ham-handed, ring-throated, but still handsome through their pint-drinker's blush. A group of fashionably anorectic students have taken over the snug.

It's the sort of drinking shop where tables are less coveted than an elbow's purchase at the bar, so it's easy enough to find a seat with a view of the door. And here he comes: wearing the usual black jeans and leather jacket, but underneath, an aviator's button-pocket shirt. Open-necked, revealing a swatch of chest hair redder than his scalp, the sage green fabric bringing out the colour in his eyes. Men have their seduction-clothes just like women, their magical garments. 'He's on a promise,' as they say hereabouts. Unless it's a Yorkshire expression. With Sam around to confuse the issue, I'm no longer sure.

Immediately he sees me he understands. His intelligence is what makes our shared history unforgivable.

'Sam couldn't make it, she asked me to let you know. With her apologies.'

How I envy the licence of men, their freedom from obligation to smile.

'I'm sorry too.'

Despite my half-drunk glass, he could easily walk out, but he shrugs, less a physical gesture than a shift in mood. 'What are you drinking?'

'A half of Murphy's thanks.'

The pub is filling up quickly now. A couple of punters try to take his seat. They're lined-up three-deep around the bar, but he's back soon enough, which means he knows the staff. His face bears the residue of recent conversation. Could be he'll deposit the glass and drink his pint with another, but I've made a show of moving my coat from the chair opposite, which makes escape harder, although not impossible.

He takes the seat without shedding his jacket.

I nod my acknowledgement of the beer and ask, because someone has to say something, 'Have you known Sam long?'

'No.' He too is drinking stout, which leaves a thin spume on his upper lip, screening the freckles. 'Do you two share a house or something?'

'She's staying with me.' A short pause. 'You know she's my sister?'

He didn't. Though he only lets it show for a second, I can guess the permutations of paranoia being worked out in his head.

'Funny you didn't spot the resemblance.'

'She doesnae have your accent.'

'She's the lucky one.'

He takes a long pull on his pint. Another swallow like that and he'll be finished.

'Aye,' he says quietly.

I'm a good socialist. I vote SNP. I did my bit for the miners; argued against the Falklands War; passed on the chance to make a killing out of privatization, though I usually had five hundred going spare. Two decades after leaving college I still sit through earnest documentaries about post-Soviet politics, and even the odd Chinese film. I feel no inclination to swap these dutiful pleasures for country house weekends spent logging dead birds in a boyfriend's game book, or sitting around a Queen Anne table planning the charity ball. But still I'm the enemy.

Each time we've met I have been aware of his scrutiny. But tonight, when looking is acceptable, he's turned away from me, his chair angled to allow him to study the length of the room. The cheapjack lighting picks out the needle-points of brilliance in his hair, taking the sandstone texture from his freckled skin and lending it, against the flattering contrast of the shirt, a buttermilk glow. For all the tautness of his scalp, his face shows the beginnings of a middle-aged pouchiness, slack pockets semi-detaching from the fierce bone. His eyes crease with something akin to warmth and, looking up, I find a man approaching us, one of those ageless types with a toddler's chubbiness of figure and the inefficient gait of drunkenness, additionally hampered by chafing thighs.

'Bobby, my man – how's it going?'

Croall lifts his hand to catch the meaty paw thrust towards him in a graceless approximation of a black salute. 'Cuddie, ya fat bastard.'

This is a Croall I have not met before: cheery, convivial, a noisy kidder-on. Grinning, Cuddie's eyes come to rest on me and I know, as you do after thirty years of typecasting, that I've just made the sexual subplot.

'Don't believe a word he tells you, sweetheart.'

This is so hilariously appropriate, and inappropriate, that I almost smirk. Cuddie detects the suppression and thinks he's charmed me. As in a way he has. His shoulder-length frizz of ash-blond hair, that plaid zip-up blouson with the fake sheepskin collar and cuffs, the buckled loafers on his feet, are flagrantly out of time; his face blooms with the rustic flush of a Shakespearian rude mechanical. I like him because all this says safety, a reason he would surely be happy with, but others, on his behalf, might not.

Croall intervenes. 'Shut it. She's on the Calico Street Committee.'

I extend a hand. 'Tracy Malleus.'

He shakes it, and takes this as his cue to join us, planting his beer on the table. Shuffling along, I clear a nine-inch section of bench and he seats himself – 'Sorry, pal' – compacting the students at the next table into an intimacy they would not necessarily have chosen. His thigh seams my skirt with a comforting warmth.

'I hear you had a rammy at the Hangman's Monday night—'

Cuddie seems confident that the lack of reaction, like the aggression before it, is mischievously meant.

'—some guy walked in on his shoe leather and left the premises on his arse, I heard.'

Croall grins, an expression of his I've rarely seen head-on. 'Someone had to teach him some manners.'

Cuddie coughs up a guffaw, glancing slyly in my direction. In Glasgow, tales of fisticuffs are often a form of flirtation. 'I don't fancy your chances with the bandits taking over Calico Street, but.' He shakes his head fatalistically. 'What do you reckon, Tracy?'

I reckon I haven't been to a meeting since Croall savaged me in the Bounty Bar, but neither of us is about to bring that up. 'If we can stall the developers for long enough they may get sick of the aggravation, but that just leaves us vulnerable to the next shark who comes along.'

Croall's tone suggests contradiction, although I've said nothing with which he disagrees. 'There's no way that supermarket's getting built. We're gonnae win this one.'

Cuddie nods, though I'm not sure whether he's supportive, or simply cowed.

'Where do you stay, Cuddie?'

'Me?' He's flattered by my interest. 'Tobacco Street.' A bashful grin. 'With my maw.'

So he's one of the natives whose homeland we're trying to save. 'What would *you* like to see there?'

Now we have a chaperone, Croall is watching me again.

'Houses. Maybe a wee café, I could live with that.'

'What about a café in a museum?' I don't need to look to be aware of Croall's reaction. 'Somewhere your ma or you or anyone who wanted could get involved in making a record of the community.'

He shrugs politely. 'Aye, sounds good.'

Croall looms across the table. 'Does it? Do you think that's important when there's half your neighbours out of work and weans selling the *Big Issue* on every corner?'

270

For the first time it occurs to Cuddie that Croall and I are not after all in complete alignment. There is a definite lessening of pressure against my thigh. Coming to his rescue, I ask Croall a question long overdue.

'I've never heard you say what you'd put there instead.'

'You should have come to more meetings then.'

Cuddie gets to his feet. 'Same again?' he checks, not waiting for an answer, jarring the students' table as he strikes out for the bar.

Left alone, the fiction of conversation is abandoned. My nerve cracks first.

'It doesn't have to be either/or, you know – alive in the community or dead in the museum.'

'We don't need it. You don't, if you belong.'

The one argument I can never refute. I believe in what I do as a missionary believes in baptism, or a doctor cleaves to the saving of lives. That is, with liberal quantities of cynicism, but an overriding compulsion. Even if we doubt the integrity of our converts, and know that the disease temporarily banished will recur, or be supplanted by one more virulent, still there is no higher vocation. I believe in the saving grace of stories. Without shaping, experience does not exist. Ask me the meaning of life and I will answer you 'to give life meaning'. But some of you are lucky enough to be born into stories already half-told.

Cuddie is back with the drinks, turning sideways to ease his passage through the scrum, a sweetly pointless stratagem since his full-bellied profile is no more slender than his shape square-on. He has brought me my half of stout in a ladies' glass. Nodding back towards the bar, he tells us 'Liam McVay's in.'

Even Croall cranes his head for a look, such is the power of a footballing demigod. Turning back, his face is briefly in profile, and one of the naked bulbs cuts across his cornea, emptying the iris of colour, flooding it with light, a transparency like the dazzled surface of a swimming pool. His gaze completes its journey and for a split second there is a quickening between us.

Cuddie sets the glasses on the table and manoeuvres awkwardly back into his seat. The students, wise to him, hang on to their pints. 'I've been meaning to tell you: Frankie's had a special delivery in from Germany, good stuff, sustainable hardwood, fan-assisted ovens, split-level hobs, all the trimmings. I said you'd gie him a bell.'

Croall grimaces regretfully. 'Mandy's got ahold of some fucking catalogue, I'll have a word, but . . '

Cuddie is shocked. '*Retail*? You're talking some cash there, man.'

'No' much change out of ten grand.'

'For fuck's sake!'

This scene falls into a bracket of irony too rich for laughter. Croall the class warrior is shelling out a shop assistant's salary for a fitted kitchen, and he's not even embarrassed. But stranger than this is the glimpse of an ordinary life, a wife, a home, a kitchen, meals. Common humanity. Like the failing elasticity of his skin, it's a disturbing idea.

'I never knew you were married,' I say.

But now I remember: his wife was in hiding.

Both men turn to look at me. It's Cuddie who puts me straight. 'Mandy's his daughter.'

So our hard man's a doting daddy.

The silence is my fault. I ought to be enjoying my moment of social sabotage, but actually I feel a little scared.

'I'm still waiting to hear what you want for Calico Street.'

Croall stiffens, maybe thinking that I'm needling him. And maybe he'd be right.

'The same as I want for every working-class area in this city: folk living in the streets their fathers lived in, and knowing their weans will be living there after them. The jobs so they can work for a living, and that doesnae mean waiting on yuppies in West End wine bars, bringing them cheese on toast they'll pay an extra fiver for if it's down on the menu as *croque monsieur* . . .'

He pronounces the hated dish perfectly, I note.

'And how are you going to make it happen?'

And so we have the row that has been rising to the boil ever since we met, the row we've all been avoiding, all us of caught between the moral summit of socialist rhetoric and the muddy foothills of the world below. Some of my generation stopped reading the papers in order to keep the purity of their views, others got real and cashed in on those gas shares. Me, I've been treading water, waiting for a line I can believe in, paying the rent with a brand of personal politics I thought no one could decry. Until I met Croall. I know what Sam would say: that he objects to the business of other people's memories because deep down he has a stake in suppressing his own. And maybe she'd be right. But to pursue this line would make it personal, and I really don't want that. There is a safety in the predictability of his arguments: the hard-nosed class interests behind economic hand-wringing, the crushing of the unions through the erosion of the manufacturing base. Against a different opponent I could be making the same case. Instead I trot out global recession, technological transformation, economic regeneration via cultural investment. The usual suspects. But the terms of the debate have no bearing on the bitterness of the argument. This fight is about something else.

'I'm sick of hearing arseholes on thirty grand a year telling us that paying folk two pound an hour in the service sector's gonnae wipe out unemployment. You cannae build an economy on cappuccino and public relations, it doesnae work, no matter how many tourists you ship in. You need to make things, real things that sell for real money—'

Sooner or later I knew we'd get back to reality. All those meetings picking my way through the ideological minefield, when I knew what was eating him all along. Nothing to do with industrial socialism. He's grieving for a bygone age of unselfconscious certainty; the real, or at least less complicated, past.

'—we're no' even any good at that, all that have-a-nice-day shite—'

'You're trying to turn the clock back thirty years . . .'

'—smiling because they might gie you a bigger tip—'

'. . . I'd like nothing better . . .'

'—going home to a house with mushrooms growing out the walls—'

' . . . but it isn't going to happen.'

The silence is shocking after the clash of overlapping voices. One or two punters at the bar have turned their heads, though whether at the noise or at its ceasing I can't say. There's a warning slippage in my bowels. I notice the hard edge of his cheekbones under that loosening skin. His outline shimmers with a faint vibration, unless it is a tremor of my own.

I was brought up in a house without manners. We never bothered with the trappings of conventional politeness. Darwin farted at the dinner table with hilarious regularity, not just tolerating but teaching us the Anglo-Saxon word. Sam got detention for saying 'cunt' in Biology, and though I went to the head to back up her claim that she didn't know any better, with hindsight I'm not so sure. She made these slips with suspicious regularity. I learned early to skirt the more obvious traps, though still liable to fall foul of the small print, the do's and don'ts which Croall seems to hold so dear.

His voice is quiet, words formed of nothing but that sheared-metal rasp. 'Is that what they taught you at private school—?'

'I didn't go to . . .'

I'm doing it again.

'—if the Jocks don't shut up, talk over them?'

Who appoints the spokesmen for a community; what insane assurance, or insecurity, pushes them into the representative role? Not the joiners: they're easy to spot with their spear-carrier anonymity, their cheerful exemption from blame. It's the others that interest me, the flag-planters and crusaders, fearless champions of the underdog. How can they not see the oppressor in themselves? Unless they do see it, and they don't care, having found what we are all seeking: just cause for behaving badly, a funnel for all the unclaimed anger, an end that justifies the means. And now it occurs to me that maybe he doesn't hate the fact that I'm female or middle-class or English. Maybe what he hates is me.

Cuddie has been growing increasingly uneasy. Now he places his hands on the table to lever himself up. 'I'm going for a piss, man.'

The bar is full to capacity, the seated crushed elbow-to-elbow, the majority on their feet. Croall gets up, pulling back the table. I stand and lean into the press of bodies. Freed, Cuddie shuffles forward a few inches and Croall, gauging the route of least resistance, places a hand on my ribcage to shift me aside. Even in this crowd, every move bringing inadvertent contact with half a dozen strangers, his touch on my body feels shockingly intimate. In his eyes I see that he has registered the possibility but without any suggestion of desire.

Cuddie pushes past us in the direction of the toilets.

'Are you staying?' I ask, not certain what I mean.

His gaze drops to a point some eighteen inches below my eyeline. 'Naw.'

He turns and starts to shoulder his way through the cram of punters. To take advantage of the path cleared it is necessary to follow closely in his wake. Close enough to sniff the black-leather scent of his shoulders, and clip his heels, and lick the freckles on that sandstone neck. Just a thought. Reaching the door he turns and, lifting his arm in valediction, shouts

'Cuddie.'

Cuddie returns the knowing leer reserved for men who quit before closing time in the company of a woman. Behind him, someone has drawn a torpedo phallus and ballooning gonads on the stick-man symbol indicating the Gents.

Croall pushes at the door, admitting a blast of diesel-tinged air that strikes the pub-fug with Alpine freshness. Outside, it has grown colder. The inner-city pavements have been walked clean of snow, but the tarmac catches the streetlights' gleam with a thin skin of black ice. I take a step, and slither. Only a pint and a half, but on an empty stomach I'm less coordinated than I thought.

Croall stands at the crossroads where he can scan the length of all four streets. Cuddie's assumption hangs slack between us. An orange light appears in the distance. He swings around. 'Where do you stay?'

He may want to annihilate me, but as a woman it's axiomatic that I'll take the first cab.

The taxi slows a hundred yards down the road, does a U-turn and drives away from us.

'I'm West End. But you know that.' If he gets the reference he isn't telling. I could always mention my fancy friends in the Ubiquitous Chip, but why bother? His back view does not encourage conversation.

'Big man, are you away?'

Startled, we both turn. Cuddie has fought his way to the door. He gives me a louche smile.

Reluctantly Croall returns from the kerb edge. 'Aye. I'll see you at Mo's on Saturday.'

Living in Glasgow, you get to learn about drunks. About vicious

drunks and happy drunks and silly drunks. Cuddie is your sentimental drunk.

'I love you, man, you know that?'

Wisely, Croall remains just out of reach, so Cuddie takes a
swaying step towards me. 'He's brand-new, so he is.' His voice
quavers on the beery brink of tearfulness. 'Brand-new.'

Croall's eyes sweep the horizon, connecting briefly with mine.
Not quite complicity, but an understanding of sorts. I could of
course start walking, pick up a cab on the way, but then I'd never
know what happens next.

Moving surprisingly quickly, Cuddie folds me into an embrace.
Once, on a daytrip to Skegness with Bridget Somers' parents, I
won a giant panda. It was stuffed with woodshavings and creaked
unyieldingly in my arms.

'You look after him, sweetheart.' His hands are planted on my
buttocks, but in his current state, he cannot really be held responsible. I can taste the curry he ate last night. 'You're a lovely-lookin'
lassie.'

He releases me from the bear-hug, only to clasp me, one-handed,
around the waist. I submit, as we do with drunks, knowing it will
soon be over. But not soon enough. He herds me towards Croall
so that we form a little triangle, Cuddie full of liquid philanthropy,
Croall's gaze trained just above his head, and me.

Cuddie's fingers palpate my armpit. 'You don't want to waste
time fighting. You're beautiful thegither.'

I look up from Cuddie's stomach to find Croall's grey eyes empty
of everything but a residual loathing.

'Gie her a kiss, man.'

Close as we are, there is enough clear air between us to offer
him a satiric handshake. Taking it, Croall pulls me towards him. I
catch the whiff of garlic as his mouth parts. Those freckled lips.
The faint click of saliva. Opening my eyes, I meet his, staring,
vacant as glass. Over his shoulder comes the clunk of the bar door
swinging shut.

I do not know how long we have been kissing, except that it is too
long. The fingers which grabbed me in that handshake have moved
on to my left breast. His mouth is hard, his tongue bludgeoning

mine with a mechanical urgency reminiscent of the first clumsy kisses of adolescence. Those days when the possibility that the other might be having a good time could override the certainty that I myself was not. Always something like arousal in the way I was left after those Calico Street meetings, a hint of unfinished business in the tremble of my hands, but all that has gone from me now. Being drunk is not a reason, and I'm barely more than tipsy, senses blunted but under control. Mostly what I feel is awe at life's ability to spring such grotesque surprises; a poor substitute for passion but perhaps more common than we think. His breathing, too, is even, his groin jammed against my belly with, so far as I can tell, no evidence of excitement.

It must be freezing out here, but windless, I hardly feel the cold. No more does he, it seems. Another exit blocked. Here we stand, locked in passionless absurdity, a churning of saliva holding out no hope of sex. Which would amount to some sort of logical conclusion. I am kissing Bobby Croall, snogging on a street corner with a man I fervently dislike, and though my skull is full of broken thoughts, I could not tell you why. The smell of his skin is in my nostrils, a complex chemistry containing a faint sour note of long-dried sweat. His hands are no longer worrying at my flesh. He's pulling back. But it's not over. He walks me into a wynd between the bar and the empty shop next door, out of the safety of the street lighting, into the virgin snow, though a patch to the left of me is discoloured by urine, canine or human, I don't know. Where are you Drew? A couple of moulded plastic refuse bins block the view from the pavement. The droning of the pub's extractor fans would cover any scream. Prostitutes get screwed or murdered in such places. And he isn't up to sex.

My back scrapes the harled wall of the pub. It was a measured shove, no harder than the ruthlessness of lust. Not applicable in this case. My foothold not quite steady, some pile of rubbish covered by the snow. He's on firmer ground beneath me, his hands in my clothing, pulling at the buttons. My mouth gapes for his neck, not out of any desire to kiss him; this is a stronger reflex, the instinct to save face. At the touch of my lips his skin jumps, his mouth fixes mine with that gnawing kiss. His hands are moving to my skirt, and now I'm not so sure of his incapacity. I could stop this. For all

277

the similarities, it is not rape. All that holds me is embarrassment, the incrimination of the past ten minutes. His fingers fumble at my clitoris. I moan, obediently, though I feel no pleasure and understand that, whatever the conventional reading of his gesture, none was meant. The kissing stops as he turns his attention to some complicated manoeuvre down below. A kite-marked foil sachet flutters to the ground, releasing the smell of latex unalloyed by the usual pungencies. My fingers stretch out to help him but he pushes them away. A sliver of pain in my left hand as the breadknife scar opens up again. Somewhere, at a great distance, prick enters cunt. Again I moan, though all I feel is discomfort, a dull pressure on my bladder because I need to pee, and a chafing because I am not wet enough, and maybe something you could call despair. His thrusts have the zestless smack of determination, his upper lip taut against his teeth, grunting with effort. I try moving towards him, in sympathy with his rhythm, but he pushes me back against the wall, the harling sharp on my spine, his bony hips striking harder, propelling that rubbery core.

Eventually he stops. I try to convince myself that he has come, that this episode of lustless violence has ended in some technical satisfaction. But I know that it has not. There is the snap of rubber as he removes the condom, followed by the scratch of a fastening zip. From his lips comes a hissing sound as he jams his hands into his pockets and walks away.

TWENTY-THREE

How strange now seems our culture's obsession with the shortness of time. Having pared myself of the distractions of routine, I can count every second of the livelong day, and I tell you now that time is endless. Not that it drags: each minute fills its allotted span and moves on, making way for the next. A simple enough insight, I admit, but I never understood it until now. And, yes, there are associated revelations I could wish to have been spared. The terror of the night, that sluggish orange darkness. The primitive loss of safety that comes with the dimming sky, so that I yank the curtains shut at the first failing of the light, assuming it ever holds sway, for there are days when the view from my window is smeared with a greenish-grey filter even at noon; on these days the curtains remain closed, the fabric carefully positioned so no trace of the outside world can leak through. There was a time when the hues and ripples of the crepuscular sky were a pleasure, a fine-tuning on my mood, now I don't care. Not for the sky, or the weather, or the people passing beneath my window, or their formulaic patter yelled across the street. We are all alone, my neighbours as much as I, our lives like those advertising flyers slipped within the newspaper's fold: cosy images of domesticity, the models thickwaisted, the interiors chintzy-cheerful, the backdrop garden not too grand; an elaborately faked normality that cannot conceal the tawdriness of the goods.

Although latterly, I have to admit, my own life is much less bland. Once you abandon the struggle to be normal, almost nothing can be taken for granted. Walking to the corner shop yesterday a black bird flew into my face and, beating it off, I found the pavement rising to meet me, the shale in its concrete sharp as gemstones, my heavy coat tightening under the armpits, palms sweating, heart hammering. The sky flashed the oyster grey of fluorescent striplights, sending the chimneys toppling towards my head, triggering the thinned saliva of imminent nausea. I cried out and hunkered down on the brown-stained paving, pressing my fingers to my throat to stem the rising tide. Opening my eyes again, the tenement opposite stood photographically still, with an eerie clarity of window frame and pantile, such precision of pointing between the stonework, and everything fractionally further away.

Standing in the kitchen now I feel the floor tilt beneath me, the walls retreating, splaying outwards from the skirting. I sit and the furniture rearranges itself, abandoning its usual deference, each object's courtly placing around the central organizing principle that is me. Or I get up and open the door to check that the hallway is still there. Which it is. This time. Sounds are subject to distortion, or a clarity I never knew. I cannot bear the radio's presumptive chatter, nor yet the hiss of absence when I switch it off. Sometimes I clap to puncture it, or shout, only to hear my own echo absorbed by the membrane of silence. At some point I eat, although it pains me to disrupt my inactivity with such a non-event. And so I pass the time, or the time passes me. Sam comes and goes. Since I never knew what she did all day I cannot say whether her routine has changed in response to this change in mine, but I sense her desire to avoid me, her pity and her profound revulsion. At four I close the curtains and count the hours until it is time to retire, although I feel as little tiredness as I do hunger. Then I lie between the bedding, not swallowed by its comforting depths but flatly exposed, a strip of flesh between alien layers, the ham in a sandwich of stale bread. Eventually I sleep, and the ordeal begins, nightmares of tongue-thickening dehydration, simple narratives in which the sinister payload is taken by lights which flicker without human hand, or walking into the kitchen to find every gas-ring on the stove alight, or, last night, a treacle-spotting of blood on night-time snow. Then the scene changed and I was shopping at an African market stall, and given in change a handful of comma-shaped stones, elephant grey, worn smooth by centuries of handling. I stood helpless, fearful of being swindled, unable to buy even a loaf of bread. Then Sam was beside me, and lifted the currency from my hand.

One morning back in our first year together Drew's paper carried news of the passing of a former colleague. A good man compulsorily retired, 'after severe depression', the obituary said. Pushing levity too far, I queried whether this amounted to breach of contract, and now I remember what he said to me. 'Depression is the result of sin.'

The first phase is the missing. All those habits never to be repeated. Our flesh folding together in bed, our fingers interlocking as we drift into sleep, the scribbletalk I'd tease him for next morning, and sometimes answer in the night, a bit-player in his dreams. That ten-minute cup of coffee before work; me preparing the papaya, or the apricots, or some other current fad, him reading out snatches from the papers, friends namechecked on the arts page or caught up in the news, fresh absurdities to add to our lexicon of private jokes. What am I to do with all these euphemisms no one else will understand?

I was lucky really. Most lovers get to the stage of forgetting why they fell in love, but with Drew I could never relax to the point of taking things for granted. I still saw him as he was, the big man whose opinions flooded the country but who in the post office shrank from taking up too much space.

I know you'll laugh, but he experienced himself as a spoiled beauty, a fall from grace that rankled in his flesh. Who can say why he ate? Maybe his mother was milkless, or his father ignored him, or maybe Sam was right and it wasn't emotional hunger but a guilty inward-turning rage. Or maybe the greed was something instinctual: life force and death wish in one primal urge. Whatever it was, in my eyes it made him perfect. Which was exactly what he needed, and the last thing he could bear.

The second phase is the witchhunt, the obsessive retrieval of all those little things you could have, or shouldn't have, thought and said and done. If only I had made more of a fuss, claimed more of his time, not been so afraid to seem too demanding. If only I'd slept with him more, worried less about Sam and the paper-thin walls, spent more time *thinking* about sleeping with him, redirected a little of the erotic fascination I frittered on Ally MacNeill. Finally, exhausted by self-recrimination, you start to consider who else might be to blame.

Couples, like siblings, agree an apportioning of the spoils. I was the bold one, he the melancholic, I the joker, he the sensitive soul, Drew the principled provincial, convinced that I had lived more of life. He believed in the romance of London, bombsites and cream stucco: a black and white movie with the dome of St Paul's somehow always in shot. And since he had never found any of this on his occasional visits to the stressful gridlocked city, he felt cheated, shut out from the splendours of a capital which, for all his love of Edinburgh, he honoured in his heart. Honoured for its scale and glamour, and hated for making him feel small. And I never saw the parallels. While he was touched by the evidence of our affinities, these were always to be set against the premise of absolute difference. If Drew was Scotland for me, what could I be but England for him? A doomed match: the love of she with too little belonging for he who had too much.

Who held the power? I was never going to play this game again, but tell me how you avoid it? He was married, but by unspoken agreement his passion was the stronger. His passion or his commitment or maybe just his fear. However it worked, the balance was in my favour, which meant I was always subtly atoning, striving for a selflessness he felt no need to match.

The third phase is the anger. A corroding heat spreading outwards through the system only to concentrate and detonate again. *He did this*. And he didn't even know what he was doing, couldn't see it as the consequence of every other thing he's ever done; all the mush he took for granted; the blind equation of his needs with simple virtue; that hurt, surprised look when they were not met; so sure that love trumped everything. Or was it me who thought like that?

And suddenly, my mind has turned full circle, back to the one irrefutable fact of loss. I never dreamed that such intensity would peter out like this. No grand finale or tearful farewells, no last cataclysmic night of sex. Just the banality of absence, the slow-dawning realization that he isn't coming back. All the things we shared, all our tastes in common: oysters at Jaconelli's, and smoked salmon blinis at Sol's, and Lowell and Lochhead and Durcan (though best he liked to hear me read Donne), and dancing in the kitchen, and eating under the stars, the pleasure taken in each other's company, and in each other's arms. And now I see it all meant nothing. Standing up, our clinches were pure slapstick, me teetering on tiptoe, unbalanced when we kissed. But once in a while, against the odds, we'd find a sort of fit: my eyes closed like a purring cat, breasts snug into his chest, the straining neck and stiffened shoulders slotted into rest, his arms wrapped firm around me. Sometimes he'd kiss my forehead, or press his lips against my brow and heal me with his breath. And all the time it was nothing. Such elaborate lies we tell ourselves.

Sam asked me to meet her at a café next to the railway station, a place smelling of stewed tea and microwaved burgers and the clogged ketchup dispensers on the tables. And though it was a peculiar choice, its joylessness seemed more bearable than the mockery of emptied pleasures at an upmarket rendezvous.

She was late. The wall clock said 12.03. The woman behind the counter insisted I had to order lunch. I chose soup. Vegetable broth, according to the blackboard. It arrived in a twin-handled bowl, a semi-luminous paste tasting of long-forgotten Chinese takeaways. The first spoonful yanked me back to my days as an underage drinker, two halves of lager in the pub and afterwards, on the pavement, the egg foo yung, never tasty even then, but cheap enough, and spiced with the promise of another life. Since child-hood I have been chasing the exotic, and only now can I admit how thin its flavour really is. I didn't know they still boosted soup with monosodium glutamate, though the cotton wool square of unbuttered Mother's Pride had been updated by a baton of powdery baguette. A square meal for one pound twenty-five. Who would have thought that I would ever need to notice? That the dispiriting weight of silver in my purse would be all I had as ballast in the world? That I would sit in a café with dyed carnations on the tables, and a distorting tape of Beatles covers, and that for these brashly cheerful touches I would find myself so grateful?

She was dragging one case and nudging the other along with her knee. Slung across her back was a new holdall, containing the surplus acquired since she arrived.

'I'm going home,' she said.

'For how long?'

She shrugged the holdall onto the plastic bench on the other side of the melamine table, and started again.

'How are you?'

In case she could tell, I said 'I didn't sleep that well last night.'

'Excuse me madam I'm sorry to bother ye—' He was a jakey, one of the dapper ones: hair wet-combed back, the stain-stiffened jacket fully buttoned, birdshit frogging on one lapel. '—I wouldnae ask but I'm just out of the hospital and . . .'

Without looking, Sam delved into her bag, bringing out two packets of Camel, one unbroken, along with a disposable lighter. 'There you go.'

He took a single from the opened pack and lit it carefully, his thumb fumbling the flint. She pushed both packets a couple of inches closer. 'Take them all.'

He looked stunned for a moment, as did I, then I realized he was composing his acceptance speech.

'They were gonnae take my leg off. I'm sixty-three, a gentleman of the road. I told them they could get to . . .'

Sam closed her bag. 'No offence pal, but piss off.'

But the monologue continued. Giving is the easy part, it's the emotional transaction we find tricky. I used to hear them out, the whole hard-luck story, however long it took, whether I believed them or not. Which did no one any favours, wasting everyone's time, upping the ante; as often as not I'd have to shrug off the arm around the shoulder, the napalm breath bearing in for a kiss. Lately I feel less inclination to sympathy, having so little for myself. He sat down heavily on the seat alongside Sam and grabbed her hand, wresting it palm-upwards and tracing its contours with a horny fingernail.

'You've a lucky hand, see your lifeline . . .'

She tried to pull away but he was surprisingly tenacious. I knew that look of Sam's. When we fought as children I only held her off, she was the one with the passion to hurt. I leaned across and laid my hand on the tabletop. 'What does mine say?'

For a moment he looked insulted, then he let Sam go. His fingers were smooth, as if coated in plastic not grime.

Head bent, revealing furrows of white scalp beneath the greasy strands of hair, he studied my palm, the longitudinal lines my fingers have recently acquired, a small callous I'd never noticed before, that drumlin scar left by playground grit. His swollen purple lips were working, although no sound could be heard. When he looked up

I saw that crystals of yellow matter had collected on his lashes. He dropped my hand and walked away, leaving the cigarettes on the table.

Sam sniggered. 'That bad eh?'

'Probably.' There was something different about her today but I couldn't work out what it was. 'So how are you?'

She raised an eyebrow. 'Blooming.'

There was an empty table the far side of the café. 'Can we sit over there?' she asked. 'Stinks here.'

I got her luggage across the room while she bought us two mugs of tea. Seated again, she frowned, wrinkling her nose. 'Not much better here.'

We were seated beneath a window and in the natural light she didn't look well. Her hair hung limp though not dirty, mascara had clogged in the corners of her eyes. I felt a stirring of superiority. Not vanity, just the cleanliness of despair.

'How long will you be away?'

She seemed to be doing some sort of calculation but in the end she didn't specify a date, saying only 'When I do come back I won't be imposing on you.'

And I thought there was nothing else that could be taken from me.

'I've never said that.'

Her mouth showed sour amusement. 'Whatever you were thinking.'

I let this pass, though it wasn't true, or at least, not unambiguously.

'Will you be staying with Janet?'

I was waiting for her to say that they were not in touch, that I was all she had.

She shrugged. 'I'm not a good houseguest. I'll find a flat. Olleren-shaw Road maybe.' Her lips had a sardonic twist. 'It'd be sort of appropriate, having a baby there.'

I laughed but it sounded like grief. Sam handed me a napkin from the stainless steel dispenser on the table. The shiny paper scratched me even as it disintegrated. She passed me a couple more. I knew it sounded hysterical, those cackling sobs.

'Is it Ally's?'

'Who else have I slept with?'

I winced at her annoyance. 'I'm sorry.' I screwed up the sodden napkins and dumped them in the ashtray. 'And you're going to keep it?'

Focusing again, I saw her take a napkin for herself. 'Yeah,' she breathed. 'Might as well.'

I was packing when he walked in. His hair had grown long enough to end in splaying strands, and the navy sweater sat oddly on his torso as if he had recently become too small for his own skin. He looked terrible, but not, I suppose, as terrible as me. I expected some protest over my departure, or at least an expression of concern, but if anything he seemed relieved.

'A change of scene will do you good. There's nothing to keep you here now.'

'Not even you.'

He looked less guilty than I expected.

To save him the embarrassment of asking I reached under the bed and found the carrier bag of clothing, the shirts and socks and underwear. I hadn't put them through the wash. He nodded, not looking at me, as he took possession.

'If there's anything else I'll post it on.'

I returned to my packing, picked seven days' worth of underwear out of the drawer, passing over the black lace in favour of the waffle-cotton thermals, then taking the sexy stuff too. Drew noticed, as he was meant to, but did not comment. Two pairs of jeans, the Icelandic sweater, my green cashmere, a couple of shirts. With access to a launderette, that would see me through indefinitely. My hand hovered over the brass cigarette box with its cache of spare buttons, safety-pins, Indian bangles, the rope-chain that leaves a mouldy circle around the neck. I left the amethyst earrings he gave me two birthdays ago, but on an impulse took the crystal.

I zipped up the bag and swung it on to the floor, clearing the bed.

'Is Sam around?' he asked, perhaps nervous of my intentions.

'Sam's gone back to Yorkshire. She's having a baby.'

For a moment he didn't know how to respond. Then he put one hand on my shoulder, a doctor's gesture across the diagnostic desk, safe from misconstruction.

'That must be hard.'

And it is, but I discovered in that moment that he had lost the right to say such things to me.

'For her it will be. The father already has one set of responsibilities.'

His interest quickened. 'Is she eligible for social security?'

Nothing brings a couple closer than discussing the misfortunes of third parties.

'Maybe she'll make him support her in return for not telling his wife.'

'I wouldn't have thought a labourer's wage would stretch that far.'

So he knew. There was an obvious question to be asked but all I said was 'Shall I strip the bed?'

He looked at me uncomprehendingly.

'You're welcome to use the place if you want somewhere you can be on your own.'

'No. No thanks. It's kind of you.'

Since when had kindness come into it?

He coughed lightly, nodding in the direction of the window. 'I wasn't sure you were in, I couldn't see the car.'

'I took it back.'

'Ah. I didn't know you could do that.'

'You can if you're prepared to flush two grand down the toilet.'

Once upon a time this would have made him laugh. Black humour was our speciality.

'What's the matter, Drew?'

'Nothing. Why?'

And then I got an inkling of it. Not guilt towards me, nor desire for another, nor a sudden late flowering of conscience over his wife.

'Oh, I don't know, maybe because Tuesday night to Saturday lunchtime this used to be your home, and for four weeks I haven't seen you.'

'You made your choice.' He had dropped the formal manner but I had yet to identify the tone that he was using in its place. 'You knew what you were doing—'

I suppressed the impulse to contradict him because there was a sliver of accuracy in his analysis. I had chosen Sam. In so far as I had not acceded to his wishes and kicked her out.

'—I didn't pick it up for nothing as it happens, but I never dreamed you'd see it as a capital asset. I tried telling myself you didn't understand what it meant, but you understood fine . . .'

The picture. He was talking about the picture.

'For God's sake Drew.'

It was the reference to the Almighty that did it, releasing that quiet crisp delivery that was as close as he ever came to anger. 'If you must swear, make it by something you believe in.'

I squinted a little, trying to take this in, and he misread my look for provocation.

'Tell me Tracy, what are we doing together? You with your novelty fundamentalist, me with my sin-on-the-side? Oh yes, you're my *partner*. Partner in what, exactly? We don't share our beliefs, we don't even share our news, little details like your getting the sack. When it comes down to it we fuck each other, and we haven't done too much of that since your sister came to stay. It was good, when we were fucking' he was getting a taste for the word 'the most fun I'd had in I don't know how many years. But like everything it seems, it has its price.'

So I was right. I always knew that Drew did not consider me an atheist, that he regarded my irreligion as an affectation that would pass. And for my part, it was hardly in my interests to challenge his belief. Was I not the one who had restored his faith? But now that same faith, the hallmark of my value, had led him to the logical conclusion: I made things matter again, and because it mattered he had to give me up.

'I may not be having a very good time, Drew, but I really don't think it's divine retribution.'

He stared at me for a second and then laughed. I simpered in a reflex of sympathy and relief, at which point he stopped laughing.

'Do you really think . . .' He faltered, as if the distance between us were too vast to be bridged by words. Then he decided to say it anyway. 'Can you not see? Your job, the car, the credit cards, all that money you owe, your sister and her bastard child . . . the way that everything you touch turns to dust. That's not the hand of God, Tracy—'

His voice dropped to a whisper, and at last I saw that what had kept him away was fear.

'—it's a curse.'

TWENTY-FOUR

I never went back, I couldn't see the purpose. I remained too familiar with the landscape for there to be any necessity of seeing it again. It may have changed, but it is not for the changes that the middle-aged return to their childhood haunts; they seek the forgotten constants, the missing stave of a railing, the post box on the corner, the uneven kerbstone to trip them back in time, and these I have never forgotten.

But now here I am, working through the checklist of the prodigal daughter, even wondering at the cliché'd smallness of it all. The ranks of slate-roofed terraces marching down the hillside look like models of themselves, the pavements arrestingly narrow, only room for one abreast. Even the horizon seems cosy, reachable. And I know it's me that got big, not the city that got small, although of course it has seen changes. Once families were fed by coal and textiles, and every child in my class had a score of second cousins, whole dynasties clustered in neighbouring streets. Now it's a student boom-town, every two-bit tech renamed a university, every local business scavenging from the harvest of degrees, and the voices behind the counter jar with the flatness of the Midlands, the nasal whine of the commuter-belt South-East. From the top of Mosscliffe Road I can still pick out the churches, the Wesleyan Reform where Lorraine Carter went to Fire Fairies, the Methodist Chapel where the Girls Brigade would meet, St George's steeple for the Brownies, but the butchers and bakers and greengrocers and ironmongers between them have gone, supplanted by craft shops and silversmiths and greetings card sellers. As a child I learned this landscape off by heart, in penance for the crime of unbelonging, and now the blandness of gentrification has made it a place where even people like me can feel at home.

For eight days I heard nothing from her, then she phoned to say that after viewing every slum in bedsitland she had finally found a watertight house. A six-month let, though she'd be gone before then.

'I thought you were looking for somewhere to see you through the birth.'

'No, I'm having it in Scotland.'

A Scottish baby. Growing into a Scottish child, to say *aye* and *naw* and *amn't I?* and *hoose*. To sing 'Three Craws Sittin' on a Wall' in a sweetly piping voice. To bring home all the playground rhymes that my neighbours in Glasgow have long forgotten but I never knew to be able to forget. I accepted long ago that I can never become Scottish, not by marriage, not by assimilation, certainly not in recognition of my services to social history, but breeders enjoy special status. By having a Scottish child, my mid-Atlantic sister had acquired rights of belonging that I never would.

'So are you managing?'

'Yeah.' She was suspicious of the question. 'Got off scot-free on the morning sickness, but I could murder for a fag. And I'm bored out of my box in the evenings.'

'Are you?' I wasn't sure if she was asking.

'Not much point sitting in the pub drinking orange juice all night, and there's damn-all else to do. It's a shame you don't fancy a visit.'

'You make it sound unmissable.'

'So are you coming?'

Sam had hurt me. Me, or my vanity, or my cosy sisterly assumptions, and I knew that, whatever the charms of Ally MacNeill, hurting me had been half the point. But such malice is a sort of claim, in the absence of any other, and I had been packed and waiting since the day after she left.

The house turned out to be in Marsland Road, a few doors down from where Donna Weston used to live. I went to her eighth birthday party, and her brother kissed me during Postman's Knock and was known as my boyfriend for the next twelve months at school, so I had a fair idea how it would look before I crossed the threshold: two-up, two-down, woodchip and shagpile-furnished, with a ground-floor bathroom tacked draughtily on the back. I used to love these redbrick terraces, so easy to draw as a child, the two windows, the door, the chimney. When I was four they introduced a bylaw which cut out the curly smoke. Of course, Sam's child will draw tenements.

It didn't take long to fall into our new routine of labour-intensive housewifery, each day filled with tasks geared to the once-simple business of keeping the body alive. Mornings I swim at the municipal pond while she lies in late, and the rest of the day we go shopping, lengthy expeditions to gather foods rich in B-vitamins and folic acid, browsing in the wholefood store for constipation-busting prunes, raiding the charity shops for baby clothes. I think of it as a marking of territory, reclaiming the streets we once walked to school, staking our claim to the new community of the consumer. And sometimes these forays yield a connection more real.

'Jacqui Palmer just served me in Boots.' Sam was bright-eyed with pleasure to be bringing back such news.

'Are you sure?'

We were outside the bakers' across the road from Highcroft Junior. Break time. Football in the boys' yard. Over the other side of the gritstone building the girls would be impersonating horses or skipping or playing out minor rituals of cruelty. Jacqui Palmer had moved a hundred yards in twenty-nine years.

'She looks exactly the same. Go and say hello.'

'What for?'

'Because you used to know her.'

'She won't recognize me, and even if she does I can't remember who she thinks I am.'

Amazing how much there is to do each day. The house is demanding as a child, what with pound coins to be amassed for the electricity, and fifty-pence pieces for the gas. Even taking a bath requires forward planning: the priming of the meter, the lighting of the fearsome barrel boiler above the taps, match after struck match extinguished at the porthole, until with an eyebrow-singeing *whoomph* it roars into blue-flamed life bringing its scalding needle-run of water. Twenty minutes to achieve a depth of four inches, then perversely it runs cold. And so afternoon becomes evening, and evening leads to bed, and sometimes we watch television in-between, though mostly as the pretext for some game. We play all the time, now: towel-flicking tig, cold spaghetti down the collar, water-squirting, pillow-fighting, hide-the-shoe, contests that have us helpless, writhing, bent double almost in pain, struggling for breath to overcome our whooping laughter. I used to laugh with Drew of course, but never quite like this, and with good reason. There is a childlike wildness to these games, but something of violence in them too, some suddenly transgressable taboo adding an edge to our hilarity. I can almost hear other children's mothers warning that it will end in tears.

Tuesday's task was a recceing trip to the secondhand pram shop. We could have caught the bus, but there was no point in saving superfluous time, and so we walked across town, along backstreets of terraces soot-darkened to scab-brown. No garden outside, no hall within, just a brick's width of wall between pavement and lounge. Spartan dwellings, it seems to me now, though I used to find beauty in their uniformity, the family snaps framed by each window: mothers ironing while singing to the radio, babies playing on the rug, dads yelling at the telly on Saturday afternoons; tiny lives I pitied and envied in the same breath.

Sam bought a baby buggy, which struck me as profligate, a waste of further purposeful excursions. Nautically striped with a clear plastic rainhood, it compacted into an unwieldy clump for the purpose of getting on buses, though we of course were returning on foot. I grasped it under my arm, then tried shouldering it like a musket. Sam raised her eyes at the saleswoman.

'No, dummy.' She restored the concertinaed metal to its original shape. 'Why do you think it's got wheels?'

And so I pushed an empty buggy through the long streets of my childhood and learned for the first time how it felt to have a perfect right to be there. It hadn't occurred to me that this prop would be a magnet to all glances, a mark of womanly continuity, a reassuring symbol in restless times. Then they discovered it was empty.

On Empire Street the men from the council were stringing coloured lights between the lampposts, a recent development. It used to be they only decorated the main street in town. Christmas was never much of a festival when I was a child. We sang carols in school, made a card for 'Mummy and Daddy', a stained-glass window in cartridge paper and coloured tissue, which we dumped in a litter bin at the end of Mosscliffe Road. For us the twenty-fifth was just another day at home. Glad when it was all over. For years now I've thought I'd rather draw the curtains, unplug the television and finish a good book, but the effort of framing a plausible alibi was never worth it, and the humiliation of the truth would have been too much.

'Now that's what I call seasonal.'

I followed Sam's gaze to the Ninety-nine Pence Store and saw a man in a Santa hat serenading a blow-up plastic doll. When we were children a tramp was lucky, like a fox in the timberyard or a shooting star. The nutters were all locked up in the asylums. Or in our annex. Now the shouters are in the suburbs; the alkies stack their empties under the wool shop window; an old boy in unmatching trainers sings 'Nancy With the Laughing Face' to a mail-order masturbation aid and is, of course, ignored. Darwin would have brought him home and found some way to reach him.

Sam's face assumed the openness she reserved for strangers. 'Hiya Lucy.'

I turned. She was a good decade younger than us and looked like a dancer, wearing those fetching layers that dancers sometimes wear. She bulged her eyes in the direction of the empty buggy and then at me. 'Lost something?'

I saw Sam snicker and felt a twinge of exclusion. 'Just getting some practice in before the big day.'

Again she spoke to Sam. 'You didn't tell me you had a nanny lined up.'

'Better than that. This is my sister, our big genetic hope. The sprog's getting my ears, his nose, and everything else from Auntie Tracy. She'll be her daddy's darling from day one, so I can piss off out to the pub in the evenings.'

I found it hard to assess the proportions of malice and simple sociable nonsense in this. Certainly Lucy saw nothing amiss.

'You wait: you'll be the gooiest mother out.'

Sam addressed her just-emerging stomach in a mock-threatening growl. 'You better hope so, kid.'

I waited until we were out of earshot to ask.

'No one you'd be interested in.'

'How do you know?'

She screwed up her face to indicate how tiresome she found this conversation.

'I can't think of a story about her.'

'You mean she's boring?'

'No, I mean she's normal.'

We decided not to take the same route home, and instead turned left through Winmoor, slum-cleared in the Sixties to make way for the high-rise estates which now, in their turn, have been brick-clad and decapitated and given party-hat pitched roofs, none of which alters their brutalist essence. Between the blocks stretch vast plains of corporation turf. Intermittent attempts at landscape gardening have long since been abandoned; even the sturdy sapling-props are gone, felled by the kids or the punishing wind that agitates such spaces. Sam turned her collar up and fingered the tip of her running nose, and there on the paved concrete pathway I found the flavour of my adolescence, a frontier-town emptiness I had always taken for teenage melancholy, not some quality inherent in the place. As if I were watching from a viewpoint high above, the estate spread out beneath me, and crossing it two specks of life, with no sound but the buffeting of the wind and the scratchy whirr of the pushchair wheels.

'Where are you going?'

She was turning up Fallow Street where the Victorian terraces start again. 'I thought we'd cut through the cemetery.'

'Why?'

'Because it's quicker.'

Between Fallow Street and the cemetery lay Ollerenshaw Road.

I have no memories of our mother, which is strange, since I was nearly four when Sam was born. It did not seem odd that we only had one parent, though I was aware of it as a source of my father's notoriety long before I grasped his fame on the wider stage. Old ladies would stop us on the street and coo and tickle and shake their heads and say it was a shame, but he was wonderful to shoulder the burden. And later, when I went to school, and learned that each of my classmates possessed a matching set of parents, I harboured this knowledge as a guilty secret, something he must never know I knew. Only once did he speak of her in my hearing, in all probability not knowing I was there. He was on the telephone. I heard the word 'Shirley', and after a spell of listening he said

'Up the Ollerenshaw Road never to be seen again.'

And that was how she gained an address in our imaginations. A fortuitous misunderstanding: we atheists too need our hallowed ground. I rationed our trips there because it was frightening and maybe I was worried that the fear might fade, leaving us with nothing but the old dull absence. More often Ollerenshaw featured in our games, an underworld we had to brave before we reached the prize. And in this way it became exciting, a mythical landscape of terror and hope, something our two-parented classmates didn't have.

And now we were back. Not as dark a street as I remembered, but menacing in its unbrokenness, no verges or trees or window-boxes and, this time of the day, few cars; just a narrow corridor stretching to infinity, with a side stop at the grave. The carriageway needed surfacing, stone setts showing through the patches where the asphalt had worn thin, though the houses looked well tended, the paintwork fresh, the frilly curtains within ten years of the fashion. The red telephone kiosk was still there, its glass protected by the same metal crosshatching, in token of a violence we never saw.

Sam seemed breathless, perhaps from keeping pace with my stride. 'You know I tried to trace her when I was in America.'

'You never told me.'

I felt obscurely usurped.

She shrugged. 'It didn't come to anything. I would have been better off trying to sort things out with my father—'

'He's my father, too,' I reminded her.

She turned to look at me. 'No, your father was someone else.'

We had reached the entrance to the cemetery, where the stone-flagged pavement ended; the paths within had been relaid in job creation scheme gravel. She gestured at the buggy. 'Want me to take a turn?'

I lifted the front wheels over the threshold of the neo-classical gatehouse. 'No, I'm fine. At least here there's no one to suspect me of matricide.'

'Infanticide,' she corrected, and it was a couple of seconds before I made the connection and we both could laugh.

'Can you believe this?' Nailed to the gatehouse was a board recommending that visitors take special note of the Egyptian obelisks, Greek columns, and Gothic chest tombs. 'It's a bloody tourist attraction.'

The cemetery was off-limits in our childhood, each entrance blocked with a makeshift barrier of wooden staves and coathanger wire. We always used the Sorrel Road gate, though I don't remember how we got over the barrier, just the breath-shortening terror I felt between those Ionic columns, and the altered state within. I gave Jane Worthington her first joint on top of the Greaves family crypt, the two of us cackling with self-suggested hilarity and trespasser's nerves. And now my den of iniquity is a community resource. The commoners' graves by the canalside have been cleared and carpet-turfed for the benefit of dogwalkers and frisbee-throwers. Only the statuary survives in its artfully planted sylvan grove, leaving those solid Yorkshire industrialists as fortunate in death as they were privileged in life.

This time of year there is no such thing as daylight. The sky is lagged with dun-tinted cloud, which puts a smoked-glass filter on the vision; the rain falls in drops with a steely core of ice. Nature is hardened, bedded in for a long tough haul, its palette so drab that the withered leaves on the beech hedge that day seemed a vibrant, gaudy brown. The grass between the graves was an obstinate, lifeless shade; the darker green of the ferns and ivy like so much painted wood. I looked up to find the twigs blurring on the bare charcoal branches, their shed leaves decomposing in the treacly mulch below. Sam left the path and, reaching into her bag, took out the kitchen scissors, returning with an armful of holly and a bushy branch-end of conifered spruce.

'What's that for?' I couldn't help the note of accusation in my voice.

'Don't worry, it's nothing to do with Christmas.'

'It looks pretty Christmassy to me.'

'Yeah well, I thought we'd put it up for the meal next Tuesday.'

My stomach lurched, though it was unlikely that Ally had been invited.

'What meal?'

As if I should already know, she said 'Our pagan feast. To celebrate the solstice.'

We had climbed the curving path up to the derelict chapel of rest and the west side of the city lay stretched before us. The Georgian snuff mill was still there, with its stately single chimney stalk and scenic miniature dam, but the curtains at its windows betrayed a residential conversion. To our right was what town planners used to call the twilight zone, jerrybuilt housing threading between small factories, Dickensian firetraps with astragalled windows and cakewalk floorboards and twisting stairways of pie-slice steps. All gone now. Those parallel lines of terraces still spilled down from Milledges, but the foreground was filled with window-less hangars of anaemic brick and corrugated steel: DIY superstores, computer stationers, cash-and-carry hypermarkets, warehouses of white goods. Sam said softly, bitterly

'So how does it feel to be home?'

Whatever her claims of cutting loose, she's carried it with her all this time. All across America. What she can't bear is that her gritty northern romanticism is as selective as my anecdotes, as bogus as her accent. Or my own.

From behind the clouds came the buzz of an aeroplane. Once anything in the sky was an event, calling for shaded eyes and pointing fingers, now we're on the flightpath.

Not sure whether I was trying to comfort her, I said 'We left, Sam. We can't expect it to have stayed the same.'

'So I have unreasonable expectations: people do. Unless they're you.' Less combatively, she added 'We both know why I came back. But he's not here now, any more than he was then.'

'He was there for you to argue with every dinnertime of your adolescence.'

'And you didn't like that?'

'That isn't the issue. You can't say he was starving you of attention.'

'I was an audience. Which was all he needed, remember? Grab-bing the megaphone on demonstrations. Making sure the waiters knew who he was. You were there that night in Paris. He had to be centre stage.'

'You're the performer.'

Her eyebrows rose and fell, acknowledging the animus in this observation. 'Have you never heard of intimate revenge?'

'No.'

She used to do this all the time. Constructing theories and giving them names and then making you feel like a moron when you didn't know what she meant.

'Parents pass on their version of the world to their children and, if they're lucky, give them the space to do their own redrafting. The others find independence through defiance, by committing the most destructive act they can imagine within the system they've been taught. Which means that even in revolt they're still compliant. You see?'

'Not really.'

She nodded, as if my obtuseness were only to be expected. 'OK, let's talk about us. What was his line on child development? That children allowed to grow up without interference would be healthy, happy, loving, free spirits. And it goes without saying that that was the way we were brought up. We were his walking proof. Well, I fucking hated him, so either his theory was bollocks or he was the last person qualified to put it into practice—'

She had the grace to join me in my laughter.

'Let me finish.' She took a deep, performer's breath. 'There are two sisters, right? And the elder one is pretty and clever and has a vocabulary of six million words, and charms the knickers – well, that'll come later – charms the *socks* off anyone within a hundred-mile radius, and she always does exactly what Daddy wants her to, she's a real Daddy's girl, and later in life she's going to go looking for men who ring those same bells for her, which is going to be a problem, but that's twenty years down the road and in the meantime things are pretty good for her. And then there's the younger sister. She looks at her options and she thinks: what's the point? Big sis has already cornered the market in children of nature, and anyway, she doesn't feel like doing what Daddy says all the time. She's not a terrible person, she's just trying to do what kids do, push out the boundaries a little, work out who she is. So how does Daddy react? He's not interested. The message is coming over loud and clear: do what I tell you to do, be what I want you to be – or fuck off. And she's a brave little kid but she's not Joan of Arc, you know. She can't fight it all by herself, and big sister isn't into joining forces, so she goes for a compromise: when there are strangers in the house or they're out in public she says "Yes Daddy", "No Daddy", she smiles for those photographers from the Sunday supplements, she's cute as pie on stage at those three-day conferences, and she's not doing anyone any favours, because, you know, she likes her share of the limelight, she likes people saying that she's a smart little sweetie and they could just take her home. She's not allergic to that at all. *But*, she can only do it because when they're alone, just the family, she fights him. It's not like she hates him. Not yet anyway. She's just trying to get a little space to breathe. But he fights back, never mind this non-interfering bullshit, he wants to flatten this kid, and she's scared, sometimes she's really scared, but she *is* a smart little kid, and she picks up on something. She knows he shouldn't be getting this angry with a four-year-old, she knows something's not right, and even though she's too young to put it into words, in her gut she knows that *he's* the kid, *he's* the needy one, she's got to love him, because he needs the proof that he's OK. And that's what the newspaper articles are about, and the television panels, and the conferences, and the lecture tours, and all the one-night stands, that's the point of the smalltown personality cult: to prove that he's OK. And why would he need all this proof? Because deep down he thinks he isn't. And she thinks: *Well fuck you, pal*. I'll play to an audience every night, if that's what it takes. I'll get the applause, I'll prove I'm OK, *and I'll still fucking hate you.*'

I was silent for a long time, as audiences tend to be after a bravura performance, even one rehearsed for the Americans.

She pulled a self-conscious smile. 'And you don't have to say it, Tracy: I know you don't remember it that way.'

But how do I remember it? Hardly at all. When she produces these epic accounts of the past, I cannot contradict or challenge her on detail, I cannot say she's wrong. In the face of her certainty my own history becomes a blank, an absence that confounds me. Even the fragments of experience I can retrieve, the names of classmates and shopkeepers, the running over of a neighbour's dog, the first creature we ever knew that died, these things just seem banal, so much superfluous detail in a world drowning in facts. I do fifty lengths each morning in the pool where I first learned to swim, and though others might hold this memory in awe, it is as remote from me as the baptism of a stranger. My life is happening in another room and I can hear it through the wall, but none too clearly. Even my dreams seem unremarkable, although I have not seen him for fourteen years, and it must be more than twice that since I rubbed my nose into the shoulder of his yellow nubuck jerkin, or felt his fingers span my ribcage as I was lifted astride the Norton. And now at night, teeth-cleaned, face-creamed, feet burning on the hot water bottle at the bottom of the bed, I feel again the joy of rising weightless between those plate-palmed hands, smelling the hot air off the engine and the tang of that salty hide, the wind stinging my hair, trees and traffic lights streaming by, my cheek pressed to his monolithic back, hard against the certainty of something bigger in the world.

For weeks she has been living here, barely a mile away, and yet it was only today that she said, as if it had just occurred to her,
'What do you say we take a stroll down Wathcote Road?'
Strange how knowing our destination transforms the streets we have been walking every day. A returnee's self-consciousness is upon me, so I see these front gardens through memory's filter, with the ornamental chimney-pots spilling lobelia and phlox, and the air teeming with thistledown and tense summer light, the wood pigeons cooing like a stuck record, a dolls' picnic set out on the earth-streaked rug, and maybe a lolly from the van if someone's mother thinks you've been good. Summer reverts to archetype in memory, like everything past. In reality, it is another of those narrow grey winter days characteristic of this place, the rain held off by a wedge of cloud like a swaddled iron bar. The eye may be hungry, but there is nothing to see; the houses have learned the bourgeois trick of privacy, the gardens reduced to a bed of stunted twigs and a mudded square of lawn. A thread of second cars along the kerbside, hatchbacks and urban jeeps, none more than three years old. We brought them here, all those years ago, we started the changes that were to make this neighbourhood a motor trader's dream. A community house full of Crazies may not be the most conventional

fillip to property prices, but Darwin gave Wathcote Road its bohemian cachet, and things escalated from there. When I was twelve the garden furniture started appearing, and fabric blinds in primary colours, and Volkswagen camper vans and 2CVs with candystripe sunroofs, and you could get *Private Eye* in the local newsagents, and rye bread in the bakers' and I knew without asking it was all on account of us, though if they hoped to become his friends they were to be sorely disappointed. Darwin was a psychiatric revolutionary but his salons were highly selective; deep down he was a bit of a snob.

And now we turn the corner, and Sam turns to catch my eye, and the street mocks us with empty familiarity. I recognize the rock garden at number twenty-three, but cannot retrieve the face of the woman who tended it. Number forty-six is now a shiatsu massage clinic, number fifty-seven a rainbow-painted nursery and crèche. Our end-terrace with its L-shaped extension has been turned into a granny farm. 'Heartlands' the signs says, in navy blue and gold.

The man at the door looks too young to be the owner. I lean sideways to see behind him, into the hall, which is designed for first impressions with a claw-footed occasional table and a sheaf of pensioner-friendly magazines. The cornicing and picture rail that Darwin ripped out have, bizarrely, been replaced. From the new ceiling rose dangles a brass and candle-bulb chandelier. Hunting prints hang in pairs on the Bourbon lily wallpaper.

'Can I help you?'

Apparently not. This is a residential home, its occupants are not animals at the zoo, and he is very busy.

'It's just that we were born here.' A lie, but he can't tell. 'Simon Malleus was our father.'

No flicker of recognition in those dull brown eyes. 'I'm sorry,' he says, unregretfully shutting the door.

Sam sniffs extravagantly. 'Lavender polish,' she says loudly. 'They use it to cover the smell of piss.'

We slouch back down the path, coming to terms with the bathos, but slowly. One last look before stepping on to the pavement. A figure is waving to us from next door's front window. Stepping over the flowerbed, I'm in her garden. She pushes open the sash and stoops to direct her voice through the four-inch gap.

'What day is it, love?'

Perhaps I only imagine Sam's snigger behind me.

'Friday,' I say, though not wholly sure myself.

And then the clock strikes noon and, turning, I see from Sam's face that she has heard it too: 'Oranges and Lemons', followed by the relentless twelve-stroke chime, and so I say, though she was ancient even then,

'Mrs Woodhouse? It's the Malleus girls, Tracy and Samantha.'

The face turns suspicious and the window closes. Foolish in the middle of the lawn, I retreat to the path; Sam waits on the public side of the garden gate.

The front door opens and on the threshold stands one of those shrink-resistant old ladies: thick-ankled, barrel-hipped, that solid bosom still riding high. Her hair, which should be white by now, is dyed the colour of dead leaves.

'Get yourselves in for a cup of tea,' she says, and the years fall away.

She puts us in the front room, with the mantelpiece photographs of her grandchildren in South Africa and the red vinyl three-piece suite with the white plastic piping and the swirling cosmos carpet in burgundy and brown. Before, she always took us to the kitchen.

Sam swivels her eyes towards the sideboard with its cardboard Christmas crib. Three wise men, two shepherds, the donkey, Mary and Joseph, the manger left empty until midnight on the twenty-fourth.

'Here we are then.' She brings the tray through, clinking with best china, a doily on the biscuit plate. The hands gripping the tray handles are so liverspotted as to seem uniformly brown, three gold rings on her wedding finger holding down the folding skin. There is a pale yellow stain on her polyester skirt. Back then she wore a pinny, a sleeveless overall in gaudy cotton with a couple of utilitarian frills.

'Sugar, duck?'

The tea is weak and greyish, the cups not altogether clean. There is a cat hair on Sam's chocolate digestive which, surreptitiously, she flicks away.

'It's all changed round here,' I say, recklessly depleting my stock of smalltalk. She nods and sips her tea and I realize she still doesn't know who we are. 'The last time I saw you, you gave me a five-pound note for passing my A-levels.'

Irritation flits across Sam's features.

'I went off to university, but Sam was still around, with our dad, Simon. You know: he ran the Two-Way House next door.'

Her face sours with old annoyance. 'A right show-off he was, always ont' telly, up on his high horse, telling us where we were going wrong. As if he knew owt about it. All those loonies next door, howling and carrying on day and night, and those poor little girls in the middle of it all.'

Beside me, I feel Sam's pulse quicken. She leans forward. 'That's us Mrs Woodhouse: Tracy and Samantha.'

Funny how she still gives me priority.

'*Millie and Mollie*,' the old lady says confusingly, her voice warm with recognition. 'Tom used to come back from his work and if that biscuit tin were empty there were hell to pay. He'd say: "You've been feeding that Millie and Mollie again"—'

I don't remember the husband, just a blue budgie that banged against its mirror in demented fashion and once every six months, for no apparent reason, suddenly started to talk. Joey, I think.

'—his wife had taken off. I don't blame her, but she should never have left those children. Tom used to say I were interfering, but there were summat funny about whole set-up. All his fancy women. And that Paki he had staying, moaning and droning and all sorts at four o'clock in the morning, and his stinking bonfires blowing ower my washing.'

Poor old Ravi, stirring up the wrath of the houseproud. I haven't thought of him in years.

Sam is prompting again, that second-sister deference forgotten. 'Do you remember you made me a nurse's doll, when I was poorly? You gave it to Tracy in case he wouldn't let me keep it. And he didn't when he found out.'

But Mrs W isn't listening. 'I wanted to ring the council, get the authorities involved; it weren't right, all three of them running round with no clothes on day and night, and all them funny folk in th'house.'

I admit I'm surprised by this accumulation of bile. Despite the small subversion of that smuggled rag doll, I always assumed Mrs

Woodhouse belonged to the club of adoring old ladies. Though their enthusiasm dwindled after the *Post* ran that story about the shit-eating.

'Tracy were his favourite,' she says unexpectedly. Sam suddenly seems larger, as if the cells in her body were expanding with vindication. 'He were always at her. It were a shame.'

'At her?'

Of course I'm aware of Sam's suspicions about sexual abuse.

'Never let her settle to owt. Calling her in, then he'd lose interest, she'd be trotting round after him like a little dog. I said to Tom "That child dun't know if she's coming or going".' She seems to have forgotten that we were those children, a mistake easily made. I too see them as separate, strangers with unguessable thoughts. 'Showing her off, making her jump through hoops. Always on about how she were special, before she were old enough to know what she were herself.'

I remember in the school hall watching other children playing. I was always aware that I was different. Better, I suppose, but worse too. Children are meant to be innocent. Darwin built a whole career on this belief. But I never was. I always knew more than I was supposed to and I always hid it to keep him happy, to keep his system intact, so he need never realize that he had spawned a freak. Which meant I was not merely knowing but deceitful as well, corrupted to the core. And still he found it in his heart to love me. It seemed like the only shred of hope I had.

'She used to watch his face, poor little lass, trying to work out what he wanted before he had to ask.'

Sam's expression clouds with sadness, a shadow in her eyes that almost makes me want to cry, and in the sharing of her sorrow I find the child that she is grieving for is me.

'Sam was the one who had a hard time.'

The old lady smiles. 'Oh she had a temper on her, a right little madam. You could hear her screaming her head off. I told Tom: one day that child's going to come back and kill him.'

Sam returns her teacup to its saucer. 'And here I am,' she says lightly.

'Any more tea?' Mrs Woodhouse lifts the teapot lid. 'I can make a fresh pot. And there's a cake that wants eating. Darren bought it me in Marks and Spencer. Thirty bob for a fruit cake . . . I cun't believe it when I saw price.'

The seam of indignation is exhausted, and with it her memories. She wants to talk of her own daughters and their successful lives, the holiday in the Lake District with her great-grandchildren last year. And after all, we owe her this much. Mentally, I allot her twenty minutes by the mantelpiece clock, but after five Sam looks at her watch and says we'll have to go. Mrs W looks suspicious again, and shows us overpolitely to the door, but when Sam is safely on the path she takes my fingers in her huge housewife's hands, as women on the street will grasp a baby supported in another's arms.

'Now I think on, I've got summat o' yours upstairs.'

This strikes me as unlikely, since I never owned anything in the first place.

'Wait on.' She turns and starts to climb the stairs.

'Don't go to any trouble Mrs Woodhouse . . .'

Back on the path, Sam is restless. '*What's going on?*'

I mime comic bewilderment, then feel guilty, irrationally anxious that the old lady might have seen. Minutes pass. Sam kicks at one of the ceramic markers bordering the blighted rosebed.

'I knew I had it somewhere.'

She's back and handing me an old grey paper bag. Inside is a pale pink crocheted cot blanket with a matching satin border, harsher to the touch than you'd want for a baby, but with that faint marzipan fragrance that we associate with new skin.

'He gave it us when our Susan were expecting Paul. You used to suck it: the ribbon were all wet in one corner. He said it were time you broke habit and he didn't want it in th'house. Paul's a policeman down at Westgate now: inspector.'

It smells of someone else's baby, its fibres bobbled by another's wash, but once it was mine, so like a good girl I say

'Thankyou.'

'She's right about the nudity,' Sam says abruptly, now we're back at Marsland Road, having completed the fifteen-minute walk in silence.

'It did no harm.'

'You think not—?'

I can always tell when she's spoiling for a fight.

'—you know, I used to get off with boys all the time, but I was just going through the motions, I never *wanted* them.'

I note the coincidence, but sexual late-starters are not so very unusual.

'I told myself all that nakedness had desexualized the body for me.' She gives a fatalistic shrug at her own stupidity. 'Maybe Mrs W should have blown the whistle, tipped off the social services.'

Very little of what Sam says actually ruffles me; she is, after all, entitled to her view. But even she knows this is garbage.

'When did it happen, then? You're the one who claims total recall.'

'There's a school of thought in survivor-work that if you suspect it might have happened but can't remember, it probably did.'

'Oh well, in that case . . .'

'OK, there's no evidence.' Underneath we're still as children, the truth still secondary to the struggle. 'No, you're right: why interfere with us sexually when he could interfere with us psychologically, emotionally and intellectually? If there was a door marked "private" he kicked it down. That's why I had no sex life till I was in my twenties: I couldn't take the risk.'

It didn't take oral history work or the indignant bluster of the abuser lobby to teach me about false memory syndrome. We constantly construct our lives anew, our memories remade at every using, an improvisational narrative with absolute licence to invent. So of course I know what Sam is doing. I've seen reminiscers reduce their lives to the simplicity of a fairytale, chasing the defining moment of mistreatment, looking to undo the wicked stepmother's curse. As artists I salute them, envy the focus of their vision, but that doesn't make them right.

'It's one woman's perspective, you know, Sam. That's all. One old woman. It doesn't even fit with what you thought before we left here this morning, but because it puts extra offences on the chargesheet you're prepared to take it on board. We never had a mother, for fuck's sake. Would we have been better off without him, in a children's home, or sent to boarding school? Sure, it wasn't a normal childhood, it wasn't a particularly *stable* childhood.

So we grew up with a sense that nothing was guaranteed. Would you have been happier as a bank teller, singing with the light operatic society, hating your husband and your family and your semi in the suburbs because you didn't have the guts to go professional? If you're looking for something to blame, I can give you twenty suspects right now, things that should have been different, and I could find you twenty people who'd had the same setback and come out of it just fine.'

'And do you think we're fine?'

'Yeah . . . I don't know . . . yeah I do. As far as anyone ever . . . it's not a question you can answer, how does anybody know?'

'By trusting their feelings.'

Good old Sam: still singing the same old song. So I take a minute to see if I can't summon an echo of her passion in the graveyard, wondering if I can find that little girl who charmed the neighbours and melted hearts and pealed with laughter just to please her daddy.

'Well?' she asks eventually, and I suppose I have to answer

'And what if I don't feel anything?'

'What do you think you're doing?' Sam's bare feet appear at the top of the stairs, attracted by the draught from the open door.

'We're out of milk.'

'We don't need it.' Slowly the rest of her comes into view. 'Only dark foods today, remember?'

'I'm not drinking tea without—'

She is swathed in a black velvet evening dress cut for a woman three times her size, the hemline flouncing crazily, the bunching fabric gathered around her midriff with a steer-head buckle belt.

'—what the hell are you wearing?'

She rolls her eyes in the manner of a child mimicking adult mannerisms. 'You're asking *me*?'

It has turned cold these last two nights, and though the house has gas fires in kitchen and living room, there is no heat upstairs. I went to bed last night wrapped in men's flannel pyjamas Sam brought back from a jumble sale, a purple cardigan holed conspicuously in both elbows, and a couple of pairs of socks. Over this ensemble is my all-concealing coat, which I'm in the process of buttoning. Unless they're looking at my ankles, they'll never be able to tell.

'Yeah, right.'

Outside the rattling windows the rain is horizontal, a front of water driving up the street, breaking against the purply-gleaming brick where the terrace turns the corner. The sky is dark as those choking days before the city became a smokeless zone. Strange that I should recall the smog and not the mother who led me through it. Sam crosses the room and closes the curtains.

'You're not going out in that.'

And so shopping is postponed because we have to dress the house, decking the cocoa-coloured tiles of the mantel with spruce and holly, embroidering the banister rail and the fringing on the standard lamp with tendrils of ivy. Then the meters must be fed so we can start preparing dinner, absorbed in the wordless companionship of garlic and steam, combining spinach and kalamata olives and anchovy fillets and soyu into an improvised pottage to be eaten with angelhair pasta purpled with octopus ink. Like those summer days of 'cooking' at Melanie Fisher's, adding measured quantities of brake fluid to a flowerpot of fermenting rose petals and black earth. Stirring with a stick. Since today is a special occasion, Sam is brewing an evilly bubbling punch to her own unwritten recipe, working from the ominous ingredients of Bull's Blood, Dubonnet, and dark rum.

She fishes a tarnished soup spoon from the pick-and-mix cutlery drawer and, scooping it into the saucepan, offers me a taste. I grimace, only slightly shamming.

'Tastes of the dentist's.'

'Maybe I overdid the cloves.' This time she brings the spoon to her own lips. 'More rum, I think.'

I grab the bottle and hold it out of reach. 'Any more alcohol and you're drinking it on your own.'

She raises her hands in surrender, then swiftly adds a slug of red wine.

'Why am I supposed to be so grateful for being a singer?'

We do this: picking up conversations started days before; it's surprisingly easy when you don't talk to anyone else.

'Because it's your gift.'

'Is that so?'

'I'm not saying you didn't have to work at it—'

Funny how long it can take to get round to the obvious question.

'—why did you give up?'

She does the small shrug of teenage nihilism. 'Why carry on?'

'Most people would give their eye-teeth to do something creative . . .'

'And what was it I created exactly?' She frowns as if to grasp a concept just out of reach. 'Apart from a few hard-ons in the front row, that is? I mean, you do that all the time, but you don't call it creative – or perhaps you do. Was that why the old boys told you their secrets?'

'You gave people pleasure, is that so bad?'

'And what did I get out of it? Yeah, they thought I was sexy, or spiritual, or dirty, or doomed, or whatever the hell they needed me to be. That didn't mean I was. I've had enough of living my life from the outside in. From now on I don't please anyone but me.'

So selfish she wouldn't even feed their fantasies on stage. So selfish, or so scared of subjection to another's will.

'And how are you going to manage that?'

She meets my eye. 'When I find out I'll let you know.'

She pours the punch into a tartan Thermos flask. 'We're ready – take this up.'

'You what?'

Automatically we chorus 'Don't say what, say pardon' and Sam explains

'We're eating in bed.'

Fresh from the high-ceilinged apartments of a tenement city, this house struck me as claustrophobically small, yet spending so much time here I find that space is redefined, taking on the infinities of childhood. I could get lost in the scuff-marks on the door of the white-painted Victorian wardrobe, spend a week counting each woodchip between window and gable wall. In such a setting it is possible to share a bed without intrusive closeness. And it is very cold outside.

She hands me the tray and, kicking off her shoes, slips under the covers fully dressed. Joining her, my feet hit a clump of cold debris at the bottom of the mattress, a book, a teaspoon, a small transistor radio. She spends hours in here, while I'm downstairs with a news-paper, staring at the stains on the kitchen wall.

She steadies the tumblers so that I can pour the punch. Just the steam off it has me reeling.

'Are you sure it's all right, in your condition?'

I lie awake each morning, waiting for the sound of retching, wondering if the silence means she might have made a mistake. There are plenty of explanations for that gently convex belly: the decision not to hold it in, an extra seven pounds, a conception to match the phantoms in her head.

'In my condition, I reckon I can do anything I like.'

'Is there a toast?'

As if it should be obvious, she says

'To the darkest hour.'

'I don't want to drink to that.'

'Yeah you do. After this it starts lightening up.'

She's been letting herself go just lately, a shit-stripe of brown roots growing in to the nylon straw, though the texture seems thicker now, which they say is some sort of sign. 'You ought to go back to your natural colour, you know.'

She stares at me disbelievingly, a mannerism I've grown used to, but still don't particulariy like. 'I don't give a fuck about my *hair*, Tracy. If you're stuck for conversation why don't we discuss your problems? Whatever it is you've been brooding over ever since you arrived.'

A rubbish bag shifting beneath my shoes, my back against the jagged wall, that kite-marked sachet fluttering down to earth.

I wind a lock of angelhair around my fork. 'Your dinner's getting cold.'

'I'll reheat it.' She lays her plate down on her lap. 'Is it Darwin?'

'He's your obsession.'

She does not deny it. 'I read the biography, you know.' A half-smile, acknowledging the implications. 'Last July.'

Just before she came to stay.

'I thought it would matter, which is why I never read it all those years. Then it turns out it's just journalism. Silly bitch had a crush on him. You can tell she was running some fantasy about what would have happened if they'd met.'

I read the book on publication, it must be ten years ago. I don't even recall the author's name. She sent me a free copy, since I cooperated with her research. All I retain of it now is that I was described as his 'grave-eyed daughter' twice. Sloppy editing, I suppose.

'That crap she wrote about the night he screwed Tony Airey's girlfriend—'

'Didn't she have a Union Jack plastic mac . . .?'

'—apparently it was a tactic to bring out the rage Airey had repressed towards his father.' She laughs nastily.

'That was how Tony saw it.'

She treats me to another stare. 'So?'

So Darwin had a healer's instinct for the weaknesses of others. He could meet them for the first time and tell them what was wrong, and then he'd pull out the thorn and they would follow him anywhere. And sometimes, if the bleeding stopped, he'd apply a little compassionate pressure to get it started again. He certainly got results. I lost count of all the waifs and strays who looked on him as dad, all the women who wanted to marry him, and of course the gays. So, yes, he probably abused his charisma, but they willingly embraced the abuse. And, who knows, maybe it did help Tony to a sort of peace.

'We've all slept with someone we shouldn't.'

'Yeah, but we don't all tell the cuckolds we're doing it for their own good – *Shit.*'

With a little metallic 'clink' both light bulbs have blown. The room is black and steeped in an eerie silence that belatedly I identify as the absence of the meter's low whirring.

'I'll go.'

'Don't bother. It's not a fuse.'

The postage stamp skylight is not its usual lurid ginger, but the wholesome shade of the countryside at night. The streetlamps are out, no television mumble through the wall. A power cut.

Invisibly I raise my glass. 'To the darkest hour.'

She coughs a little as the fire-water goes down the wrong way. The bed lists as she leans over and places something on the carpet.

'Not hungry?'

'Don't want to poison the little bastard before he sees the light.

Assuming any of us get to see it again.' A slithering sound as she fusses with the covers. 'If you had one prematurely you could still get yours out first.'

It may only be whimsy, but this is not a game I care to play.

'Why not?' Her innocent voice. Which of course is anything but.

'Because I'm too old now.'

'Not quite.'

'And I don't think Drew has fatherhood in mind.'

'Have you asked him?'

'I'd have to see him first.'

'Yeah.' Some movement beside me. 'I'm not counting any chickens either, if it comes to that. We could pool resources, save on childcare: two can't be that much more work than one.'

After weeks of responsible abstinence, she's drunk on two glasses of punch.

'Whom do you suggest I get to impregnate me?'

'I'm sure Ally could be persuaded.'

She had to take him from me, but now she wants to share. In fantasy at least.

The mattress pitches as she leans across me, reaching for the flask on the bedside table. A softness against my arm which might be her black velvet breast. 'You could have had him, you just made it a little too obvious that you saw him as beefcake. The boy wants to be loved for his mind too.'

They have discussed me. A thought shaming and gratifying in equal parts.

'And you're the woman to do it?'

The sudden aromatic warmth of the punch, an unsteady trickling as she pours it out.

'That's the question. Whatever happens I can't see us shacking up together. Which means there's an opening for you. And room for a little one.' She settles back onto her side of the bed, shuffling over as our legs accidentally touch. 'What do you say?'

Some alteration in the air tells me she is smiling, so she may not be expecting my answer. And although it's not a new thought, said out loud it surprises me too.

'I don't want to create another human being to go through life feeling like me.'

I know I told her I felt nothing, but always there were the shadow feelings it was necessary to deny. That I wasn't blithe enough, or wild enough, or sufficiently spontaneous; that to wake up less than lovable was to forfeit my conditional visa as a foreigner on this earth. So yes, for what it's worth, I think that Sam is probably right: Darwin needed us to be perfect – or, at least, to be admired. Which is not to say I share her lust to blame. His life's work was a dyke built against we will never know what terrors, a barrier between his children and the world. He was doing it for us. It's just that he had no sense of us as other than himself. Sam forced him to see the distinction and paid a terrible price – although, as it turns out, not quite so terrible as mine. Strange that I should live under the premise of absolute freedom, when my very desires were determined by his wishes. *You're on your own*, he said, though his will, like DNA, was threaded through my being. *Please yourself*, he said, but I had no self to please. Maybe that was my intimate revenge.

Sam's smile, if that's what it was, has gone. 'And you still think I'm unnaturally obsessed with him?'

'No, I think it's perfectly natural, given that you missed the end.'

There is such a thing as dying time, agonizingly slower than those hours filled with the restless ephemera of living, and yet, considering its emptiness, insultingly swift. Sitting by the bedside, clothes tightening in the heat, studying the tripwire cables, the dented Anglepoise above the bed, the poly bag of glucose fluid eking into the arm. After so many years of not looking, the uncooked-sausage fingers and citrus-peel nose came as a shock, yet at the neck where the stroke had forced his posture into heedless discomfort, the flesh was smooth and mottled like a baby's, with a faint purple crazing under the translucent greyish white. All the visitors in the ward were prone to squeamishness, that sudden imperative to taste fresh air, then, ten minutes later, the shamefaced slinking back. We all had nausea and spots before the eyes. Nothing so simple as the sight of blood or the sniff of antiseptic, just the proximity of damage.

'You should have brought me home.'

'*What?*' Even after so many months of cohabitation, I'm still surprised when the curtain is drawn back. I am the enemy, cheating her of some birthright, blocking out her light. I suppose she always felt that way. 'I told you he was dying.'

'You said he was unconscious, that it wasn't worth coming back.'

Did I? It was fourteen years ago. I don't remember. Maybe I was trying to keep his death for myself. Maybe I thought she was seeking permission to stay away. Whatever, it's too late now, so to change the subject I ask

'What's the score with Ally?'

My voice still sounds unnatural when I say his name.

'We're "being adult" about it, taking some time to think it over. He said he'd have to spend Christmas up there, break it to Mhari in person. Basically, he wants to road-test her again before making up his mind, and I'm supposed to stay in Glasgow, waiting by the phone.'

The room smells of evergreen and stale sleepy air, with an undertone from that heap of dirty washing in the corner. Sam pregnant has a stronger scent, as if a swab from the valley between her breasts were lodged within my gullet. As a teenager I always knew when she was menstruating, her sticky hormones swamped the house.

After the pause her voice is almost tender. 'He's a nice enough guy, pretty much the nicest. Not that that's saying much. I can't expect anything better to come along – the sex is tops – but it's like I'm covered in polythene all the time. I can see him opening up like people are supposed to when they're in love, and all I feel is resentful. Like I'm helping him to be himself at the expense of me being me. And we all know what that reminds me of—'

Actually I don't, but let's hope that she means Darwin.

'—anyway, I sort of lost interest once I'd bested you.'

If I concentrate I can smell the cool breath of the fir cones on the carpet.

'Is that a joke?'

'Depends whether you think it's funny.'

'I don't find anything very funny at the moment.'

'Tell me about it,' she slurs in an American drawl.

Sam always regarded my happiness as pathological, a nervy teetering high, a fizzing cocktail of hormones set off by imminent crisis. And now it looks as if she was right.

315

She says, this time without ironic intonation, 'What's wrong, Trace?'

The very question I would like answered. So many possibilities, none of them good, so many imponderables and teasing loose ends. Euan told me that my sacking was political, and its one-off nature seems to bear that out, but none of the officers hated me enough and the councillors barely knew me. Unless it was a lobbying job. Croall must have the contacts. Bella Monzie: who can say, I never bought Drew's line that she didn't know. The tabloids are full of vengeful wives cutting the crotch out of the old man's suits, pouring vintage cellars down the drain. She could be crazy enough to have trashed the car. Or maybe it's nothing personal. Workers lose their jobs, drivers hit and run, every day. But the painting was not an accident.

'Drew reckons I've been cursed—'

'Does he?' I can sense that killer eyebrow springing to attention.

'—and I think he might be right.'

Her voice is distant, wary. 'And why would you think that?'

I have never been the superstitious type. In a world of cheesecloth hippies comparing auras, unhappy housewives who have to hope There's More To Life Than This, presidents who won't talk arms control on a Tuesday because the holder of the other global arsenal is a Gemini, I've been a freakish minority. When Drew sprang his melodramatic announcement I felt nothing but embarrassment. But I'm running out of explanations.

'What about good old bad luck?'

'I've never believed in it—'

Not in luck, nor in fate, nor in any external pattern, though I might have been better adjusted if I had. Deluded but more sane. The bedsprings creak beneath me, Sam is rocking gently on the mattress.

'—I don't know. I don't know anything any more except—'

Sam stops rocking.

So what if my first words were lisping wit, and I was weaned on the honey of praise, and Hockney painted me in blue gingham shorts on a yellow canvas deckchair?

'—that I'm empty inside.'

All at once we're blinking in the light. Downstairs the meter starts to whirr. Next door's television surges into song.

Sam's right hand is inside her velvet neckline, holding one soft breast. 'I'm sorry,' she says. 'I'm sorry, I'm sorry, I'm sorry.'

'Are you sure you want to go?'

It's a little late to ask me with the minicab at the door, but I appreciate the gesture.

'I need to get back, sort things out.'

She proffers a Tesco's carrier. 'I made you sandwiches. There's a couple of cans in there as well. Seeing as it's New Year's Eve.'

'They'll have drunk the buffet dry by Darlington.'

'That's what I thought.' She can't wait to see me go, get the parting over and done with. 'Will you be OK on your own?'

I was about to ask her the same question.

Outside, the cab-driver hoots his horn. I lean over her shoulder so that we can exchange cheek-warmth without touching.

'All right, love?' says the driver, slipping into gear. I wind down the window. Sam waves awkwardly from the door.

'Give Drew my worst,' she calls.

In the midst of unbelief I have found a secret superstition. This is the first time I have failed to leave the past behind; the first new self that has not let go the attachments of the old; the first lover to resist relegation to the status of dinner party anecdote. I could say I miss the sex, but that's not quite true, although I think about it all the time. The end of an *affaire*, like the beginning, is marked by erotic fascination.

I might be washing up, or cooking, or just sitting down and marking time, and suddenly I'm reliving our second night. That delicious thing he did that seemed to be a papery insect scuttling across my skin, the wonderful distraction at my lower lips, fingers probing the aperture, tongue bewildering my inner thigh with asymmetrical sensation. I feel these caresses now as if he were naked beside me, although I was never to experience them again. By the time I was relaxed with him the patterns had been laid down, a wordless negotiation had established what we did and did not do. And now I mourn that insect, some foreign body from a desert place, a cicada perhaps, or the strange animated herb Sam once found in a plate of vegetable dansak. What happened to it? Did he get lazy? Had I put him off? Or was it that novelty wrought a miracle of sorts, a twenty-four-hour bloom, and it was my nerve ends, not his technique, which subsequently blunted?

I've tried all the usual ways of dealing with unwanted passion. Psychology, finding fault, dismissing the one fixed point of reference in a universe of lies. But then I picture his face, the bruised shadows of his eyesockets, that narrow ridge of nose, his acreage of smooth cheek furrowed in smile, or that sudden spasm of expectorated laughter. Drew gave me the most vivid brush with happiness that I have ever known. And whatever the flaws in the life we wove together, however clearly its unravelling was foretold, no matter how dysfunctional our reasons, although the mind is quick to defile its purest memories and scar tissue soon numbs the open sore, I know he loved me. And I will not let that go.

TWENTY-FIVE

I had packed with the usual hope. That once the key had turned inside the lock and the door blundered open over the molehill of mail, I would find the life within quite changed during my absence. Or my own self altered, the life within outgrown. And of course I was disappointed. If also relieved. My first task was to halt the mortgage repossession. I found Sam's travellers' cheques on the marble washstand, a rectangular hole in the furring of dust. Next came the need to reestablish friendships. Four seemed a viable number. And this paid unexpected dividends, when Euan took me to a Burns supper at the home of Alex the freelance proof-reader, who put in a word with Sandy the desk editor, who agreed to give me a trial. The following three weeks were spent correcting misplaced punctuation, then a fortnight's fact-checking on a pensioners' handbook, and a month after that I progressed to freelance editing (more comma-chasing, but at a higher rate of pay). It's not much but it meets the interest payments and connects me, however tenuously, to the world. And one happy byproduct of the single state is that it costs me less to live. A pot of ratatouille can last me the whole week. Once a fortnight the budget stretches to a bottle of Soave and a packet of chocolate gingers, and with my municipal season ticket I still manage a regular swim. I approach each day with a convalescer's carefulness, reading a little, and watching the news, and learning to live without the companionship of my own reflection. (Gina took the mirrors. I know she'll dine out on the story, but it seemed the surest way.) I am experimenting with ordinary pleasures: the first scent of earth after the winter, the crocuses on the sliproad embankment like garish litter in the unmown grass, a palely flaccid salmon steak marked down at the supermarket. Yesterday was a good drying day.

There is a terrible safety in expecting the worst. Sometimes it seems a definition of depression, sometimes it seems like peace. No clamouring hopes. No wondering when it will all come right. Or is it that by taking my nasty medicine like a good girl, I am trying to empty the bottle? It takes time getting used to the idea that I am the sucker most deceived by my own lies. That it is possible to be unhappy and at the same time to live tolerably well. An unsettling perspective on my past. I have spent forty years filling my life with brightly coloured incident, trying to be normal, and now I wonder if I was not driven by the suspicion that others might be as empty as myself. I read once that the clinically depressed have a highly realistic outlook on the world; it is the happy sane who stand deluded. Newspaper paradox. A cheap intellectual model, if much in my thoughts of late. By expecting the worst, I protect myself against it. By believing my life is without structure or meaning, I bed down in the comforting context of crisis. Even this style of swithering monologue, with its hint of mental unravelling, has a reassuring familiarity. In reminiscence we encounter it all the time. My special talent was for cutting through the knot so that the fraying dropped away.

I know I have been cursed. But I cannot yet believe it.

I never thought about the fact that Drew had swallowed all this stuff. The religion had its uses, but the spooks I just blocked out. It was how I avoided classing him as insane. And now I find myself choosing between rival paths to the asylum. Conspiracy, persecution complex, suspecting all my friends, searching the crowd for the fixated stranger, the nutter with a grudge. I once took a call from an abusive restaurateur. A table had been ordered in my name, the diners served with lobster and Chablis, then they did a runner. It could have been a joke. We inhabit an ambiguous universe.

Something has stripped me of my life, my small belonging, leaving me with nothing but the memory of my love. That unworldly good only I can shed, by painting his faith as childish shadows, his passion mawkish sentiment, the self-regarding attachment of a fool. It was not enough that he should feel, for feelings change or go in disguise, or are snagged in a depressing skein of reasons, resemblances, emotional puns, the insulting tribute of transference. I needed starker proof, mystic communion, the smoke of eternal fire. I might not believe what he believed but I could believe in his belief and, through that, find it in my heart to love. Sometimes, some things matter. Once you comprehend the enormity of the blessing, it is not hard to accept the possibility of a curse.

For three months I steered clear of Ricky and Yolande, purposely avoiding the places I thought they'd go. And then, knowing the dangers, I drifted along to the Day of Action, losing myself in the crowd around the trade union floats and the African drummers and the kathakali dancers and the Amnesty cage imprisoning some conscience-stricken thesp we were supposed to recognize from *Take the High Road*. Of course she was there, touting leaflets for her Maoist splinter group, revelling in so many enemies all together in the same place. She was surprised to see me, but what surprised me more was the flash of animation in her face. Maybe it was just the carnival atmosphere, the small insurrection of spending a wintry day outdoors. She enquired after Sam's welfare, but failed to ask about Drew. She knew, then.

'You'll have to come over to the house.' An invitation never issued before. 'Ricky's away in Dundee the now, but he'll be back Friday night—' She winced and suspended conversation until the pipe band had passed by. 'What are you doing Saturday?'

It was agreed that what I was doing Saturday was dining at their flat. Seven o'clock. (I wondered if this meant a long evening, or if I'd be out of the door by nine.) Just before she resumed her leafleting, ignoring the sodden mat of discarded paper underfoot, she touched my arm as if she really liked me.

Yolande and Ricky live above a travel agents just off Sauchiehall Street, an urban fantasy of an address, with a cinema, three night-clubs, two casinos and a 24-hour takeaway all within five hundred yards. And yet up the stair and inside the flat I felt oddly removed from the hub of things. Ricky was out, and Yolande frying auber-gine slices, leaving the far side of the room dimly visible through a greasy veil. She sat me at the kitchen table, a battered example of farmhouse pine lacquered in mauve gloss paint. The floor was stripped to greyness, the varnish long since scuffed away. A candy-stripe durrie spread its second geography of ridges over the uneven boards. The rosé she poured me was weak and perfumed, heady with the memory of my student days: tinned tomato risotto scoffed crosslegged on the carpet, a couple of slackly rolled joints, and something cheap that poured from a prettily shaped bottle.

'Ricky's away faxing my strip to the paper.'

I nodded, not sure whether she was explaining his absence or just flagging up her superior ideological purity. As if I needed reminding. In my teens and early twenties there were people who cultivated me because I was Darwin's daughter. Mostly I could tell from the start, but with the Savilles it was weeks before I caught that look of expectation on their faces and realized what they were waiting for. Their kitchen was just like this. Shelves of pulses, huge Kilner jars of lentils and beans and dried apricots and wheatgerm and spaghetti turning greyish with old age: all so dusty you could be sure they were never used. Just kept waiting, like Yolande's Coal Not Dole coffee mugs and the ANC women's section recipe book and the CND tea towel, for the start of the post-revolutionary perfect world. Above her fridge was a poster of a white-haired Uncle Sam with the slogan ¡Manos Yankis Fuera de America Central y del Caribe! A pegboard to the left of the cooker displayed a Steve Bell strip torn out of the Guardian, and a couple of the householder's own cartoons. The one I understood showed Michael Forsyth as Bonnie Prince Charlie in drag, with Margaret Thatcher as his Flora Macdonald. Not the wittiest of allusions, but the clumsiness of the agitprop made it possible to ask

'What was it you did in Chile. Politically I mean?'

Disorientated by the leap from olive oil to politics, she hesitated, using the back of her wrist to push a strand of hair up off her shiny forehead. 'Literacy work, mostly.'

I wondered if I'd misunderstood. 'Teaching people to read?'

'Uh-huh. We tried to get a basic numeracy class going too, but it never took off.'

So much for Molotov cocktails and the Kalashnikov under the bed, those electric nights in the torturer's cell. How had I never clarified this before? Because I was frightened to ask a question that exposed my ignorance, my acronym-blindness, my shaming lack of a coherent position on the various liberation struggles around the globe? I never could quite get my head around internationalism. And a heroine of the people was still a social asset, even if I felt so inadequate beside her that the subject was never broached.

The click of the latch announced Ricky's return.

'Hiya gorgeous.' He bent down to kiss me, chastely, on the nose.

'Hey, that's my shirt.'

Yolande consulted her chest, as if this was news to her. 'It was in the dirty basket, and I'm frying.'

'Do I care?' He wrapped his arms around her from behind and started to undo the buttons. Yolande wriggled but stepped back from the blue flame, into his embrace. There was a moment's silence during some transaction that had no need of words. She tutted in a manner suggestive of sluttish acquiescence and I caught an unwanted glimpse of bedroom roleplay.

'OK, you fry; I'll change.'

Ricky took over the spatula and addressed himself to the task with unnecessary absorption. I studied the walls, which had been painted a very long time ago in a colour which no longer has a name. The books were obviously Yolande's, and the hand-thrown jug, and the Moroccan leather pouffe, and that grubby Indian rug. Apart from a newish compact disc player there was nothing I could identify as his, and plenty that I guessed he would disown. That cheeseplant for a start.

'How's your singing sister?'

His face seemed free of subtext.

'Big and getting bigger all the time. Moaning because her feet stink and the curl's dropped out of her pubic hair.' In the old days this would have got a reaction. Or would it? I had never been left alone with him before. Funny that we should be friends and fail this basic test of friendship. 'She's coming back, if you hear of anyone with a ground-floor flat to rent.'

'I'll ask around.'

Yolande returned dressed in a pair of jeans too wide in the ankle and too short in the leg, topped off with a matted mohair jumper. For once the cleavage wasn't on show. Ricky ceded his place at the stove and, filling an Irn Bru bottle at the sink, watered the cheeseplant.

It was a pleasant evening, not much hilarity or heated debate, but relaxing enough for none of us to worry when the smalltalk petered out. They were different at home, their noncommittal relations a clear statement of commitment; they were together:

matter of fact. By the end of the meal we had covered most of the subjects people of our age and class discuss when they don't have children. Music and movies and politics and books, all reduced to the level of celebrity gossip, so that the silicone-moulded rock recluse is dissected with the same paperback psychology as the cabinet minister or the mutual friend. It's what passes for community these days. There was only one sticky moment, when Ricky mentioned a sparkly-suited greed-show host who had joined the anti-motorway lobby and was now living up a tree.

'He was on television the other day. Said he'd fixed up a stand-in so he could get away to film the *Royal Variety Performance*. Prick. What was it I saw him on . . .?'

He tapped the table, trying to remember, and because I knew he'd get there in the end I said

'It was *Revelations*. He was Drew's first guest.' Ricky and Yolande exchanged brief glances. 'Have you seen him?'

I had a feeling Ricky was about to say no. Yolande lit a joss stick to cut through the smell of oil. 'We had a drink with him last week. He was looking well.'

She looked me in the eye, awaiting my next question.

'Good,' I said.

The conversation turned to holidays. They were thinking of Barcelona.

It was while Ricky was grinding the coffee beans that I asked Yolande about the curse.

'What?'

We were sitting on the prewar sofa with the boobytrapped springs which she had tried to neutralize by setting a double layer of newspapers under the all-concealing throw.

'When you did my tarot.'

The wine had left a rosy fingerprint on either side of her nose. 'I thought you didn't believe.'

'Maybe you converted me. You got everything right.'

'Did I?'

Those inflatable lips hovered on the brink of a smile. She thought I must be joking. Unless she had privileged information.

I asked her 'Do you believe in curses?'

She glanced over at Ricky, working up a sweat over the rotating handle of the grinder. 'I've seen some things.'

'And if—' I abandoned this phrasing. 'Do they last indefinitely?'

'Not necessarily.'

'But to be certain, you'd have to find the person who'd done the cursing?'

Her gaze just skimmed my shoulder. 'I wouldn't.'

'So what am I supposed to do?'

'Get on with your life.' For a second I sniffed the sulphur of her old animosity. 'Like the rest of us.'

It was clear that she considered the subject closed, but there was something I still needed her to tell me.

'You know that famous client you had, the one who got my reading—' Her face was so blank that I wondered if she remembered. '—it was the only reason I let you do my cards, then Ricky went and lost the list so it didn't prove anything anyway . . .'

'Aye, well, there was nothing to prove.'

'How's that?'

'You didn't draw the same cards.'

I wasn't sure I believed her. 'So who was he?'

'*Jesus*, Tracy.' I think we were both taken aback by the force of this, though Ricky did not look round. She moved her face closer, dropping the volume again. 'Just let it go.'

There was a groan from the corner as Ricky straightened up, puffing out his lips in self-congratulatory exhaustion. 'Remind me, Yo: why don't we buy ready-ground like everybody else?'

The first time I saw Drew again I nearly cried aloud. There he stood, just the same, in his green suit and the two-tone peacock shirt missing its last-but-one button. Though you can't tell that on screen. He was talking to a designer-clad geneticist who claimed to have disproved the existence of God and for a moment, as the camera almost caught his eye, I thought he was going to mention postmodernism. He hated peach-lipped scientists dressed in three shades of vanilla putting him right on air, although such loathing is not necessarily exclusive of desire. If she smiled at him in the green room, who knows where it might have ended? Maybe Ancona Street. He must have moved in by now.

The following Sunday he chaired a debate on euthanasia and I knew that he would laugh, make some blackly comic remark, but only once he was safely off-camera. And then I heard the doorbell and found Euan on the stairhead. His glance flipped away from the television as if I were watching a blue movie. I picked up the zapper and blacked out the screen, although the video recorder continued to purr.

'I'm away up to the cottage in a fortnight. My sister's in Spain so there's a bedroom free if you're interested.'

'It's good of you Euan, but . . .'

'Fresh air, good food, plenty of walking. Or stay in bed all day if you like.' He dropped the breezy tone. 'You need a holiday, Tracy—'

I always knew Euan liked me, but it never occurred to me that his affection would outlast my entertainment value.

'—if you don't believe me, just look in the mirror.'

I thought about explaining, but decided better not.

'And I'd be glad of the company.'

'If you're trying to stop me watching *Revelations*, you need to know that they get it up north too.'

He smiled, showing the sparse patches in the Errol Flynn moustache he has decided to regrow. 'Moira doesn't have a television.'

The Highland palette always astonishes, so different from the silver streets of noirish Glasgow, or the blue-black stone of the sunstruck capital. Here is the Scotland you find squared-off by gilt in the underlit museums of small provincial towns. Five hundred hues of brown, acid yellows that loosen the saliva under the tongue, the lurid green of sphagnum moss, so unexpectedly pleasant to the touch. Lichen like spilled facepowder, or charred paper, or circles of distemper painted on the rock. Glowing bracken under a canvas sky. The piebald mountains with their polyfilla cracks of snow.

We did the usual things city-dwellers do north of Stirling. Went for walks laden like Sherpas. Lay on wind-battered hillsides watching the clouds. Combed the guidebooks for references to log-fires and fiddles, then settled for a gassy lager in the nearest bar. Nicknamed everyone we met more than once. Hugged stiffly when we said goodnight. And, on a whim one Wednesday morning, stopped at the lochside bothy and booked our forty minutes on a seal-spotting tour.

The skipper was a sinewy pensioner in a tourist-pleasing hat embellished with a fraying of scrambled egg. He winked at me with obligatory roguishness as he handed me aboard. His vessel was a former fishing boat with a valiant diagonal of bunting strung from mast to prow, and red paint thickly layered over its rust sores and deck splinters. The timetable, it soon became clear, was a quaint local fiction: we would sail when he considered the number of passengers warranted the expense of fuel. Euan and I each bought a waxed paper cup of weak tea, added a furtive nip of brandy from the hipflask, and prepared ourselves for a wait. I counted every one of the twenty-three punters as they stepped aboard. That quartet of Canadians on the ancestor trail, the northern English couple smiling in incomprehension at the accent of the first mate, a family of seven from Bonnyrigg, two old ladies with binoculars, the screaming toddler and his hollow-eyed parents, a speccy youth in a baseball cap, the arm-locked lovers taking alternate bites out of a Danish pastry. I saw Euan clock the Finnish girls in their flashy yellow survival gear and selfishly hoped they weren't staying in the locale. Finally, the boat's engine rattled into life.

On shore it had been calm, even balmy, but out on the sea loch a scalpel wind made small incisions around the eye, shaving the cheek, insinuating through three layers of jumper and my waterproof sleeve. The captain began his commentary over the popping mike, the jokes worn thin with repetition, although the passengers still laughed. Leaning against the stern rail, I squinted under the brightness of too much sky.

'Don't look now, but I've just spotted an old friend.'

Of course I looked. Drew was standing on the far side of the deck. My heart kicked in my chest, cheeks roaring with a heat fiercer than the brandy burn. I was conscious of my saltblasted complexion, the hairwash I hadn't bothered with last night, my mansize rainproof padded to a fit by all that wool, and still I felt the familiar tug of narcissism, the siren's fatal compulsion to beguile.

'If you'll just move over to starboard ladies and gentlemen.'

The portside passengers shuffled over. I saw out of the corner of my eye that Drew was not among them.

'*I know you're on the television, Mr Monzie, but the selkies won't put on a private show.*'

The passengers tittered and swivelled their heads. Two teenagers I had attributed to the Bonnyrigg family, a girl with the volcanic skin of puberty, and a much shorter, younger boy, stared at the deck with ferocious indifference. Another famous name would have turned the situation, pulled some hokey stunt to make the crowd his own, but not Drew. His features showed the same lust for invisibility I read on the faces of those children. A family resemblance, I surmised. I touched Euan's sleeve and obediently he sidled towards the Finns. I watched our progress through the water, followed the brief lifespan of the fluorspar curl of wake. Knowing him so well I could predict his every movement.

'I suppose it's fate,' I said, without looking at him.

'How've you been?' he said, without looking at me.

'Bad, but getting better. Thankyou for asking.' I had, of course, rehearsed what I would say, though this was nothing like it. 'And yourself?'

'Oh, I don't know—'

This had a provisional sound, so I waited while he searched for a reply. The cold had brought a hint of fever to his face, a whitish waxy look with a rouge spot on each cheek. Sometimes when we made love his skin would take on such alarming contrasts and secretly I'd resolve to acquire some basic lifesaving techniques. I never did get round to it. His hair, worried by the wind, seemed stringy against his skull. So no, he wasn't looking too hot either, but still there was the size of him, the sheer substantiality of that almost unfeasible bulk. I always honoured the animal mystery that kept all that ballast aloft.

'—it feels like I've spent the past month doing nothing but shifting cardboard boxes.'

'From Bella's,' I supplied, since he wasn't going to. 'Into Ancona Street.'

This threw him.

'I knew last time we met,' I added gratuitously.

Still he would not look at me. We passed the circular cages of the salmon farm, the fish leaping, their instincts intact despite the hopelessness of their rearing, silver flesh convulsing with the gravity-defying drive to spawn. Above us the triangular pennants on the bunting were rippling frenziedly. I allowed the pause to lengthen. He hated deliberate silence as children hate the dark.

'Why didn't you say?'

I knew him inside out.

'Because I didn't want to upset you, Drew. I always put you first.'

'Really?' He stared at the water giving back its exact replica of the thousand greys of the softly wadded sky. Gruel and fleece-wool, chewed gum, squirrel, swarf. 'That wasn't my impression.'

He never used to judge me. Until my moment of sacrilege, pricing the icon, trying to offload my sad-eyed alter ego. Who was not to be so easily shed.

Since he probably hated me anyway, I asked

'Have you got someone else installed?'

How was it that we had never had a row? Walking out, yes, and sulking, and those peevish words the last time that we'd met, but no honest-to-goodness, screaming-the-walls-down row. Which in a sense has left us unconsummated to the end.

He closed his eyes briefly. 'That would rather defeat the object.'

Just then the wind changed direction, catching at his coat so that it flapped against my leg. That navy cashmere I had so often cooried into and even once in Ruchill Park, having climbed the hill to see the city spread beneath us, worn draped about my shoulders. Inconceivable to stand so close to him and yet not share his warmth. Though the wearer shun me, that coat must surely take me in its arms.

'Too cryptic for me, darling,' I said.

He checked over his left shoulder as if this remnant of our old familiar lingo might have carried above the wind, but Donalda and Cameron were orbiting adolescence's solitary planet. Our fellow passengers had now gathered in the prow.

'They seem nice kids,' I added, reverting to formality.

I felt a turbulence within Drew's airspace and I knew he was unnerved that I had guessed. For an intelligent man he had an extraordinary faith in the stupidity of others. Or rather, he needed to believe in his own opacity until the moment he chose to be revealed.

'I'm afraid they don't think their father's so nice.'

'They feel you've treated her badly?'

He looked away to the north, leaving me only his rubber ear and that padded neck with its guillotine crease. He was right, of course: it was none of my business.

The boat was drifting towards what seemed to be a slick of brown weed until my eyes adjusted to the fact that every inch of its surface was covered with inert brown sludge-coloured bodies. And then, as the pewter sunlight broke through the cloud-cover, they came to life, languidly stretching and twisting and scratching, changing position with that ungainly sack-race lumbering. Imagine living in the freezing lava of the Atlantic and still loving the sun. I once sat on a harbour wall on Islay, barely ten feet away from a colony of seals basking on the heated metal of a sewage outflow pipe. Even in proximity they remained strange: muscular slugs overlooked by evolution, creatures so contextless and self-contained in their beautiful solid blubber that they held an obscure erotic charge. At the other end of the boat the trippers exhaled a collective *aaah*. Too early in the year for furry pups: maybe they found the adults sweet, though at this distance they looked hairless, industrial, faintly obscene. The biggest bull, a mottled blue like old inner-tube corrupting in the air, stared at us impassively before opening his mouth in an intimate pink-tongued yawn. Not so different from us after all.

I shut my eyelids against the relentless light. 'You know, I never thought you'd do it.'

He made a sound that was almost a laugh. I opened my eyes to find him monochrome beside me, his face leached of fleshtones. Grief seemed to coarsen his skin, stealing its elasticity, enlarging the pores like lateral slashes of rain across a train window, the suddenly visible stubble dragging his cheeks into jowls. I squeezed the rail to stay my hands from touching him.

'They had a dossier listing my movements. Restaurants, concerts, walks in the park. Photographs too.' He seemed to be telling the seals. 'Don't worry: you're fully clothed.'

So I was right about being followed.

'How come they never printed anything?'

He clouded, then caught my meaning. 'It wasn't the papers. It was a private detective, hired by the True Reformed.'

'But you left years ago.'

For a minute he almost forgot his grief. 'This is Scotland,' he said drily.

The boat's long wash was curving now. We were returning to the jetty.

He shrugged. 'Anyway, they achieved their objective.'

'Which was what?'

He hesitated. 'I was going to start preaching again.'

A path with which I was always incompatible. 'And you never thought to let me know?'

'I didn't think you cared.'

I wasn't letting him away with this. 'No, Drew, you were setting me a test. I was supposed to divine what was going on through telepathy and make a fuss so you could be sure I loved you.'

Although, on reflection, there was a percentage for him in either outcome. Drew is after all a romantic, in love with the idea of loss.

He lifted a meaty hand to rub his eyesocket. 'Have you noticed how the wind feels like it's punching us in the head?'

I ignored this, though as it happened he was right. 'So you rolled over to stop them feeding you to the tabloids.'

'They would have gone to Bella.'

'But you left her anyway.'

'She doesn't know about *us*.' I had my doubts about this. 'Believe it or not I was thinking of you.'

I doubted this, too. 'You never know, I might have enjoyed my starring role in a scandal—'

I felt him jar at the levity, and his posture became a little less collusive.

'—I always wondered why you needed to believe I was so frail.'

This seemed to amuse him, in an acrid sort of way. 'I never doubted your toughness, Tracy. Not after I met your sister—'

And now finally he turned to look at me, without admiration or infatuation or sentimentality or lust, or any of the expressions I used to associate with love. But candidly, levelly, a look I had seen before and brushed aside, as we choose to discount that which does not suit our purpose. And at last he said something utterly unexpected.

'—but you so badly need to believe you're good.'

I felt my chest split open like a ripe fig, peeling back the skin of me to offer up the fruit. What if he really knew me, what if there was a real me for him to know?

'Dad.'

I turned. Cammie and Donalda were watching us. Behind them, I saw the Scots pine growing on the lochside, the red and yellow paintwork of the ticket collector's bothy.

'Come here you two,' he said with seamless joviality, and for the first time I understood what it meant that he had children. 'And meet my friend Tracy.'

I tend to feel nervous around adolescents, knowing their pitiless eye. Beneath that scoured forehead with its irrepressible contour of spots, it was possible to see the woman his daughter would one day become. The boy, with his huge front teeth and his paper-white nose with its five perfect freckles, was anyone's guess. Both had Drew's hair, though I did not care to search for further clues. Donalda smiled in a close-lipped way that might have been suspicion, or just a habit-forming brush with orthodontics. Cammie studied his trainers. No one could think of anything to say.

The captain unlatched a gate in the starboard rail where a straggling queue was forming. My ex-lover's children walked away to join it.

'Pray for me,' I said, though he'd think I was being facetious.

He leaned forward and in a sudden fervid gesture pressed his cheek hard against mine. I felt his whiskers' rasp, his breath warm in my ear.

'I miss you,' he said.

The boat berthed, jarring against the jetty. Deliberately I held back for Euan, allowing the Canadians to come between us, so that on the pier Drew had to turn and look for me and then to call quite loudly

'It wasn't Fate. It was Phemie. She wants to see you.'

TWENTY-SIX

I knew that I would find her, even without an address. That teatime visit on an afternoon of freakish snow was one of the stations of our courtship, every detail of it precious, and although for ease of storage the memory flashed up as a single brilliant tableau, I knew I could retrieve the rest. All I had to do was retrace the route we took from the Quaich that day and surely the street, and in its turn the closemouth, would draw me in. I could have spent an afternoon in the library poring over the electoral roll, or waited to check the address with Drew, but I had promised myself I would not see him again until – what? Let's just say I had a notion to follow the sequence of events; for once in my life I would put my trust in fate. So much for fate. I walked street after street in search of Phemie's tenement until in the end I could not even be certain which way we had turned out of the Quaich. I bought a map in the newsagents and scanned its half-familiar names, tried dowsing a nail file over the relevant page. Nothing. Another half hour and I abandoned hope. And now I'm late for Sandy.

I have developed a liking for my new boss, with her long straight back and her dull brown ponytail and the expensive clothes which transmute upon her frame into poor copies of chainstore polyester. Though well into her fifth decade, she has yet to leave the state of girlhood; there is a straightforwardness about her that gives time spent in her presence the wholesome air of the paddock, a smell of sweet apples and hay. The gossip is that she once had a husband whom she loved enthusiastically and, just as wholeheartedly, left. These days she shares her bed with a health and safety inspector called Sue. They've just moved into a new house, a semi-derelict semi-detached on Lochinvar Drive, bought in defiance of the surveyor's recommendations. Sandy is working at home this week while men in navy blue overalls rip up her floorboards and spray dust over her walls. The daily visitations of a string of tradesmen, each sorrowfully shaking his head over his predecessor's shoddy work, provide a bubbling source of comic anecdote, but her gaiety transmits over the telephone line with a wheezy undertone, as if a crying jag were waiting for the moment she replaced the receiver. In an attempt to lighten the despair we're both too polite to acknowledge I have bought her a present, a tulip-shaped lampshade of marbled glass. Still in its Oxfam bag to minimize any sense of obligation.

Lochinvar is one street away from MacKendrick Avenue. And it is a measure of how things change that only now, as I catch sight of the black and white sign jutting from its street-corner lamppost, do I realize how close I am to Bella's house. On impulse I turn right, following the route I have traced so often and so furtively, taking advantage of my newfound citizen's right to roam. A plumber's van is parked on this side of the empty street, a roofer's on the other: a sure sign that just around the corner lie the clement months when this douce suburb will echo with the clink of extendable ladder, the whine of hovermower and hedge-clipper, the housepainter's whistle and the blackbird's song. A sky of featherbedding and old rags, with the soft air and the already leafy trees, makes the street itself an interior, and fleetingly I have a foretaste of the Scottish summer, its stillness, its enigmatic boredom, the focusless anticipation in the rows of blank-windowed houses under its flat white tepid sky.

Entering the cross street, my way is blocked by a road gang, an orange truck with a vat of tar and a dinky diesel-driven roller patching a workman's trench across the junction. The crumbled black asphalt is compressed to a steaming blue and, as the roller retreats, a wall of vapour rears up across the road, curling to rejoin the air. I could skirt the fresh tarmac and move on, but there is a quiet compulsion about this respectable residential street with its eldritch curtain of mist, so I stand and watch the roller return, the vibrations of its progress pricking the arches of my feet, and as it depresses the freshly laid surface another inch, a second haar rises to block my vision. The road gang trundle off to their next assignment just down the street, the vapour dissipates, and Phemie is standing on the other side.

'Here you are,' she says, with that precise enunciation of hers.

'Here I am,' I echo, meaninglessly, staring at her white PVC mac and matching sou'wester and bright yellow rubber boots. The coat reaches down to her ankles, and is rolled thickly at the cuffs, the hat covering her head like a bucket. Over the past couple of days the weather has been changeable, prone to sudden showers of needle rain while the sun turns the pavements to blinding silver, but surely this outfit amounts to overprecaution.

She crosses the gently steaming frontier. 'What have you brought me?'

She is looking expectantly towards my handbag.

I take out my purse, but evidently it holds no interest. Now my hairbrush, make-up bag, keys. Behind me is a mossy, flat-topped garden wall. I spread my possessions along it. Chequebook, diary, tissues, packet of mints, don't ask me why I'm doing this, single earring, safety-pin, abalone button, two paracetamol, Sam's birthday crystal.

Phemie picks up the crystal in tiny caramel-coloured fingers with a slight arthritic curve.

'A joke present from my sister. For warding off the evil eye.'

'I know what it is for,' she says.

We appear to have omitted some crucial stages in the etiquette of the chance meeting: expressions of surprise and pleasure, enquiries after each other's welfare, the gossipy exchange of news. She is turning towards MacKendrick Avenue and seems to expect me to accompany her. I scrabble my possessions back into the bag.

'I'm going this way,' I nod towards Lochinvar Drive. 'I have an appointment.'

'Nothing that can't wait.'

She doesn't even glance at me for confirmation.

I fall into step, feeling conspicuously tall, as if she were a child and I her mother. For a mad moment there I was about to reach down and take her hand. The pavement is dark beneath the linden trees, yet above us the new leaves are a tangy electric green, hanging limp as laundered hankies, not yet stiffened by summer's lacquer of dried sap and grime. Something so touching about the city spring: hyacinths sprouting in the cupboard, the muted green of the waking turf, cherry trees showy as June brides with their overblown bouquets.

'You saw Drew—' I blurt, though I promised myself I wouldn't.

Her head is barely level with my chest, which means I cannot see her face or indeed any other part of her within that waterproof tent. Her hands have vanished up into the sleeves. I have a sudden conviction that whatever is walking beside me is not Phemie at all.

'—I saw him too, bumped into him on a boat. Ha,' my laughter sounds as falsetto as Sandy's over the phone. 'I'm surprised he didn't jump ship for fear that I might drown us all.' I wait in vain for the polite echo of mirth. 'He thinks I'm cursed.'

'He told me.'

'The problem is, I can't think of anyone who would care enough to curse me.' And what else did he say? That he was afraid to touch me? 'Unless it's my sister.'

'But you won't let it be your sister.'

A funny way of putting it. 'I didn't know it was my choice.'

I suppose we both must look like crazies, her in that outsize lollipop lady's raincoat, me stooping within earshot, right-angled at her side. Thankfully there's no one here to see us.

'Where are we going?'

She halts and pushes at a wrought-iron gate. 'We're here.'

Too late I see whose garden we are entering.

'I can't, Phemie.'

She pulls off the sou'wester to reveal hair cropped very short, almost crew-cut, and standing up as if charged with static. Emerging from under that enormous hat her head is comically small, tiny as a grapefruit. The blood flow under her scalp, clearly visible through the fine white bristle, makes her seem luminous. Huge silver rings are looped through the shirred flesh of her earlobes.

'Bella won't mind. She's away, making the most of Andrew's week with the children. And we should take shelter.'

The soft depths of the sky have been replaced by a casting of lead just above the terracotta pantile of the roofs. The light is strangely intent so that everything, the bootscraper on the front doorstep, that scratch in the maroon paintwork of the door, the nap on the lamb's tongue straggled by the last shower of rain, possesses a cinematic clarity. She leads me along the side of the house, past the dustbins. At the end of the back garden, over the stepping-stone flags set into the uncut lawn, beyond the Anderson shelter pressed into service as a garden shed, is a bower enclosed by an apple tree, a mature horse chestnut of impressive girth, and three flowering cherries, one pastel-blossomed, the other two a blaring bubblegum pink. Between the trees is a threadbare oval of grass, a sicklier growth than the shaggy lawn, and a fishpond with a couple of etiolated goldfish screaming silently beneath its surface. My eye strays to the kitchen window, but all that is visible is a bottle of washing-up liquid and a square of blue-emulsioned wall.

Phemie drops her hat underneath the horse chestnut. I move to join her but she lifts one spindly finger to arrest my progress. Guiltily I glance back towards the house.

'There's nobody home,' she says. 'Now, would you bring me that box?'

The cardboard carton is under a lean-to by the kitchen door. Sinking my fingers into the mound of privet clippings I feel a jag and the sudden disproportionate misery of drawn blood. Rose-prunings too. The box is too heavy to lift, so I bump it over the grass to the spot under the cherry trees where Phemie is building a mound of sticks and sawn-up branches. I make haste to help, dragging the wood from a neatly stacked pile by the creosoted garden fence. Even with two of us, it takes several minutes. Phemie removes a long forked stick from the mound, then digs deep into the right-hand pocket of her voluminous raincoat. Of course I knew it was a pyre, but the small gold lighter shocks me even so.

'No one will bother us,' she says, reading my thoughts.

The privet crackles and a flame takes hold. We stand silent, rapt in the awe of fire, its voracity and precarious life. When finally I look away Phemie is no longer at my side. I scan the empty garden, panicked, expecting to hear the sirens any second, but the door of the Anderson shelter opens and she emerges holding a bone china sugarbowl, pale cream with navy and gold bands, missing one of its daintily angled handles. Wedding present ware. Bending to the fishpond, she fills the bowl with water and sets it on the ground. Then, tying the nickel chain to the forked stick as if fashioning a fishing rod, she dangles Sam's crystal into the seat of the fire.

I crouch beside her, breathing in the woodsmoke. 'Was it Bella?'

'Would you wish it to be Bella?'

'Not now.'

Her lips twitch, a mannerism that might signal disapproval, though I prefer to read it as amusement. 'Do you have a silver fivepence?'

I consult my purse. 'Only a twenty.'

'Put it into the water.'

We wait. Then with a flourish she lifts the necklace clear of the fire. The crystal has clouded, its transparency crazed by a thousand tiny fissures. She drops it into the bowl. The water sizzles faintly. I snigger. Nervous, I suppose.

'You see?' she says as if confirming something she has known all along.

The coin is resting on the bottom of the sugarbowl, beside the crystal. Phemie drops the stick into the fire, the bark bubbles as it detaches from the unseasoned wood.

'The coin has not stirred,' she observes. 'You are forspoken.'

The curse of the favourite, blighted by undue praise.

'Sam will be pleased,' I say.

Seven months since my sister reentered my life. Nine since a stranger walked into Gil's salon and walked out with my hair. Four years since I sang a snatch of Cole Porter with a small-screen celebrity in a bottle-green suit. Fourteen years since Darwin's death. Thirty-six since I gained a sister, and mislaid a mother. Forty-one since I was born. I would have said that I had lived a happy life, apart from the pain. A bit of a crowd-pleaser, but enjoying the show. The fact that I was hollow only made the surface all the more precious. And now it seems I was always on a false trail.

This close, Phemie's most striking feature is not that translucent skin or her childlike frame, but a pure intelligence that communicates itself even when she does not speak.

'We'll need the shawl now, Tracy.'

What shawl?

She glances down at the Oxfam carrier containing Sandy's lampshade, which I have wrapped carefully in the baby blanket returned by Mrs Woodhouse. All these old ladies I've looked to in my life.

The blanket swings three times over the fire before she winds it tightly once, twice, thrice around my neck, securing it with one of those tinny heart-shaped brooches given away by some showbiz charity on fundraising days. The fabric smells scorched but is wonderfully warm.

'Give me your jacket.'

'It's going to rain.'

She looks up at the lowering sky. 'Not rain,' she says.

I hand her the jacket.

'Now the rest of your clothes.'

I laugh, and her expression takes on a nuance of astonishment.

No sign of life behind the gloomy glass of the neighbouring houses, a thicket of buddleia screening us from the garden to our left, that creosoted fence concealing everything to our right but the top half of a child's blue plastic swing. I'm wearing a black all-in-one that, from a distance, might be taken for a swimsuit.

Phemie folds my shirt, jacket and trousers into a tidy pile on the ground, and stands waiting.

'Everything except the shawl,' she prompts.

No one would wear a swimsuit in a suburban garden in April anyway.

'Lie down.'

The grass is dry and almost warm, crepitant beneath me, prickling my bare skin. Phemie kneels and reaches into her left-hand pocket to find a small commercial drum of salt. She pours a white stream into the bowl of water and stirs it with a forefinger. The blue veins across the back of her hand seem threaded not under but over that orange glaze of skin. I feel the calm that overtakes me at the ministrations of women: the shampoo girls, my dentist with her sterile diamond studs, the cosmetics counter geisha who once smothered me in slap. She dribbles lukewarm wetness over the soles of my feet and the palms of my hands, draws her finger across my forehead and, finally, insinuates it between my lips. Brackish water with the metallic taste of money. The rest of the saline hisses on the fire.

'What are we doing?'

'Restoring you to yourself.'

'And if there's nothing to restore?'

Did I mention the colour of her eyes? There isn't any. Just the black pupils returning their intelligent non-response.

When I was twelve and the miners still had the power to commit the nation to darkness, I decided to call on my friend Gillian. Amazing how unfamiliar the housing scheme was without light. I made it as far as the doorway by keeping one foot on the path and the other on the ragged grass verge, so busy trying to avoid the dogshit that I came upon the concrete step unexpectedly, jarring my foot against its unseen edge. Feeling the contours of the porchway with one hand, I stepped out confidently into nothingness. I still remember that plunge into vacancy, the hit in my stomach and the long long wait. I had time to plan my funeral, and to savour Sam's regret, and to register this endless drop as punishment for my badness, and to know just as we do in dreams that if I could only quell my fear I might never feel the impact. Afterwards, when they found me, they clucked with relief: it was only ten feet. Weeks later I went back to that stairwell, when the missing balustrade had been replaced, and dropped a five pound bag of potatoes over the rail. Barely a second before it reached the bottom. Only ten feet, but an eternity of not knowing. I made sure I never felt that way again. Or only once, when I allowed the sea to take me in the hope of saving Drew. And a third time, now.

Looking up, I can see Phemie's nostrils flaring delicately with each indrawn breath. Behind her the blossom is brilliant against the leaden sky. She gets to her feet and walks to the shelter of the horse chestnut, and suddenly as if on cue the air turns wersh, the wind blows with a cyclonic whirling that takes up the debris on the grass, yanks next door's swing into spastic jolting, agitates the cherry twigs in crazed helixes of motion, the ravaged flowers weak as tissue paper against the storm. The sky is raining cherry blossom, petals falling like confetti, swirling in the frenzied currents of air. A crack of thunder triggers a rattling in the trees. My hand catches a constellation of exotic sugar. A moment to grasp the wonder of this and then it is hailing in earnest, pelting as if to reach some quota, stinging my bare breasts, bruising the tender flesh of my outstretched thighs, piercing my flinching eyelids. And through the sharpness I could swear I feel Drew's stubble grinding my cheek, Sam's soft flesh against my arm, the pitch and roll of the mattress, all the pivotal moments I have fumbled or missed. Down the street a dog barks relentlessly, and then another, and then a distant siren, to be joined by a descant of yowling cats. Above me trees are swaying, flames leaping and spitting, the fluttering touch of the cherry blossom commingling with the ice bombarding my skin, every nerve electrified by the soughing wind. I can feel my lungs inflating with each breath, feel the oxygen firing my blood, the blood threading through the fine capillaries, joining wider tributaries, veins feeding the heart. And with the same breath panic has me by the throat. The shawl's brace has turned from support to suffocation, pressing on my windpipe, immobilizing my jaw. I am tearing at the layers of blanket, nails splintering in the stitchwork, until with an absurd and liberating *ping* the brooch flies free and my noose unfurls. The fabric hits the fire, one corner curling, blackening, the pink satin ribbon shrivelling. Phemie's face glimmers in the shadows under the tree. There is a smell of burning wool and a faint fleeting taste of marzipan as the flames take hold.

I am lying on the ground, feeling the hummocky turf against my back and the hail and the petals and the wind's shivery caress on my skin, the smell of fresh earth and scorched wool in my nostrils, my left side freezing, my right cheek and arm and thigh searing with the lick of fire, and in the same moment cooled by the kiss of the wind. When did my body start shaking beyond control, every muscle quivering, tremors in my thighs and fingers? Over by the tree Phemie is keening. The notes merge with the boisterousness of the storm and the percussion of the leaves and the clamour of the birds and animals and the whooping car alarms, and I do not understand why the very dead do not wake with it, for I have never felt so alive. The sound is vibrating in my chest, my mouth stretched huge as if in shout, and now I see that I too am this noise, this unstoppable welling of outside and in, this fullness that aggravates its own hunger, this abundance that I always missed though I could never define it, this addiction I will feed every moment for the rest of my life.

I walked down Calico Street today and in the new piazza, where the old men like to sun themselves outside the video rental, I bumped into Mary Duffin. She was on her way to see the Maggies. They meet every Monday in the twenty-four-hour bingo. The chairs are better upholstered than Magellan Street and they get free tea and coffee and chocolate fingers too. I had Sam's baby with me – Shirley, our mother's name – so I had to explain that yes, she was gorgeous, but no, she wasn't mine, although I have seen my share of changes. I miss the old girls, and it would have been good to catch up on the gossip, but I was expected round at Drew's. We keep our separate households out of choice these days. He likes the safety of his harmless secrets and, after forty years spent on the surface of my skin, it turns out that I greatly relish mine. Though for all my good intentions, it's not easy finding time to be alone. Every other weekend Cammie comes to tea, and Donalda's slowly softening, and I'm singing in a choir, which I've yet to tell Samantha. Drew is preaching the odd Sunday now at his local Church of Scotland, and seems the happier for it. He's even started on a diet, in fact he's lost ten pounds, and although sometimes I grieve for my shrinking storybook giant, I hope he sticks it out.